KING EDWARD'S RING

A WEST AFRICAN YARN OF ADVENTURES MORE OR LESS TRUE

BY

PEREGRINE ATBUSH

"We will talk of Africa, the world's final chance of adventure. . . .
Oh, there's some fun left in this old globe yet."
—*Life the Accuser.*

King Edward's Ring is a story by Peregrine Atbush, published at the office of the *East Anglian Daily Times*, Ipswich. The scene is laid in the West African bush, and the hero's adventures are numerous and exciting enough to satisfy the most excating reader.

Scotsman, 6 July 1908

King Edward's Ring, by Peregrine Atbush (Ipswich: *East Anglian Daily Times*). This story is described as "A West African Yarn of adventures more or less true". It concerns a ring belonging to the ancient family of Riversley, which two centuries ago got into the hands of "Ye Quene of Ibibio, a black people of Guinee". The hero describes his adventures in search of the ring, and eventually he marries Pleasance Riversley, who inherits the house and estates of her family.

Country Life, 11 July 1908

This is an unpretentious sort of story, yet it has merits too seldom found in work put forth with a greater flourish of trumpets. The author is evidently well aquainted with Nigeria and its natives, and without being tediously informative contrives in the course of his story to give us some very interesting glimpses of the country and of the native life and ways of thought, besides spinning a very readable yarn. Here and there the hand of the amateur is betrayed by resort to a wild improbability to pull the story through, but for the most part the story has an extraordinary air of simple truthfulness. Indeed, the present writer, while reading the book, has repeatedly had the strong impression that it might almost be a chapter from Mungo Park. Evidently Mr Atbush has been drawing on his own personal experiences, and he had done so to such good purpose that he should be recommended to try again, avoiding next time such far-fetched coincidences as the finding of a bottle of hair-dye in his hero's baggage just when he wanted it for a native chief.

Evening News, 23 July 1908

Published by Jeremy Mills Publishing Limited,
22 Occupation Road, Lindley, Huddersfield, HD3 3BD.

www.jeremymillspublishing.co.uk

First published 1908.
This edition © Jeremy Mills Publishing Ltd, 2006.

ISBN 1–905–217–22–6

Photograph opposite:
By kind permission of the Trustees of the British Museum.

FOREWORD

Charles Partridge was born at Offton Hall on 10 February
1872 and brought up in the Georgian house in Tavern Street,
Stowmarket where he died nearly 84 years later. He was the
elder son of Charles Thomas Partridge of Stowmarket,
Raydon and Shelley Hall, iron and timber merchant, and
proud to trace his descent through nine generations of
Suffolk Partridges who had farmed their lands within sight
of Stoke by Nayland church tower since Tudor times. He
spent and thoroughly enjoyed the years 1884–86 as a boarder
at Ipswich School under the Revd F.H. Browne, then new as

headmaster. Conscious that he followed in the footsteps of Henry Rider Haggard (at the school 1869–72), he quizzed older Ipswichians about Haggard, eliciting the information that he had told some of his earliest adventure stories after lights out in the School House dormitories.

Partridge never forgave his guardians (he used the word to spare his parents' feelings) for moving him, in the belief that the Suffolk climate did not suit him, to a school which he steadfastly disdained to name, referring to it merely as 'in the Sheers'. He did not enjoy the new school, in his opinion much inferior, and retained a lifelong loyalty to Ipswich School. It delighted him to be made President of the Old Ipswichian Club in 1950, which gave him the opportunity to make after-dinner speeches long remembered for their length. Another thing he kept to himself was his middle name which began with 'S': 'a stupid name I parted with years ago', and he always insisted on the simple address 'Charles Partridge, Stowmarket, Suffolk'. Stanley is not a bad name for a pioneer in Africa.

After graduating at Christ's College, Cambridge in 1895 he joined the Colonial Service as Assistant District Commissioner, Southern Nigeria, later to become Political Officer and District Commissioner. A keen anthropologist, he became in 1903 a Fellow of both the Anthropological and the Royal Geographical Societies. His acute powers of observation and prodigious memory led to his writing, during his first home leave in 1904, *Cross River Natives: notes on the primitive pagans of Obubura District*. This work the Colonial Office gave him permission to publish, for though he had only been in the Protectorate for three years, he wrote with complete authority. His book was greeted as one of the best written by an Englishman on 'a race of primitive people'.

As Resident in Ibadhan in about 1910, he was involved in an incident with far-reaching repercussions. He heard that the German anthropologist and Atlantis hunter Frobenius had by violent means obtained the Olukun Head, having found it in the sacred grove of that sea-deity. It was 'a head of marvellous beauty, wonderfully cast in antique bronze, true to the life, encrusted with a patina of glorious dark green'.

Partridge took police with him to intercept the expedition and compelled the collector to return to Ife and surrender the head and other spoils to the Oni, the tribe's paramount chief. Forty years later when the Nigerian government had at last given full effect to his ideas, his action was described as 'far in advance of his time in his enlightened attitude to the preservation of native antiquities'. Partridge himself assembled an important collection of artefacts by totally ethical means and presented it to Ipswich Museum.

He also caused a stir when living with the pagan Igaras, far up into the interior. Their king died, and received a splendid funeral, at which, but for Partridge's stubbornly prolonged presence, they would have sacrificed his wives and eunuchs. The stand-off was effective.

After the Great War, when he was a Lieutenant on the Special List serving in Salonika, he resigned from the Colonial Service and returned to Suffolk to devote thirty-five years to historical research. On the basis of articles on the history of Ipswich School written during his Cambridge days and published in its Magazine he was elected a Fellow of the Society of Antiquaries in 1904, and then became an overseas member of the Suffolk Institute of Archaeology. Back in Suffolk he became an active council member until he fell out with the secretary, the Revd Harold Augustus Harris of Thorndon. He abruptly resigned withholding the last part of a work of which the Institute had already published three sections. He contributed regularly to the *East Anglian Daily Times* under the pen-name 'Silly Suffolk' and a lively collection of his pieces was published in 1925 under the title *Prose and Poetry*. He also contributed a glossary of over 40,000 Anglo-Indian words to the *Indian Antiquary*, a task demanding infinite patience and perseverance.

Much of the foregoing comes from his only obituary, written by Wallace Morfey for the *Old Ipswichian Magazine* in 1956. Morfey seems not, however, to have known about Partridge's only novel, written very much in the Rider Haggard style, but published privately, for no publisher at the time would accept it, in 1908. *King Edward's Ring* has as sub-title 'A West African yarn of adventures more or less true', and as such it makes compelling reading. Under the apt pseudonym Peregrine Atbush (but further evidence of misguided modesty) it is

Dedicated
(without permission)
to the Reader (Readers sounds presumptious!)
with pluck enough to read it from beginning to
end this 'Yarn' of adventures in the West
African Bush which no publisher has had the
pluck to publish!

Although the book could 'be obtained [for one shilling] at all the Railway Station bookstalls of Messrs W.H. Smith and Son, and Messrs Wyman and Son' the only copies so far traced are in the British Library, the Suffolk Record Office at Ipswich, Ipswich Museum and the Ipswich School Archives.

A new generation of readers may now enjoy the lively fast-moving plot, knowing that the author of *Cross River Natives* had a keen eye for detail and a fluent writing style. Suffolk yeoman Partridge was no radical, but he understood and respected the indigenous people of West Africa, working with them and trusting them whenever it was possible and appropriate.

The one footnote in the book should be clarified. The story begins and ends in Suffolk and the author attempts to give the fictional Riversley family substance by referring readers to the second edition of *The Suffolk Traveller*, 1764, page 421. In fact copies of that edition end at page 340.

John Blatchly July 2006

KING EDWARD'S
RING

Contents.

DEDICATED

TO THE READER (READERS SOUNDS PRESUMPTUOUS!)
WITH PLUCK ENOUGH TO READ FROM BEGINNING TO
END THIS "YARN" OF ADVENTURES IN THE WEST
AFRICAN BUSH WHICH NO PUBLISHER HAS HAD THE
PLUCK TO PUBLISH!

KING EDWARD'S RING.

CHAPTER I.

I SET OUT ON MY QUEST TO THE LAND OF THE CANNIBALS.

> "He either fears his fate too much,
> Or his deserts are small;
> Who dares not put it to the touch,
> To gain or lose it all."

"Now, papa," says Pleasance, "we are ready to 'talk ancestors,' so please read us what the old book tells about the ring."

So the Squire reads as follows:

"This Parish is remarkable for a Family who take their Name from the Place, the Family of the *Riversleys*, who have long had their seat at *Riversley* Hall. Of whom that ancient Chronicler *William le Menteur* doth relate as follows, viz., 'In A.D. 1339, or 12 *Edward* III., the King of *England* did invade *France*. . . . To take the Town of *Saint-Pol* he collected a great Number of Boats, in which he placed his Archers, and had them rowed up to the Palisades of Wood with which the Town was enclosed. They shot so well that no one dared to show himself at the Windows, or anywhere else, to defend it. With the Archers, there were those who with sharp Axes, whilst the Archers made use of their Bows, cut the Palisades, and in a short Time did so much Damage that they flung down a large Part of them, and entered the Town by Force. Among those of the *English* who by their Bravery did most distinguish themselves was an Esquire named *Walter de Riversley*, whom the King did make a Knight-Banneret, and upon whom, as a special and particular Reward for Valour, he did confer a fair Ring, being a Turquoise-Stone of a rich blue Colour set in Gold and having the royal Badge or Device of a Griffin, which said Signet-Ring the King did take from off his own Finger, and it did afterwards become an Heirloom with the Descendants of this Sir Walter de Riversley.' From him is descended the present Proprietor, who hath a fine Seat in this Parish."*

" Sir Walter's banner hangs up in the hall," says the Squire. "I will show it to you some day."

" And the ring, papa!" exclaims Pleasance; "do please show us the ring."

" That I cannot do, my little daughter," he replies. "King Edward's ring has been lost for over two hundred years. You have often heard how Riversley was sacked and partly burnt by the Roundheads in 1651, and how Arthur Riversley, a young man of thirty, then head of the family, fled into France and joined the Court of Charles II. He took with him the casket containing the ring. Those were troublous times. Not knowing where he could safely deposit it, he transferred the ring to his finger, and wore it day and night. Travelling in Spain on the King's affairs, he was seized by Moorish pirates and taken to Algiers. He escaped, and managed to get aboard a Portugese ship bound for the Guinea Coast. There he was joined by another young Englishman named Daniel Wood, and they had many thrilling adventures.

" This Daniel Wood, Dick," adds the Squire, turning to me, "was, your father thinks, brother to an ancestor of his."

" And the ring, papa?" cries Mistress Pleasance.

"Listen, I will tell you," continues Mr. Riversley. "Years afterwards, when Charles was on the throne, and, Arthur Riversley having long been given up as dead, his brother Thomas was living here, Wood arrived in Riversley, and confirmed his companion's death. He narrated their adventures to the Squire, who wrote them down in a book which I have here, and finished by telling how Arthur Riversley, worn out with fever and fatigue, had died and been buried at a place called Iboku, a village on a cliff some forty miles up from the mouth of a great river on the Guinea Coast."

" That's West Africa," says Jack.

" He brought back Arthur Riversley's walking-staff, a long stick of some hard native wood, grotesquely carved with lizards and human faces, with brass rings round the lower end, and scratched with the initials 'A.R.' You know it well; it hangs up in the hall above Lady Ann's picture."

"'Poor Lady Ann who saw the ghost and died with fright," Pleasance informs me in an aside. "But please go on, papa."

* Kirby's *Suffolk Traveller*, second edition, p. 421.

"Daniel Wood also brought with him a long strip of narrow cloth, coarse and durable, and dirty-white in hue.   On it, using apparently a pointed stick dipped in a dark blue dye, Arthur Riversley had printed the following words."

The Squire turns over the pages of a manuscript "History of the Riversley Family,' and shows us children this inscription and sketch:

YE RINGE IS IN YE HANDS OF YE QUENE
  OF IBIBIO

A BLACK PEOPLE OF GUINEE WHOSE
  MARKE IS

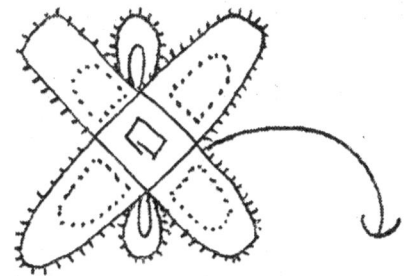

                    ARTHUR   RIVERSLEY
APRILL 1677.

We are spending a fine summer evening under Queen Elizabeth's oak in the park at Riversley.   On the rustic seat that surrounds its trunk sits Mr. Riversley, "the Squire," with his little daughter Pleasance at his side, and we two boys —Jack Riversley, the heir, aged twelve, and I, Richard Wood, the rector's son, and the Squire's godson, aged eleven—are lying on the grass.   Jack's sister Pleasance is two years younger than her brother.

"And where is the ring now?" asks Pleasance.

" Still in the land of Ibibio, as far as we know," replies her father; "perhaps on the finger of some man-eating monarch or dusky queen."

"Has nobody ever tried to recover it?" we all inquire.

"Yes; three attempts have been made, all without success, and all bringing disaster upon those attempting its recovery. Arthur Riversley's nephew went out in 1681, but died of fever on the Gold Coast.   Fifty years later the heir of the family and his next brother were shipwrecked and drowned off the Kru Coast, while on their way to find the Ibibio country. Lastly, in 1792, or thereabouts, Edward Mann, whose mother was a Riversley, undertook the quest, but was so badly bitten by a crocodile in the Calabar river that he died of his wounds soon after reaching home. He, however, got as far as discovering that the Ibibios are a cannibal tribe dwelling in the hinterland between the Niger and the Cross river. Since then no attempt has been made, and——"

"I wish I were a man," interrupts Pleasance, "for then I would sail away to the Guinea Coast, and have lots of splendid adventures, and at last get back the ring from the dusky Queen of Ibibio."

"When I grow up," exclaims Jack, "I will recover it, and you, Dick, must come with me."

"No, Jack, that won't do!" says the Squire. "Your duty lies at home. You are the last male heir of the elder branch, and I hope that you and your descendants will carry on the old line for many a generation. If you should lose your life in such a quixotic quest, the Holworth Riversleys would, on my death, succeed to this property, and I would rather that the old place should be burnt down than that it should go to them. They were Roundheads and Hanoverians in the past, and now they are Whigs, and so-called Reformers."

"But it would be great fun to get the ring," says Mistress Pleasance. "I wonder if the Queen always wears it!"

Jack, who has been knitting his brows thoughtfully, says, "If I were to die, Pleasance would be left. She would have Riversley, and she's as good a Tory as you are, sir. She would marry, and——"

"No, my boy," says the Squire, "no, she would not inherit. The Riversleys of Holworth would get the estate. When you are older, I will explain it all to you."

"Please tell us now, papa," says Pleasance. "I want to know why I can't inherit. Please leave out all the long words, and we'll try hard to understand."

"Well," he replies, "if you are very attentive, and don't interrupt, I'll try to make you understand it."

So we settle ourselves into attitudes of attention, and Mr. Riversley begins:

"King Edward's ring became the greatest heirloom of the Riversleys, and was handed down from generation to generation. It was kept in a casket, whose whereabouts was known to only the head of the family, his eldest son on coming of age, and their lawyer. In Henry the Eighth's reign, Sir Thomas Riversley pulled down the old mediæval hall, built the present house, and greatly improved the estate."

"He was knighted on Flodden Field," says Pleasance.

"Do be quiet," says Jack.

"He also," continues the Squire, "made a very long will, by which he strictly entailed Riversley in the main line from father to son. He had four sons and an only daughter named Pleasance, who was born ten years after her youngest brother, and became the delight of her father's old age."

"Just like me," says Mistress Pleasance in an aside.

"The brothers were all rather wild, fonder of roving and fighting than of staying at home, and this—so tradition states —caused the old Knight to add the following peculiar clause to the entail. I will read it over to you. Our family historian has shortened the long legal phrases, and put it all into fairly plain English."

"'If at any time the owner of Riversley have no son or other male issue, but have a daughter, she shall inherit on these conditions, namely, that she remain unmarried until she reach the discreet age of twenty-five years, when, choosing from among her suitors a good man and true, she shall go before the King, and, presenting unto the King the jewel known as "King Edward's Ring," shall beseech the King's grace to sanction their marriage and to bestow upon them the manor and lands of Riversley, whereupon the said bridegroom shall lay aside his own name and arms and adopt those of Riversley only. If the King do not approve her choice, or if she remain unmarried for twelve months and a day after her attaining the said age of twenty-five years, or if any other of the said conditions be unfulfilled, the manor and lands of Riversley shall pass to the next male heir of the family.'

"So much for Sir Thomas's entail."

"And did Pleasance's brothers all die? And did she marry a good man and true and inherit Riversley?" asks Jack.

"No, my boy," replies the Squire. "The third son eventually succeeded his father, and from that day to this there has always been a male heir, and Riversley has descended in unbroken line from father to son, although several times, as now, there has been an only son to inherit it."

"And if I were to die," continues Jack, "Pleasance could not inherit because the ring has been lost."

"That's it, my boy; that's just the difficulty. A hundred years ago, when my grandfather had three daughters but no son—he afterwards married again and had several sons—the case was submitted to the lawyers. They decided that, according to the terms of Sir Thomas's entail, no heiress could claim priority over a male heir unless she should fulfil *all* the conditions, including the production of 'King Edward's Ring.'"

Then Pleasance stands up, and, facing her father, exclaims, "It's very unfair, papa! I hate entails, and lawyers, and

stupid wills.   Since you won't allow Jack to go, *I* will go.
I will recover the ring, and you shall come with me, Dick."

*   *   *   *   *

I, Richard Wood, am recalling to mind the above scene as
I pace the deck of the "Africana," bound for West Africa.

It is the twelfth day since we steamed out of the Mersey
on the 25th of June, 188—, and I am getting ample leisure
to think over the whole of my past life, and to review the
circumstances which have sent me on this voyage.   Some of
my friends have called it "a wild-goose chase," but I must ask
you not to pronounce judgment until you have been placed
in a similar position yourself.

This is my first voyage, and, indeed, with the exception of
a winter spent in provincial France, I have never been out of
England before.   I have, therefore, all a traveller's experiences to learn.   Mankind is the most interesting of all
studies: the pageantry of life is so vastly entertaining that
one sometimes wishes one might be always a spectator, instead
of having to divide one's attention between playing one's part
and watching others play theirs.   Fortunately, however, for
the good of our great Empire, most of her sons are of the
opinion, and act up to it, that

"One crowded hour of glorious life
Is worth an age without a name."

But this is a narrative of adventures, and not a philosophical
treatise, so I must finish talking about thoughts and get on
with the story.

It is, as I have said, the twelfth day of the voyage.   We
have skirted the ill-famed "Bay"—which, however, proved to
be as calm as a mill-pond—passed the Canary Islands, and
are now getting our first view of the dark continent.   It
is the coast of Senegambia, and it looks very much like the
coast of anywhere else.   The low cliffs are mostly bare, but
are clothed here and there with trees.   The highest hill,
Cape Verde, has a light-house on its summit.   Through my
glasses I can see a few small villages and a few isolated
houses.   Miles out from land, two fishing-boats are tossing
about on the waves.   Each boat contains four natives, wearing dun-coloured clothing and scarlet fezes.   We are getting
into the "rainy belt," and expect a great deal of rain.

This evening there is a most glorious sunset—one of the most
beautiful I have ever seen.   It creates in my mind a vivid
picture of the old oak in Riversley park, with the Squire
and the three children grouped before him, and so I go over
again, word by word, the telling of the history of "King

Edward's Ring." That was fourteen years ago, and here am I setting out to recover the ring from the land of the cannibals.

To make everything plain to the reader, I must recall other pictures of the past.

* * * * *

Twelve years have passed away since we "talked ancestors" under Queen Elizabeth's oak. My mind's eye is looking into the Blue Chamber at Riversley Hall—a large, low room, lighted with two oriel windows filled in with diamond-shaped panes. The setting sun is streaming through them, staining the white coverlet of the bed with gules, azure, and or of the armorial shields emblazoned on the glass. On the bed, propped up with pillows, lies Jack Riversley; his sister Pleasance, now a beautiful girl of two-and-twenty, stands near the window, and I am sitting by the bedside.

In rescuing a little child from a hole in the ice, my friend Jack was himself submerged, and struggled so long before rescue arrived that he contracted pneumonia, and the doctors have given up hope of his recovery.

"Promise me," he is saying, his hand grasping mine, "promise me, Dick, that you will undertake the quest which you and I, with Pleasance as witness, vowed to follow to the end. I cannot live another month, and I am the last of the older line of the Riversleys. It would break the Squire's heart if the old place should go to the Holworth branch. In three years' time Pleasance will be twenty-five, and then, unless she produces the ring, she will lose all claim to this property."

"O! don't worry, dear Jack," Pleasance exclaims. "Nothing matters if you don't get well again. Of course you will get well. *I* have never believed the doctors."

"Let me finish, Pleasance," he says. "Listen, Dick. This very year you and I were to have set out for the Ibibio country. We have talked of it and planned it for years, but it is all over with me now, and you must go alone. . . . I have no strength to say much. Promise me that you will do your best to recover King Edward's ring."

"I promise, Jack."

"Thank you, old fellow," he says, pressing my hand, and looking into my eyes with a look which I never forgot. "And now, Pleasance, I want you also to promise me something. Promise me that when Dick returns with the ring you will cease your disdainful ways and——"

* * * * *

The same room, the same figure on the bed, the same

stains of gules, azure and or on the white coverlet. There is
a brighter flush on the sick man's face as he joins together
the hands of his sister and his life-long friend.

"Dear old Jack!" says Pleasance. "you have been as blind
as Dick himself. Whether he returns with the ring or
without it, I promise."

*　　　*　　　*　　　*　　　*

Six months later. A lawyer's office. Mr. Stubbin, the
Squire's solicitor, is talking, and I, dressed in deep mourning,
am listening to him.

"The Riversley estate, being entailed, could not be mort-
gaged," he is saying; "but Mr. Riversley has from time to
time been obliged to mortgage all his other property, and I
fear that, at his death, Miss Riversley will be left almost
penniless. The estate will then go to his kinsman, Sir
Frederick Riversley of Holworth, which, as you know well,
lies on the other side of the county. The late Sir Frederick
was an ardent Whig."

"'He successfully opposed Mr. Riversley for the borough
of Ipswich, I believe?" I remark.

"He did," replies Mr. Stubbin, and continues, "Earlier
in life they were rival competitors for the hand of the same
lady, and, in that contest, the Squire was the winner. The
present Sir Frederick is a less zealous opponent of Mr.
Riversley's views. He has, in short, made overtures for
Miss Riversley's hand, and has offered to espouse the Tory
cause. This, and the unforeseen prospect of the old place
still remaining the home of his daughter and her descendants,
have won over the Squire, and he ardently desires the consummation of this proposed marriage."

"And Miss Riversley?" I inquire.

"Miss Riversley is in great distress. Anxious to give her
father his heart's desire, she yet refuses to accept Sir
Frederick, asserting that she has promised her hand to you,
Mr. Wood. I, my dear sir, am instructed to—to—request
that you will give back that promise."

"Are you speaking on behalf of the Squire or of Miss
Riversley?" I ask. "On the death of her brother, Miss
Riversley and her father went abroad, and, as you know, are
still away. I have not seen them personally for several
months."

"'It is Mr. Riversley who is instructing me,' the lawyer
replies.

"Then tell him," I answer, "that I refuse to consider his
request until after my return from West Africa, and that it

will then rest with Miss Riversley as to whether or not she be released from her promise."

   *   *   *   *   *

The same landscape as in my first picture. The two figures standing under Queen Elizabeth's oak are those of Pleasance Riversley and Richard Wood.

She points to the Queen's motto carved in deep letters on the back of the rustic seat—SEMPER EADEM.

   *   *   *   *   *

The next day. S.s. "Africana" steaming out of the Mersey.

CHAPTER II.

DOG TOWZER IS INTRODUCED, AND INTRODUCES AMO ILORIN.

A fortnight after leaving Liverpool we again sighted land —a monotonously-flat coast fringed with trees, the surf breaking white on the sandy beach.

In the afternoon we anchored off Monrovia, the capital of Liberia, and lay in perfectly calm water about a mile and a half from the shore. Among the palms on the beach were a number of low, thatched huts.

The reason for putting in here was to engage a gang of Kru boys to work the cargo at other ports further along the coast.

The steam whistle signalled our arrival with a long fiendish shriek, and we soon saw a bustle on the beach, followed by the launching of many canoes and two big surf-boats. The former were very light, in shape exactly like the half of a huge pea-pod, and so narrow that the occupants, sitting behind one another, almost touched the sides with their sides. Some canoes contained only two or three, while others were almost full.

They passed round to the starboard side, and there a scene of animated confusion prevailed.

The "boys" who came to swell the numbers of our crew were more dressed—less undressed would be more accurate—

than their friends who paddled them out, but some of their young brothers were quite naked. These last, after taking leave of their elder relatives, gave us some amusement by diving for coins thrown from the steamer.

I had been recommended to engage a Kruman as my servant. Several came aboard on the look-out for masters. From among them I engaged a youth who informed me in fairly understandable English that his name was Tom Peter. I chose him for his good-natured, though ugly, face, and for his herculean proportions, denoting strength which might be useful in an emergency. Referring to an old note-book, I am able to give his exact measurements: Height, 5 feet 10 inches; chest, 41 inches; waist, 33 inches; biceps, 12¾ inches; thigh, 23 inches; neck, 16 inches.

He induced me also to engage his small brother, Jim George, who, he informed me, was a skilful valet. Of this pair, more hereafter.

Anchor was weighed, and we put out to sea again.

I must now introduce to you the faithful comrade who accompanied me to the West Coast, so, without further delay—dog "Towzer," the Reader. I hope that, during the course of our adventures, you will learn to like and respect one another as greatly as I like and respect you both. More than that I cannot say!

Dog Towzer is a well-bred fox-terrier with shapely body and legs, round, clear eyes, set sufficiently far apart to inspire trust, and an expression as alert as it is intelligent. He soon became a favourite with everybody on board, and the good-natured Captain allowed him the run of the whole ship. On the first night, he was confined in the cook's galley, but, somehow or other, he managed to break loose and find his way to my cabin. Awaking at dawn, I saw him lying on the floor. He opened his eyes, rapped his stumpy tail on the ground, winked knowingly at me as much as to say, "Yes, here I am," and then went to sleep again.

For some peculiar reason known only to himself, he took quite kindly to the Kru "boys." Whether it was that their bare legs and feet made him feel akin to them—I noticed that he declined to have anything to do with the natives in civilised costume—or whether it was their open-air meals and huge appetites that won his doggy heart, it is, as I have said before, impossible to know. Anyhow, he liked them, and they liked him, and he spent a good deal of his time among them and the deck-passengers. He especially attached him-self to my cook, Tom Peter, whose afternoon siesta on the deck he used frequently to share, Towzer's white coat forming the pillow for Tom Peter's woolly head. If, however, Towzer arrived late, and found the cook already asleep, he took his turn by softly resting his head on Tom Peter's great bare chest. At night, he never deserted his white master for his black friends.

Passing the Ivory Coast, we anchored, on the nineteenth day of the voyage, at Axim, a port on the Gold Coast. During nearly the whole of the preceding day, it had rained persistently. It was about 6.30 a.m., rainy and misty, and the place seemed reeking with damp; but the weather soon cleared up and the sun came out. Here we took a great many native passengers aboard, and also landed some Europeans, getting a good deal of amusement in watching the ascent of the former from the surf-boats to the deck, and the awkward descent of the latter. Some of the new-comers were Mohammedan traders going to Lagos, taller and far more intelligent-looking than the Krumen, and wearing togas of coloured cotton gracefully draped from the shoulders.

In the afternoon we reached Sekondi, another place on the Gold Coast. From the steamer it looked clean and well-kept, the European houses large and white, and the native dwellings built of mud, with thatched roofs, and palm-trees in among them. The same animated scenes occurred. The boatmen here use short, three-pronged paddles and sing as they ply between the shore and the steamer. There is a wild strain of real music in their monotonous chants. They wear nothing but a loin-cloth, above which they are of fine physique. Their long, muscular backs, gleaming with splashings from their paddles, fall and rise all together with the utmost regularity as they dig the waves with short, sharp thrusts.

We lay here till the middle of the night, and some of us sat up on deck enjoying the cool breeze and the bright starlight. I dozed for a few minutes, and dreamt of home, and, awaking, found it difficult to realise that I was really nearing the land of the cannibals. For centuries we Woods have been yeomen in the same neighbourhood in Suffolk, living a peaceful, stay-at-home life. I used to think that it would be almost impossible to break away from the strong bonds of Heredity. Yet I have broken the chain, and here I am, many hundreds of miles from East Anglia, having put my life and "all" to the touch on a quest as full of possibilities as were the quests of the days of chivalry. It was pleasant to be absolutely free and independent, the air felt thick with adventures, and it was a fine thing to call at port after port and see—or, at any rate, know—that the Union Jack was floating supreme on shore.

The next day we called at Cape Coast Castle and Accra.

B

The former looks from the sea like a miniature Constanti-nople. Its houses—European and native picturesquely com-mingled at the expense of sanitation and health—slope up from the beach, and the surrounding country is hilly and densely wooded. Accra is quite different, presenting a long, straggling appearance with all its buildings standing on the same level. At both ports we shipped more native passengers, and at the latter place the purser bought pine-apples, which proved to be a refreshing addition to our bill of fare.

On the twenty-first day after leaving Liverpool, we dropped anchor in Lagos Roads, and, circumstances being such that the "Africana" had to spend twenty-four hours there, I took the opportunity to go ashore and call on a college friend who was private secretary to the Administrator of the Government.

Tom Peter and Towzer accompanied me, the former being anxious for me to buy him "cloth,'" and also assuring me that, without his protection, probably both I and my dog would, as new-comers, be taken advantage of by "dem sabby-book [educated] niggers," and that they might even "chop [eat]" Towzer!

I found my friend by no means overwhelmed with work, his "Chief" being down with fever, and he prevailed upon me to stay the night with him at Government House. Lagos is the largest town on the West African coast, but there are far larger native towns in the interior. I do not intend to trouble the non-skipping reader with my first impressions of this semi-European, semi-native community, nor is it my intention to tell you what we had for dinner, or exactly how many mosquitoes I caught or did not catch under the dia-phanous curtain or net that hung around my bed.

Let it suffice me to say that all went well until early the next morning, namely, at 7 o'clock, an hour after I had risen, when Tom Peter, whose yearnings for cloth had been rather upset by seeing and coveting the white trousers and white, gold-buttoned "mess-jackets" of the "boys" at Government House, came up to me rather excitedly—a negro never rushes up—and exclaimed, "Dem soldier-man go t'ief [thief, steal] dem dog Tuza, sar!"

"Here's a mild adventure to begin with!" thought I; my friend Hall inquired "What's this palaver about?" and Tom Peter gave us the following graphic account of it.

"'I go for market, sar," he said. "Dem dog go foller me. He walk close my legs, like so," indicating, with his hand, that Towzer had kept close to heel. "Dem soldier-man—he be *bad* man!—he lib for market. He look dem dog; he like 'em. I no t'ink he go t'ief 'em. I buy plenty t'ings. I

lib for buy s nall, small beef [a small piece of meat]. I no
sabby dem man foller me. I look [see] my bruder; I no look
'im for long time [it is long since I have seen him]. We lib
for talk. Den one time I t'ink 'Tuza!' He no
lib! I hollar. Den dem mammy what sell beef, she
say 'What's matter?' Den she say, 'Dem Amo, dem
long man, he buy beef—dem dog t'ief it—den Amo, he
go quick, he catch dem dog, he put 'em for bag, he run for
bush.' Den I hollar 'T'ief, t'ief!' I run; plenty people
run; we find [look for] 'em, we no look [find] 'em.''

This explanation ended, Hall at once called an orderly, and
despatched him with a note to the head of the police depart-
ment. In a very short time, a smart corporal and three
constables arrived, and my friend explained the whole matter,
and, on behalf of the Governor, issued instructions that they
were to do their utmost to recover my dog and to capture the
thief. Tom Peter volunteered to lead them to "dem mammy
what sell beef," and off they started.

Four hours later, when we, having finished "breakfast," were
sitting on the verandah smoking cigarettes and talking of
things in general, the corporal appeared with a grin of satisfaction on his face, and, saluting the Police Magistrate, who
had been lunching with us, said "We catch him, sar!"

Our host consenting, the Police Magistrate ordered that the
man should be brought before us. The first to arrive was
dog Towzer, who, breaking away from Tom Peter's custody,
rushed up to greet me, looking rather muddled, but apparently
none the worse for his escapade. Then came Tom Peter, but
in what a state!—his cloth clotted with mud on the left side
from hip to knee, his singlet (vest) torn off the right shoulder
and hanging in tatters, blood oozing from a nasty wound on
the right arm, and his face and hands all dirtied with mud,
perspiration, and blood.

"We catch dem t'ief, sar!" he cried exultingly. "He be
bad man, plenty bad. He fight plenty; I fight; I pass him
for strong [I proved stronger than he].''

Then, escorted by a rabble of men and boys, who had been
admitted as "witnesses," came the prisoner, handcuffed, and
guarded by the three constables, whose uniform bore signs of
rough treatment.

The prisoner himself presented a deplorable appearance.
After getting on his track, they had followed him along the
outskirts of the town to a small, dirty hamlet situated a mile
or so away, and there, after having been chased from one compound to another, he had turned at bay, and fought the whole
band of them, until, at last, Tom Peter, who had been rescuing Towzer from durance vile in a dark inner chamber, had

joined the assailants and brought the matter to a close. Tom
Peter, motioning the others to stand aside, had tackled him
single-handed. After battering one another with sticks, they
had wrestled on the ground, and eventually the thief had been
overcome and put in irons.

He was, as the seller of "beef" had said, a "long man."—
six feet two inches in height, I judged, and deep-chested and
broad-shouldered in proportion. During his flight and subsequent struggles, he had discarded or had had torn from him
all his clothes except a scanty loin-cloth, dark blue in colour.
His splendid proportions and long shapely limbs were thus
fully disclosed to view, and I thought him the best-built man
of his size that I had ever seen. His arms, ironed together
at the wrists, hung down dejectedly, he kept his head low
with chin on his breast, and his whole attitude betokened abject
despair.

On his being brought to a standstill immediately in front
of us, we could see that he had suffered considerably in the
fight. His skin was scratched and bleeding, and smeared
with dirt and blood. From a long cut on the side of his
head the blood was still dripping, and he had a similar wound
on the right thigh.

"This is an old offender," said the Police Magistrate, turning to me; "his name is Amo Ilorin; he comes from Ilorin, a
Yoruba town far away in the interior. He is always getting
into trouble, and, in short, has spent more of the last four
or five years in than out of prison. When he first appeared
here from the north, he was recruited for the constabulary,
but, after a year's service, was dismissed for repeated acts of
insubordination. He won't return to his own country, and
insists on staying here, though he is so unpopular with the
native staff at the gaol that I'm afraid he gets more than his
share of dirty work and punishment when undergoing sentence there."

Then, looking at the prisoner, and addressing him through
an interpreter, he continued, "The last time you were arrested
for larceny, Amo, you were sent to prison with hard labour
for twelve months, and I warned you that, if you did it again,
I should transfer the case to the big Judge [Chief Justice]
in the Supreme Court, and recommend a severe sentence and
a flogging. Your past record is so bad that you will probably
get at least five years this time. Take him to prison, Corporal,
and tell the gaoler to send him before me to-morrow."

I ventured to interpose. "My dog is the cause of this
trouble," I said; "would you allow the man to be asked if
he has anything to say for himself?"

"Certainly, if you wish," was the reply. "Ask the prisoner,

Foster," said the Police Magistrate to his interpreter, "if he wants to say anything."

Amo Ilorin lifted his head, and, raising his chained hands, wiped away the blood from his left eyebrow and cheek. He looked to be about my own age. There was a hunted, sullen expression in his great eyes. He spoke to the interpreter, who turning to us, said, smiling,

"He says he does not care how much you flog him—you may kill him, if you like—but that he cannot spend five years in prison, and that, if you send him there again, he will kill himself. He says that his mother will pay plenty money if you will fine him and not send him to prison."

As the interpreter finished speaking, an old hag made her way through the little crowd, leading two goats, and carrying a cloth tied up into a bundle. Handing over the goats to a girl who accompanied her, she flung herself on her knees, and, untying the ends of the cloth, poured out a medley of coins on the ground, and, pointing to them and the goats and fowls —the girl had flung down half-a-dozen fowls with legs tied together—began to gesticulate to the Police Magistrate.

"She says," interpreted Foster, "that she will pay all her goods for her son's release; that she is a slave in the house of Mamodu Latopa; that her days are drawing to an end, and that her son Amo stays here to perform the sacred rite of burying her, and that, if you put him in prison, she will die soon and alone in this foreign country and will be buried like a dog with no one to mourn for her."

Then the prisoner, laying aside his defiant, sullen attitude, pulled himself up, and, using his fettered hands as freely as that condition permitted, and looking from his mother to us, and from us to his mother, poured out sentence after sentence of what, though I could not of course understand one word of it, was the most impassioned eloquence and pleading that I had ever heard.

The Police Magistrate yawned and said, "Well, what does it all mean? Cut it short, please, for we are getting rather tired of this."

"He says he is young and full of strength; that he does not like to live in the small, small prison, but likes to move about in the big world, free to go anywhere. He begs you to let him stay and bury his mother, and to take all their goats, and cloth, and fowls, and money instead of sending him to prison. He says that, if you no agree to that, you must send him and his mother over the great sea to the land of Ibibio, and sell them there as slaves, so that his mother may die in her own country and her spirit be born again there."

"Ibibio!" I exclaimed, "ask him what he knows of Ibibio."

But here the old woman broke in. Standing up, and leaving her money scattered on the ground, she addressed us with much animation. To emphasise her words, she brought her arms, body, and head into play in such manner that their movements almost anticipated the interpreter's rendering.

"She says," the man translated, "that she is the daughter of a big [*i.e.*, important] woman who lived far away over the great sea in a country called Ibibio. That long ago, when she was a girl, but almost ready to go into the fattening-house, there was war in her country. Her mother's village was burnt, and she herself was seized and taken to Efik, where she was sold to a man, a trader, from this country. He took her over the great sea—she was full of fear, she says—and brought her here and sold her to another man. Then, after many days of travel, she was taken to a very big town ——"

"Ilorin," interrupted the prisoner, who was following the narrative with interest; "I was born there."

"At Ilorin," continued Foster, "she became handmaid to the principal wife of a great chief, who had many horses and sheep, and a new wife every moon. She found favour in his eyes and bore him two daughters and then a son. This son now stands before you. When Amo grew up, he was bigger and stronger, and had a blacker skin and a longer neck, than all the other sons of this chief, so that his father loved him much and gave him a horse and a gun. But she herself, she says, grew old, and then this chief saw her no more. The other sons of the great chief and their mothers became jealous of Amo, and so they agreed among themselves and seized him and his mother, and sold her to Mamodu Latopa of Lagos, and sold Amo to the Bini people."

Here the prisoner again interrupted.

"He says," Foster told us, "he says that he was taken to Benin, and that the king there, seeing him to be a big and a strong man, would have made him one of his eunuchs; that he, in the presence of all the court, thanked the king for this proposed honour, and so deceived them all, and so escaped. Then he returned to Ilorin to look for his mother, and then hid himself, but was betrayed, and almost captured again. Then he went to many towns of the Yoruba country, and at last he came to Lagos, and found his mother in the house of Mamodu Latopa. She being an old woman, he stayed here to bury her."

The prisoner said something to his mother, and she answered him.

"What are they saying?" inquired the Police Magistrate.

"I don't know, sir," replied Foster; "but I think they speak their own country language."

"Ask him," I said, "if he understands the Ibibio speech."

"He says he understands it small [a little]," interpreted Foster; "that his mother taught him the language of her own people, and that he and his mother speak Ibibio when alone together."

"Luck has befriended me," I thought to myself, "for, no sooner do I set foot on African soil, some four or five hundred miles from my destination, than I find two people who can speak the Ibibio language, one of whom was actually born and brought up in that inaccessible country. Moreover, they are both evidently extremely desirous to go there, and might prove of great use to me. I am told that negroes are never 'grateful,' but I feel quite willing to risk an experiment. If I can obtain the prisoner's freedom through my intercession, and arrange for the return of his mother to her country, I may win their gratitude, and thus perhaps help on my own ends." These thoughts passed through my brain in far less time than it has taken me to write them down.

I had told my friend Hall something of my quest, so I said to him, "This fellow might prove very useful to me. If you will send all these people out of hearing, I should like to discuss it with you and Mr. Philipps."

So interpreter, police, prisoner, and rabble were sent away to sit down under the trees, and we three fell to discussing my proposal.

The Police Magistrate at first rather demurred at my offer to take this notorious prisoner out of the hands of the law, but, when I proposed to redeem Amo's mother and take her with me also, and so remove from Lagos the cause of her devoted son's persistency in remaining there, he fell into agreement with me. They both thought me very rash in taking such a ne'er-do-well under my wing, but, being men of the world, they admitted the truth of my observation that "the so-called 'black sheep' of human kind often turn out to be particularly white if only treated in the right way. When a fire smokes, blame the stoker, not the fire."

Hall obtained the assent of the Governor—I cannot recollect whether "Governor" or "Administrator" was the title then in vogue at Lagos—to my proposal, and, meanwhile, the Police Magistrate sent a message to summon Mamodu Latopa, owner of Amo's mother.

She and her son, the interpreter, police, and rabble having again been called up before us, it was explained to them that I, "the white man with the moustache," was on my way to Old Calabar and Ibibio, and that I proposed spending several months at the former place in order to pick up some know-ledge of the Ibibio language before continuing my travels. If Amo and Adiaha (the old woman's name) would swear to serve me faithfully, and teach me the Ibibio language, and help me in the Ibibio country, I would intercede with the Government for his release, and would redeem her from her master, and would take them bc'h with me.

Down on their knees in front of me they both fell, with their foreheads touching the ground. Hating a "scene," and feeling very uncomfortable, I asked the interpreter to make them get up, which he did. The poor old lady seemed more dazed, than frenzied, with joy. Her son conducted himself with quiet dignity, but said "T''ank you, sar," and gave me a look with his great eyes that, somehow or other, reminded me of my poor friend Jack Riversley's look when I promised him to undertake the quest.

Adiaha's redemption was easily arranged with Mamodu Latopa, and I paid over the money.

Before doing this, however, the Police Magistrate adminis-tered to mother and son a solemn oath that they should serve me faithfully in all things and should never return to Lagos again. First, they were both sworn on a Bible. Then the interpreter suggested that they should also be sworn on the woman's own "juju," which, he said, she wore around her neck. The old woman was decently clothed in a series of dark blue wraps, gracefully draped in the fashion favoured by Mohammedan women. Round her neck she wore a necklace of elephant's hair. Attached thereto, and hanging between the breasts, was an object about the size of a hen's egg, but longer and flatter, bound round with copper wire. This, the interpreter explained, contained, wrapped in cloth, a fragment of some relic belonging to her mother's family, by whom it was greatly reverenced. It had been tied round her neck a few days after birth, and she attributed to it the preservation of her life through all the dangers of the past.

Detaching this pendant, the old woman passed it three times round her head, and then, touching it with her lips, re-swore the oath administered by the Police Magistrate through the interpreter. Then her son followed suit.

It was now two o'clock. The "Africana" was to weigh anchor at six p.m. Adiaha was sent off to collect her goods and chattels, and Amo, who was to remain under police custody until embarkation, was taken away to be washed, and to have the wound on his head sewn up and dressed. Tom Peter was also sent to the doctor.

My host and his other guest gave me much kind advice

as to taking quinine, sleeping under a mosquito-net, changing immediately after getting wet, and "Above all," they said, "*don't worry*; the mind acts on the body, and more than half the battle in West Africa is to keep cheery and hopeful."

They went with me to the beach to see me off. Amo was already in the boat, handcuffed, and guarded by the corporal and one constable. Adiaha, however, was still ashore. The boatman had refused to embark her goods, and no wonder! She had five goats, a cat—yawling dolorously, it being tied too tightly round the loins—at least a score of fowls in a huge flat basket, a couple of ducks, two heavy wooden boxes, and a large assortment of pots, pans, calabashes, sleeping-mats, and other domestic utensils. Everybody was wrangling, Tom Peter foremost of them all, and Towzer was trying to worry the cat.

Our arrival somewhat mended matters, and we then learned that the chief cause of commotion was that the old lady had left her parrot behind, and, having failed to enlist a runner in her cause, was threatening to return to the town herself. She was, certainly, most unreasonable! She threatened to drown herself, to kill herself, to do anything, in short, except behave like a sensible being. At last, however, I hired another boat, and we bundled them all in—Adiaha (still protesting!), goats, cat (still yawling), fowls, ducks, boxes, "and et cetera" as they say. Towzer wanted to go in that boat as escort to the cat, but this was not allowed.

So, taking farewell of our Lagos friends, we pushed off to the branch-boat (steamer), which took us to the "Africana." On boarding her, the irons were taken off Amo's wrists, and he became a free man attached to my service. I never had cause to regret this arrangement, and I often had reason to congratulate myself on it.

Many a time has my wife said to me, "If you hadn't taken out Towzer with you, and if Towzer hadn't been stolen by Amo, you might never have found the ring, and you might have been eaten by the cannibals!"

To which I always reply, "If you hadn't given me Towzer, I should never have taken him out with me."

CHAPTER III.

THE TAMING OF AMO.

As soon as we were out to sea again, I took stock of my little native following. Jim George, the cook's small brother, had remained on board in charge of their "box." Tom Peter's wound had been well dressed, and gave him but little pain. Amo, however, had fared worse. The doctor had shaved the left side of his head and sewn up the long cut, but, though he would not admit it, it was evident that the pain was still considerable. The wound in his right thigh, which had also been sewn up, was not so severe. He said his body felt "sick all over," so I sent him to lie down.

Adiaha had forgotten the loss of her parrot in the anxiety of getting all her live stock and household goods safely on board. She gathered them around her on the for'ard deck, and I was pleased to see Tom Peter helping her assiduously. "How quickly," I said to myself, "these natives fraternize, and what a good fellow Tom Peter is to do so much for the old woman!" On remarking this to the Skipper, who was also leaning over the rail watching the deck-passengers, he laughed and said, "Your 'boy' is not doing that for nothing!"

After dinner, Tom Peter found me strolling up and down, and said to me, "Dem woman like me, sar. I no let dem Lagos boys humbug her for beach [on the beach]. I help her plenty. She dash [give] me one goat." So the cook's goodness was satisfactorily explained.

He had, however, come to report that Amo was "plenty sick, he lib for talk fool-palaver," which meant that he was delirious. I followed Tom Peter down the companion-ladder, and we threaded our way among sleeping natives curled up in every attitude on the deck. An awning had been stretched over them as a protection against rain, and the air underneath was somewhat close. Poor old Adiaha, worn out with the excitements and anxieties of the day, was sound asleep amidst her worldly goods. The cat, however, was awake, and glared at me out of a dark corner.

Amo had placed his sleeping-mat and pillow apart from other passengers, and had wrapped himself up in the long blue wrapper which, together with a cast-off pair of soldier's breeches and a scarlet fez, he had added to his scanty costume before entering my service. But, tossing about in his sleep, he had uncovered himself, and now lay with the upper part of his body exposed to the cold night air. He was talking and muttering and clenching his hands as if again living through all the incidents of the fight. I felt his forehead; it was burning hot. His heart and pulse were also thumping abnormally.

Leaving Tom Peter there, I went in search of the ship's doctor. He, though deep in a rubber of whist, followed me at once, but seemed rather astonished when I led him to the deck-passengers.

"Fever," he said, "that's all. I will give him a dose of salts and twenty grains of quinine, and he'll be all right to-morrow."

So the doctor administered the medicine, and it seemed to quiet him.

By the morning, however, the fever had increased instead of abated. He was very ill. The continual chatter and confusion on the for'ard deck made his delirium worse. I had noticed on the poop a quiet nook walled in on three sides with cargo, and it now occurred to me that this was the place for Amo. So, the Captain consenting, a gang of Krumen carried him there, and the Third Officer—a pleasant, jovial, young fellow whom I had got to know rather well during the voyage—had an awning rigged up, and so made it quite a snug retreat.

Here—to cut a long story short—I spent the greater part of the next three or four days, including the nights, nursing Amo. Tom Peter, and, sometimes, little Jim George, relieved me during part of each night, and at meal-times. His mother was of but little help to us, for, as soon as she had left her goats and other goods to visit the poop, she began worrying over their safety, and so became such a nuisance to everybody, that we eventually did all the nursing ourselves, but allowed her to see her son for a few minutes every day.

The Captain, the doctor and crew, and all the other European passengers thought it very absurd in me to take so much trouble about "a native"; but, leaving humanity out of the question, they had not perhaps so much at stake as I had.

The passage from Lagos to Old Calabar took us nearly a week. We lay forty-eight hours off the mouth of the Forcados river, some ten or eleven miles out at sea, waiting for the branch-boat to come out to us, to tranship passengers and mails for the Niger. Our first sight of the coast of the country now known as Nigeria was ushered in by a glorious sunset, which, acting on my Lagos friends' hopeful maxim, I regarded as an omen of good luck. I sat on the poop in the fading light, gazing at the tree-fringed shore and wondering what was in store for me in the mysterious inland country.

About two o'clock in the second night, Tom Peter came to my cabin and roused me with the report that Amo "lib for die [is dying], sar." Putting on a dressing-gown over my pyjamas, I hastened round to the poop. The fever-stricken man had left his mat and crawled to the side of the ship, and was leaning against the rail, apparently in a dead-faint, and almost naked, for he had thrown off the blankets with which we had covered him. The moon was casting a myriad of dancing lights on the sea; her beams burnished the muscles of Amo's great shoulders and the graceful curves of his long, shapely limbs. We half led, half carried, him back to bed.

"I t'ink," said Tom Peter, "I t'ink he fear debil plenty much. Debil humbug him *plen*-ty. I t'ink he lib for —what you say?—jump for sea."

We wrapped him up once more. His temperature was 103 degrees. I gave him a drink of milk and soda, and he sank down with a sort of groan. Tom Peter fetched me a blanket from my cabin, and I sat there until the moon faded and the first faint signs of dawn appeared.

The rising and the setting of the sun are two of the most beautiful spectacles vouchsafed to us in all the wonderful pageantry of this life of ours, and I sometimes comfort myself with the thought that, when I become old and lose, as I must, the keener feelings of "glorious life," I shall still enjoy to the very end delights such as the majestic beauty of great trees, the music of the brook, the yearly procession of English wild-flowers from yellow Spring to purple Autumn, the soft radiance of sunrise and the rich splendour of sunset.

At dawn, Amo ceased his restless movements and mutterings, and dropped off into a quiet sleep. Tom Peter, with Towzer as pillow, was lying on his back on the other side of the poop. His lusty snoring, together with the dog's fainter refrain, blended into a duet which the most charitably-minded critic could not in truth call musical.

Between 7.30 and 8 o'clock, Amo awoke fully conscious. His forehead was cooler, and I found that his temperature was gone down two degrees. I helped him to sit up. By this time, I had found out that he could both understand and speak English a little. Pointing to the side of the ship where we had found him during the night, I said "Bad, bad," and shook my head and frowned.

He replied, "I beg you, sar. Me be plenty sick. Debil humbug too much. I t'ink I lib for die. Dem big fish [shark] go chop me. You no go, sar, I beg you!"

"All right, old fellow," I said, patting his shoulder. "I won't leave you. Them devil fear white man too much;

white man pass [is stronger than] devil. I think you live for get well. Sabby [do you understand]?"

"Yes, sar," he said, with an attempt at a smile; "white man be all same [the same as] God," and he turned his great melancholy eyes up to the sky. He sat looking at me for a time, and then, his head nodding drowsily, I made him lie down again, and he fell into a quiet sleep, which lasted until the sun was high in the heavens.

By this time we had left Forcados far behind, and were steaming eastward for Bonny. That same evening we anchored off the mouth of the river, waiting for the flowing tide to carry us safely over the bar at daylight. I had had my camp-bed brought up from the hold and unpacked, so that I might sleep on the poop, and thus keep to my promise of not leaving Amo. He, however, protested, "I beg you, sar. Me no be fool any more. You no fit for sleep here."

But, feeling pretty certain that he would not attempt suicide again through fear of the "devil" of sickness, and that my near presence was sufficient security, I slept with my usual abandonment of the cares of life. I awoke only once. The moon was shining full into our little retreat. Amo had tossed off the blanket from his right shoulder and side, and, while gently replacing it, I waked him, and he said, "What's matter?" Then, realising what I was about, he laid his hand softly and hesitatingly on my arm and said, "Me t'ank you, sar. You be all same bruder for me. S'pose you die, me die. I like you plenty, sar."

Then I gave him my hand, and we swore a silent, but mutually-understood, oath of friendship, a friendship which has lasted—well, which still lasts. You will see in the sequel—if you have patience to follow this yarn to a close— that Amo Ilorin proved willing to die, not only with or after me, but for me.

The Bonny river, as are all those on this coast, is fringed with luxuriant mangrove-swamps, and the eye soon wearies of their grey-green monotony. Bonny itself is quite a small place, consisting of a cluster of European houses and "factories" with a native village on one side. I landed for an hour or two, and was interested in the tropical shrubs and flowers. I gathered a blue flower growing wild, resembling our water-violet. The native village consists of a collection of low mud hovels with trees and little cultivated patches in among them. Towzer and I stared at the natives, and they at us. They struck me as being a very queer-looking lot! Some of the children were tattooed or painted all over. Dogs and fat little goats went about here and there. The huts seemed full of naked children. The women wore no clothing above the waist, and were ugly creatures. Several old cannon lay about. The "streets" had open drains with liquid filth running therein, but the smell was really not very bad. I noticed a bread-fruit tree covered with green fruit.

My first impressions of the natives of the "Oil Rivers" were far from favourable, these people being of poor physique, and, judging from their faces, as low in intellect as in physical endowments. On getting back to the ship, I remarked this to the Skipper, and he said that the natives living in these Europeanised coast-towns were "the scum of the country," who, having added the white man's vices to their own, had become one of the lowest types of humanity.

The next morning we entered the mouth of the Cross River, or Calabar estuary, but, a little up, we ran on to the flats, and there stuck fast. Every effort was made to get the steamer afloat, but, though she somewhat shifted her first position, she refused to continue her passage until flood-tide the following morning. We were all weary of the long voyage, and twenty-four hours in a drizzling rain within some forty miles of our goal was the climax of dreariness and weariness.

However, to air another hacknied piece of philosophy applicable to West Africa, "all things come to those who wait," and so we did at last find ourselves moving on between low banks of mangroves churned by the coffee-coloured water disturbed by our paddle-wheels. All around, as far as the eye could see, lay these mangrove swamps. Rain fell heavily at intervals, and rain-clouds filled the sky; it was what one calls "April weather" at home. Higher up, the low banks give place to cliffs on which stand the native suburbs of Old Calabar.

About noon we anchored off Duke Town, and at 3 o'clock I went ashore to pay my respects, and to present a note of introduction, to the British Consul, Mr. Johnston. I did not at first tell him of my projected visit to the Ibibio country, but stated that I wished to spend a few months at Old Calabar in order to study the language and customs of the natives. (I ought, before now, to have told you that, prior to leaving England, I had been informed on good authority that the language of the Efiks or Calabarese was almost the same as that spoken by the Ibibios.)

Mr. Johnston was most courteous and obliging, and helped me in every way. Until I could find quarters of my own, he insisted on putting me up in his own bungalow, and extended his hospitality, not only to my two Kru servants, but to Amo, his mother Adiaha, and all her goats, fowls, ducks, and other effects. Towzer and the cat were of course included.

Amo's fever had left him, but he was weak and shaky from the effects of it. His wounds were healing satisfactorily.

It was in the latter half of July—I forget the exact day—when we reached Old Calabar, and I stayed a week with the Consul before getting into a house of my own. It was the middle of the wet season, and a very wet season it was! Having jotted down in my note-book the results of meteorological observations taken at the Consulate, I give them here so that the exact and scientifically-minded reader may judge for himself. That year the rains began in the middle of March, and the total rainfall for that month was 8.22 inches. In April, 8.61; May, 16.87; June, 14.87; July, 21.81; August, 26.14; September, 22.37; October, 5.49.

Thanks to my host's assistance, I acquired the loan for one year of a "compound" built on the hill at the back of the European "factories" which here fringed the left bank of the river. For this I paid the extremely reasonable rent of three shillings a-month! A compound is a collection of huts or rooms forming altogether the residence of one family. When isolated, as mine was, they are usually surrounded with a fence or stockade within which are shanties for live stock and little patches of vegetable-garden. The walls are built of wattle and clay, and the roof is a framework of stalks of the wine-palm (*Raphia-vinifera*) thatched with mats made from its leaflets. The floor is of clay beaten hard, and still further hardened by the application of cattle-dung. Clay couches and seats are raised according to the architect's fancy, and strong bed-platforms and shelves are made with palm-stalks.

My compound was fairly clean and in good repair—above all, no leakages in the roof. Before taking up residence therein, I had it thoroughly swept and re-swept—rafters, walls, floor, nooks and crannies. Then I had the walls whitewashed inside and out, the doors—of unpainted deal, and made by a carpenter at one of the factories—painted green, and the enclosing stockade thoroughly overhauled and strengthened.

The whole enclosure was rectangular, and had only two openings, a large entrance in the middle of the side facing the sea, and a small exit at the back. Passing through the gate, and walking up between double rows of pineapple-plants and lemon-grass to an open doorway, one obtained admittance to a little courtyard, twenty feet long by fifteen broad, surrounded by a verandah and the three principal rooms occupied by me and my stores. A passage on the right, closed at each end by a door, lead to the kitchen and the Kru boys' quarters, and a similar passage on the left lead to Amo's room. Adiaha had a couple of rooms at the back, and was allowed to keep her cat, fowls, and ducks within the enclosure, but I could not tolerate the smell and bleating of the goats, so they were billeted with a neighbour.

Here I lived nearly four months, that is to say, up to the middle of November. I made the acquaintance of all members of the little European community—Government officials, missionaries, and commercial agents, but spent as much time as possible among the natives themselves, being anxious to further my ultimate ends by getting to know their language and customs. Their tradition is that, about two hundred years ago, their ancestors lived in the Ibibio country, but were driven thence during a civil war to form new settlements, first on islands in the Cross River, and then on different parts of the mainland. One section of these refugees came down river, entered into friendly relations with the Kwa tribe, and built Iboku (Old Calabar).

You may perhaps remember that it was at Iboku that Arthur Riversley died and was buried by his friend Daniel Wood. I made inquiries as to the first white men who had visited the place, but the "oldest inhabitant" could tell me no more than that it was "long ago, before our fathers came here."

One day, however, walking about the modern European cemetery which occupies a palm-crowned eminence overlooking the river, I noticed a rough block of stone half-embedded in one of the angles formed by the buttress-roots of a huge predominating silk-cotton tree. What first drew my attention was what appeared to be a rude cross chiselled thereon. Clearing away the bush and grass, and digging away the earth, Amo and I found an inscription below the cross:

A. R.

1677.

I afterwards had this stone excavated, raised, and cleaned, and the cross and inscription painted white. Then, and not till then, an old grey-haired Efik remembered that he had heard his grandfather say that in the old times a family of Kwas living down the river used to pay a yearly pilgrimage to this tree and sacrifice a goat at the stone. He called it "Isu Makara" (the white man's altar). In clearing away the rubbish, we had found a number of bones, including several goats' skulls.

My chief instructor was a young educated Efik, rejoicing in the high-sounding names of Asukwaw Ekpenyong Ephraim Adam Duke, son of an important member of one of the principal "Houses" of the Efik tribe. He spent two hours with me every morning teaching me the language, and used often to accompany me in my walks, explaining everything new that fell in my way. Amo was my constant attendant, and he, and, later on, his mother also, helped to carry on my education.

Amo became quite a character in the place, and I at first feared that the local belles, attracted by his superb physique and his "long neck" (one of the chief points of the native standard of beauty), would be the cause of continual "palavers." One of Adiaha's great wooden boxes was really her son's property, and contained his wardrobe, a heterogeneous collection of clothing amassed during his travels, and the pride and joy of his heart. Attired in one striking costume after another, he used to take his walks abroad, envied by all the other dandies of Duke Town, and admired by every female eye. But Amo was by no means susceptible of these dusky ladies' charms, and, like many a smart frequenter of Bond Street and Piccadilly, he dressed more to please himself than to attract the other sex.

He, however, being human and a negro, did not altogether escape the wiles that beset his daily progress. After extricating him from several peccadilloes, and disbursing, according to local custom, money to appease the injured parties and to defray the cost of the necessary "sacrifices," I lectured the delinquent, and then arranged his marriage with a damsel of the Duke House, and was "best man" at the ceremony. After this, harmony prevailed. Madame Amo lived under her mother-in-law's wing, and cooked her husband's "chop" and kept his room clean. She was not allowed to share in his box of finery, but he bought her cloth and beads, and she held her head high among the up-to-date smart set.

I used often to join Mr. Johnston in his afternoon walk. He had a cultivated eye for colour and for beauty of every kind, and drew and painted with considerable skill. He also took much interest in the fauna and flora of the place, and I gathered from him information about animals, birds, trees, and plants, which was afterwards of great service to me. I told him the whole history of my quest, and he used his utmost endeavours—but, of course, in vain—to dissuade me from it.

"My dear fellow," he used to say, "you are attempting an absolute impossibility. The days of miracles are over. The hinterland, on even this bank of the river, is unknown and full of communities of savages hostile to one another and inimical to Europeans. The Ibibio country, lying on the other bank, is absolutely a *terra incognita*, and even Efik traders fear to go there. The Ibibios are proverbial for all that is inferior or evil—the very word 'Ibibio' expresses reproach and disdain. They are said to be cannibals, and to indulge in the worst forms of human sacrifice, and their whole country is in a constant state of warfare. Even if they were as peaceful and harmless as—suppose we say—the Dutch, the odds are a hundred to one you would never find a ring lost over two centuries ago. I cannot, of course, restrain you from going, but I do earnestly request you not to go."

The Consul, however, at length realised that I was not to be turned back, and then he was most kind in helping me with advice and suggestions. It was he who recommended that I should become a member of the "Egbo Society," a form of secret society predominant among the Efiks, and said to extend far up the Cross River, and even into parts of the Ibibio and Ibo countries.

"There is a wonderful freemasonry among all members of this society," said Mr. Johnston, "and it is greatly due to it that Efik traders can safely ply their trade a week or ten days' journey up the Cross and Aweyong rivers, and also visit the Aros who live up a 'creek' which joins the Cross River near Itu. Its secrets are zealously guarded, but I understand that no man able to pay the regulated fee is refused admittance. There are various grades, and the more you pay the further you are admitted into the Egbo cult. I am told that a fully-initiated member pays as much as £1,000 in fees before he attains to the highest grade. I should certainly advise you to join it. I quite think that you would gain rather than lose prestige by doing so, and it may prove to be of real service to you."

So I joined the Egbo Society. Before setting out on my quest, I had enlisted my "all" in the cause. My godmother had left me a little fortune of £7,000, and an important firm having a large "factory" or depôt at Old Calabar had agreed to become my local bankers. With the Consul's help, I tried to be admitted to the highest grade, and offered to pay considerably more than four figures for the privilege, but I was unsuccessful. No foreigner, they said, might advance beyond the second grade, the fee for which, including that for lower grades, was £700. They also charged me another £100 for being a white man! They were equally—in fact, rather more—opposed to admitting Amo to the first grade, and, indeed, seemed very reluctant to allow him to ascend as far as the second; but the offer of an extra fee of £50 ultimately prevailed, and he and I went through the same ordeals together. This affair cost in fees alone £1,550. As the sequel will show, it was, however, a good investment.

Most honourable, Reader, you do not, I am sure, for one moment expect that I should tell you any of the secrets of the Egbo Society.   Anyhow, I certainly have no intention of doing so.

Poor old Adiaha took out a new lease of life, and, in her position of housekeeper to the white man whom all the people got to know so well, and of mother to his magnificent major-domo, became a matron of considerable consequence.   I presented her with another parrot on condition that she kept it out of my hearing, and her cat presented her with a litter of kittens, one of which accompanied me back to England, and was grandmother of the sleek tabby now sitting on my writing-table.   The old lady's goats were also prolific, and her hens laid eggs for my breakfast, and all things prospered with her.

After much consultation with Amo, I eventually decided not to take Adiaha with us, but to leave her in charge of the compound at Old Calabar and of Madame Amo.   We did not know what lay before us, and so judged it best to have as few incumbrances as possible.   Later on, Adiaha could return to her own country to lay her old bones in the ancestral burial-grove.

Tom Peter and his small brother would also be left behind. On hearing that my destination was "the bush," my cook, chosen, as you may recollect, partly for his muscular strength, had intimated that he would rather not accompany me—"Me no fear, sar; me strong too much.   My bruder be small pickin, he no fit to go for bush.   S'pose he sit down for [remain at] Calabar and I no lib, dey go sell him for slave."

There were, as Tom Peter knew quite well, other Kru "boys" there who could have taken charge of Jim George during his big brother's absence.   The fact was that the champion who (helped by police and rabble) had overpowered Amo at Lagos, was in a desperate funk at the very idea of going among cannibals, and there was much to be said on his side.   I risked much to gain much ; Amo hoped to find a welcome with his mother's people, and to pave the way for her return ; but Tom Peter had nothing to gain in exchange for the possibility of becoming an entrée at an Ibibio banquet. So I found a situation for the two brothers at one of the "factories," their new master undertaking to send them back to "we country" (the Kru coast) at the expiration of a year.

Tom Peter begged to take care of Towzer for me, but, though I at first entertained his proposal, I in the end did not part with my four-footed friend.

In place of the two Kru boys, I engaged two Efik servants named Okun and Etim.   From the head of my Egbo "lodge," I hired two very large canoes, each provided with a crew of twenty paddlers and a headman who was also steersman.   Last, but by no means least, I engaged an interpreter named Alfred Ikong, for Amo and I were not yet fluent in the language.

Adiaha had from time to time told me all that she could recollect of the people and country where she had spent the first thirteen years of her life.   It was, she said, divided into two sub-tribes called Anang and Ikono, the former ruled over by a queen, and the latter by a king.   These two sections were always at feud with one another, but, on certain great annual occasions, a truce was declared and mutual festivities took place.   She herself belonged to the Anang section, and her own mother had been queen, but had been deposed when Adiaha was quite a little girl.   Her girlhood had been very uneventful—fetching water and firewood, going to market with her mother, carrying yams from the farm, and dancing "offiong" on moonlight nights in the dry season.   Then came the terrible day when their village was raided, her mother shot down, and she and other children carried off and sold. Her mother's name was Adiaha Ediaw Ituen, and their village was Ikot-Afia-Ete.

I asked her if she had ever heard her mother speak of a ring different from what the women usually wore.   She replied that, when her mother was queen, she had many beautiful cloths and fine beads and jewels which she had yielded up to her successor, but that she had no recollection of any particular ring being mentioned.   She remembered, however, that the queen of Anang was sometimes styled "Adiaha Makara," which means the white man's eldest daughter.

CHAPTER IV.

A CROCODILE AND A FAT BRIDE.

On the fourteenth of November, which happens to be Pleasance's birthday, we set out from Old Calabar.   Alfred Ikong brought with him two small boys to attend to his own wants, and I allowed Amo to bring a youngster named Otu, the crown of whose head was just on a level with his master's waist. Otu was plump, but as lithe and active as a kitten, and it was not often that he kept his "master" waiting for anything. All told, my following numbered fifty men and boys and dog Towzer.

My kit and stores, including several cases of articles to be distributed as presents, were contained in fifty packages of various kinds, which we divided equally between the two canoes. None of them exceeded sixty pounds in weight, the average load of an Efik carrier. We went practically unarmed, as behoved a peaceful mission. In my boxes, however, were a brace of revolvers—one for Amo—and five hundred rounds of ammunition. I carried at my belt a long hunting-knife of the finest Sheffield steel, and Amo and Ikong had each a matchet and a strong clasp-knife, the latter given them by me. The object of my expedition was generally understood to be the opening-up of trade between Old Calabar and the remoter parts of the Ibibio country.

Mr. Johnston and all our friends, European and native, assembled at the beach to take farewell of us and to see us start. Adiaha was, as usual, a disturbing element. At the eleventh hour, i.e., at 5 a.m., she had become possessed with a violent longing to accompany us to the land of her birth, and had created such a commotion in the compound that some of the fowls had flown over the fence and the cat and kittens had taken refuge on the roof. Finally, we had been obliged to lock her up in an inner room, but liberated her when we left for the beach, and she followed us screeching about her burial and her "ekpo" (spirit or ghost). When taking leave of her son, she removed from her neck the pendant upon which she had been sworn at Lagos and gave it to Amo to fasten to a girdle of beads which he wore round his loins.

It was 7 o'clock when we pushed off. We were delayed a good half-hour by one of the paddlers having casually forgotten to bring his paddle! This, by the way, is a typical instance of the unreliability of the happy-go-luck negro, the "careless Ethiopian" as an experienced African traveller calls him.

How glad I was to be off! The sun was shining on the broad expanse of the river, the morning breeze blew fresh and cool, and the little Union Jack hoisted at the stern of each canoe fluttered exultingly. Three paddlers out of each crew had been told off on orchestral duties, for a canoe without music would be like a stage-coach without a horn. One beat with two sticks on a flat drum of hard wood resting on his knees, another beat a double sistrum or gong of iron called "ngkong-ngkong," and the third vigorously shook a rattle of basket-work filled with seeds and pebbles and called "nsak." This music is of a primitive kind, but they keep excellent time, and really the result is by no means unmelodious. One of the headmen started a song, and the two crews joined with one accord in the chorus and sung right lustily.

"What are they singing about?" I asked Ikong.

"I don't know, sir," replied the interpreter, whose sleek overdressed appearance and airs of educated superiority had already rubbed me up the wrong way. "They are singing one of their country songs, but the words are unintelligible to me."

"Rats!" I exclaimed, which was of course equally "unintelligible" to his cultured understanding. The paddlers were members of his own House, and their country songs were his country songs, but he wanted to pose as having forgotten everything except the veneer of Europeanism acquired at the mission-school.

"Dem canoe-boys," explained Amo, "sing 'Makara [white man] go for bush, Makara catch [has] plenty box, plenty cloth lib for box. Makara be all same debil, he no fear Ibibio; s'pose Ibibio chop [eat] Makara, Ibibio be too much sick.'"

"A cheery prospect for both the eaters and the eaten!" I said with a laugh. "Tell them, Amo, to sing one of their 'offiong' songs." (Offiong in the Efik language means the moon, and also a dance danced by moonlight.)

So, with grins which displayed unrivalled rows of gleaming teeth, they dug their paddles into the water and sang "When the girls return from their fattening, we play and sing—we sacrifice a dog for Adiaha [the eldest daughter]—we eat plenty of yams and drink much palm-wine."

This refrain was sung over and over again, now by the paddlers on one side of the canoe, and now by those on the other. Then a deep-chested voice would sing a few of the words as a solo, and then both crews, with our Efik servants to swell the chorus, would burst in and almost drown the roll and rattle of the band.

Amo had pleaded to take the whole of his wardrobe with him, to which I had consented on condition that his big box should be left behind and his things packed into two smaller boxes.

The costume donned by him to delight the eyes of those of his friends who had assembled on Calabar beach to bid him farewell reminded me of a dressed-up figure meant to represent Robin Hood which I had seen in a procession of "Ancient Foresters" in a little country-town at home. He (Amo) had got into a pair of buckskin breeches so tight for him that he must have suffered agonies in getting them to meet round his middle, and his small valet had quite failed to button them at the knees. He wore a white vest, and over it a discarded cavalry tunic of scarlet cloth braided with yellow stripes across the chest. A shortage of two inches in the sleeves was a trivial defect, but a similar space where breeches and tunic should have overlapped was a sartorial difficulty which he had surmounted by twisting round his waist a broad scarf of a brilliant orange hue, the ends of which hung down at the left side. His legs below the knee were bare, but he wore dark blue "sand-shoes." On his head was a large soft wide-awake of black felt, with an orange band round the crown, in which was stuck a plume of six nodding peacock feathers, the insignia of his rank in the Egbo society. As if to enhance the effect of this tight-fitting and gaudy costume, he carried loosely over one shoulder the dark blue wrapper worn by him when he came aboard the "Africana."

His get-up was that of a highwayman of romance, and must have been extremely hot and uncomfortable, but he carried himself with his usual stately dignity.

Towards the bow-end of these dug-out canoes, the natives build a little deck, and over it erect a shelter roofed as are their huts. Here we stored those of my packages that required protection from rain, and here I sat in my deck-chair viewing all that was to be seen. By hugging the banks, we made about one mile an hour against the stream.

About noon we moored our canoes to the bank of a little fishing hamlet in order to cook our midday meal. The paddlers quickly set to work to collect firewood and prepare their yams and fish for the pot. I had my chair put under a tree, and entered into conversation in his own language with one of the headmen. Towzer lay on the ground at my feet.

"Well, Usua," I said, "how do you like my dog? Don't you think he's a better animal than your own breed?"

"I don't know, master," he replied, "I have never eaten white man's dog."

He had understood my words, but not my meaning. The Efiks eat dog-flesh, roasting the body whole in its skin over a slow fire.

Knowing it to be useless to explain, I asked him questions about his food (a favourite topic), and he said, "We boys eat all flesh that falls in our way, but on most days we get only yams and fish. Snake is good to eat, and sometimes Abassi [God] sends us a bit of elephant."

"What about crocodile," I said; "is he good eating?"

The boy expressed horror, and exclaimed, "We never kill crocodile!"

"Why not?" I inquired. "Surely the crocodile is a bad thing that ought to be killed."

"My father's 'ukpong' [soul] lives in a crocodile," he replied, "but nobody except the 'abia-idiong' [medicine man] knows in which particular crocodile it lives, so we avoid killing any of them lest we should kill that one and so cause our father's death."

"Suppose," I said, "suppose you were to find a dead crocodile lying on the bank; would you take it home and eat it?"

"No," he answered, "it is forbidden."

"When your father dies, what will happen to his crocodile?"

"It will die at the same time," he said, "and of the same kind of death. Two years ago our father became lame in his left leg, and it happened in this wise. A white man at one of the factories saw a big crocodile snatch a small girl who was washing calabashes in the water on the beach. He fired with his gun, and hit it in the leg, so that the blood came out and made the water red. From that day our father was lame."

"And the little girl," I inquired.

"The crocodile dropped her, and the white man picked her out of the water. When our father heard of it, he commanded that the cloth and all the beads and charms then being worn by the child should be collected and thrown into the river to appease the anger of the disappointed crocodile. If he had not feared the wrath of the white Consul, he would have had the girl herself thrown in, as was our forefathers' custom. I myself saw the white man shoot at our father's 'ukpong.'"

"On which side was the crocodile hit?" I asked.

"On the right side," he replied.

"But you told me," I said, "that your father became lame in his *left* leg. How do you explain this?"

Usua wore a puzzled smile as he shook his head and answered, "I don't know, master, but the medicine-man knows."

Merry shouts came up from the riverside. Some of the paddlers, having thrown off their cloths, were enjoying a bathe, splashing one another with water, and playing a sort of polo with an empty gin-bottle. Just above them, two or three of the smaller boys, including little Otu, were quietly washing their cloths. Towzer, who had left me, was barking at the water's edge in enjoyment of the fun.

Suddenly a scream and a cry of "fium" (crocodile) arose, and a stampede was made for the shore. A crocodile had seized Otu by one arm and was dragging him into the water. Grasping my knobbed stick of English oak, I rushed down and jumped in, but was just too late. The monster had made off with his prey. None of the Efik canoe-boys attempted to do anything except yell. I was out of my depth, and found myself struggling against the current. Then dog Towzer came to the rescue. He knew I could swim, and so didn't trouble himself about me, but made straight for the retreating crocodile, and bit him on the nose. The ugly beast turned his head, and, making a snap at his assailant, loosed his hold on the poor boy, who, almost unconscious through fright, was swept down to the canoes and there rescued by a paddler.

Where was Amo all this time? On getting to land, he had unwound his waist-scarf and taken off his tight tunic, and had then thrown himself on his mat in the shade of a tree to enjoy a much-needed sleep, for he had been up half the night superintending our final packings.

The paddlers' yells waked him, and, just as I, trying in vain to reach Towzer, was expecting to see the crocodile's great jaws on the dog's body, Amo made a tremendous leap from the bank and disappeared under the water near the monster's tail. The beast's attention was again diverted, and it turned its head, but, at the same moment Amo drove his knife into its side, and, with a mighty splashing, it crimsoned the river with blood, and then, struggling against the current, was carried down and caught in the branches of a snag just below where our canoes were moored.

Little Otu was more frightened than hurt, but his arm was bleeding where the crocodile's teeth had pierced the skin. I tied my handkerchief round it, gave him a drink of brandy, and had him laid on a mat on the bank to await further attention. Towzer had escaped scot-free, and came out of the water shaking himself and wagging his tail. Then he rushed off along the bank and began to bark at the crocodile's body.

Acting on my orders, the canoe-boys fetched rope; and, throwing nooses over our scaly enemy, hauled him to land. He was still alive, gasping for breath and spurting out blood. We gave him the coup-de-grâce, and then stretched him out and measured him——8 feet 3 inches from the tip of his snout to the tip of his tail.

Amo's white vest and breeches were stained with blood, and our clothes were of course dripping wet. I soon stripped, and was rubbed dry and warm, and put on other things; but Amo's valet was just then incapable of assisting his master, and one of Ikong's boys, pressed into the temporary vacancy, proved so unskilful that Amo took at least five minutes to get out of his soaked buckskins, and I believe that ultimately something harder than hard words fell on the head of "da... damn fool-boy what lib for sabby book."

While this unparliamentary scene was taking place behind a tree on the bank, I was dressing and binding up Otu's arm. He almost forgot the pain in his delight at becoming an object of so much general attention. Towzer, however, was the hero of the hour. The paddlers now regarded him with awe; some were of opinion that he was a "devil," and others thought he had acquired bravery by having eaten a leopard, the king of beasts in their category. Towzer thoroughly appreciated all this adoration, and, in royal fashion, levied tit-bits of yam and fish from his admirers. He and Otu became great friends.

Then I had the crocodile skinned, and, when you visit me at Riversley, I will show you the result. It hangs up in the hall, under Lady Ann's portrait, and next Arthur Riversley's carved walking-staff.

"Well, Ikong," I said, "why didn't you help us against the crocodile?"

"I am not amphibious, sir," he replied, "and ——"

"Do you mean you can't swim?" I impatiently interrupted. "Do, please, speak plain English, and not try to choke yourself with long words!"

"Very well, sir. I was about to say that members of the House of Ikong have from time immemorial refrained from killing the crocodile."

"Why?" I asked.

"That I cannot explain, sir. The prohibition has been handed down from generation to generation from remote antiquity. As Holy Writ saith 'All that have not fins and scales in the seas, and in the rivers, shall be an abomination unto you.' The crocodile, sir, has scales, but legs instead of fins."

"And you, my friend," I thought, but did not say aloud, "have the gift of the gab, but lies and humbug instead of truth and plain-dealing."

However, he was really rather amusing, so I made up my mind to enjoy the humours of his pedantry, and to "pull his leg" instead of continually "sitting on him."

So I replied, "Very true, Ikong. I am glad to find you have such powers of observation. I shall be obliged if you will always kindly point out to me any idiosyncrasies in fauna and flora that we may happen on in the course of our peregrinations. You, of course, understand me?"

"Certainly, sir," said he, with a gratified smile; "idiosyncrasies were one of the branches of study in which I qualified before terminating my education."

"Right—O!" I said. "Now pay attention, my learned friend—idiosyncrasies or no idiosyncrasies, I prefer plain dealing to lies, and I require you to tell me the truth even if such a course be abnormal to you. I have lived four months in your country, and I am not a fool. The real reasons why you did not take part in the crocodile palaver are, first, that you are somewhat of a coward, and, secondly, that you believe the creature to be an 'ukpong,' the abode of the bush-soul of one of your people. Come now, tell me, isn't this your belief?"

"I am a Christian, sir," he replied.

"Yes, yes," I said, "I know that; but we all believe a good many things not contained in the Bible. Trust me, Ikong. I am not trying to laugh at you. I am genuinely interested in the ancient beliefs and customs of your country, and, in exchange for what you tell me, I will tell you about those of my country. There are many Europeans, men of education and culture, who hold beliefs very similar to those held by your people. Ghosts, for example—I have never personally seen one, but a new experience is such a luxury that I live in daily expectation of thus enlarging my circle of acquaintances. The old house in which my grandfather and his father were born is said to be haunted by a lady who wears a rustling gown. I went there, and slept in a certain room on purpose to see her, but didn't. So don't be afraid that I shall mock at what your instructors look upon as 'foolish superstition.' I quite understand that you are greatly superior to these 'bushmen,' and that your head is full of knowledge which they don't possess. But I am sure you have not forgotten all that has been handed down by your ancestors. Tell me, has every boy a bush-soul?"

A little flattery sometimes goes a long way. Ikong consented to forget, for a while, his knowledge of isms and idiosyncrasies, and to instruct me in what, had I thought to call it anthropology, he might have been willing to regard as a subject worthy of a place in his curriculum of "education."

"No," he answered; "sometimes he does not get an 'ukpong' until he becomes a man."

"How does he get it?"

"Sometimes he dreams of a certain animal, and then it becomes his bush-soul; sometimes he goes to the medicine-man, who tells him what animal or other thing he should sacrifice to. Sometimes he has the same 'ukpong' as his father, and sometimes that of his mother, but he may have quite a different one."

"Where does your own bush-soul live, Ikong?"

He gave a sort of half-ashamed laugh, but replied, "It lives in a hippopotamus far away in a certain water, and this particular hippopotamus keeps himself very quiet. I got it in a dream, and I often dream that it is tempted to its death with all kinds of food, which, however, it always refuses."

"And so," I said, "you, of course, never kill these animals or eat of their flesh?"

"O, yes," said he, "I do. I shoot them, and I eat the meat; but my own hippo cannot be killed."

"My people," I said, "used long ago to believe that every tree contained a spirit, and that the moaning of the wind through the branches was the voice of this spirit. Has your country anything like that?"

"Yes," he said, "in one of our plantations at Iboku we have a great tree. Once upon a time fifty men began to cut it down, but it bled, and, when it was half down, it rose up again, and then they left it. One of their number was lost, but the medicine-man [abia-idiong] restored him."

"Do many bush-souls live in trees?" I asked.

"No," he replied, "they live mostly in animals, but there is one tree which is good for the 'ukpong.' We call it 'etufia.' Its trunk attains to a great height before there are any branches or leaves, and it has a smooth red skin [bark] which easily peals off, so that men cannot climb it. If a bush-soul gets into this tree, it reaches a great age, dying only when the tree itself does."

"Suppose a man fells the 'etufia?'" I inquired.

"Then the man who owns the bush-soul will die," he said, "and you will hear the tree groaning. If you break off a branch, the man will be only sick."

On the evening of the fourth day, we reached a place called Itu, which lies on the right bank of the river, some fifty miles above Old Calabar. We had slept each night at various settlements on the riverside, one night at a place called Ikunetu. Ikong and his boys, and most of the paddlers, used to sleep ashore. I had my bed with its mosquito-net put up on the little roofed-in deck of one of the canoes, and Amo occupied the other, the two canoes being alongside. My two "boys" slept in my canoe, and Otu in Amo's; also three paddlers remained in each canoe to guard the contents. I'm afraid that nobody but myself slept much, for, as Amo said, "Dem flies humbug too much, sar. S'pose me lib for sleep, dey make palaver for my ear—buzz, buzz. Den dey go chop me, sar. I t'ink mosquito be pickin debil."

Itu village stands on a cliff some three hundred feet above the river, and clothed up to its summit with trees and bush. Its people belong to the Ibibio tribe, but on the beach which stretches from the foot of this cliff to the water's edge are a number of compounds built and occupied by Efiks from down river, who come here to buy slaves and trade. At this time,

Itu was a noted slave-market, for to it were brought men, women, and children seized or taken in pledge from the upper parts of the Cross River, from the interior of the adjoining Ibibio country, and from the remote hinterland then continually raided by the Abam mercenaries of the all-powerful Aros or Inokuns of Ibum (now "Aro-Chuku") and Obinkita.

We approached the beach in grand style—flags fluttering, paddles flashing rhythmically, orchestra putting forth all its strength, and lusty chorus singing: "When Efik men paddle, the sea-cow hides his head, but the fish come out to play." Now the Efik and Ibibio word for the sea-cow (maniti) is "itu." Their song had therefore a double meaning! I myself have seen fish leap so high out of the water as to land themselves in a passing canoe.

A score or so of canoes of various sizes were moored to the beach, on which lay, scattered about, empty palm-oil puncheons, bags of kernels, and the refuse of the morning's market. I had been recommended to spend a few days there, chiefly to get advice as to my further movements from the chief, a man of some wealth and importance and of considerable rank in "Egbo." So, leaving the headmen and paddlers in charge of the canoes, we threaded our way through the little Efik settlement—the lanes and spaces between the compounds were littered all over with rubbish and ill-smelling filth!—and ascended a steep path leading up the face of the cliff.

The chief's compound was on the top, at one side of the open town-place, round which were grouped other dwellings, and in the middle of which stood a great cotton-tree. Chief Udaw Idiong was a middle-sized, middle-aged, man with a rather prepossessing face and quiet manners. He placed the Egbo-house at my disposal, and there I lived for a few days.

Itu, being on the Cross River, and at the mouth of the river Enyong, an important waterway of trade, had more or less assimilated the "civilization" of Old Calabar. Its people were plump and of better physique than the inland Ibibios, and, in dress, both men and women followed Efik fashions. Efik traders had introduced the bread-fruit tree, cocoa-shrub, and lemon-grass. The Egbo-house was roofed with corrugated iron, as I found to my cost in the heat of the day, and inside, over a doorway, was painted in rough English characters: "KING UDAW IDIONG EKPE HOUSE." The chief had a son whom he had sent for a few years to the mission at Calabar.

On the second afternoon after our arrival, Amo said to me, "Plenty men lib for beach, sar. Dey go play. Dem chief's son go marry fat woman. O, sar, she fat pass eberyt'ing! She be all same pillow. I beg you come look 'em, sar."

So I went. On the way down, Ikong explained in his pompous way, "Marriage nuptials are about to be celebrated, sir, between Mr. Samuel Augustus Wilkinson Ekpo, second son of the head-chief here, and a young lady of the family of Efiong Eyamba of Iboku."

"Is the bride so very fat?" I asked.

"I, sir," he replied, "should describe her as embonpoint. Her family being wealthy, she has been able to remain nearly a year in the fattening-house."

As we neared the bottom of the hill, we could see a crowd of people massed together in the main thoroughfare of the beach-hamlet. Drums were being beaten, and horns blown. There was a buzz of many voices, and a nodding of coloured plumes among the sea of black heads. When we arrived, the people made way for us, and I found myself to be a sort of counter-attraction to the bridal party.

On the ground stood a large European arm-chair, plentifully furnished with cushions, and provided with a little roof of palm-leaf mats raised on poles. Near by stood the bride, one hand grasping an arm of the chair. She was short, and, as Amo had said, just like a pillow in her enormous fatness. Though her only article of clothing was a wide girdle of hundreds of hawk-bells strung together, few of her charms were exposed to view, for, from head to foot, her body and limbs bore a mass of finery and jewelry of every description—ribbons and gewgaws, gaudy ornaments and tinsel, feathers and little bells. There were at least a score of bracelets on her arms, and she wore necklaces, leglets, anklets, and finger-rings. To crown all, she had on her head a structure into which were stuck a dozen or so of huge plumes of the most gorgeous hues, similar in everything but colour to those fixed to horses' heads at old-fashioned funerals at home. Although quite a young girl, her size gave her the appearance of a middle-aged woman. Her skin was rather light-coloured, and her bones were everywhere covered with pillows of fat—her eyes disappeared into her cheeks, and her cheeks fell on to her shoulders, which, with her back and sides, were simply padded with rolls of adipose flesh. Her arms rivalled Sandow's in bulk, but were almost shapeless with fat. Her face wore an expression of placid indifference.

"Plenty fine mammy, sar!" exclaimed Amo. "She no work, she no play, she no go for market, she no cook chop. Ebery day for eight-nine [eight or nine] moons she lib for house in dark, dark room; all dem time she lib for sit quite [quiet]; dem small pickins pass chop for her; she chop too much chop, she sleep, she chop plenty more chop, den she sleep agen."

Near the bride stood five or six small, slim girls, her brides-maids. They wore bright loin-cloths, to which were attached little hawk-bells, beads, feathers, and as many gaudy odds and ends as they had managed to acquire."

"Where is the bridegroom?" I asked.

"Probably," said Ikong, "he is arranging with the lady's parents the final details of the marriage-settlements."

"I suppose you mean," I said, "that he is paying over the last instalment of his purchase-money; but I have learnt enough of native customs to know that this does not generally take place until at least several days after the consummation of the marriage."

"I t'ink he lib for drink tumbo," said Amo; but at that moment Mr. Samuel Augustus Wilkinson Ekpo arrived upon the scene.

He had certainly been drinking tumbo (palm-wine), and a great deal of it too, and probably gin had also been in circulation. He was dressed "up to the nines," as an English bank-holiday 'Arry, whose get-up he somewhat resembled, would have said. He was a short, thick-built, young man with face much inferior to his father's. He wore baggy black trousers, black boots a size too small for him, a bright pink cotton shirt, an orange-and-green silk scarf round his waist, a large "christy-minstrel" collar, a huge blue bow-tie, and a stiff straw-hat, with white muslin twisted round the crown and hanging down behind. A heavy (? gold) watch-chain and two sparkling rings completed his attire.

He leaned on a friend's shoulder, and, coming up to me, gave me a rather insolent stare. However, I had been staring at his bride, and "a cat may look at a king." So I saluted him in his own language, and said, that, hearing the chief's son was celebrating the joyful event of marriage, I had come down to wish them good luck, and to present them each with a little gift.

Then, calling my boy Okun, I took from him the articles I had brought with me and duly presented them. To the gallant bridegroom I gave a ratan-cane with a heavy silver knob, and to the fair bride I handed, open, a parasol of scarlet silk fringed with white lace. Mr. S. A. W. Ekpo struck an attitude, and raising his hat, bowed, and thanked me in tolerable English. The lady almost blushed, tried to smile out of her mask of fat, and languidly raised a ring-laden hand to take her gift; but one of the bridesmaids fore-stalled her in this act of exertion, and held it proudly over

Miss Eyamba's nodding plumes.   She was now the happiest
woman there, for my gift enabled her to outrival all her rivals.

I had done the right thing, and was received with acclaim.
The bridegroom sent for palm-wine, and then and there—but
after him, in accordance with the native custom that the host
must drink first to show absence of poison—I drank their
health, first spilling some of the liquid on the ground.

"Tell them," I said, hoping to get some fun out of Alfred
Ikong, "tell them I pour my congratulations upon their
hymeneal altar, and wish them long life, unbounded felicity,
and an innumerable progeny."

Whether my learned interpreter understood me or not, I
don't know, but he was quite equal to the occasion, for, commanding silence with uplifted hand, he poured forth an oration
which lasted so long that the bride had to be re-seated, and
her spouse provided with a support for his other shoulder.

The speech ended, I returned to my quarters, after giving
Ikong and Amo permission to stay and enjoy the festivities.
These, accompanied by music and dancing, lasted far into the
night.   I wisely forbore to ask for my interpreter and major-
domo again that day, and I was not surprised that on the
following morning they both seemed out-of-sorts!   I made no
comment thereon.

CHAPTER V.

A MIDNIGHT ADVENTURE.

From Chief Udaw Idiong I learned that the beginning of
the Anang country—the country of Amo's mother, and of the
"Quene" in whose hands Arthur Riversley reported King
Edward's ring to have been—was only one day's journey
inland from the river Enyong, but that the principal town was
said to be much further inland, and on the other side of "a
great water."   He, as the Consul at Old Calabar had done,
tried his best to turn me back, saying that the natives of the
interior were fierce and treacherous, making human sacrifices
and eating human flesh.   He was quite sure they would not
tolerate a white man among them.

"Will not the 'Egbo' carry me safely through?" I inquired.

"No," said the Chief, "they know not Egbo. It is only we living on the banks of the river, or a few miles inland, who have bought Egbo from the Efiks. The people of the interior have different societies and different jujus. They greatly fear Ekpenyong-Ibriitam, the big juju of the Aros."

"I go peaceably," I said. "I want to talk to them about trade with the white merchants of Old Calabar."

"They care nothing for trade," he replied; "but are you a wise man, a doctor, can you make sick men well again?"

"I have some wonderful medicines with me," I cautiously answered, "medicines whose virtues are known only to white men, and I can bind up wounds and set a broken bone."

"Then," said the Chief, "if your mind be still strong to go into Anang, go as a doctor, but do not give away your medicine as the mission-men do, but sell your skill for much money. If you give them medicine for nothing, they will suspect you come to seek something other than wealth; but, if you take cattle and goats and manillas from them, they will understand you."

Now, as you will see later on, Udaw Idiong was a cunning man, seeking his own ends rather than my welfare, for he hoped to obtain, through me, cattle and goats and manillas for himself!

"I will," he continued, "give you one of my men as guide, the son of my own sister. He shall go with you, and tell the people of your skill in curing sickness and mending broken limbs."

Then he called a young man named Akpam Etuk Udaw, and I agreed that he should accompany me.

"Moreover," said my host, "he will see to it that your Efik servants and followers do not play you false. When your interpreter, whom you call Alfred Ikong, was full of gin last night, he talked of the riches he would get and of the wives he would marry through having entered your service. You are my stranger [guest], and have won my heart; you have joined our Egbo, and are therefore entitled to receive help and good counsel from us. Be watchful and wary, Makara. Trust not these Efiks. The desire of my heart is to see you back again in safety, sleeping once more in my village."

It was finally decided that we should not try to enter the Anang country by the road which started from a place called Okopedi, a mile or so above the mouth of the Enyong, but should go in our canoes far up the river, two days' journey, to a village called Use, where there was a big Egbo-house, and from where there was said to be a road to the capital of the Anangs.

Early the next morning, it being now the fourth week in

D

November, we left Itu, taking with us Akpan Etuk Udaw, usually called Akpan, and his "boy." In return for his hospitality, I presented the Chief of Itu with an English mayor's chain of office, made of brass and enamelled in colours.

Wishing to learn something of the character and capabilities of my "guide," I had him with me in my canoe, and placed Ikong in command of the other. Akpan proved to be far more communicative than the learned Alfred. He was, in fact, quite eager to give me information, which helped greatly to break the monotony of our slow passage up the river. He knew the names and qualities of every tree and plant, and all about birds, snakes, and monkeys.

I had warned Amo to watch Ikong and Akpan very carefully. Amo was the only one of my staff whom I really trusted.

Both banks of the Enyong are clothed with bush to the water's edge. It is more dense on the left bank; along the right bank for many miles runs a path which is under water in the rainy season. Many fine trees raise their majestic heads above the walls of luxuriant vegetation that quite block all views of the country beyond.

The band continued to discourse sweet music, but there was less singing. Perhaps they had not yet recovered from the orgies attending the wedding at Itu, or perhaps their minds were at work on what the next day might bring forth.

"Look, master!" cried Akpan in his own language, "I see a snake in the water."

I looked. A small black snake was swimming near the canoe. It tried to get in, but the paddlers drove it off.

"Tell me, Akpan," I said, "what is the Big Juju in the Aro country?"

Akpan looked rather scared. "Nobody knows, except the juju-men," he said, "but some say it is a very big serpent."

Then Amo pointed out another swimming snake, which dived and disappeared. Then we heard monkeys, but could not see them. A pair of large black-and-white birds ("inuen-abasungko") passed us, skimming over the water like swallows. From an overhanging branch a kingfisher, a flash of gorgeous blue, dived twice with a splash. We passed a canoe paddled by two women; with them was a white cat whose mewings waked dog Towzer to instant attention. On the surface of the water floated a number of little plants with long roots and velvety leaves which I called "water-cabbages."

"Are they good to eat?" I inquired.

"No," replied Akpan, "but I think fish like them."

Then we talked about monkeys, and he said, "There are not many monkeys here, and there is said to be none in the

Anang country; but at the back of Itu, in a country called Itamm, they are quite plentiful, for all the people there are forbidden to kill or to eat them, so they go freely about the towns and into the houses. We sometimes call that country Ebok-Itamm." (Ebok means monkey.)

"Why are they forbidden?" I asked.

"They have a story," he said, "that long ago all their women were barren, and they began to fear that their race would die out. Then they went to a famous medicine-man [abia-idiong] and besought him to help them. So he told them what sacrifices to make, and he also told them never to kill or to eat monkey any more. Then they did as he told them, and their women began to bear children again. This is what I heard in their village called Eikum."

"Any elephants in the bush here?" I inquired.

"No, master, not one," he said.

"But in the old days," I continued, "when your grandfather's grandfather was alive—were there no elephants here then?"

"I have heard old men say," he replied, "that very many years ago a few lived in the thickest part of the bush. Far up the river, at the back of Ikpe market, there is a village called Ina-Enin, which means the place where elephants sleep. There are still great trees and much swamp there, but nobody has ever seen an elephant there."

"Where did you get this ivory?" I said, touching his bracelet.

"I bought it at market," he answered. "There are plenty of elephants in the Uwet country across the river. Also the Inokuns bring us ivory from far distant parts of the Ibo country."

We spent the first night at Asang, a large village of thickly-clustered compounds, built on a sort of island surrounded by swamps at the head of a little creek. It reminded me of parts of the river Deben in Suffolk. Its banks were fringed with bright-green rushes, and on its placid surface floated many water-cabbages.

Asang was then a centre of trade, its people going far up the Enyong to buy oil and kernels from the inland Ibibios and from the Inokuns. It was also a place to which captives were brought before being sold at Itu. During the wet season they had but little chance to escape, all paths into the interior being under water, and they—chiefly people from inland parts—being entirely ignorant of the use of canoes and paddles. They went about unshakled, to all appearances very indifferent to their fate.

The head-chief received me in his compound. He was a big, stout, clumsily-built man, with hair and beard plentifully sprinkled with grey hairs. He had great ugly eyes, thick protruding lips, and an evil expression on his face. He stank of gin. His dress consisted of a wrapper of shabby black velvet extending from the loins to the ankles, and another wrapper of large squares of scarlet and blue velvet sewn together, which he wore flung over his shoulders. His head was bare. On each wrist was an enormous ivory bracelet.

He received me sitting, spat on the ground, and asked why I had come. Then I remembered I had not given the Egbo sign of my second-grade rank. I gave it, and his attitude immediately changed. He pulled himself up, made a sort of apology, and sent for palm-wine. We drank together, and fell to discussing the prospects of trade.

Later on, the chief assigned me my quarters at one end of his own compound, and I spent the evening writing up my journal.

I slept soundly, but dreamed that my canoe had been upset in the creek, and that I was struggling with a crocodile on the muddy bank. The stench of the mud seemed to trouble me more than the crocodile did. I awaked. There certainly was a strong smell of mud, and a hand was pulling gently at my sleeve.

A voice, it was Amo's, whispered, "Me lib, sar. Softly, softly! Dem Ikong do bad t'ing. I foller, I look 'em. S'pose you come, sar, I go show you."

I was about to strike a match and light my lantern, but Amo stopped me. "Plenty quite [very quiet], sar!" he said. Then he brought me my breeches, socks, and leggings, but made me put on light sand-shoes instead of my heavy boots. Nor would he allow me to wear my grey flannel shirt, but handed me a short dark coat. Then he guided me along the verandah to a corner of the compound, where there was a passage so narrow that we had to proceed sideways. It was closed at each end by a "bamboo" door, and led to the rubbish-heaps which these people, ignorant of the laws of health, and to spare themselves steps, allow to accumulate in near proximity to their dwellings.

My guide signed to me to bend low and to follow him. So, creeping close to the ground, from which a medley of evil smells arose, we made our way towards a clump of plantains. There was no moon, and clouds almost obscured the stars. Their fitful gleams, however, showed me that Amo had nothing on except something dark round his loins. As I crept along behind him, his body stank overpoweringly of mud. Once, I put out my hand in the darkness, and it touched the handle of his matchet. He was armed.

Arrived safely behind the great plantain-leaves, we stood up

Amo whispered, "Ikong and dem chief, first dey gib plenty gin to we. Akpan and his boy drink plenty. Okun and Etim [my "boys"] drink plenty. Me no drink, me humbug 'em, me 'tend me lib for sick [I pretended to be sick]. I put hand for belly, I make noise like so." (He groaned.) "Den I go for my mat, I call Otu, we sleep. Den I talk softly, softly, for Otu. I say 'Me be your master. S'pose you be good boy, I gib you plenty cloth.' Dem boy like me plenty. Den he 'gree [agree], and I go swear him. Den I say, 'Go look Ikong and dem chief, come tell me what t'ing they do.' Dem boy go. He be small small pickin, he fit for go softly too much. Den he come back. He call me. I foller. We go for bush, we catch [reach] big water. He say 'look 'em.' I look lamp lib for oder side. Dem boy say 'Ikong and dem chief lib there.' Canoe no lib; we find 'em, we no look 'em."

Here we were interrupted by a rustling close at hand. We kept quiet for a few minutes, but nothing happened. It was probably only a lizard.

So Amo continued, "Den I make Otu sit so," touching his neck and shoulders. "We go for water. Water smell bad too much. Water be plenty high [deep], so high," touching his middle. "Otu fear crocodile, but I t'ink dem no lib for dat water. We catch land. Dirt [mud] lib too much. We foller dem lamp. Dey go for juju-house. O, sar, dat be bad place! Plenty head," touching his head, and meaning skulls, "lib dere. All dem canoe-boys lib for dat place. I t'ink they go swear 'em. Den I make Otu sit down for bush, I come for you. I beg you, sar, we go look 'em."

Amo told me his tale in far shorter time than it will take the patient reader to understand my attempt to reproduce his "pidgin" jargon. His knowledge of English had improved since joining my service, and he could now understand at least the meaning of almost anything that I said to him, but could not speak it well. When excited, he relapsed into the above kind of jargon.

"Can't you find a canoe?" I said, for I did not enjoy the prospect of wading through a cold swamp in the dead of the night.

"No, sar," he replied, "I carry you all same Otu."

I had been thinking over the situation quickly in my mind, and a plan had occurred to me.

Sit down here, Amo," I said. "I shall be back one time [directly]."

Then I crept back to my room, and, taking off my clothes, put on a complete suit of black tights which I had brought from England with me. The sleeves came down to my wrists and the collar came up to my chin, so that the whole body was covered except the head and hands. Into the pocket of the vest I slipped a white handkerchief and a little box of white toilet-powder. I also took the precaution to strap round me a leathern belt with revolver and ammunition-pouch attached.

Then I rejoined Amo. "You be all same debil, sar!" was his criticism of my appearance.

We reached the water's edge. The feeble starlight showed the swamp to be full of bushes and reeds, and the smell was very bad. Hundreds of frogs were croaking their midnight hymn. A night-bird gave a prolonged mournful hoot, and the breeze murmured uneasily among the rushes. It was a fitting night for deeds of evil.

I mounted on Amo's shoulders, folded my arms across my chest, and sat perfectly still. He carried me safely across, but had no little difficulty in getting through the mud on the opposite bank. Then he set me down, and I told him to fetch Otu, and to tell him not be be afraid of me.

Meanwhile, I opened the powder-box, and rubbed plenty of powder all over my face, ears, and hands, and tied the white handkerchief turban-wise about my head.

Amo returned with Otu. The little fellow was shaking with fear and clinging to his master. My appearance did not tend to decrease his fears, but, after a time, we quieted him, praising him for his bravery and promising him "plenty fine t'ings," as Amo said.

During his master's absence, Otu had lain concealed in a thicket commanding a view of the juju-house, and this is what he had seen. Led into the building by the chief and Ikong, the forty paddlers and Ikong's two boys had been ranged along the clay benches which ran around the interior, and ordered to sit still and say nothing. Then a fire of sticks had been made in the middle of the floor, and, oil having been poured on, the whole place was brightly illumined. Then a case of gin had been brought out and opened, and all the boys had been invited to drink. So they drank for a long time, until the gin was quite finished. Just before Amo had fetched the boy to me, Otu had seen a big "devil" enter the juju-house, and had been filled with fear.

We patted him on the back, and I showed him my revolver, and Amo pulled out his matchet, and then we and him near the water's edge, and told him to lie still and do nothing until we should return to him.

Then Amo and I crept up through the bush towards a light which, rising and falling from afar, gleamed fitfully among the trees. It was the fire in the juju-house. I followed close behind my guide. Sometimes, where the ground was open, we crept along on all fours, sometimes we passed swiftly from tree-trunk to tree-trunk, and so at length reached the thicket.

The leaping flames made every detail of the interior plainly visible to us. It was an oblong room, open at the entrance-end, but closed by a wall at the back. On each side was a mud wall three feet in height, but between the top of these walls and the eaves of the roof there was an open space. Down the middle of the room was a line of posts supporting the high-pitched roof. The central post was imbedded in a circular mass of clay painted with geometrical designs. Nearly the whole of the back wall was covered with a screen of animals' skulls, those of goats and cattle predominating, and in this wall were two small doorways over which hung mats of fibre. On the top of the round block of clay, arranged so as to encircle the central post, were about a score of human skulls. The flames played on their polished fore-heads and empty sockets, and they seemed to grin with diabolical fixity.

Music, so weird and unearthly that I cannot find words to describe it, came from behind the building, and ever and anon arose the monotonous chanting of a human voice.

Scattered about on the floor lay a dozen or so of empty gin-bottles, and behind them, huddled together on the clay seats, were my paddlers.

"Look, sar!" exclaimed Amo in a whisper, "dem debil lib!"

The mat covering one of the little doorways had been raised, and into the room had stepped the most extraordinary-looking figure that I had ever seen. Not a square inch of his skin was anywhere visible, for he was clothed from head to foot—my description is based on subsequent knowledge—in a tight-fitting suit of fibre and reeds plaited together, in-cluding gloves and a sort of boots of the same material. Hanging down before and behind, to represent beard and locks, were long streamers of fibre, bleached almost white. Over his face he wore a huge grotesque wooden mask, stained black, with the features picked out in white. This was sur-mounted by a rough wig of fibre which overhung his fore-head. Concealed under this fringe were apertures for his eyes, and, just below these apertures, were false eyes made of small round pieces of looking-glass, then a newly-imported article up the Enyong. In his gloved hands he carried a coil of native rope.

The music ceased, and the Figure raised an arm as if to enjoin silence on his audience already as silent as the grave.

"I am 'Idem Inyang' [the spirit of the waters]," said the Figure. "I feed on the flesh of men, and drink their blood. It is I who upset canoes and drag underneath those who struggle in the waters. Crocodiles are my servants. They wait upon me and catch men for me to fatten and eat. Crocodiles are my children. I fondle them as mothers do their babes. Every seventh moon the people of the Enyong feed me as I love best to be fed. You men from Iboku [Old Calabar] have heard how they tie a man round and round with rope, and throw him into my arms. See, men of Iboku, see these skulls that smile so gleefully at you. These are the heads of those whom the people of Enyong have thrown in to me."

Here, pointing to the circle of skulls, he laughed long and loud, and the paddlers huddled closer together.

"Ha! Ha!" he shouted, "you may well fear, for have not you cause to fear? Ten days ago did I send one of my crocodile-sons down the Enyong and into the big river to catch me a man that I might devour him. Three days ago word was brought to me that my son had been killed by the white stranger, the man with the moustache, and his black follower from over the sea. I heard, moreover, that men of Iboku who paddle his canoes helped to take my son's body from the water, and to skin it for this white man. Then my anger was aroused, and I swore vengeance on those murderers. Fate has put you into my clutches, and this night three of you must die. Choose then, men of Iboku, choose which of you shall give me their flesh and their blood. I have finished."

With another burst of fiendish merriment, the Figure disappeared behind the hanging mat.

Five minutes passed away, but none of the wretched gin-sodden boys moved or spoke.

Then the Figure re-appeared, and, with an angry gesture, threw the coil of rope down on the floor. "My wrath boils over like an untended pot!" he exclaimed. " Will you tempt me to claim six victims? Choose quickly, I command you. Choose quickly, and bind them, that I may throw them into the river to feed me and my children."

Again he withdrew. The music re-commenced, accompanied by a strange rattling noise, produced, as I afterwards learnt, by shaking bunches of human arm and leg-bones. Not one of the canoe-boys spoke a word. They were speechless with fear, and huddled closer and closer together as a flock of sheep in an east wind.

Another five minutes elapsed, and then the Figure appeared for the third time, and, again commanding silence, addressed them as follows, "Men of Iboku, my heart is sad for you. You are people of the waters, you love to swim and paddle, you are not as these land-loving Ibibios are. Again have I turned your crime over in my mind, and I now see clearly that it is not you who should pay the penalty, but the white man and his tall servant. Upon them, and them only, shall my vengeance fall. I will spare your lives, men of Iboku, on this condition, namely, that you take, all of you, a solemn oath to move neither hand nor foot in aid of the white man except in so far as my servant Ikong may command you, and that, on your return to your own country, you breathe not a word of what shall befall this white stranger, his man Amo, and his goods. Let all those who agree to take this oath go down upon their knees."

Down they all fell in much disorder. Some were so dazed with gin and terror that they entirely collapsed, and sprawled on their faces on the floor, while others, falling sideways, charged into their neighbours with telescopic effect along the whole line. The two headmen, however, managed, somehow or other, to restore order, and eventually there they all knelt, one-and-twenty of them on each side of the juju-house.

The Figure retired behind the curtain, and returned bearing a clay pot which he placed on the fire, and stirred the contents with a short stick. In a few minutes it began to boil over with much bubbling and hissing, and emitted a most horrible stench.

"This pot," said the Figure, "contains 'mbiam' [juju medicine] of the deadliest nature. Herein are the gall of the leopard, the fangs of the 'asabo' [a large snake], the blood of an Albino child, the juice of many poisonous plants, and scrapings from the skulls of all those men whom I and my crocodile-children have devoured. But the pot is not yet full. It cries for food, and you must feed it."

Then, with a pair of scissors in one hand and a small calabash in the other, he passed down the ranks of kneeling boys, and clipped their finger-nails and their hair, and gathered the clippings in his gourd, and made each boy spit into the gourd, and then he emptied the contents into the pot, and stirred vigorously.

"Ha! Ha!" he laughed, "the pot is fed, she licks her lips at the dainty morsels."

The pot certainly bubbled and squeaked most gruesomely, and the odour was so nauseous that, though my hiding-place was at least twenty yards away, I had to hold my nose. Amo, and those inside the building, seemed quite unaffected. Negroes can endure smells which would make many a European sick.

Dipping his stick into the nasty mess, the Figure brought it out tipped with a substance resembling tar. Then, going up to the circle of skulls, he fed them all by smearing it on their upper row of gleaming teeth. (The lower jaw of every skull was missing.)

"Ho! my beauties!" he cried. "You shall taste first at our banquet. The soup is good. These men of Iboku have flavoured it as you like best."

He stirred it again.

"Listen!" he shouted. "Your oath shall be this. Each of you must swear that he will help me, Idem-Inyang, to take my vengeance on these two men, that, to accomplish this end, he will in all things obey my servant Ikong, and that he will keep the whole matter deep at the bottom of his heart so that no other man shall know aught of it. If you swear and keep this oath, I will not punish you for your share in the death of my son, and all will go well with you. But, if you do not swear, or, if swearing, you break the oath, though it may be by only the wink of an eyelid, then will your fate be indeed terrible, for then this 'mbiam' will torment your body, the ghosts of these men," pointing to the skulls, "will meet you at every corner after dark, and my children the crocodiles will watch your goings and comings and at last drag you beneath the water to my torture-house. Do you all swear?"

"We all swear," they replied.

"There are two-and-twenty skulls," he continued. "Get up and come up eleven at a time, and let each man place his hands on two skulls, and, the others remaining silent, let each man, one by one, speak the words of the oath in a clear voice."

So the boys, quaking with fear, came up in four companies, eleven in a company, but only nine in the fourth, and every boy, laying his two hands on the shiny tops of two skulls, repeated after the Figure the words of the oath imposed upon him.

Then they retired to their seats, and the Figure once more stirred the contents of the pot.

"Kneel down again," he cried.

They obeyed.

The Figure stepped out into the open, and, waving his arms about, gabbled a string of long words, from which I gathered that he was calling upon the spirits of the air, of the trees, and of the swamp, witnesses to the oath just sworn in the juju-house, to take vengeance upon any boy who should venture to break it. He rattled on at a pretty good rate, and every now and then I caught the names of local deities and spirits, and even of constellations—Ngkuku-Ekpo, Ekpen-yong-Ibriitam, Ekpe-neyene-ukut-etibi-enang-idibi, etc., etc.—but, at last, having finished the Efik mythology, and probably wishing to impress his hearers with a final flourish, he astounded me by appealing with much impassioned eloquence to "Shadrach, Meshach, and Abed-nego, permutations and combinations, Mediterranean and subterranean, Numbers and Deuteronomy, idiosyncrasies, principalities, and powers!"

Having exhausted both voice and imagination, Ikong—for, of course, the Figure was he—re-entered the building, and, while he recovered his breath, gave the contents of the pot a final stir."

"Stick out your tongues," he cried to the kneeling ranks.

They obeyed. Dipping his stick into the horrible brew, he began dabbing it on to their extended tongues. Some of them gave a cry of pain as it burnt them. One dip of the stick did not go far along the line, so Ikong had to return again and again to the pot.

"Enough of this! Now is my time," I thought. Whispering to Amo, I handed him my belt, revolver, and pouch.

Then, leaving the 'thicket, I advanced quickly to the entrance of the juju-house, and, waving my whitened hands up and down, and protruding my deadly-white face—as white as the turban which concealed my hair—I broke into peals of the most fiendish laughter and yells that, I flatter myself, ever disturbed the denizens of the West African bush.

What the terrified inmates saw was a human figure with a skin many shades blacker than their own, but with head and hands of unnatural whiteness. This figure was wildly animated, rolling its eyes, gnashing its teeth, and dancing like a bear on red-hot bricks.

The effect was instantaneous. Their night of terror had reached its climax. Screaming and shrieking, pushing and tumbling over one another, they rushed for every exit. Most of them disappeared over the low side walls, but a few escaped through the two little doorways at the back, and two or three, almost maddened with fear, rushed past me and so out at the open end of the juju-house. I made straight for the circle of human skulls, and with them pelted the flying boys in snowballing fashion. What fun it was! What a noise those old skulls made as they hit the bony part of some wretched fugitive, or struck the hard clay walls and floor!

My first shots were aimed at the "Spirit of the Waters." He was in as great a funk as his late victims, and turned yelling to escape through the curtained doorway, but I caught him a hard blow on the back of his neck, and down he fell, and, falling, caught his foot in a log, and so upset the pot of "mbiam." The boiling liquid poured over Ikong's foot, and, had it not been for his boot of fibre, he would have been very badly injured instead of sustaining merely a painful scalding. He lay on his face yelling with fear and pain.

Only Ikong and I were left in the room. A whistle from me, the signal agreed upon, brought Amo to my side, and we quickly bound the scoundrel's feet together, pinioned his arms behind his back, and left him lying on his face.

Then, with torches in our hands, we explored the back of the building. The two little doorways gave admittance into a small chamber, a sort of chancel to the nave in which the night's ceremonies had taken place. It was provided with clay seats, and in the wall separating it from the large room was a small circular aperture through which Ikong's accomplice, the stout chief of Asang, had probably watched the performance. It was he, of course, who had played the musical accompaniment. An open door at the back of this inner chamber indicated how he and some of the paddlers had managed to escape into the bush. This door had been so hastily and roughly opened that it hung on only one hinge. The place was full of juju objects—skulls and bunches of human bones, empty gin-bottles, pots full of stinking messes, bundles of fusty herbs, drums, and other musical instruments. In one corner I picked up a whip of hippo-hide.

Amo and I spoke to one another by signs only, for I wanted to pose as a spiritual visitant, and to conceal our identity from the learned Ikong. Re-entering the larger room, we cut away as much of his fibrous costume as was necessary for our purpose, and then Amo administered half-a-dozen stinging lashes with the little whip. Then, Amo lifting his head, and I his feet, we carried him out and laid him on the ground, face downwards, behind our thicket.

Then we returned to the juju-house, and, each taking a burning branch, quickly ignited the thatch in different places. As soon as we had satisfied ourselves that the flames had taken good hold on the building, we stealthily retired into the bush, and, going in the same manner as we had come, retraced our steps to the water's edge. We found little Otu huddled up in his hiding-place. It was important that we should recross and regain our sleeping quarters before the return of the chief and Ikong and the runaway paddlers. I therefore told Amo to carry Otu and give me the lead through the swamp.

"No, sar, I beg you," said Amo, "me fit for carry all two [both]."

And this is how it was done. I mounted on to Amo's shoulders and sat as before, my legs hanging over in front, steadied by his left hand and arm. Then Otu climbed up our backs and so mounted on to my shoulders, and, placing his hands on the top of my head to steady himself, kept them there. I supported him with my left arm, and with my right hand grasped Amo's right hand stretched up to me Thus we crossed the swamp in safety, and gained the further side. Then, dismounting, we crept in single file through the bush and over the dung-heaps to the little passage, and so regained mv room.

I gave them both some whiskey, cautioned Amo to remove from his body all traces of the night's doings, and to look after Otu, and dismissed them both to Amo's room. It was 2.30 a.m. I stripped off my black garments and locked them up in a box, removed all remains of powder from my face and hands, went back to bed, and soon fell asleep.

CHAPTER VI.

A "MIRY CLAY."

It had been arranged that we should leave Asang early on the morning after our arrival there, but the night's adventure had upset everything.

At 6 o'clock I was waked by Amo instead of, as usual, by one of my two boys, and it was Amo who that morning brought me the cup of cocoa with which I used always to wash down my daily 5-grain tabloid of quinine.

"O, sar!" he said, with a delighted grin all over his face, "plenty palaver lib for town. Dem big chief lib for sick, dem Ikong lib for sick, dem canoe-boys—some lib for sick, some no lib. Dey no sabby we make fool palaver; dey t'ink you be debil, sar; dey fear debil too much!"

"Where are Okun and Etim?" I asked.

"Dey be sick for head dis morning. Dey drink plenty gin last night," he answered.

"How is Otu?" I inquired.

"He lib for cook your breakfast, sar. He sick small small He no fit for talk. I dash him fine coat. I t'ink you go dash him, sar?"

"Yes, Amo," I replied, "and the sooner the better, so bring him here."

Otu entered my room with a conscious air of displaying

unusual finery upon his small person. His every-day attire up to the present had been simplicity itself—just a loin-cloth and nothing more, except such articles of jewellery as a brass bangle on his wrist, a hawk's bell attached to an old boot-lace round his neck, and another bangle round one ankle. But now he wore Amo's "dash," a shabby scarlet waistcoat furnished with brass buttons. It was many sizes too big for him, and hung about him like a sack, but he was as pleased as a newly-breeched English boy, or a débutante in her presentation-frock.

"Good-morning, Otu," I said, "you look very fine this morning."

Otu had assumed dignity with his finery. Not deigning to smile, he drew himself up, and, saluting as he had seen Amo do, said "Gooder-mornin', sar. Me lib."

"Good boy," I replied in his own language, "I and your master think you are old enough to be treated as a man, so we took you into our secret last night. You must never tell anybody about it. You must be deaf and dumb about it. Do you understand?"

"Me sabby," he replied, saluting again, and displaying further evidence of his linguistic attainments.

Then I gave him two white singlets (vests), a leathern belt, a piece of blue-and-white cloth, and a red fez.

Taking them, he saluted gravely, and said "Gooder-mornin', sar," which he meant for an expression of thanks.

Then I explained to him that, if the other boys should see his new things, they would suspect something, and that therefore he had better let me lock them up for him, he retaining the waistcoat only. To console him, I gave him a little clasp-knife.

A boy entered and handed me a slip of paper addressed in pencil "To His Honour Mr. R. Wood Esquier." Inside was written, also in pencil,—

Sir,

I have the honour to inform Your Worship, these with my respecks, that last night, the — ultimo, a lady of this town engaged in culinary operations overturned a mess of pottage over one of my foots, which have necessitated considerable pain to me, compelling also the postponement of my matutinal visit to you, Sir. I also beg to inform that certain of the paddlers have too much inebriated themselves. Awaiting Your Honour's respectable commands.

I am, Sir,
Your Worship's faithful obedient Interpreter
Prince Alfred Plantagenet-Ikong XIII.

When you come to visit us at Riversley, you shall see this delightful epistle, the only communication with which Royalty has ever honoured me.

"Tell Ikong I'll come and see him," I said.

Then I dressed and went to him.

His Highness the Prince lay on his face groaning pitifully. One foot was bandaged. Two women of the place sat at his side ejaculating sympathy at every groan. Over his head was suspended a bunch of rubbish consisting of bones, shells, dried herbs, and such like.

"Well, Ikong," I said, "this is very unfortunate. You seem to be in pain."

"Oh! Oh!" groaned the sufferer, his face in the pillow.

"Come, Ikong," I said, pulling at his sleeve, "turn over and let me look at you."

Very carefully the poor wretch turned over on his side, and presented to me such a face that I had much difficulty to refrain from laughing. As is the custom with these people when sick, he had painted white circles round his eyes, and, "for juju" (as Amo explained), he had had his hair dyed red with camwood, and had had horizontal lines painted across his forehead with some yellow pigment.

"Come, what's the matter?" I inquired. "Surely you are not making all this trouble about a scalded foot."

"No, Sir," he said, "my skin is sick all over. I am bewitched. Last night, while holding a little service among these poor heathen, as is my wont, the devil himself appeared —as Holy Writ saith, 'he goeth about like a roaring leopard' —and, although I abjured him not to torment us, he ——"

"Upset a mess of pottage over your foot?" I inquired.

"No, sir," said Ikong, "in my epistle to you I have already explained that ——"

"O, yes," I interrupted, "I remember it was 'a lady engaged in culinary operations.' Is this the lady?"

"Yes, sir," he replied. Then, speaking to one of the women, "Go, Adet, and bring the pot you overturned."

"Stop," I cried, "I am quite satisfied, and don't want to see the identical pot. Devil or no devil, you seem rather upset, and, as some of the paddlers seem also to have suffered, I will put off our journey till to-morrow morning, when you and all the others must be ready to accompany me."

Then I mustered the paddlers, but only thirty-seven of them turned up. They presented such a "sketchy" appearance that I no longer tried to restrain my laughter, and the rag, tag, and bobtail of Asang were quite willing to act as chorus. There they stood all in a row, some with white circles round their eyes, some with leaf-plasters over cuts and bruises sustained during their headlong flight, some rubbing an injured limb, and others with hands supporting their aching heads.

"Where are the other three?" I asked.

One of the headmen stepped forward, and explained that in the evening they had gone to the bush to "play," that a "devil" had suddenly appeared and chased them, that they had scattered themselves in all directions, some running against trees or into prickly bush, some falling into the swamp, and some into the arms of "bad spirits."

"Those who drink bad spirits," I said, trying to be funny, "are very likely to meet with bad spirits." As they didn't, however, understand me, this remark fell quite flat!

"Well, and the other three?" I inquired again.

"Dey no sabby what place dey lib for," replied Amo, who had been about collecting news; "p'rhaps they lib for bush, p'rhaps they lib for water, p'rhaps they lib for die."

At this point, two of the missing paddlers appeared round the corner, one carrying the other, two miserable-looking objects, their loin-cloths tattered into rags, and their bodies muddy, scratched, and bleeding. One of them had sprained his ankle. They had spent the night among the rushes on the other side of the swamp, and had remained there until, hunger overcoming their fear of crocodiles, one had carried the other across.

Ikong's two boys had rejoined their master, but the missing paddler had never returned. They searched everywhere for him, but found nothing. Probably, we concluded, he was eaten by a crocodile. His name was Tua-Mbom.

I took part in the search, and thus discovered that the juju-house stood on a long narrow island, the landing-place of which was at the end furthest removed from the point where I and Amo had landed. The chief and Ikong and the forty-two boys had gone there in one of our big canoes. The two scoundrels had decoyed them thither under the promise of gin and "play," and then, having fuddled them all with drink, had treated them as described in our last chapter.

In did not trouble about Chief Enia-Eke of Asang. Amo reported him, "Sick too much, sar. Plenty wife go cry for him, sar. He say white man bring bad debil for dis town. He t'ink dem debil lib for your box, sar. I say, 'My master sabby plenty medicine, he pass idiong-master [abia-idiong, native doctor], I t'ink he pass all dem bad debil what lib for bush.' O, sar, when I make my eyes go sleep," closing his eyes, "I look you lib for dem juju-house. You holler. Dey run. You harl [hurl] dem heads at 'em. O, sar, how dey run!"

Amo exploded with half-restrained laughter. He was, however, very discreet, and though, during the next day or two, I often detected a look on his face which betrayed merry thoughts within, he kept his merriment to himself, only giving it vent when he and I were alone.

Early the next morning we pushed off from Asang. The chief gave "sickness" as the excuse for not seeing me off, and, with his message, a goat as a farewell offering. I replied suitably, and sent him a present of cloth.

It took us the whole day to reach Use, or rather the beach on the riverside used by the Use people, the village itself being two or three miles inland.

The higher up the Enyong we went, the more varied became the scenery and the more interesting the ever-changing panorama of bird and insect life. Naturalists would, I am sure, find it a very productive field for their researches.

A little way above Asang, low bushes take the place of the big trees and thick bush of the lower reaches of the river, and over them you have a continuous view of the heights of the Utut-Obio country. Masses of "water-cabbage" separate the open river from the swamps on the right bank. Here on a branch sits an usari-bird (kingfisher), while just below, picking at a cabbage, is a brown bird as large as a thrush. Higher up, on the left bank, we pass a beach called Esuk-Itu, and here the paddlers put forth all their strength, for, but a few miles inland, is the notorious grove of Ekpenyong-Ibriitam, the great juju of the Aros ("Long Juju"). The band cease their drumming and beating, the voices of the canoe-boys are hushed, and they keep their heads low and averted.

All around us lies a great expanse of swamp, but the high waters of the rainy season are rapidly going down, and everywhere trees and bush are appearing once more. Just ahead of our canoe flies a bird with wings of a brilliant brown colour, a diver called "edinim-inyang"; many dragon-flies are playing over the bright-green weeds at the bank; on the gaunt arm of a snag sits a pair of blue-black swallows; we pass under an overhanging bush and catch sight of a green snake just above us, and, further on, another of the same species drops from a bough into the river and swims rapidly across the water in front of us—a distance of about one hundred yards. Where the water has receded, the lower branches of overhanging bush are leafless and mud-stained, and from them hang dirty river-weeds.

But we leave behind us the swamp-bordered parts of the river and again pass between defined banks, several broad straight reaches which are rather monotonous. The scenery

E

reverts to that met with below Asang. Looking back, we view in the distance a well-timbered ridge of hills, said to be in the Aro country. We see several large birds of the wader family named "ukut-ubum"; we pass on the right bank a little settlement of Asang people called Ikot-Offiong; a small green crocodile lies asleep on the mud, but, remembering last night's experiences, the paddlers pretend not to see it, and I say nothing, but silently admire the fern-like leaves of the ngkara-palm.

On a burnt tree-stump sits a gorgeously-blue kingfisher; a dragon-fly wings its way past us, and from point to point ahead of us flies a grey pelican called "ikpang" by the canoe-boys, but "enang-itong" by Akpan of Itu; the riverside timber increases greatly in size, and there are "bamboo" fish-traps built at intervals along both banks.

We pass another Asang settlement, a place called Ntan-Obu-Ikot-Ukpe, on whose beach men are busy hollowing out canoes from prostrate trunks. Many birds are twittering in the bush; we see another wader ("ukut-ubum"), and then pass a small dug-out propelled by a fisherman at its stern. The setting sun illumines the trees on the left bank; the chattering of birds increases, and at length swells into a chorus of evensong. We are passed by a party of Efik people in a canoe returning from Ikpe market; they are singing and beating a drum, and their paddles keep excellent time; "obudo" fish are jumping near the bank; the sun, a globe of fire, disappears from view, and all Nature seems to hush during the short half-hour of twilight.

Just as the inky pall of night was descending upon us, and the orchestra of frogs was beginning to tune up, we arrived at Use beach, and were all very glad to disembark and stretch our legs after the cramping confinement of the canoes. The quiet, uneventful day on the river had done something to restore my men to a normal state of mind and body. I had engaged two new paddlers to replace the one lost at Asang and the one with the sprained ankle.

They quickly had fires lighted and pots boiling, and I, after thoroughly enjoying a most refreshing hot "tub," got into my deck-chair and read my favourite chapters of *John Inglesant*. It was, fortunately, a non-insect night, so it was possible to read by the light of a lantern without becoming the one and only point of attraction for every winged creature of the neighbourhood. Dinner was soon ready, and by 8 o'clock we were all in bed and some of us already asleep.

An old maxim says "Six hours' sleep for a man, seven for a woman, and eight for a fool." My own rule is to take eight only when I cannot get nine. On this particular night

I took nine and a half, and was very glad of them, and felt infinitely fitter for them.

We were all astir soon after 5.30, and then I held a council of war. Akpan was the only one of the party who had been to Use. He said it consisted of five hamlets all close together on a hill about an hour's walk inland, but that a very bad "sea of mud" lay between us and them. He said they were quiet people, and had a big Egbo-house.

Ultimately I decided to leave five boys in charge of each canoe and of the greater part of my baggage, and to set out with all the rest of my following, taking with me sufficient kit and stores for twenty-four hours only. So we started in single file, Akpan leading, I next, then Amo, and then our boys and paddlers, the latter acting as carriers. "Prince" Ikong had begged to remain on the beach, pleading that his foot was much too bad to permit of his walking. I, however, would not trust him out of my sight, and so lent him my hammock, and he thus rode right royally in the middle of the line.

After following the winding path for rather over half-a-mile, we emerged from the bush on to a tract of land cleared for cultivation. At the foot of the gently-sloping hill on which we stood lay a little valley now filled with black mire to a breadth of about a hundred yards, and on the other side the ascent was clothed with clumps of tall grass and a few scattered trees. Still further inland was a much higher hill crowned with palms, plantains, and several gigantic cotton-trees, with the thatched roof of a hut visible here and there.

Just as we reached the edge of the swamp, a very large bird, a wader called "okumbe," arose from a tussock of reeds and winged its flight towards the river.

Amo wanted to carry me through, but this I would not permit him to do. He and Akpan went in first, and floundered about trying to find the best passage. Amo described it as "bad all over." In most places it came up nearly to his knees. The Use people had planted a crop of koko-yams in the mud, and our guides at last found that, by setting our feet on these plants and on the roots of grass growing here and there, we could cross safely.

The only members of the party who required to be carried were Ikong, little Otu, and dog Towzer. I told headman Usua to take Towzer across, and consigned Otu to the shoulders of the other headman, who was half-a-head taller than most of his men.

I was wearing old boating "shorts"—knickerbockers coming down to within three inches of the knee—and had substituted for ordinary boots a pair of rubber snow-boots, which protected all the lower part of the leg. It was weary work toiling through that swamp, for every now and then, where there were no vegetable stepping-stones, it was necessary to plunge knee-deep in the mire, and it was by no means an easy task to get one's legs out of it. Though the sun was still low, and a cool breeze was blowing, I became very hot and perspired freely. Those of the carriers who had recovered from their experiences on the juju-island seemed to enjoy this crossing, laughing at one another's struggles, and shouting advice as to the best course to follow.

Just as I had reached the further side, and was being pulled out of the mud by Amo, Towzer began to yap furiously. I turned round. He was riding on Usua's shoulder tail fore-most, and could thus see everything taking place behind him.

"I t'ink he look dem okumbe," said Amo, pointing to a large bird, probably the mate of that already mentioned, which had just risen from the swamp. "Dem arms make plenty noise," and he flapped his own up and down to represent the movement of the bird's wings.

But Towzer did not cease his yapping. On being set down on the ground, he ran up and down along the bank, putting his front paws in the mud and then withdrawing them as if afraid to venture.

Akpan suggested that perhaps the dog had seen a rat and wanted to go back and kill it.

By this time all were over except Ikong and his four carriers. They had an awkward heavy load, and had followed a course a little to the left of the others.

"Come, fall in," I cried, "Amo, count them, and see if all the loads are here."

So they fell into line, and Amo carried out my orders.

"All lib 'cept Ikong and dem four boys," he said, pointing to the hammock, "and 'cept Otu. I no look Otu."

"Where is Otu? Who has seen Otu?" I asked, "You brought him over, Ensa. Where is he gone? What does he say, Amo?"

"He say he no carry dem boy, sar. He say dem boy lib for him back small small [only a short time]. Den dem boy no look dem small knife what you dash 'em. Den he run for beach for catch [to get] dem knife."

"Did anybody else see him go?" I inquired.

Nobody spoke.

"Did nobody see Otu go back to the beach?" I asked again.

Ikong's hammock had just reached the bank, and he said, "Yes, sir, I saw him. He called out he would return immediately."

All this time Towzer had continued to run along the bank, barking and whining, and trying to get on to the mud. As Ikong finished speaking, the dog made a jump, landed on a little hillock of grass, and was preparing to jump further ahead.

"He sees something," I cried. "Perhaps Otu has fallen in, and this fellow is lying to us. Go, Akpan, help the dog, and let him guide you."

Akpan sprang forward, but Ikong interposed. "The dog is mad, sir," he said. "This country is not fit for European dogs; they always go mad. I think he has seen an 'idem' [spirit]." Then, turning to the paddlers, he continued, "If Akpan goes back into the swamp, he will bring the idem's wrath upon us. Remember Asang, and Idem-Inyang."

"You d—— scoundrel!" I cried. "You have been up to some of your foul tricks. I will get to the bottom of this."

Then, pulling out my revolver, and stepping up to him, I pointed it at his head, and called on Amo to cover Ensa with his.

"The first man who moves," I cried, "I will shoot him dead. Now listen to me, you boys. *I* was the 'devil' who frightened you all two nights ago. I followed you to the juju-house, hid in the bush, and heard the whole thing. Ikong was 'Idem-Inyang.' I heard the oath he made you all swear. You went up to swear in four companies, eleven, eleven, eleven, and nine. The next day I wrote a full account of it to the big Consul at Old Calabar, telling him the names of the chief and Ikong and also to what Houses all you boys belong. Before we left Asang, an Itu boy took my letter down in a small canoe to Chief Udaw Idiong of Itu, who by now has sent it to the Consul. Therefore, if any harm befall me, or Amo, or my servants, or even my dog, you will be arrested on your return to your country, and will be punished accordingly."

The four hammock-bearers were so astounded at this, that they lost their balance, stumbled, and out fell His Highness Prince Alfred Plantagenet-Ikong the Thirteenth. At my action and words, his face had paled to a dirty olive-green colour. He fell on that part of his body which had received the well-deserved flogging!

Then, remembering that all these boys were members of Egbo, I gave the sign of the society, and continued, "I have purchased the second grade in Egbo, I know 'ebungko' and 'awtungaw-kawidem,' and I have seen the mysteries of 'etakefe' [the inner shrine, or chancel]. My man Amo has also attained to the second grade. You have heard that the big Consul will punish you if anything befall us. I now tell you that Egbo also will punish those who do any injury to members as high in grade as we are. This man Ikong is only of the fourth grade. Besides being your temporary master, I am your senior in Egbo, and, as such, I call upon you all to obey me and not this scoundrel."

"Go, Akpan," I said, "follow the dog, and you, and you, and you," pointing to three stalwart carriers, "go with him."

Amo and I stood with our revolvers cocked and pointed, covering Ensa, the prostrate Ikong, and the whole party, while the four men plunged into the mire. Helped by Akpan, Towzer led them back along the course taken by the hammock-bearers. On reaching the deepest part of the swamp, he stopped short, wagged his tail, and gave a series of excited barks. Then we saw Akpan stoop down.

"I have found him!" he shouted. "He is half-buried in the mud. I think he is dead."

It would not have done for Amo or me to leave the party on the bank, so I sent the hammock and six more paddlers to Akpan, telling them to bring Otu to me as carefully as possible.

Here Ensa broke down and whimpered, and kept on pointing at Ikong.

"What does he say?" I asked.

"He say," explained Amo, "dem man make him fear debil too much, so, s'pose Ikong go tell him for kill Otu, he fit for do it. S'pose Ikong no lib, he no do it."

"Look here, Ensa," I said, "you cannot get away from me. The best thing you can do for yourself is to tell me the whole truth. I quite understand that Ikong has made you afraid of him."

So, while Otu was being dug out, he told me everything. When we started to cross the swamp, Ikong had made his bearers wait until last, and, calling Ensa back, had whispered to him, reminding him of his oath, and ordering him to throw Otu head foremost into the deepest part of the mud. Accordingly, on reaching the middle of the swamp, Ensa had tipped the boy over backwards, but he had fallen on his side. Then as the mud was closing over him, he had cried out, and Ikong, leaning out of the hammock, had hit him hard on the side of his head with a heavy stick, and had killed the boy—so Ensa thought. Ikong had ordered the four carriers to "obey and say nothing," and had hastily concocted the story about Otu returning for his knife, and had finished by saying "Push on quick, I will find a way to bury him deeper."

Without further ado, I ordered the paddlers to tie Ikong and Ensa hand and foot. My appeal to Egbo had completely cowed them, and they obeyed my order promptly. I also had Ikong gagged.

Next I turned my attention to Akpan and his helpers, just then reaching the bank. Otu's little body lay in the hammock, and Akpan was carrying the dog. Both being set down, Towzer at once made for his friend Otu, and began licking his face. Poor little fellow! What a sight he presented! His whole body, except the right side of his head, and his right shoulder and arm, was caked thick with stinking black slime, and his mouth and left eye were plastered over with it. Had he sunk in half-an-inch deeper, his nostrils would have been covered, and he would have died of suffocation. On his right temple was a nasty wound, covered with blood, the result of Ikong's blow.

"Water!" I cried. "Is there no water near here?"

"Yes, master," replied Akpan, "at the top of this little hill the ground slopes down again to a stream."

"We will take him there," I said; but first I freed his mouth from the mud, and poured down his throat a few drops from my brandy-flask. His pulse was beating feebly.

Then we resumed our march, Otu's body occupying the hammock, while our prisoners were carried on the shoulders of four men apiece. Amo and I walked at their side, our revolvers in our hands.

It was as Akpan had said. On gaining the top of the hill, the path descended to a little stream. Here I called a halt, and had a fire lighted, a bucket of water put on to be warmed, and my canvas bath prepared. The water was soon ready, and we first scraped and then washed all the mud off Otu's body and limbs. He was unconscious, and, not knowing then, as I do now, that the negro, like the cat, has nine lives, I feared that the blow had affected his brain.

Towzer put himself forward, and aided us by licking Otu wherever he could get at him. This was the second time that the faithful dog had saved the boy's life.

I tried to revive him by rubbing his arms and legs with whiskey, and at last he opened his eyes, stared around, and said "Gooder-mornin', sar." Then I knew that he was all right.

Up to this time, we had seen nothing of the Use people. We were now within half-a-mile of their dwellings, but the narration of what happened to us there must be carried on to the next chapter.

CHAPTER VII.

TRIAL BY EGBO-COURT.

When we had all crossed the stream where we had halted to remove the mud from Otu's body, I sent Akpan and two paddlers forward to take my compliments to the chief of Use, and to announce to the people that a white man skilled in medicine was about to visit them. The path up the hill on which the village was built passed between a number of little huts used for the storage of their crop of koko-yams.

A hundred yards above these huts, I called another halt, and we sat down awaiting the messengers' return. The country all around was hilly and well-timbered, especially towards the river, across which, in the' northern distance, appeared ridge after ridge of wooded heights.

At the end of half-an-hour, Akpan and a score or so of natives arrived. One of the latter led a white goat. Akpan held in his right hand the white handkerchief which I had lent him to carry as a token of peace. Had he returned with it in his left hand, it would have been a sign (so we had agreed) that the natives were disinclined to be friendly. Their spokesman advanced and prostrated himself, while his companions stood quietly a short distance off.

"Welcome, white father, welcome, great abia-idiong [medicine-man]," he said. "Okun Ibanga, chief of the Use people, bids me welcome you to our villages. News of your skill in medicine has come before you. Our canoes visit all markets as far as Itu. Our boys saw you there, and they heard tell of your wonderful medicines, and of your witchcraft in healing broken bones. We are your sons, we beg you to accept this goat, we beg you to sit down in our midst, for many of us are sick."

I was seated in my deck-chair. "How is it," I said, "that your chief himself comes not out to welcome me? I am, as you say, a medicine-man of great learning and skill, and, just as the strength of a full-grown man surpasses that of a small child, so do my medicines surpass your 'idiong.' I am not pleased. Your chief, if he wish me to sit down in his poor village, should have come out himself to beg me to do so. I cannot take this gift except from his own hands."

I frowned and lay back in my chair, inwardly much amused at the ridiculous "side" I was putting on.

The spokesman, Udaw Ibanga, retired to hold a brief consultation with his companions.

He was returning to me, but I held up my hand and

stopped him, and told Akpan to act as messenger between us.

"He says," explained Akpan, "that their father the chief is an old man and sick, that otherwise he would have come out to lead you to his dwelling, but that he has sent his second son to offer you, as a token of respectful welcome, a goat so white that, though five men should examine its skin for five days, they would not be able to find a black hair thereon."

In a low voice, I asked Akpan if he had seen the chief, and, if so, if he was really sick.

"I saw him, master," he replied; "he is an old man and lame, but he is sick only with fear. I would counsel that you proceed to the market-place they call Umaw-Ama, and there sit down and call the chief to you. It is good that he should leave his hut to salute you, for, if you go first to him, his people will think he is greater than you. He is a great Egbo-man, but you are Makara [white man], and must not yield to him."

This was sensible advice, and I acted upon it. "Tell Udaw Ibanga," I said, "to lead me and my men to their market-place. There I will sit down and cook my food. If his father the chief wants me to do him the honour to remain a short time in his village, he must gather all his people together and meet me there. Then I will accept his gift and be friends. The white man never breaks his word."

So we formed into line again, and followed our guides. To reach the market-place, we had to pass through a hamlet called Ntaiket. Through the high fences which surrounded each compound many curious pairs of eyes gazed upon the first white man whom they had ever seen!

The market-place called Umaw-Ama lies midway between the hamlets of Ntaiket and Esen-Edi, and is an open space of irregular shape shaded by trees. Choosing the shady side, I gave orders that everybody should here cook their food, and my own servants set to work to prepare mine. Amo mounted guard over our two prisoners; Akpan went with Udaw-Ibanga to the old chief; and poor little Otu, watched over by Towzer, lay on a mat beside my chair.

The Use people, seeing that we were unarmed and engaged in the eminently peaceful occupation of cooking, and that I, though a pale-skinned medicine-man of such great repute, looked not altogether unlike a human being, gradually ventured out of their retreats and gathered around us. First came only the men, but, after a time, women and children joined them, and took up their stand at a safe distance on the bank behind their husbands and brothers. They were very quiet and orderly, watching my every movement and whispering comments to one another.

Men, women, and children wore each a wrapper of thin Manchester cloth, tied round the loins, and reaching down on an average as far as the knees. Some of the adults had a second cloth tied shawl-wise over their shoulders, or otherwise arranged around the upper part of the body. Most of them were bare-headed, but a few wore a cloth twisted like a turban round the head. Those few men who had travelled as far as Itu were more up to date in their attire, and could thus be easily picked out in the throng, the distinguishing article of dress being generally a white vest, but in a few isolated cases a shirt or shabby coat took its place. The six or eight dandies of the assembly wore stocking-caps, and carried cheap umbrellas. The other men carried long thin walking-staves, and some of them had a satchel of fibre suspended under the left arm across the back.

Their personal ornaments were many and varied. Some, both men and women, wore elephant's-hair necklaces, on the front part of which were threaded one or two long beads. One woman, who boldly advanced into the front of the men, had, besides bracelets and finger-rings, a brass bangle just below each knee, and several copper bangles round each ankle. With the exception of a small patch of hair at the back, her head was shaved entirely clean. With her was a young girl wearing nothing but strings of white cowries round her loins. Other girls wore only a single row of them, and I noticed that others wore below their knees or around their ankles little circlets of dried grass.

Neither sex went in for elaborate hair-dressing, either wearing it quite short or having it shaved into various patterns. In a few cases, all the hair was shaved off. One boy had a native-made comb stuck into his wool.

I had finished "breakfast," and was reading, with one eye on my book and the other on everything else, when Chief Okun Ibanga arrived. His appearance was heralded by the blowing of a long horn, the musician walking in front of him and sending out blasts first one side and then the other. The old man was leaning on his son Udaw's shoulder, and carrying in his hand a native broom. Behind them were Akpan and "the court," a dozen oldish-looking men and as many youths and boys.

The little procession came along very slowly, for the chief was, as Akpan had truly said, old and lame. I took no notice of them until they were halfway across the marketplace, when I laid aside my book and prepared to be gracious. The chief limped as if in great pain, and was trembling and evidently much afraid. I felt sorry for the poor old man, but, knowing that my safety and success depended greatly on how I should play my part—people nowadays call it "bluff"—among them, I sat tight and did not allow good-nature to overcome caution.

Coming up to me, Chief Okun Ibanga, still clinging to his son for support, bent down and laid the broom at my feet.

"Ete [father]" he said, "I have heard of the power and wisdom of the white man, but you are the first of your race upon whom my eyes have ever looked. I salute you, and welcome you to my village. I lay at your feet the symbol of my rank and power. Take it, that I and my people may become your children."

"Pick it up and give it to me, Akpan," I said.

Then I ordered that one of my boxes should be brought and placed in front of me, and then I motioned to the chief to sit down.

"I salute you, Awbong [chief]," I replied. "I come from the big Consul who rules over the Efik people. I am a great medicine-man, and visit your country to learn what sicknesses trouble you, and especially to study a sickness which makes men so drowsy that they sleep themselves into death. You have done well to come out to salute me. I am your stranger [guest]; I do not come to usurp your power. I have accepted your 'ayang [broom],' but now I return it to you," and, so saying, I handed it back to him.

He looked much relieved. Then he beckoned to his men, and they led up the unblemished goat, and also deposited at my feet fowls, eggs, and a large quantity of yams and plantains.

"Thank you," I said, "I accept your offering as a sign that friendship is established between us."

Then, calling to my boy Etim, I told him to take away the goat, and tie it up under the trees where its bleating would not disturb me, and I gave similar orders about the other things.

Something, however, was wrong. The chief and his people did not look happy.

"What's the matter, Akpan?" I inquired.

"They want you to touch their gifts," he explained. "Unless you touch them, you have not shown all the people that you accept them."

"Right—O!" I said, "bring them all back."

Then I laid my hand on the goat, fowls, eggs, and other produce, and a sort of murmur of satisfaction passed through the crowd.

A man advanced carrying a large clay pot, and set it down near the chief. Another brought several little gourd-cups and other drinking utensils.

"I beg you to drink palm-wine with your children," said

Okun Ibanga. "It is the custom of our country to offer it to the stranger, who, if he comes in peace, will drink it with us."

I of course agreed.

The ceremony was performed with the utmost punctiliousness. The pot, a shapely vessel ornamented with a series of concentric circles round its neck and a sort of net-pattern on its bowl, was placed between us on a ring or circular stand of plaited grass called "ekara." To keep flies and dust from getting into the wine, the open mouth of the pot was stopped with a small round calabash or gourd. The chief's own butler officiated. Removing the gourd, he stuffed some fibre into the mouth to act as drainer, and then, tipping it up, poured out the liquid into half a calabash halved lengthwise, and thence, draining it again through fibre, into one of the little gourd-cups. Before presenting this cup to his master, he spilt some of its contents on the ground.

The chief took the cup, spilt more of the wine on the ground, called on Abassi (God) to bless my visit to them and to cement peace and friendship between us, and drank what was left. Another cup was handed to me, and I followed suit, pouring out a generous libation to the spirit-world, and wishing them "good crops, prosperous markets, and plenty of children." These wishes I spoke in their own language, slowly, and in a loud voice. All the people heard me, and replied with a sort of "hear! hear!" of satisfaction.

Then the cups were re-filled and passed round to my men and to the principal members of the chief's personal following, and so we emptied the pot.

This important ceremony concluded, I asked the chief how long he had been lame, and what had caused his lameness.

"It began eight moons ago," he said. "I was returning from the beach, some bad spirit put poison in the swamp, and it got through my skin, and has never left me."

"Let me look," I said.

The chief put out his right leg, and showed me a kind of carbuncle growing just above and behind the knee. I felt it. It was as large as a turkey's egg and hard at the base. It was smeared with a green mess, and, just above it, was tightly tied a circlet of twisted grass.

"I think I can cure you," I said. "Why have you tied this grass round your leg?"

"To prevent the sickness from getting up into my body," he replied.

Then I told him that, wishing to understand as much as possible of their beliefs and customs, I had joined the Egbo

Society, and had, together with my man Amo, been admitted to the second grade.

"Many years ago," he said, "we bought Egbo from Efik traders who came up to visit us, and we have a fine Egbo-house here. I have ordered my boys to clean it out so that you may sleep and live there."

"Bring up the prisoners," I called to Amo.

So Ikong and Ensa, the former still gagged, and both still bound, were brought up and laid on the ground before me. I told the whole story to Chief Okun Ibanga, and finished by intimating it to be my wish that their case should be tried and punished by members of Egbo, Ikong having broken their code by conspiring against two members far senior in rank than he.

It was agreed that the case should be deferred until the following day.

Opening negociations having thus been brought to a satisfactory close, I told the chief that I should be glad to retire to my quarters. Before leaving the market-place, I said to the people, "Those of you who are sick may come and see me to-morrow morning."

The Egbo-house to which I was conducted was so "fine" and I spent so many days in it—nearly a fortnight—that I wrote in my journal some descriptive notes from which I draw the following account.

It was an oblong building, open at one end, and closed at the other, with low side-walls, and a high thatched roof. There was a space of several feet between the eaves and the top of these side-walls. It was thirty-six feet long by twenty-seven broad, and three feet of its length were walled off at the back so as to form the "etakefe," inner shrine or chancel. The two principal posts which supported the roof were each imbedded in a huge square altar-like mass of clay carved on front and sides with geometrical patterns painted black, white, red, and yellow. That surrounding the front post was six and a half feet square. The front side of the "chancel" wall, and both sides of the side-walls, were painted with vertical stripes of the same four colours. A low earthen seat ran along both sides of the house.

On each side of the second post stood a strange-shaped clay erection surmounted by a pair of bush-deer's horns, and to one of them was attached a rope which hung down from the roof These were built there "to protect the house." On a stand in front of the first post and its clay block was a large "obodum" drum, four and a half feet long, encircled by a string of the skulls and jaw-bones of goats and dogs. Several smaller drums lay here and there.

But the principal furniture of Use Egbo-house consisted of an extraordinary series of statues or images carved out of blocks of "ebo" wood, painted with the same four colours, and arranged in due order around the building. They were representations of "Ekpe" or Egbo and his attendants—"the children of Ekpe's house."

The tallest figure was that of Ekpe himself, five feet four inches in height, standing on the top of the block in front of the first post. He wore a real loin-cloth, necklace and anklets of fibre, and a bell tied on to the cloth behind. Carved out of the wood was Ekpe's hat, a flat thing, worn on the back of his head, and ornamented with rays radiating from the centre. His outstretched right hand grasped a whip, and his left was behind his back nearly touching the bell. To the post behind him was nailed his many-coloured tight-fitting suit of European cotton, knitted by the natives.

There were eleven other figures, including those of two "Ibom" or horned snakes of over five feet in length, the executioner with his knife, the gong-beater with his gong and stick, the drummer with his drum, a woman with a calabash on her head, another carrying a drinking-horn, a group of "Ekpe's children," and so on.

These images had been then but lately put up. They were all, as I have said before, painted black, white, red, and yellow. The general effect of this temple of Egbo rites, this hall of statues, was very weird and strange. The chief and his people saw nothing incongruous in placing it at my disposal as a temporary dwelling-house. "Superstitious" though the negro may be, he is at the same time extremely practical, and sees no irreverence where no irreverence is intended. That I myself was a member of the Egbo Society made no difference whatever; any stranger of importance would have been allowed to quarter himself in the Egbo-house. You must not therefore please compare me with those soldiers of the Roundhead party, who, during the civil war of the seventeenth century, quartered themselves and their horses in our churches.

"You were right," I said to my host; "you have indeed a fine Egbo-house. Who carved all the images for you?"

"A man living far away in the Ikono country," he replied. "We paid him thirty goats for his work."

"And how much," I asked, "did you pay the Efik traders for your Egbo?"

"Eight slaves," he answered with as much unconcern as a modern millionaire would speak of ten-pound notes.

"And these slaves," I continued, "where did you get them?"

"Six we bought from the Ikono people," he replied, "and two were women of this town who had given their husbands so much trouble that they had to get rid of them."

The house had been sprinkled with water, and swept out fairly well. On going in, however, I found that the wooden figures were covered with dust and filth, and told my boys to brush them down, and give the whole place another thorough cleaning. They began operations, but soon had to leave off, for numerous bees had chosen the angular corners of the bodies and limbs of the Egbo images as suitable depositories for their honeycomb, and greatly resented interference. So I had to countermand my order, and the bees, as if in gratitude, granted us a peaceful share of their abode.

We converted the long narrow inner room into a prison, for I did not think it advisable that the arch-scoundrel Ikong should be kept far out of my sight. Chief Okun Ibanga arranged that some of his men should relieve one another in acting guard over the prisoners, and thus Amo was once more free to attend to other matters. The chief also lent me handcuffs and leg-irons of native make, and we of course ungagged His Highness the Prince.

I sent Akpan and a mixed party of paddlers and Use boys down to the beach to bring up all my stores, and, before darkness set in, I had them all safely lodged in the Egbo-house.

Besides the two prisoners and their guard, I arranged that Amo, Otu. my two boys Okun and Etim, and the other head-paddler—the last that I might keep watch over him—should all sleep under the same roof as myself. The chief's own compound was near at hand. He placed one side of it at the disposal of the thirty-eight paddlers, and also undertook to keep an eye on Ikong's two boys. Akpan and his boy also slept in the chief's compound. Towzer attached himself as nurse to Otu, and considered so much licking to be a necessary part of the cure that I doubt if Otu had ever felt cleaner.

That night I put a very hot yam-poultice on the old chief's leg, and, bandaging it tightly, told him to lie as still as possible.

Early the next morning we held a court to try Ikong and Ensa for their attempted murder of Otu, and to try Ikong alone for his conspiracy against me and Amo. It was held in the open air under the shade of some great trees growing near the Egbo-house. No women, but all members of Egbo, including those of the lowest or "ekung" grade, were allowed to be present, and the assembly embraced several prominent Egbo officials from the neighbouring inland village of Aka, which had also bought Egbo from the Efik tribe.

Okun Ibanga, helped by a sort of jury of six old men, presided, and I was prosecutor and chief witness.

On being asked whether he pleaded guilty or not guilty, Ikong said, in English, "I am a British subject and a Christian. I have been arrested without a warrant and by order of one who has no jurisdiction whatever in this country. The whole affair is illegal. Under such circumstances, I decline to reply to any interrogation whatsoever. As a Christian, I scorn the superstitious, idolatrous, and iconoclastical [so he said!] procedure of this heathen court. I appeal to the British Consul at Old Calabar. I shall say no more."

Then he drew himself up, made a movement as if to fold his arms across his chest, forgetting for an instant that they were fettered, and assumed an expression of disdainful indifference.

I explained to the court something of what he had said, and then, looking at Ikong, said in English, "You know as well as I do that British jurisdiction has never yet been extended to the Ibibio country. You know, too, that, among all races of mankind, be they black or white, "heathen" or Christian, the taking of human life, except in war, is forbidden. The attempted murder of Otu was only the first step in some foul scheme concocted by you against me and my man Amo. Otu is, as you know, brother to Amo's wife. Where native laws are good and just, the British Government does not interfere with them. The Ibibio tribe is closely related to your own Efik tribe and, while in this country, you are subject to its laws. Your trial will proceed."

On the same question being put to headman Ensa, he became very voluble, laying all the blame on to Ikong, and disclaiming any share in the attempted murder of Otu except that of obeying the order of an Egbo senior whom he had taken an especially solemn oath to obey in all things.

Witnesses were sworn on a certain sacred "juju" belonging to the old chief, who kept it usually concealed somewhere in his compound.

Ikong's four hammock-bearers, examined separately, all gave the same evidence; that they had seen Ikong instructing Ensa, who carried Otu, to keep in the rear of the others, and that they had seen Ensa thrown Otu into the mud and Ikong strike him hard on the head with a loaded stick (produced). Then Amo told of Towzer's barking, and of my sending Akpan to follow the dog, and of Ikong's attempt to prevent my order being carried out. Finally, Akpan and those boys who had helped him, told the court how Towzer had led them to Otu, and how they had found him all but suffocated in the mire, and with a bad wound on his head.

Ikong refused to say anything whatever, but Ensa corroborated the witnesses' evidence, and, again pleading that, according to Egbo code, he could not have done otherwise than obey a senior's command, threw himself on the mercy of the court.

The president and six members retired to the Ebgo-house, and there held a private consultation among themselves.

On their return, they re-assumed their seats, and Chief Okun Ibanga made known their judgment.

"We find them both guilty," he said, "of an attempt to kill the boy Otu, who is a free-born member of the Duke 'House,' and also a member of Egbo, though only of the 'ekung' or lowest grade. Both the accused are not only Egbo members, Ikong having been admitted to the fourth grade, and Ensa to that just above 'ekung,' but also belong to the same 'lodge' as their victim. They were therefore attempting the murder of one related to them by the closest ties of Egbo, one whom they had sworn to treat as a brother and to protect and avenge in every ill that should befall him. All of you here present, from the Makara, the great medicine-man, to the last-initiated member of the 'ekung' grade, are members of the Egbo Society, and have been instructed in its laws. If the boy Otu had not been rescued by the cunning of the white man's witch-dog, called 'Tuza'"—here Towzer, who, by the way, was the only non-member present at this Egbo court, pricked up his ears and wagged his stumpy tail—"he would probably have died, and then, according to our law, these two men would have been put to death. But, though the boy still lives, theirs is a very serious crime."

At this point headman Ensa fell down on his knees and began to howl and cry, but his guards dragged him up again and made him keep quiet. Ikong remained immovable in body and in expression.

"We find," continued the president, "that, though Ensa was breaking one of the most sacred of our Egbo laws, he was acting under the order of a member several degrees his senior, and we have therefore decided to treat him leniently. Instead of selling him as a slave to the Aros—the punishment which his crime deserves—we think it sufficient to banish him for ever from the Egbo Society, so that he may never again enjoy its feasts and festivals, or avail himself of its protection and privileges."

Here one of the jurymen spoke to the president, who, after a whispered consultation with the others, added "All fees paid by him on entering the society and on higher initiation to his present grade are of course forfeited to his own 'lodge.' "

Then, after a short pause, he continued, "We cannot show

F

any leniency towards the other prisoner, Ikong. He refuses to plead, he refuses to give any reason for his attempt to kill the boy. We have heard that the white men who rule over the Efik people forbid killing just as we forbid it, and yet this man—who is learned in the language and ways of the white men, and who has cast off the religion and customs of his forefathers, and sacrifices only to the white man's God— has attempted to kill a boy who has done him no wrong whatever! We pronounce upon him the sentence decreed by the sacred code of Egbo—that he be banished for ever from the Society, that his right hand be cut off at the wrist, and that he be sold to the Inokun people of the grove of Ekpenyong-Ibriitam ['Long Juju']. I have spoken. The court is dismissed."

CHAPTER VIII.

THE CANNIBAL-EXECUTIONER.

Had a thunderbolt fallen at my feet out of the then cloudless expanse of sky, I should not have been more astounded than I was on hearing this judgment. "Of course this must not be carried out," I said to myself; "such punishment is barbarous and inhuman, contrary to all the dictates of christianity and civilization!"

Ikong, on hearing it, had at first looked incredulous, and then almost amused, but in a few moments I noticed that his face assumed that same dirty olive-green hue which had come upon it when I had frustrated his attempt to prevent the discovery of Otu's body, that his knees trembled, and that into his eyes crept a look of the deadliest terror.

Then I stood up and addressed the assembly.

"Chief Okun Ibanga, chiefs and officials of Egbo, and people of Use," I said, "I understand your language better than I can speak it. I have understood everything that has been said here this morning. I too am, as you know, a member of the Egbo Society. I have, however, been initiated only as far as the second grade, whereas Chief Okun Ibanga, and also his right-hand colleague the Chief of Aka, are fully-initiated members of the first grade. I therefore am their junior, and, according to Egbo law, am not entitled to criti-

cise or to dispute anything decreed by them. I am here as
your stranger [guest], and a stranger should not make comment upon what his hosts say or do. Besides, however, being
your fellow-member in Egbo, and your 'stranger,' I am a subject and servant of the great White Queen who lives over the
broad sea, whom all white men reverence and obey. She
makes known to her people the wishes of all-powerful Abassi"
(I pointed up to the sky), "the same mighty God whom you
yourselves worship from afar, for He looks down upon us all,
black men and white men alike. In the old days, the days
of your grandfathers' grandfathers, we white people knew not
the will of Abassi, but sent our ships to your country and
bought men and women and sold them into slavery, and,
long before those days, we too used to cut off the right hand
for far smaller crimes than attempted murder. Our wise
men, however, learned that such actions were displeasing to
Abassi, and for many long years we have ceased to do thus,
and so Abassi has blessed us and made us the greatest nation
upon the whole earth. We have, moreover, tried to teach
other nations what things are pleasing and displeasing to
Abassi, and the great White Queen sends her servants all over
the world to make known what Abassi tells her. The big
Consul at Old Calabar makes known the Queen's laws to the
Efik people, and they are beginning to understand and to
obey. Abassi has told the Queen to forbid slave-dealing and
such punishments as mutilating the human body."

At this point, I was interrupted by a murmur from the
whole throng, a murmur of decided disapproval.

"Listen to me, men of Use," I continued, "listen to me, a
servant of the great White Queen. I have heard the judgment pronounced by the president. It is just and right to
find both prisoners guilty, it is just and right to punish Ensa
leniently, and it is just and right to punish Ikong
with great severity; but I appeal to the president and other
chiefs to give him punishment different from what has been
decreed. He is a man of some rank and position, and belongs
to a wealthy Efik 'House.' I would advise that you banish
him for ever from Egbo, that you send him to be imprisoned
for a term of years in the Consul's gaol at Old Calabar, and
that you impose on him a very heavy fine, which, if he cannot
pay, I undertake shall be paid by his family. By imposing
such a sentence, you will not only please Abassi and the Consul, but you will add a large sum of money to the funds of
your own 'lodge.' I have finished, and await your reply."

Chief Okun Ibanga and his six colleagues again retired to
talk among themselves, and I drew Amo and Akpan aside to
ask their advice as to what was to be done.

They both quite failed to understand why I should object to the carrying out of the sentence.

"Dem man be bad too much," said Amo. "He no fit for lib. S'pose I be big Egbo-man, I go kill him one time. He get bad heart. He try for kill Otu, and he t'ink for kill you and me, sar. S'pose dey no sell him for slave, he go catch plenty bad men, and he go kill we, sar."

Akpan's opinion was that it was unwise to attempt to interfere with the usual course of Egbo law. He thought the sentence just, and even lenient, for sometimes, he said, such crime was punished with additional mutilations. He pointed out that these people knew nothing of white man's law, and cared nothing for any threats that I might make. I was the first white man that had ever visited them. They were an independent people, subject to no control, and very treacherous and savage if opposed. Our own safety and the success of my quest might depend upon my attitude in this case.

"Suppose," I said, "they insist on carrying out this sentence—can we do nothing to prevent it?"

"What can you do, master?" said Akpan. "Only you and Amo are armed, and only with small guns [revolvers]. All the Use men have guns in their huts. Your paddlers would not dare to fight for you. I and my boy come here to trade sometimes, and do not want to make palaver with these people. What can two men do against hundreds?"

"And what do you say, Amo?" I inquired.

"S'pose you lib for fight, sar, me lib for fight. S'pose you no fight, me no fight. Me fit for kill plenty men, but me t'ink dey go kill we all two 'fore we finish." This was Amo's reply.

So I returned to my seat, and thought it over, and was obliged to come to the conclusion that, if my arguments should fail, it would be useless and foolish to oppose the strength of two men armed with revolvers—"and, by the way," I suddenly remembered, "our revolvers are at this present moment locked up in one of my boxes in the Egbo-house"—against hundreds who, though having only matchets and sticks with them, could quickly fetch their guns and have us entirely at their mercy. And then, besides probably losing our own lives, we should in no way benefit the prisoner, and should probably imperil the safety of all the paddlers and our personal servants.

"And, after all," I thought, "this Ikong is a great scoundrel. He did his best to kill poor little Otu, and he had doubtless planned some scheme for getting rid of Amo and me. I will try further argument, and, if that fail, I must realise that this is such a 'primitive' country that, unless crime against life and property be punished severely, it would be quite impossible to maintain peace and order."

A few minutes later the president and jurymen returned, and silence fell upon the court.

"Makara," said the old chief, "we have held secret consultation together, and we have carefully weighed your words. This man Ikong has done evilly towards one of your boys, and has moreover conspired against you yourself and your tall servant. Yet you ask us to spare him, to permit him to return to his country, and to impose a fine on him instead of cutting off his hand and selling him into slavery. We have, as I said before, thought deeply on what you propose, but we cannot understand why you should wish to make the punishment easier for him. He has sinned grievously against Egbo, and must pay the penalty as Egbo law ordains. We know nothing about the Consul's prison at Old Calabar. This is not a crime that can be atoned for by a payment of money. Besides this, we have no guarantee that the money would be paid—we know nothing of the prisoner's family or 'House.' Egbo was brought into this village by my grandfather, and it is our duty to perform the rites and to administer the laws as handed down by him. If we should judge a case and publicly pronounce a sentence, and then afterwards make such sentence lighter, the people would say among themselves that Egbo is become weak, and that the judgment of its elders veers about like the wind. By such actions, Makara, we should spoil our country, for evil-minded men, no longer fearing punishment for their misdeeds, would then eat up all the land. I have finished. The sentence of Egbo must be carried out."

Then took place what was to me the most painful incident of the whole proceedings. Ikong suddenly lost all self-restraint, and abandoned himself to the wildest paroxysm of hysterical fear. Throwing himself down at my feet, he grovelled and wallowed, imploring me to forgive him, promising with many religious oaths to serve me and slave for me with the utmost fidelity, beseeching me to threaten the Use people with war and annihilation unless they should release him, and even begging *me* to go down on my knees on his behalf!

I stopped him as soon as I could, made him get up, and said to him, "Though you don't deserve it, Ikong, I will do my best for you, but I am afraid they will not listen to me. You yourself have brought this trouble upon you. You are doing your case no good by making this degrading exhibition of yourself. If you have to suffer, play the man, and hope for a possible escape."

Once more addressing the assembly, I said, "Chief Okun Ibanga, elders, and people, I too have given this matter most careful consideration, and I find that there is much good in what the president has said. You owe your present state of peace and security to the wise laws handed down to you by your forefathers, and you are right to act so that these laws may be respected and obeyed. But, as time goes on, the wisest and the best of laws must change as all things change. Abassi teaches us new things which were unknown to our forefathers, and at the same time He teaches us to put away things which our forefathers reverenced. In the name of Abassi" (I pointed upwards), "and in the name of the great White Queen, I ask you not to mutilate this man, and not to sell him into slavery."

Then I resumed my seat.

Another whispered consultation took place, somewhat interrupted by the murmurings of the mass of the people. I noticed that some of the men were slipping away to their huts and returning with their guns.

Chief Okun Ibanga arose. "Quiet!" he shouted.

Then, looking at me, he continued, "As our forefathers have taught us, so must we do. You tell us, Makara, that the Abassi whom you white men worship is the same Abassi whom we ourselves reverence. This I know not, but I do know that it was Abassi" (he looked upward) "who taught the Egbo laws to men who lived long ago, and that, in upholding these laws, we are but carrying out the commands of Abassi. The law must take its course. The people are already murmuring at the long delay. The prisoner must lose his right hand in the presence of all the assembled children of Egbo, who will thus see that Egbo is strong in the land and must be obeyed."

I could say no more. Interference would have been vain and foolish. I had to submit.

The "executioner" and his assistants took Ikong and led him to a shed opposite the open front of the Egbo-house. As soon as they laid hands upon him, he began howling again, and, as they dragged him away, he poured out in English a torrent of imprecations and filthy language upon me and everything connected with me.

I had already observed this "shed." It consisted of an oblong space surrounded by a seat or low wall of clay, a foot in height and a foot in breadth, over which, supported on slender posts, was a roof thatched with the usual materials. It was called "efe-ngkuku-ekpo," which, translated literally, means "the shed of the shades of ancient fathers"—i.e., the place where they sacrificed and prayed to the spirits of their departed chiefs. From the rafters hung several human and animals' skulls, and on a sort of shelf were drums and other articles of Egbo ceremonial.

But the most noticeable object was on the floor. It was the rudely-made clay figure of a man lying at full-length on his chest, with the head so raised that his glass eyes (fragments of looking-glass) were visible to anybody standing in front of him. The hands and feet had been broken off and lost. It was about four and a half feet long, and was called "ibok-ukpong," meaning literally "medicine of the soul." I had wondered what it was for, but had made no inquiry about it. The clay used was the ordinary reddish-brown clay of the district, and it was unpainted.

"You go, Akpan," I said. "I will stay here. I don't want to see it done. And you, Amo, go and prepare water and bandages, and get my medicine-chest ready. I will do what I can for his arm."

So they went. Akpan, however, returned almost immediately. "I beg you to come, master," he said. "I think they are going to kill him; but, if you come, they will not dare to do so."

Deeming it advisable to comply with this proposal, I made my way through the crowd surrounding the shed, and had my chair placed just outside.

"I have come here," I cried out, "not because I approve of the sentence, nor out of curiosity, but because I wish to make sure that the prisoner receives only the punishment decreed by the president."

They had stripped the wretched Ikong of all his clothes, and were offering him a drink of gin, for to render the victim as insensible to pain as possible is a custom common among negroes, and tends to show that they are not so fiendishly cruel as they are sometimes accused of being.

Ikong was trembling like an aspen-leaf, and was at first unable to comprehend what they were offering him. Then he shook his head, and looked furtively round as if seeking a channel of escape. They put the bottle into his hands, but they shook so much that he could not get it up to his mouth. Then the "executioner," a stout jovial-faced man with a horrible squint in one eye, took it from him, and, first spilling a few drops on the ground and taking a sip himself, held it to Ikong's mouth and made him swallow some of the contents.

The fiery liquid produced a rapid effect. Ikong ceased his trembling and whimpering, pulled himself together, cast a scowl of hatred at me, and, taking the bottle into his own hand, put it to his lips and in a few gulps emptied it. Then he threw it in my direction, but failed to hit me. It went a yard or so to the side of me, and was caught by one of the crowd.

Chief Okun Ibanga motioned to the people to stand somewhat back. Only Ikong and the executioner and his assistants were inside the shed. The chief himself and his colleague stood near my chair, and Amo and Akpan were with me.

Ikong had drunk so much gin that he reeled and would have fallen had they not caught him. Two men took him by the arms and two by the legs, and laid him out flat on his chest on top of the clay figure. Ikong, being about a foot taller than the figure, did not fit well, but they made his head rest on the dummy's head, and stretched out his legs and arms to cover those of the dummy. Each leg was kept in its place by a man holding it at the ankle, and there was a man at each arm, and a fifth sat straddle-wise across the victim's back.

"See," said the executioner, pointing to the right arm of the figure, "Ibok-Ukpong has no right hand, but we will soon give him one!"

At these words, he drew from its goatskin sheath a very bright matchet, and, stepping out of the hut, flourished it about before the people, and then presented its edge to the president.

"Yes," said the old chief, "it is sharp enough. Do your work."

The executioner re-entered the shed, and, kneeling down with his back towards us, took in his left hand the four fingers of Ikong's right hand, and, bending them slightly upward, and pulling at the arm, raised the matchet with his other hand and at one blow severed off the victim's right hand.

Then, springing up and standing on the little enclosure-wall of the shed, he brandished aloft the dripping trophy, and cried, "Thus do we punish those who break the laws of Egbo." He then flung it down at the president's feet. I turned away my head, nearly sick at the sight.

The executioner's eyes glared. He protruded his portly form, and rubbed his wet fingers all over his skin. The lust of blood was upon him.

"Ha!" he cried springing back into the shed. "See here, and here, and here," and he pointed to the missing left hand and feet of the clay figure. Ibok-Ukpong still wants a hand and two feet. Let us make him whole again. We have a willing victim here. He likes his bed so well that he already sleeps, I think. Come, let us finish our job."

But I interposed. Laying my hand on Chief Okun Ibanga's arm, I said, "Listen, Awbong [Chief]. The sentence of the court has been carried out. You ordered that only one hand should be cut off. Justice has been satisfied. Would you bring shame on your court by permitting this man to exceed your judgment? Stop him, I beg you."

The chief advanced to the front of the shed, and, spitting on the ground, cried out, "It is finished. The decree of the court has been executed. Take away the prisoner, give him medicine, and see that he do not escape."

Turning to the executioner, he said, "Take your reward, and go."

The man looked disappointed and surly, and cast a glance at me which was anything but friendly. Pointing to the victim's little pile of clothes, one of the perquisites of his calling, he ordered an assistant to gather them up, but first he wiped his matchet on them. Then, returning it to its sheath, he picked up Ikong's hand by the fingers, and, swinging it backwards and forwards as he walked, strode out of sight, disappearing into one of the neighbouring compounds, and leaving a trail of blood behind him.

The crowd was already dispersing. The old chief came up to me, and, touching my shoulder, said, "I could not do otherwise, Makara. The people demanded it. We chiefs have but little power to contradict them. They, and all of us, believe that our lives depend on carrying out the ordinances of our forefathers."

"I bear you no ill-will," I replied. "Help me to attend to the prisoner's arm."

Ikong was in a swoon. With the assistance of a native doctor whom the chief sent to me, I tied the bleeding vessels, and cleansed and bound up the mutilated stump. Then they carried him away into a sort of prison built at one corner inside the head-chief's compound.

Early that morning, before the trial, I had put another steaming-hot poultice on Okun Ibanga's leg, and he had told his principal wife to have fufu (yam pudding) on the fire all day long, and every hour or so, carrying out my instructions, she applied a fresh poultice.

To reach the Anang country from Use, you have to pass through the district of the Ikono sub-tribe, over whom, as Amo's mother had informed me, a "king" ruled. Use and several neighbouring villages, including Aka, belonging to another sub-tribe of the Ibibio-speaking people, and, living near the river Enyong, they had for many years been visited by Efik and Enyong traders, and had thus adopted Egbo, and certain innovations in dress and household affairs, the influence of which had tended to make them somewhat less "savage" than their inland neighbours. This state of affairs had been explained to me at Old Calabar and at Itu, so that I was quite prepared to meet with greater difficulties the further I should advance into the country.

My plan was to win the confidence of the Use and Aka people, and thence to make my way to the "capital" of the Ikonos, and so to eventually reach the Anangs. The Use villagers looked upon the Ikonos as "very bad men, always fighting and killing people." Their king was said to be a stranger or foreigner, who had many wives, and lived at a place called Ikot-Abassi, which, being interpreted, means "the people of Abassi" (God's people).

When the paddlers heard that it was my intention to go as far inland as the Ikono country, they one and all informed me that nothing whatever would induce them to accompany me.

"Dey fear too much," said Amo. "S'pose dey go for dem bush, dey t'ink dey neber look deir own country no more. Dey say plenty debils live for dem bush. Dey say dem big king go chop [eat] man ebery day."

My two servants, Okun and Etim, also declined to brave the dangers of such a journey, and of course Ikong's boys were no longer required. Akpan and his boy, however, as already agreed upon at Itu, would accompany me. Otu was rapidly recovering under Towzer's attentive care. I asked Amo if the boy feared to go with us.

"No, sar," he answered, "he no fear. I ask him. He say he lub me and you plenty, and he lub Tuza too much. S'pose dem dog go for bush, he fit for go. S'pose, he say, dem bad men chop dem dog, den he go kill plenty men 'fore dey kill him. O, sar, dem small boy make me laugh too much!" Amo was greatly amused at his small valet's boasted prowess.

Akpan's boy could cook a little, and Otu had picked up similar knowledge, first from Tom Peter at Old Calabar, and then from my present cook Okun. Their respective masters agreed to lend me their services, and Amo himself would superintend the stores and everything else. If the Ikonos should be willing to receive me, they would probably provide me with carriers, each village in its turn sending me on to the next village.

I therefore permitted the paddlers and other boys to depart. Before they left, I appointed another headman in place of Ensa, who, though allowed to return to Old Calabar, went home in deep disgrace. By them, I sent a letter to my "bankers" of "Jemima" Factory, requesting them to pay the paddlers' wages (sixpence each per diem), and to settle with the owner for the hire of the two canoes. In thus "burning my ships," I was depriving myself of the best means of return to civilization.

By them I also sent a letter to Mr. Johnston, in which I gave him a full account of our proceedings since leaving Asang, including Ikong's punishment, and the banishment of headman Ensa from the Egbo Society. I asked him to make known the latter fact to the head of the delinquent's "lodge" at Old Calabar.

I instructed them to pick up at Asang, on their way down the river, their comrade who had been left there to recover from his sprained ankle, and I myself paid off the two Asang boys who had been there engaged as substitutes. Finally, I "dashed" them a head of tobacco each, and told them to get back to their country as quickly as possible.

After their departure, our number was reduced to only six, namely, I (Richard Wood), Amo, Otu, Akpan, his boy Ima, and Ikong. I should, however, have written seven, for dog Towzer was of course still with us.

A few days after Ikong's trial, the executioner brought a clay model of a right hand and added it to the handless body of the figure called "Ibok-Ukpong." Squinting at me he remarked with a horrible grin, "I said I would give him a new right hand. Before many moons are finished, I will give him feet and a left hand also." Many people heard him say this.

As I have said before, I spent altogether a fortnight in the Egbo-house at Use. Every day sick people came to me, not only from the five Use villages, but from neighbouring communities of the same sub-tribe. I managed to set a few broken bones, and was also successful in sewing up cuts and other wounds. Most of those who came to me were suffering with cutaneous diseases, chiefly yaws, a kind of eruption, which, though certainly contagious, most often owes its origin to their unsanitary dwellings and disregard to cleanliness. The application of boric acid ointment effected many cures. Several extraordinary cases of elephantiasis were brought to me, but for these I could do nothing.

My principal patient, however, was Chief Okun Ibanga. The hourly succession of hot yam-poultices was certainly softening the tumour, but by no means so quickly as I had hoped, and I was beginning to fear that, unless I could think of some other treatment, my reputation as a doctor might suffer seriously.

The solution of this difficulty came about in the simplest possible way. One morning, while eating an egg at breakfast, my thoughts turned to eggs at Riversley Rectory, and then to an old woman named Sally Martin from whom my father used often to buy them. I pictured to myself old Sally's cottage in the lane, and then remembered how, in our childhood, Pleasance and Jack and I used to visit her, to see her hens and ducks, and to hear her stories about witches and ghosts. Then, all of a sudden, I jumped up from my chair, exclaiming, "I have it; I will cure the old man after all!" I had suddenly remembered how Sally Martin had quickly cured Jack of a similar trouble on the back of his neck which our local doctor had been treating for days without success.

"My goodness, gracious, Master Jack!" she had said—I can even now see and hear her saying it—"Them doctors don't know nothen at all. Jest you come to old Sally, my dear, and she'll soon put yer right agen. I aren't no scholar, and I don't know no Laten, but I do know a thing or two that my old grandmother larnt me."

Whereupon the old woman had broken a fresh egg, made a hot bread-poultice with a "doke" or impression therein, poured the white of the egg into the doke, and clapped it on to Jack's neck.

"There, Master Jack," she had exclaimed, "that'll hurt yer good tightly, I'll be bound; but jest yer let that alone, and that'll soon cure that old boil."

Sally was proved to be quite right. Her poultice had such "drawing power" that one application had been sufficient to cause the breaking of the carbuncle.

This forgotten incident of long ago thus suddenly occurring to my remembrance, was welcomed by me as being the probable way out of my dilemma.

CHAPTER IX.

"THE SPIRIT SHALL RETURN UNTO GOD WHO GAVE IT."

It was on the tenth day after the trial and mutilation of Ikong that I remembered old Sally Martin's cure. During this period I had been turning over in my mind the possibility of saving Ikong from being sold into slavery. Every day I had attended him in his confinement, and done what I could to ease the pain. He, poor fellow, was in great dejection.

"I am ruined for life, sir," he said to me. "What good is a man who has lost his right hand? I am disgraced in the eyes of all my people. A still worse fate awaits me. The Inokuns will buy me, and take me to Ibum, not to live and work there as a slave—this" (holding up the stump) "makes all work impossible—but to sacrifice me in the juju-grove of Ekpenyong-Ibriitam ['Long Juju']. No one ever returns from there! O, sir, I beg you in God's name, help me to escape from this awful fate."

I pondered it over in my mind. He was strictly guarded, day and night, and, to prevent his running away, they had passed his feet through circular apertures in a very heavy block of wood and fettered them together on the other side. My appeal at the trial on Ikong's behalf had made the Use people suspicious of my intentions towards him, and I had an enemy in the executioner, whom I had balked, not only of the pleasure of further mutilating his victim, but—horrible to relate!—of a *meal*.

This is how I found it out. On the day after the trial, as I entered Ikong's prison at one door, the executioner went out at another, and I noticed a peculiarly unpleasant smell, but said nothing about it. Afterwards, however, I asked Amo what it was.

Amo laughed and said, "Dem man what cut off Ikong's hand, he go mock Ikong. He cook Ikong's hand for fire; he sit down for dem prison, and he go chop dem hand. S'pose dey cook man, fingers and dis" (sticking out his tongue and touching it) "make plenty good beef."

This is actually what had occurred. The plump and jovial-faced executioner had roasted Ikong's hand, and then, going to the prison, had sat opposite his wretched victim, leering at him with his squint eye, and gnawing the flesh from the bones! I had, therefore, by my intervention, deprived him of three-quarters of his intended feast.

Akpan informed me that negociations were already in progress for Ikong's sale to certain Inokun traders who frequented Umaw-Ama market. I could see that Akpan himself rejoiced in Ikong's fall. From the first, they had been rivals for my favour, and the learned interpreter had on a certain occasion called Akpan something which meant "uneducated bushman," which insult had never been forgiven by the latter. I could not therefore take Akpan into my confidence.

Nor did I feel any surer of Amo's sympathy. Ikong's perfidious treachery, overheard by us on the juju island at Asang, had hardened Amo's heart against him, and he also

considered that Ikong's cold-blooded attempt to murder little
Otu had not been punished any too severely. I could per-
suade Amo, and probably compel Akpan, to aid me in any
scheme that I should concoct, but it would have been but
half-hearted aid, and so I did not call upon them.

One course remained open to me, and this was to secretly
obtain the assistance of Chief Okun Ibanga himself.

I had taken rather a fancy to the old man, and had had
several long conversations with him. He seemed to live a
life somehow apart from his people, and his thoughts were
often engaged in speculating upon the mysteries of existence,
and upon

> "That undiscovered country from whose bourn
> No traveller returns."

I recollect one occasion in particular. It was a warm
sultry night, and the chief and I were sitting in the open
space opposite the Egbo-house. Amo lay stretched out on
the ground beside me. The moon was full. Her beams
penetrated into the Egbo-house, and cast an unearthly light
upon the painted images. The whole pageantry of the
heavens was spread out as a map. Never had I seen the
"Milky way" more crowded with dim shapes. The "Plough"
was upside down. Perhaps nothing brings home and England
nearer to the imagination of the absent traveller than the sight
of this friend familiar from childhood's days. All Nature
was hushed and still, but every now and again, carried on
the breeze from a remote hillside village, came the roll of the
tom-tom and the full-voiced notes of an "offiong" chorus.

I asked him about his ancestors and the past history of
the Use people.

"Long, long ago," he said, "our first forefather came here
from inland parts. The country was covered with forest
and thick bush, in which elephants roamed, but the last of
them was killed long before I was born. Afterwards he had
a wife, and they built their hut where my compound now
stands. Their children multiplied and spread all about the
country. When my father died, he hoped his spirit would
meet those of our first forefather and his wife."

"And you," I inquired, "do you expect to meet them and
your father in the spirit-world?"

"Of course," he replied, looking up to the heavens. "We
believe that our spirits go first to Abassi, but that, after
living with Him for a time, they return to this earth and are
born again."

"Do they," I asked, "always return to the same village?"

"No," he answered, "it depends on what has happened in

their former life here. If the spirit was happy here, it returns to its old village and compound, and is born again into the body of an infant, but, if it lived unhappily, it goes to dwell in another community."

"Do all the people hold this belief?"

"Certainly they do," he said. "Sometimes when a woman's baby dies, she cuts off a finger, so that she may recognise its spirit when it returns to this earth, for, if her next child be born with one finger missing, she knows that the spirit has returned to her. What do you white men believe, Makara?"

"Some believe one thing, and some another," I replied. "There are some, but these are only a few, who believe that after death the spirit lives no more. Most of us, however, believe in the continuance of life after death. Many are content to hold exactly the same belief that their fathers and grandfathers held, but those who think much thereon, and study the ancient books of the past, and the beliefs of all the nations upon earth, realise that man—black man and white man alike—knows really nothing of the life to which the spirit passes after death."

"And you, Makara, you yourself," he inquired, "what do you think about it?"

"I certainly believe in a future life," I said, "I believe that life is immortal, that every form of life exists for ever. I look upon life as—as a ——"

Against a neighbouring tree stood a long ladder formed of stout palm-stalks with narrow rungs of the same dovetailed into them.

"See that ladder," I continued, pointing to it. "It seems to me that life is like a ladder with many rungs. Each rung is what we call a life. Men are for ever climbing this ladder. Sometimes they go up a rung, but sometimes they go down. The space between each rung is what we call death. We pass from rung to rung, but can see no rung except that on which we are standing, nor can we remember anything of what happened to us while we stood on the other rungs. Do you understand me?"

"Yes, Makara, I understand," he replied; "but it is very difficult. For many long years I have wished to hold communion with my father's spirit, but" (he looked round on all sides, and lowered his voice) "though I buried his body with all customary rites and sacrifices, and erected a fine 'ngkweme" [spirit-house] for him, and though I have through all these years made periodical sacrifices and prayers as our forefathers taught us to do, my father has never spoken to me, nor do I know where his spirit lives. I am chief priest over the

Use people, and they look upon me as a medium between them and the spirit-world. Therefore they obey and fear me. I have never told them that my father's spirit, and those of more ancient forefathers whom we worship, never appear to me."

His voice died away in a mournful cadence. Truly this frank confession was an unveiling of typical priestcraft and sacerdotalism!

"And your father," I ventured to inquire, "where do you think his spirit now lives?"

"I do not know," he sadly admitted. "Life and death, Makara, are deep mysteries which even we priests cannot understand. Sometimes, in the rainy season, when our valleys are filled with mist and we cannot see the hills beyond, and then the sun comes forth, and the mists slowly fade, and there is revealed what has been hidden there all the time— sometimes I stand alone and watch the fading mist and wonder if death, which some men call 'black,' may not prove to be like the glorious sun, who burns away the mist and shows us clearly what lies beyond."

The old chief ceased speaking, and sat pensively gazing at the expanse of hilly country lying stretched before us in the moonlight.

"Perhaps," he continued in a low tone, as if speaking to himself, "perhaps my father's spirit still lives with Abassi in the sky, or perhaps he has all these years been displeased with us his children, and so has chosen to be born again in some other community. I cannot tell. He never comes to me. I make sacrifices, but get no reply. Perhaps death will make it known to me."

The chief's musings brought to my remembrance a stanza of Fitzgerald's translation of the *Rubáiyát*:

"Strange, is it not? that of the myriads who
    Before us pass'd the door of Darkness through
        Not one returns to tell us of the Road,
    Which to discover we must travel too."

After this particular conversation with Okun Ibanga, I used sometimes to refer to it when alone with him.

"Don't you think," I would say, "that perhaps your father has been taught in the spirit-world by Abassi that some of the sacrifices and other customs practised by your forefathers are not suitable for these later times, and that therefore he is displeased with you, and so does not return? Abassi has taught the great White Queen and her wisest men that human sacrifices, mutilations, and slave-dealing are displeasing to Him. I would suggest that you make an experiment. Discontinue these things for a few years, and see if such change will produce a favourable result."

I poured out this advice drop by drop, and had of course too much tact to mention Ikong's case in connection with it. The old chief said little, but was, I could see, pondering upon it.

One day, however, he said to me, "If you will give me some sign that what you white men teach is sent you from Abassi, I will cease to practise these things. Otherwise, I cannot forsake the customs and laws of my forefathers."

"Give me time," I replied; "you ask a difficult thing. I must think it over."

This was two days before my recollection of Sally Martin's cure, two days spent in planning scheme after scheme, but rejecting them all.

I determined to use the old woman's recipe as the "sign," and to lose no time in applying it.

So, going to the chief, I said to him, "If I, with Abassi's help, can extract all the poison out of your leg in three days' time, will you receive it as a sign that He wishes you to cease from human sacrifices, mutilation, and slave-dealing?"

"Yes," he replied; "cure me in three days' time, and I will believe."

Now, the means of cure was extremely simple, but it never does for a doctor to allow his patients to penetrate "behind the scenes"—bread-pills, swallowed in the belief that they are a mixture of three things of lengthy Latin nomenclature, would often be ineffective if the patient knew their real composition. So I soon planned a little "hokey-pokey" accompaniment to my medical treatment, and this is what it was.

First of all, I told the chief that he must send messengers to every compound and every hut of the five Use villages, to tell every man, woman, and child old enough to walk alone, to bring each of them a hen's egg to the Egbo-house the following morning.

So he called his Egbo runners, and in the name of Egbo they went forth—north, south, east, and west. The people were told that their chief's recovery depended on their obedience to the order.

Early the next morning they began to arrive, and by eight o'clock the large open space was packed with hundreds of them. Standing at the entrance to the Egbo-house, I called upon them to come up one by one and deposit the eggs in native baskets borrowed for the occasion, and then to remain until I should address them.

"Before you put your eggs into a basket," I cried, "you
G

must rub the shell gently behind your right knee, for that is where your chief's sickness grows."

They all solemnly carried out my directions, though many mistook left for right until my assistants Amo and Akpan directed them what to do.

This finished, I addressed him as follows:

"Men, women, and children of Use, your head-chief, Okun Ibanga, is very sick with a bad leg. It is difficult to make him well, but I have invoked Abassi's aid, and I call upon all of you to assist me. From these eggs, I shall select one for use in making a powerful medicine. If you wish your chief to recover, you must carefully carry out my further orders. During this and the next three days no wanton destruction of life must take place within the whole Use community—no goat, pig, dog, chicken, fish, lizard, snake, rat, bird or fly of any kind whatsoever must be killed, not even a mosquito or a jigger. Also, every one of you who crosses the chief's compound or this open space must limp with his or her right leg, and so establish sympathetic relationship between Okun Ibanga and all his people. I, for my part, will apply a wonderful medicine. If Abassi wishes your chief to recover, the cure will be wrought within three days. If, however, it fail, it will be because some of you will have displeased Abassi by omitting to carry out the instructions now given you. If any living thing die accidentally, the cure will not be affected thereby. I have finished. You may go. Remember all I have said."

So they departed.

Most of the eggs were what we should call "bad." The negro himself prefers them so! For my purpose, I selected the freshest I could find, broke it, and poured the white into a cup. In another cup I dissolved in water a tabloid of potassium permanganate. Then I sent my hammock to the chief's compound with a message that all was ready. He was brought to the Egbo-house, and with him came his wife carrying her pot of hot fufu. She made a poultice, and I made a "doke" in it, and therein poured, first the white of the egg, and then enough of the other liquid to impart a deep purple colour to the whole thing. Then I clapped it hot on to the carbuncle, bandaged it tightly round and round, and had my patient carried back to his hut. I ordered that nobody should visit him except his principal wife.

When I saw him an hour later, he said, "The medicine bites me very much. I think the devil inside is trying to get out."

In the afternoon I put on another similar poultice, and in the evening a third.

All day long, I had been greatly amused to see men, women, and children limping through the chief's compound and across the space opposite the Egbo-house.

The third poultice soon proved effective. I stayed with the chief. He called out, "The devil has broken my skin. I can feel him running away."

His wife removed the bandage. The tumour had broken, and much pus was exuding. I squeezed it, and at length extracted a hard core as thick as my little finger and half-an-inch long.

"See," I said, "here is the devil. Tell your wife to take it away and bury it deep in the ground. Your leg will be nearly well again by the day after to-morrow. The medicine has done its work. Abassi has sent you a sign."

I washed out the wound with potassium permanganate, and put on a simple yam-poultice. This treatment was continued during the next two days, and by the third day the place was almost healed.

That same day, Okun Ibanga called all the people together and addressed them outside the Egbo-house. He said that Abassi had given to him, their chief, a sign that He was pleased with the great white doctor's visit to Use, and that they must learn and obey Makara's teaching.

Then a pit was dug in the middle of this meeting-place, and therein were cast all the eggs except the three used in the cure. The smell created by this final ceremony was such that "the great white doctor" was exceedingly glad when the pit was filled in again!

Afterwards, I had a private talk with my patient. "Abassi has given you a sign," I said. "It is fitting that you should give Him a sign of your gratitude, and of your determination to carry out your promise."

"You mean Ikong?" he inquired.

"Yes," I said, "that's what I mean."

The chief looked rather troubled. "I dare not do it," he said. "If I set him free, the people will be angry, and seize me, and punish me in his stead. What can I do?"

"Let us consult together," I replied. "Two heads are often better than one. If we two can arrange a scheme for freeing him unknown to anybody else, will you consent to it?"

At last he consented, and we arranged a plan of escape for Ikong

Had he been able to use both arms, he might, on getting away from Use, have paddled himself in a small canoe down the Enyong. This, however, was now impossible. Now, every week a party of people from Asang used to come up the river in their canoe to attend Umaw-Ama market. They used to sleep on a beach just below Use, and return home early the next morning. Ikong knew these people, and, if he could join them, would thus be able to get away.

When dressing his wound, I talked it all over with him in English, with such gestures that his guards must have thought I was discussing medical details. Ikong himself was too experienced an actor to betray by his face or voice the joy with which he entered into the scheme.

On the next market-day, the chief, who alone kept the key of Ikong's fetters, conveyed it to the prisoner concealed in a lump of fufu. Two men were always on guard at night inside the prison. That day Okun Ibanga gave them very salt fish for their rations, and managed to drug the bottles of water (empty gin-bottles) which they took with them when assuming duty.

The old chief used often to go at night to a grove just outside the village, where he was supposed to perform certain juju rites for the good of the whole community. On the night in question, an hour or so before dawn, Ikong liberated himself from his fetters, and, stepping over his sleeping guards, crept out of the prison and through the compound and, as agreed upon, joined Okun Ibanga outside. The chief led him by a back way to the juju grove, and thence, by paths known only to the Use people, on to the well-worn track leading to the little beach where the Asang traders were sleeping. There he left him, and so Ikong escaped. The chief returned to his own hut.

To protect myself and Amo from suspicion, I had set afloat a report that a leopard was visiting the Egbo meeting-place at night. So they built a big trap, and, at my special request, two men of the village, with loaded guns at their sides, had for several nights watched from inside the Egbo-house. They were so keen to kill the leopard that I felt pretty certain they would not fall asleep. I thus provided witnesses to prove that, on the night of the escape, Amo and I had not left the Egbo-house.

The next morning there was a great outcry. The guards on awaking had found that Ikong was gone, leaving behind him the fetters, but locked. (Ikong had taken the key with him.)

Chief Okun Ibanga was foremost in expressing indignation. He went to find his key, kept in a secret place known only to himself.

"My key is missing!" he cried. "Somebody has taken it. It was here when I went to bed last night. Later on, when all the village was asleep, I visited the juju-grove. During my absence, somebody must have stolen it," and he looked suspiciously in my direction.

"Call those men who watched last night for the leopard,"
I cried.

When they came, they both swore that they had kept
awake all night long, and were quite certain that neither I
nor Amo had left the Egbo-house. Thus was suspicion turned
away from us.

I turned it in another direction.

"It may be the work of the executioner," I said. "He
has perhaps carried off the prisoner so that he may give
'Ibok-Ukpong' feet and a left hand. Let us go and see."

So we went to "the shed of the shades of ancient fathers,"
and the people looked, and, behold! the clay dummy with
glass eyes was *no longer maimed*—feet and a left hand had
been added! We examined them. They were not yet
hardened, and bore evidence of having been hurriedly made
and quickly baked in a fire.

"Arrest Umaw Afai the executioner" shouted the chief,
"and arrest the two guards who fell asleep and thus made
possible the prisoner's escape."

The executioner trembled in every limb, for he knew well
how unpopular he was. "Some enemy has done this thing,"
he cried, "or perhaps it is the work of a bad spirit. The
prisoner has escaped through witchcraft, but I smell his blood.
He is not far from here. If you look for him now, you may
find him."

"Put them in prison," ordered the chief, "and let everybody search for the runaway."

So these three men were arrested and put in prison. Then
all the people went hither and thither seeking for Ikong.
The women and children searched every compound and hut,
and the men went to the adjoining bush, and their yam-fields,
and the beach. Messengers were sent to Aka, and, at my
suggestion, two canoes were launched and kept on the river
all day long in case the fugitive should not yet have taken
to the water.

By this time, Ikong was probably miles away down the
Enyong. The search was continued until evening, when
men and boys returned from all parts of the neighbourhood,
unsuccessful of course. The chief caused it to be publicly
announced that the next day the three men under arrest
would be put to the ordeal of boiling oil. If found guilty,
they would suffer the usual penalty. If found innocent, it
was probable that Ikong's mysterious escape, and the incident
of the clay feet and hand, were the work of witchcraft. So
the people went satisfied to bed, looking forward to the ordeal
of the morrow.

On the following morning it accordingly took place, but,

as I was too ill to witness it, I will not attempt to describe
the ceremony from hearsay, lest those Europeans who have
visited the country since it has become a centre of British
administration, and have thus acquired a more exact knowledge of Ibibio customs, should accuse me of inventing "traveller's tales"! It is sufficient for me to tell you that, as
previously arranged between the chief and me, all three men
were found guiltless and acquitted. I hope it was a lesson
to Umaw Akai to moderate his lust for blood.

It was Chief Okun Ibanga himself who had instructed me
to lay suspicion on the executioner, and to advise the people
to examine the figure of "Ibok-Ukpong." To tell you the
truth, I was as much surprised as anyone to see the additions of two feet and a left hand, and you may be sure that
I took no pains to conceal my surprise. The people saw I
was genuinely astonished, and this also helped to rid me of
all suspicion.

I was quite at a loss to understand how these additions
could have been made. I happened to have noticed that,
on the afternoon before Ikong's escape, the figure was still
lacking both feet and left hand. The open space in which
the shed stood was a public thoroughfare much-frequented
until nightfall, and during the whole of the night in question
the two leopard-watchers, concealed in the front part of the
Egbo-house, had been awake and on the alert within only a
few yards of the figure. How, I said to myself, could anybody have entered the shed, open on every side, without their
knowledge?

Of course I asked the chief to explain it.

My question brought a peculiar smile to his face, and he
replied, "It is a mystery, Makara. I cannot tell you everything. We people of the bush know just a few things which
are still unknown to even the wise doctors of the great White
Queen, who, you tell me, lives over the big sea. Perhaps,
Makara—perhaps, I say—when you have climbed higher up
your ladder of life, these mysteries will be made known to
you. If I were to tell you all my secrets, and you were
to tell me all yours, we should no longer be men of power and
influence! Nay, Makara, ask me no more."

I laughed at the old chief's manner of eluding inquiry, and
did not trouble him any further thereon. Probably, I
thought, he modelled the clay feet and hand at night in his
juju-grove, and probably he managed to add them to the figure
while the watchers unconsciously dozed for a few minutes.
It is, however, a fact that most negroes, including many educated members of the race, firmly and sincerely believe that

their chiefs and medicine-men have the power of becoming invisible upon occasion.

It was not until long afterwards that I heard something which throws further light on the incident. The cunning old chief had not instructed me to cast suspicion on the executioner merely to withdraw it from ourselves. He had had another object in view. Umaw Akai was a man of ever-increasing wealth, and, although generally disliked by the Use people, was also increasing so rapidly in power and influence that Okun Ibanga had begun to fear him as a rival for the chiefship. So, using me as his unconscious tool, he had cleverly brought about the executioner's arrest, and, having thus got him into his power, had that same night forced him to pay a very considerable bribe in exchange for a promise of acquittal from the ordeal.

I have said that I was too ill to attend that ceremony. The fact is, I had been poisoned, and, had not I detected the symptoms at once, and known what to do, I might never have survived to write this yarn. The usual emetics having failed, I dissolved in hot water some common brown toilet-soap. It formed an opaque green liquid, five or six tumblers of which produced the desired vomiting. It was quite the nastiest drink I have ever swallowed!

I do not know who poisoned me. Perhaps it was some member of the executioner's household. Perhaps, however, it was the old chief himself. Don't be shocked, good Reader. This is a wicked though a very delightful world. Why not? I was his sole fellow-accomplice in effecting Ikong's unpopular escape, and he was about to turn it to his own ends and thereby obtain wealth and a political victory. Dead men tell no tales. To help "Makara" higher up his ladder of life was safer than to have him remain at Use!

CHAPTER X.

THE DANCE OF THE GHOSTS.

We had now been a fortnight at Use. I was anxious to push on to the Ikono country, and the poisoning incident increased my desire to go. I could see, too, that the chief would be glad to get rid of me. He no longer looked me straight in the face. Perhaps, I thought, it was really he who poisoned me.

The poison had been so short a time in my system that I soon recovered from its effects, though for twenty-four hours or so I suffered a good deal of pain. The next day I was almost well again.

On the same day, as I was discussing with Amo and Akpan the desirability of sending a message to the "King" of the Ikonos, two strangers arrived accompanied by a son of the chief of Aka. Each of them led a goat.

Udaw Enaw of Aka introduced them to me. "These men," he said, "have come to our village from Chief Esien of Ikot-Abassi. There are many other Ikono men sitting down in Obo market-place, but, according to our custom. they may not cross the swamp that lies between us and them. These men bring you goats, and have a message for you, Makara."

I saluted them, and asked them what they wanted of me.

They were wild-looking youths, below the average height, and of poor physique—thin, but muscular, arms and legs, narrow foreheads, and an almost straight line down the side of the body from arm-pit to knee. Their fashion of hair-dressing was the same as that of the Use people, namely, the hair shaved off into patterns. They also wore the same articles of jewelry, but their loin-cloths were of home-woven straw-coloured fibre. They came unarmed.

Their bearing was more independent than that of the Use people. There was no cringing on their part. They went through a sort of salute with the right hand—probably taught them by their more experienced chaperon from Aka—and then delivered their message in a direct straightforward manner.

"Our chief," they said, "sends us to salute you. We have heard of your skill as a medicine-man, and of your magic in taking the poison out of Chief Okun Ibanga's leg. The Aka and Use people whom we meet at Obo market have told us all this. Our chief sends you these goats, and a bullock which awaits you the other side of the swamp, and begs you to visit him. He says he is sick, and would fain consult with you. No white man has ever entered our country, and it is only because you are a doctor that we permit you to visit us."

"What reward does your chief propose to offer me?" I asked.

"If your medicine makes him well," they answered, "he will give you three slaves, but if you refuse to take them —for we have heard that white men no longer require slaves —he will give you their value in manillas. Also, many of our people are sick, and they will pay you manillas, and goats, and fowls for your medicine."

(Manillas are a form of currency long since made for and imported by European traders. They are made from an alloy of metals, are crescent-shaped, and of various sizes and values. The only variety used for purposes of trade in the Ibibio country is that called "Okpoho Ibibio" by the Efik people. Their value is about sixteen to the shilling, and each of them weighs about three ounces.)

Never be in a hurry with primitive peoples. They don't understand and often misinterpret haste.

"Give my compliments to your chief," I said, "and tell him I will think over what he proposes. He must, however, send me two bullocks before I will come, and he must send many carriers to take my loads, and in every village through which I have to pass there must be water and wood ready for my use. Moreover, the road must be cleaned for me, and bridges over streams must be made good and strong."

The messengers' faces fell. They were disappointed that I had not at once agreed to accompany them.

"Our chief is a great man," they said. "He is the most powerful chief in all the Ikono country. He likes to have his wishes carried out with no delay."

"I, too," I replied, "am a great man. He who possesses medicines and skill such as mine goes only where it pleases him to go. I will send one of my men back with you to your chief. If he return with a favourable reply, and report that roads and bridges are cleaned and repaired for me, I will visit your chief. Otherwise, I cannot go into the Ikono country."

They were obliged to agree to this. So I sent Akpan with them, first carefully instructing him to observe the attitude of Chief Esien and of all the Ikono people. I declined to take the goats until Akpan should return. The messengers therefore left them at Aka.

That afternoon I packed up, and we left Use and proceeded to Aka, about a mile and a half further inland. Here also was a large Egbo-house containing another series of painted images, including two snakes each ten feet in length. In it I spent the next three days awaiting Akpan's return.

On the fourth day he arrived, and, with him, the two messengers.

"Our chief salutes you," they said. "He sends two bullocks, and fowls, and eggs. He knows you are a great medicine-man, and has commanded his people to give you carriers and to do all your bidding. During the last two days all the Ikono people—men, women, and children—have been cleaning the roads, and making the bridges good for you."

Akpan confirmed what they said, and, in a private interview with me, reported that Chief Esien was most anxious to see me, and was preparing for my reception. He was a big man, Akpan said, not so tall as Amo, but very strong, he thought. He was not an Ibibio, but an Abam, an Ibo-speaking tribe living northward of the Aros, and somewhere near Bendi. These Abams, he said, were of physique superior to that of all other neighbouring tribes; they loved fighting, and were employed as mercenaries by the wealthy Aros of the "Long Juju."

Early the next morning we departed from Aka, boys of that village carrying my loads as far as the little market-place called Obo. I left my bullocks and goats in charge of the chief of Aka. About half-a-mile out of the village, you obtain from the saddle-backed ridge along which the path runs an extensive view of numerous hills and valleys all around. The general "lie" of this part of the country is as rough as a cobble-stone pavement at home—some geological upheaval of long ago has formed so many superfluous hills in every direction that the country resembles a Normandy pippin stuck all over with almonds.

Obo market-place lies between two pieces of swampy ground, and is a sort of neutral site where the two sub-tribes of Use and Ikono agree to meet on friendly terms for purposes of mutual trade and profit. Here the Aka boys left me, handing over my loads to a crowd of Ikonos. There was also an escort of twenty or thirty men carrying guns—long "danes," cap-guns, and a few Snider rifles.

Then we set out. We had come southwards from Use. We continued in the same direction as far as a place called Aba-Edeap, then went south-eastwards to another village whose name I do not recollect, and then crossed a deep rapid stream called Ibum, which means "great." The bridge consisted of tree-trunks resting on short horizontally-placed poles supported on piles. On each side was a somewhat insecure fence of "bamboo" poles. On reaching the further side, we again changed our course, now proceeding to the north-west, and so continued until our journey's end.

After marching for two hours, I called a halt under some trees on the bank of a small stream. I reckoned we had covered about six miles. Here my carriers, escort, and servants bathed and cooked their food.

Everywhere the "road," a mere winding track three or four feet wide, had been cleaned for us. Although we saw but few huts, and even fewer people, I judged from the extent of cultivated land that there was a large population. The dry season, lasting from the middle of November to the middle of March, was now fairly set in; a few "afternoon" farmers were still gathering in their yams, but the majority had already stacked their crop, and were now burning and clearing the bush for planting purposes. The Ibibios are an agricultural people, their chief crops being the yam, maize, cassava, pepper, koko-yam, and gourd. After harvest they allow the land to lie fallow for at least three years, but often the period extends to six, eight, and even ten or twelve years. This system of course means that each village requires a great deal of land. Consequently, the whole country has been cleared of virgin forest, and the only big trees left standing are those that shade town-places, market-places, and burial-groves. The oil-palm, however, flourishes abundantly throughout the country, and in streams, swampy places, and planted near dwellings, the wine-palm is also very abundant.

There is no town anywhere in the Ibibio country, but there are many small villages, communities consisting of a number of compounds separated from one another by belts of bush and little cultivated patches of koko-yam and okra. A collection of such compounds forms, as I have said, a village, outside and around which lie large communal yam-fields and acre upon acre of "ekpene," i.e., bush which has grown up on fallow land.

Though main "roads" generally pass through the "village" itself, the huts of the villagers are so concealed by bush, fences, and clumps of plantain. that it is difficult, for the traveller to form any true estimate of the population. He may sometimes go through a large village without seeing a single inhabitant. Every village is a community within itself, independent of all the others, with its own town-place, and head-chief. The latter may be compared to the *maire* of each little village community in provincial France. Often a village is split up into several quarters, each under a minor chief. Also, each compound has its headman. The chiefs and senior headmen form the parliament of the community.

Our road took us through several villages, but our column attracted hardly any attention, the people being too absorbed in the daily routine to trouble to come out to see even such a rarity as a "white man." In every town-place, however, there were a few loiterers, who stared at me and exchanged greetings with my escort.

About an hour and a half after resuming our march, we came, early in the afternoon, within sight of our goal, Ikot-Abassi, the principal village of the Ikonos, and residence of Chief Esien. It stands on a long ridge of hill which can be picked out from neighbouring heights by marking the three gigantic cotton-trees, two living and one dead, which occupy its summit, and the exceptionally large number of cocoanut-palms which its people have planted among their dwellings. By the road we had followed, Ikot-Abassi was about twelve miles from Use, but, as the crow flies, it is much nearer.

Just before we entered the village, we passed across a tract of ground, half-a-mile in length, which was being burnt and cleared for yam-planting. The bush was still smouldering here and there, ashes and charred sticks lay about, and the trunks of palms were black and scorched.

Just as we entered the village, a peculiar blast as if from a horn was heard.

"What's that?" I inquired.

"Ekpo, master," said Akpan. "I think they have a big 'play' to welcome you."

Just then two creatures rushed across the path in front of us—two such weird-looking creatures that I wondered if they were men or animals. They certainly had the legs of men, but the upper part of their bodies seemed to be covered with hair or something similar. Towzer ran forward and barked.

My escort laughed, and I said, "What are they, Akpan?"

"Ekpo, master," he again replied. "At this time of year many villages play Ekpo. Women are not permitted to see them. If they catch any woman on the road, they flog her and fine her, and sometimes sell her, or even put her to death."

Now Ekpo means ghost or disembodied spirit. It must not be confused with Ekpe, the Egbo Society. The latter is said to have been brought to Old Calabar from the Kamerun country, whereas Ekpo ceremonies are one of the principal features in the religious system of the Ibibios, from whom Efiks trace their ancestry. There is, probably, however, some philological affinity between ekpo and ekpe. Ekpe means leopard as well as "Egbo Society."

Akpan's explanations were, however, interrupted by a tremendous outburst of music. During the last few miles of our journey, we had heard, coming from the ridge on which Ikot-Abassi stood, the roll of many drums, muffled, however, by the trees and bush which separated us from the drummers. As we had come nearer, it had ceased, but now it broke out again, and the noise was quite deafening.

We passed under one of the three great cotton-trees. Amo pointed upward, and, looking, I saw built in its topmost branches a sort of hut-platform with a series of ladders leading up to it from lower branches. On this aeriel structure stood a man with a horn, and in front of him was suspended a drum. This was the village watch-tower. He had been observing our approach, and had signalled information all over the village by means of his horn and drum.

Turning a sharp corner, we suddenly entered upon an unusually good piece of road. It was about three hundred yards long, ten feet broad, and perfectly straight, and ran between an avenue of trees of various kinds whose branches met overhead. About half-way along this avenue, an arch, or, rather, narrow roof of "bamboo" and leaf-mats spanned the road from side to side. It had been put up to protect from rain the rudely-modelled clay figure of a man which lay on its back across the road. At his feet was an ants' nest some three feet in height, and a large clay pot. Under the roof, tied to its apex, was a bundle of "medicine." I afterwards learnt that this figure and its accompaniments were believed to protect the village from harm—no enemy stepping over the image and passing beneath the "medicine" could do the villagers any injury, not even if he should shoot at them with his gun, for the shot would be ineffective. They also believed that the ants' nest was "brother" to the man's figure, which had lain there as long as the oldest inhabitant could recollect.

The above details and information were collected by me afterwards. All my attention on this my first entry into Ikot-Abassi was given to the group of people who were awaiting me on the further side of the arch—not just beyond it, but at a distance of forty or fifty yards down the avenue. I could see quite a number of women, and behind them a big man and half-a-dozen other men.

"It is Chief Esien," Akpan shouted. He had to shout because of the never-ceasing tremendous din of the drumming.

I at once ordered a halt. The two guides, I, Amo, Akpan, and half my armed escort had passed through the arch. All the others remained on the opposite side. I had my chair fetched, and sat down then and there. Etiquette is important all the world over. The nicest people are those who never "pose," but they are often beaten in the race of life by those who do.

Then I sent Akpan forward with my compliments. Meanwhile, I took closer stock of the people ahead of me. There looked to be about thirty women, ranged in lines one behind another, five or six in a line. They all wore blue-and-white loin-cloths, and turbans of the same round their heads, and were loaded with beads and jewelry. Each carried a fan of bush-deer skin. They were moving their feet with a sort of "mark time" action, swaying their bodies gently from side to side, languidly oscillating their fans, and singing something in a minor key.

Behind them, and towering above them, were visible the head and broad-shouldered bust of a man who wore a cap of some spotted animal's skin, with something blue and white around it, and a white necklace. Behind him were bare-headed men armed with spears.

Akpan was gone several minutes. He appeared to be conferring with the chief.

Suddenly the drumming ceased.

On his return to me, he said, "The chief salutes you. He asks you to come forward and drink palm-wine with him."

"Tell him," I answered, "that he must meet me half-way. I am not a smaller man than he. I will advance alone. Let him also advance alone. We will meet midway and salute one another."

My message was received with a sort of wail of dismay from the women, and they, with the spear-bearers, crowded round the chief and seemed to be imploring him not to leave them. He, however, shook them off, and I could hear him laugh and say, "I fear no man; let me go."

Then he spoke some word of command, and the women formed into ranks again and continued their singing.

I stood up. Amo pulled my sleeve and whispered, "No go, sar! I t'ink dey go kill you."

Then for the first time since I had known him, I was angry with Amo, and, shaking him off, exclaimed, "Let go, you fool. You will spoil the whole thing!"

As soon as I began to walk forward, the chief scattered his women to both sides, and advanced to meet me.

He was a splendid-looking man in the prime of life, in height about 5 feet 11—nearly three inches shorter than Amo. He had a bull-neck, unusually long muscular arms, equally strong-looking legs, and chest and shoulders so tremendously deep and broad that they were almost a deformity, especially as he was small round the waist. Round his loins was a leopard's skin, and I could now see that his tight-fitting cap was of the same. He wore anklets and bracelets of triple rows of white cowries, and three strings of them hung round his neck. Around his cap he had a sort of coronet, consisting of a strip of blue cloth with leopards' teeth sewn thereon. In his left hand he carried a long carved walking-staff, very similar to Arthur Riversley's.

I have said that the chief and I advanced to meet one another unattended, but this is not strictly accurate. On each side of him walked a small boy, bare-headed, but in other respects miniature copies of the chief, for they wore loin-cloths of bush-cat's skin, and triple rows of cowries round ankles, wrists, and neck. I, on my part, was attended by dog Towzer, who followed unabashed though uninvited Neither of us could reasonably object to such escort.

Chief Esien bore himself right royally, and moved with

the graceful ease of an athlete in thorough training. He was clean-shaven, and looked about six-and-thirty years of age. He had rather good features, lips not too thick, a short upper lip, and small ears. I liked the way his eyes were set into his head, and his expression was straightforward and manly.

We saluted one another in the Ibibio language, and, by some common impulse, our hands went out together, and we shook hands in thoroughly English fashion. As we did so, our eyes met, and a second mutual impulse—something in the humour of the situation, I suppose—brought a smile into them, and we both laughed. I noticed that he had hazel eyes full of expression—a most unusual feature in a negro, most of them having black eyes, dull and lustreless. Afterwards, however, I noticed a few other natives with eyes of the same colour.

This was indeed a good beginning. If two people agree in their sense of humour, they will agree in most things. Instinct told me that I might trust Chief Esien. There was nothing petty in his face. He looked cheerful and sensible, as broad-minded as he was broad-shouldered.

"You are sick?" I inquired.

"Yes, a pain in my back," he said; "but we will not talk about it now. My people have got ready a big ekpo-play for you to see. Let us go to the town-place. They are all there. But first I must send away these women," and, so saying, he returned to them.

Meanwhile, I called Amo and Akpan to me, and gave them instructions as to our loads. Amo looked rather crestfallen.

"You made a mistake, Amo," I said. "Don't do it again. Always remember that a white man must never show fear. Those who never show fear make others fear them. This chief is pleased to see us, and will treat us well."

The women were disappearing along a side pathway. I rejoined the chief, and he and I, walking abreast, led the procession. The two small boys kept very close behind him.

At the end of the avenue we turned to the left, and entered another, narrower but longer. It was fairly straight, and, a quarter of a mile ahead of us, I could see a large open space with hundreds of people therein. Just then the drumming began again, and made conversation quite impossible.

At the end of the avenue we passed under an arch beneath which a bundle of "medicine" was tied, and entered the large town-place of Ikot-Abassi, an open space of irregular shape shaded by another of the three huge cotton-trees, and by a picturesque medley of such trees as the ukana (oil-bean), the okono (much used in religious rites), and the cocoanut and oil-palms.

Chief Esien led me across the middle of this arena to a shady spot under a clump of okonos. The carriers and escort followed, and seated themselves on the ground behind us   My chair was brought, and the chief sat on a chair of his own, a unique specimen of native workmanship which now stands in the hall at Riversley.

Ranged on our left in a semicircle under the trees was the orchestra, consisting of forty or fifty drums of the "nting" variety, and a xylophone called "ikun."   Most of these long drums were attached to poles stuck upright in the ground, and behind them the drummers sat, stood, or knelt.   Some drums had two drummers apiece.   These youths had their brown skins painted black in every imaginable pattern or geometrical device.   Each drummer had two short sticks with which he vigorously beat the instrument in front of him.   The "ikun" consists of a number of short lengths of hard "unaw" wood placed crosswise on top of two parallel sections of plantain-stalk, and is beaten in the same manner as the drums.   They kept excellent time, and were very serious and keen about it.

Behind the band, and all round under the trees, stood thousands of men and boys, gathered from other Ikono villages to see this big Ekpo-play.   Some of them carried cheap European umbrellas!   No woman was present.

At the end of the town-place opposite to the orchestra there was a gap in the ring of spectators kept open for the entry and egress of the dancers.

The drumming stopped as we took our seats.   Then, after a short interval, during which my host and I drank palm-wine together in the presence of the assembled multitude, Chief Esien raised his staff, and, at that signal, the boys struck their drums with one accord, and made music which was really thrilling and stimulating.

Then there issued from the gap at the opposite end a procession of the weirdest-looking creatures that could possibly be imagined.   They came in single file, and I counted thirty-two of them.   They looked "all head and shoulders" on a pair of slender legs.   Their legs, arms, and stomachs were bare, and blackened with wood-ash (all details I learnt afterwards); round their ankles, and just below the knees, were tied circlets of feathers and fibre fringes; they wore several loin-cloths, with streamers of cloth hanging down at both sides, and thereto were attached a sheathed matchet and a bell, the latter dangling down behind.   Bunched under their arm-pits and around the middle of their bodies were bundles of fibre; grotesque masks concealed their faces, and they wore long beards of bleached fibre, and huge shaggy wigs of grasses and fern-like creepers, which hung down low on shoulders and back. The masks were painted black, and on some of them the features were picked out in yellow and white pigments. One mask had great wooden teeth, and one of the monsters had stuck a yellow marigold on each side of his wooden nose. Several wore bracelets of white fowl's feathers. They all carried a bow and arrows.

These awful-looking monsters pranced into the arena, and, after making a preliminary round, with a special flourish as they passed before the chief and me, retired in single file as they had come, and disappeared through the gap.

Then a pair of them returned, and danced and pranced to the din of the drums, waving their arms, shaking hands with one another, and brandishing their matchets in the air. The next pair went through the same antics, but had laid aside their bows and arrows, and carried small European looking-glasses. Another pair held each an iron sistrum or gong on which they beat with a short wooden stick. This went on until all of them, sixteen pairs, had gone through the same performance. It soon became monotonous. Chief Esien watched them with quiet indifference.

The music ceased for an interval, and the chief informed me that the monsters were having a rest.

Just then Towzer, who had been chasing lizards in the background with more enjoyment than success, raised a great barking. He had found something at the base of the great cotton-tree.

"Go, Amo," I said, "and see what he is barking at."

Amo returned and reported, "Big snake lib for hole, sar. He no like dem dog. I t'ink dem snake get pickins. S'pose I go shoot 'em, sar? Asabo be bad snake."

Turning to the chief, I said, "There is an asabo in a hole over there. My dog has found it. My man wants to shoot it."

Chief Esien roused himself. "It is forbidden," he said. "We never kill the asabo. It is our 'ukpong [bush-soul].'"

So I sent Amo to call Towzer off, and to bring him back to me.

"Tell me about your ukpong," I said. "I have no wish to kill anything that is held to be sacred."

"I am a foreigner," replied Chief Esien, "an Abam. We have a different language and different customs from these Ibibios, but since I became their chief, I have learnt to do as they do. We never kill or eat this snake. When we celebrate the feast of new yams, asabos come into our huts and do us no harm. We feed them with yam and eggs, and if we pick them up they do not bite us."

H

"Do all the Ikono people have the asabo for their bush-soul?" I inquired.

"No," he answered, "this village has it, but other villages have different things. Ibak-Asi has the rat, and Abiakpaw the bush-cat. When men from those two villages disagree, they revile one another by calling out 'Eku [Ye rat!]' and 'Atan [Ye bush-cat!].' The Ibak-Asi people kill and roast rat to sell in the market, but do not eat of it themselves."

"If they kill the rat," I said, "it cannot be their ukpong. How is this?"

"It is not their ukpong," he replied; "but I cannot explain. I am a stranger here. I know, however, that they are forbidden to eat it; the rat is their 'ibet [prohibition].' "

Suddenly the drums struck up again, and the performance was continued. As the monsters, or professional dancers, did not at once appear, a few amateurs, youths in ordinary attire, stepped out from the ring of spectators and gave us specimens of their skill. Their limbs being unencumbered with Ekpo paraphernalia, they were more agile than their predecessors. Each performer executed a pas-de-seul, twisting and contorting his limbs as he deemed most fit. One plump man, who was pointed out to me as an abia-idiong (medicine-man), danced with quite marvellous agility.

After five or ten minutes of this kind of thing, the drummers struck a peculiar note, and the professional performers began to re-appear.

First came several oldish-looking men, who, Chief Esien explained, were the conductors of the performance. They "ran the show." They were not dressed up, but they carried weapons and played an active part. One old man with much yellow powder on his face carried in one hand a bunch of little rattles ("ekput") and in the other a bell. He shook the rattles, and jingled the bell. Another had a bow and arrows, and another a drawn sword. A fourth held a long green wand. These headmen pranced about in front of the drums, and two of them drew their matchets, and advancing against one another crossed weapons two or three times.

Then followed the shaggy "ghosts," not two at a time as before, but singly. As each of them approached the orchestra, he of the green wand pointed it at him, and in a loud voice exhorted him not to do harm of any kind whatsoever to any living member of the community. At the same time, he of the bow and arrows kept making pretence to shoot the dancing monster. This pair met each Ekpo as he entered the arena and followed him up and down, keeping at a safe distance from him, but never taking their eyes off him until he made his departure through the gap. Each monster concluded his dance by rushing up to the line of drummers, shaking his weapons at them, and kicking up his legs almost into their faces.

It was not until the whole thirty-two of them had been through exactly the same antics that the performance was brought to a conclusion. The band finished with a furious flourish, and I felt much relieved that it was all over. I think Chief Esien felt the same. He had yawned a good deal towards the close.

If you ask me to explain this ceremony, I must reply that I cannot do so satisfactorily. I was so engrossed with other things just then that I did not make particular inquiries. I am of belief, however, that it is akin to an Efik ceremony of which I had heard at Old Calabar. The latter is called "Ndok," and is performed at the beginning of the dry season in every alternate year. Its object is to drive out of the compounds and villages the ghosts of all those who have died since the last "Ndok." It is accompanied by noise of every description; but, unlike the Ibibio ceremony of Ekpo, it takes place at night.

I leave it to scientific anthropologists to establish affinity between these two ceremonies; but I strongly suspect that the monsters who danced before us at Ikot-Abassi were meant to represent the spirits of those of the villagers who had died since the last great dance.

CHAPTER XI.

HUMAN SACRIFICES.

Chief Esien of Ikot-Abassi lived in the middle of a large square compound, kept always perfectly clean by a company of small boys called "the King's sons." They were not really his children, but were pages-of-honour enlisted from all the Ikono villages, and were generally the sons of chiefs. There were twenty-four of them. Their principal duty was to be is constant attendance, day and night, on Chief Esien, and for this purpose they were divided into twelve pairs who relieved one another every two hours. They performed various other duties, such as keeping the royal compound and huts clean, fetching the king's water and wood, and preparing his bath. They were under two instructors, minor chiefs of the village.

Esien's own dwelling consisted of a large room used as a sort of council-chamber, with two smaller rooms built at the back of it. The huts all round the compound were occupied by his thirty-five wives and their children.

He allotted to me and my men a small but well-built and clean compound situated about a hundred yards from his own, and there I lived nearly three months.

Early on the morning after our arrival, the chief, with two boys in close attendance, came to visit me. He hoped that I had slept well, and was satisfied with my quarters.

I thanked him, and replied that I had had a good night, and was quite comfortable.

"Walking," I added, "is fine exercise, and, after yesterday's march of twelve miles up and down your hills, I was glad to get a long night's sleep. Do you go about the country much?"

"No," he answered. "I am never permitted to leave this village. It is one of the laws that the king of the Ikonos must never go outside the bounds of Ikot-Abassi except as a dead man, when they carry his body to the royal burial-grove."

"How then," I asked, "do you take exercise? You look well and healthy, and your limbs are those of a strong man who is constantly using them."

"I wrestle," he replied.

"And you have strained your back?" I inquired. "Is that the sickness about which you want to consult me?"

He smiled. "My sickness can wait," he said. "It is better to-day. When the pain returns, I will tell you."

He wore the leopard's skin round his loins, and the cap, but his coronet of leopards' teeth was laid aside. He had also discarded his necklaces, but wore the anklets and bracelets. He certainly looked to be in perfect health. There was no spare flesh on him, and his skin shone with a satin-like lustre. Amo subsequently informed me that, after his morning bathe, Esien was every day rubbed all over by his boys with an oil extracted from the kernel of the nut of the oil-palm.

"Many of my people are sick," continued the chief. "I beg you to cure them. I will see to it that they pay you for your medicines. I like you, and I hope you will stay here a long time. I will show you all things in this village, and, whenever you will, you can visit the other villages of the Ikono people."

So I began doctoring operations, and many came to me to be cured. Thus my medical and surgical knowledge, rudimentary though it was, proved of infinite service to me. Without it, I could not have peacefully entered the Ikono country.

Chief Esien led a fairly strenuous, though confined, life. Besides having to keep his numerous wives in order, he sat in court five days out of every seven, to hear and determine "palavers" from every part of his kingdom. All his villages had their own separate chief and council, by whom ordinary cases were settled; but, when a verdict could not be thus obtained, or when one or both of the parties refused to accept the judgment given, the case was transferred to their tribal head, who was Chief Justice as well as King. Of course he levied fees on litigants, and this added considerably to his revenue. He also superintended the care of his cattle and goats.

Twice a day, early in the morning and late in the afternoon, he repaired to an open stretch of greensward shaded by many palms, which it was a duty of "the king's sons" to keep short and in good order. Here for an hour or two he would wrestle with anybody who would stand up to him. If any man threw him, he gave him a bullock; but from those whom he threw he demanded only a fowl. The reward was so tempting that candidates came from all parts of the Ikono country, and also Anangs and Ibos.

When wrestling, he exchanged his leopard's skin for a pair of fibre drawers, but never removed his tight-fitting cap. He also took off his bracelets and anklets of cowries. Of course he did not wrestle the whole time. In the intervals between his own bouts, he delighted to sit and watch a good match between two of his men. Wrestling was the national pastime, but women were not permitted to be present at it.

Esien himself was extraordinarily agile and expert, which, added to his powerful strength, made him almost invincible. Some of the elders of the community were always present in an umpiring capacity. Only twice during his "reign" had a decision been given against him. One of these defeats was attributed to a slip on wet grass, and the other to a new "trick" employed by an Ibo from the Ungwa country. Seldom putting forth all his strength, he would "play with" his opponent as long as he required the exercise. Sometimes he would tackle two men at a time. On one occasion I saw three youths struggling with him for twenty minutes without being able to overcome him.

After we had attended two or three of these matches, Amo said to me, "Dem chief be strong too much, sar, but me t'ink me fit for pass him. Me pass him for head [in height]. S'pose me go try, sar?"

"Certainly," I answered; "though he will probably prove too strong for you, it ought to be a good match."

So Amo stood up to Chief Esien.

I doubt if the multitudes who thronged the amphitheatres of ancient Greece ever saw a finer pair of athletes than those two negroes who stood before me on that stretch of greensward silhouetted against the sky. If men may be compared to horses, Amo, with his long shapely limbs and neck, and perfect symmetry of form, was like a thoroughbred racer, while the chief, with his bull-neck, strong muscular limbs, and massive chest and back, was like a powerful cart-horse.

They brought to my remembrance the fine description in the twenty-third book of *The Iliad* of the wrestling-match between Ajax and Ulysses, and I could almost hear my father's voice reading me Homer's sonorous lines. Unlike that classical contest, however, which lasted so long that the spectators wearied of it, the match between the Yoruba and the Ibo was of the briefest duration. After displaying in their preparatory movements a series of beautiful attitudes, they grasped one another, first by the wrists, and then round the shoulders, but then, all in a moment, the struggle was brought to a close by Esien seizing Amo round the loins, lifting him bodily off the ground, and so throwing him over his back and on to the ground behind.

Amo fell with rather a crash, and lay stunned for a few moments, but, by the time I had reached him, he had picked himself up again and scrambled to his feet.

There was a good-natured grin on his face as he exclaimed, "Dem chief pass me for strong. I t'ink he be all same el'phant. S'pose me lib for wrestle ebery day for ten-twelve days, me fit for try him agen."

I explained this challenge to the chief, and he and Amo shook hands upon it. Amo bore no ill-will for his defeat.

The third day after our arrival was the market-day called Addita. This market was held every fifth day on the point of the Ikot-Abassi ridge furthest removed from that by which we had made our entry. It lay about a mile from the royal compound.

Chief Esien had offered to conduct me to it, so, accompanied by our respective suites, we set out for it about 9 o'clock in the morning, the hour when it was usually most crowded.

A big yam-field separated the village from Addita market-place. Long before we reached it, we could hear the hum of innumerable voices coming therefrom. Its site was a grove of trees, standing on the extreme point of the ridge, and encompassed on all sides by land either just going out of cultivation or just being cleared for a new crop.

We passed out of the bright sunshine into the cool gloom and comparative darkness of this grove. The clearing was of large extent. It was kept always free from weeds and grass, but trees and clumps of okono grew all over it, thus forming shade grateful to those who frequented it. It was thronged with people, the noise of whose chattering made conversation rather difficult. A peculiar smell filled the place, a smell like that of putrid meat or rotten eggs.

"What's this smell, Amo?" I said.

"Me t'ink dey sell plenty beef for market," he replied. "Plenty t'ings lib here for ground what make bad smell."

We turned to the right, and began a round of the place. It was by far the largest West African market that I had yet attended, and contained much that interested me. Vendors, chiefly women, squatted on the ground behind their wares, over which, set out to the best advantage, they chattered and haggled with the ever-changing stream of purchasers. The "master of the market" came up to pay his respects to us, and it was evident that a certain degree of order and regulation prevailed. I learnt that every village whose inhabitants were regular attendants at Addita had assigned to it a certain section of the clearing, that each of these sections was sub-divided into little areas confined to certain kinds of merchandise, and that every "stall-holder" had his or her fixed place of which they took possession immediately on arrival. These arrangements helped to prevent confusion and disputes.

Owing, however, to the evil machinations of Inokuns from the Ibo country, who, as already explained, fomented discord in order to encourage slave-dealing, the whole country was extremely unsettled. Women and children never came to market without an armed escort of their menkind, for, otherwise, they might be seized on the road and sold to the Inokuns. In among the trees on the outskirts of the crowd, I could see men and boys carrying guns and matchets, the latter often held ready drawn. They were waiting to escort their women and unarmed relatives back to their villages.

"How," I inquired of my host, "how do you chiefs manage to maintain order and peace among such a vast crowd of people, many of whom are armed?"

"We make them fear 'mbiam [juju medicine]," he replied. "Sometimes, however, the 'mbiam' loses its strength, and then there is fighting in the market, and people are killed and wounded, while some with their goods are seized. Then the market has to be closed, for traders fear to attend it any longer."

The merchandise displayed before us was very varied. There was just room for us to pass in single file between the rows of squatting women. Here, on both sides, were baskets filled with the satin-skinned kernels of the oil-palm, varying in shade from pale lemon to the deepest orange; here were old gossips with eggs, green stuff of various kinds, and white cassava dumplings; here sat an Inokun youth presiding over a little store of Manchester cloths, looking-glasses, padlocks, and a few umbrellas; then a row of fish-sellers, their stinking goods impaled on long sticks; here a boy with live bats cruelly suspended by their wings from a stake stuck upright in the ground (sold "for idiong," as Amo explained); then an Inokun girl, her hair dressed high into a fan-like crest, offering for sale half-a-dozen brass bracelets; then quite an array of clay pots; then yams, plantains, a fowl or two, baskets, salt, native-made string, edible snails, mushrooms, etc., etc.

Half-way round the circle we arrived at the butchers' quarter. The nauseous smell had seemed to increase as we moved on, and I quite expected to see a great display of "high" meat. It was not so, however; this side of the market was not nearly so crowded. About a dozen men sat behind bits of flesh—"beef," as Amo called the whole collection—impaled on wooden skewers. There were lumps of venison and beef (bush-cow), lights and liver of pigs and other animals, and a few unsavoury odds and ends, including a dead puppy. All these delicacies were more or less high, but their united odours were insufficient to account for the awful stench which pervaded the whole place.

"What is this bad smell?" I inquired, turning to Chief Esien. "Are there any dead bodies in the bush? It is so bad that I shall be sick if I stay here any longer."

"O!" said he, with a laugh, "do you find it so very bad? It comes from two men whom we sacrificed here ten days ago —that is all. The market had been closed for five years because of fighting, but we had a big meeting and opened it again. Come, I will show you."

Leaving the outer circle, we turned round and made for the middle of the market. Tree-trunks and clumps of bush had previously hidden from us the gruesome sight that was now presented to our view.

In the very middle was an ukana-tree and a clump of okonos, and round their bases, as around those of other similar clumps, was a mound of earth gradually formed by the accumulation of rubbish swept up and deposited there at the close of each market-day. From two branches of the acacia-like ukana there hung, head downwards, over this mound, the bodies of two men. The stench was, to me, almost overpowering. Holding my nose, I went as near to them as I could endure. They were each suspended from a brass rod (another form of currency) bent into pot-hook shape, one end of which was passed over the branch and the other through a hole made in the heels of the victims.

On the trees above us were perched several vultures, who, when the market was ended, would swoop down to continue their ghoulish feast. Glutting themselves on the corpses were a number of scaly millepedes.

There those two bodies hung, every now and then gently swaying as the wind caught the branches of the ukana, and all around hummed the din of the market, thousands of men, women, and children absolutely indifferent to this horrible spectacle and loathsome smell!

"Truly the negro is a philosopher," I thought to myself.

Towzer had stopped short on seeing the corpses, and had retreated behind me, where he stayed crouching and growling at my feet.

The chief said, "This is the sacrifice we made when we re-opened the market. We also put 'mbiam' across all the roads. All men now fear to do anything bad here. We have made it a good market. The 'mbiam' was strong."

Little Otu had been pointing to one of the bodies, and saying something to Amo.

"What is it?" I inquired.

"O, sar!" said Amo, "dem boy say he sabby dis man." pointing to one of the victims. "He say he sabby dem ibory what lib for his arm."

I looked more closely. Their wrists were tied behind their backs. One of them had on his left arm a thick ivory bracelet with a peculiar pattern and a lizard scratched thereon.

"Well," I asked, "who does he say it is?"

"He says," continued Amo, "he say dem man what lib for dead, be all same dem canoe-boy what we no find for Asang. We t'ink crocodile chop him, sar."

I called Akpan. "Look," I said, "do you recognise this bracelet?"

Akpan went up to the body.

"Yes, master," he replied, "it is Tua-Mbom's. He was the paddler we lost at Asang. I often noticed it on his arm. And see," he continued, pointing to a long scar on the right shoulder, "I know him also by this mark."

"Where did you get this man?" I asked the chief.

"We bought him," he replied. "He was sent to me by an Enyong chief with whom I trade."

"Is this chief's name Enia-Eke, and does he live at Asang?" I inquired.

"Yes," said Esien, "you are right. The slave hanging here was sent to me from that place twelve days ago."

Thus was that chief's perfidy still further revealed! Either the missing boy had been discovered in the bush after we had left Asang, and then sold into slavery, or the old scoundrel had managed to seize him before our departure and keep him concealed from us.

"Were these men killed before they were hanged up like this?" I inquired.

"No," replied the chief; "but we gave them plenty of gin. It would not have been right to kill them."

"Did they die quickly?" I continued.

"I don't know," he answered; "but some boys said that they passed through here two days afterwards and heard one of them moaning."

"Let us go," I cried. "I have had more than enough of this!"

So we went.

As we left the market-place, I noticed on the ground at the foot of a tree a human skull flanked by a clay saucer and a block of stone.

"Who was he?" I asked.

"That," replied the chief, "is the head of the man who was sacrificed here when Addita was first opened many years ago. His spirit watches over the market, and we give him fufu and gin and palm-wine."

"What will you do with the skulls of your new victims?" I inquired.

"We shall wait till they fall to the ground," he answered. "Then we shall place them at the base of a tree, just like this, and we shall give them food and drink."

"And the other bones?" I said.

"They will also fall to the ground," he continued; "but we shall not trouble about them. Perhaps the dogs or a leopard will eat some of them; perhaps they will lie there till they rot away. See here," pointing to a brown half-gnawed thigh-bone, "this is what is left of the first man sacrificed here."

"Do you always sacrifice a man when you open a market?" I asked.

"Yes," he replied; "unless such sacrifice be made, it is not properly opened, and will not be good. In seven days from now an old market called Ederiobo, which lies beyond those hills" (he pointed westward) "is to be opened again. Five villages who have long been at strife have agreed to meet there peaceably to re-open it in the usual manner."

"Will they sacrifice a man?" I inquired.

"Three slaves," he said, "for it was a very bad palaver that stopped it. I have given them one of the three, and they will buy the others."

On retiring to my compound, I thought the matter over, and determined to do my best to prevent this sacrifice. The next day I laid the following plan before Chief Esien.

"I am a white man, and a great medicine-man," I said. "Suppose I offer to open Ederiobo market myself, and throw strong 'mbiam' on the ground—would they spare the lives of those three slaves?"

At first he said that any alternative was quite out of the question, that, as their forefathers had taught them, so must they do. But, after further argument, he gave in; and sent messengers to summon the five head-chiefs of the villages in question.

When they arrived, we learnt that they were disputing among themselves as to the number of victims. The mass of people demanded five instead of three, *i.e.*, one for each village. There was so much difference of opinion that it seemed doubtful if the re-opening of the market would ever be achieved. This dispute, however, paved the way for my proposal, for at length, after spending a whole day in squabbling over their customary procedure and arriving at no satisfactory conclusion, they agreed to consider the alternative I offered them.

The details were arranged as follow. I was to provide five pure-white fowls, and repair to Ederiobo. They were to have it cleaned prior to my arrival, and to meet me there with all their people. The "master of the market" would then sacrifice the fowls, and I would pour my "powerful mbiam" across all roads leading to the market, and pronounce a curse upon anybody who should ever again do any deed to "break" it.

On the day of the ceremony, we set out early from our headquarters. We travelled in a north-westerly direction, and it took us about an hour and a half to reach our destination. Ederiobo lay in a grove of trees in the midst of the five villages. As we approached it, I expected to hear the murmur of many voices; but absolute silence reigned. We entered it. It was everywhere overgrown with grass and brambles—not the slightest attempt had been made to clean it!

"Patience!" I said to myself. "In this country of the *non*-strenuous life, they never do to-day what can be put off until to-morrow."

So I sat down under the trees, and, calling five of my followers, sent one to each of the five villages to inform their respective chiefs with my compliments that I had arrived and was awaiting them and their people.

One by one the runners returned, and Amo reported to me, "Dey all say dey lib for come, sar."

"So does Christmas!" I thought. Some months' experience of the negro mind had taught me that "lib for come" was a very elastic phrase.

So I ordered all my party to spend the interval in cooking their food.

An hour later, people began to arrive, and in two hours' time each village was fairly well represented.

The reason, they explained, why they had not cleaned the place ready for me was that they could not agree as to which village should begin the work! Even now they had not settled this point.

"Show me your five sections," I cried.

Then "the master of the market," Ekandem Udaw Offiong by name, pointed them out to me, and I went to the middle of each, and plucked up a weed from each, and taking the five roots in my hand, threw them all together into the bush.

"Look!" I exclaimed. "I have begun your work for you, so there is no further cause for dispute. Let every man and boy bring his matchet and clear the place."

The people laughed, and then I knew that things would go well. Hundreds of them set to work, and in a very short time they had cut down the brambles, rooted up the grass and weeds, collected everything into heaps, and deposited it, either just outside the market-place, or on the mounds of former refuse accumulated around the bases of trees.

Then followed the sacrificial ceremony. I handed the five white fowls to Ekandem, who wore round the crown of his head the ring of an "abia-idiong," and had his face, chest, and arms daubed with white and yellow pigments. He stood beside a mound in the middle of the clearing, grasping the fowls by the legs, three in one hand, and two in the other. To hinder their struggles, the two legs of each fowl were tied together. Then the people thronged around him, and he passed the fowls down the faces and chests of all that could get near him.

"Why is this done?" I asked.

"To make them strong, and the market good," Akpan explained. I imagine, however, that the fowls were looked upon as a sort of "scape-goat," and that those who crowded round Ekandem were thus transferring their "sins" prior to the sacrifice.

Then five men, one from each village, stepped forward with drawn matchets. These particular representatives had been picked out because they had played an active part in the fighting which had "broken" the market. The officiating priest handed four fowls to an assistant to hold, but retained the fifth. Then one of the matchet-bearers came up and cut its head off, and Ekandem, taking the dripping head, smeared it on the executioner's forehead and chest, and then threw head and body on to the mound. Grasping another fowl, he went through a similar ceremony with the next man, and so on until five quivering bodies lay scattered about on the mound behind him.

Now my turn came. Amo assisted me. I stood on a little eminence in the midst of the people. Taking in one hand a large glass tumbler, I filled it nearly full of water. Then, while Amo held it, I produced with much serious deliberateness my silver matchbox, and took therefrom two tabloids of potassium permanganate, and dropped them into the water.

All the people watched me with breathless interest.

Slowly I stirred it round and round with the handle of my tooth-brush, and so continued until the water became quite purple. Then I added a few drops from a bottle of Worcester-sauce, and finally poured in a little brandy from my pocket-flask. My "powerful mbiam" was quite ready.

Ederiobo was approached by five "roads." At the point where each of these roads gave access to the market, I performed the same ceremony, which was as follows. Standing with my face to the thronging crowds who filled the clearing, I drew a line across each road from side to side with Amo's matchet, and called out in a loud voice, "I open Ederiobo market once more. May it be big. May many traders come to it. If any person from any of these five villages" (naming them) "do any bad thing which will again break the market, may this mbiam deal with him." Then I poured some of the liquid all along the line.

This ceremony, as I have already said, was gone through five times.

As soon as it was concluded, some of the people shouted, "Ederiobo is now open again. We will call it the White Man's market."

Then we returned to the place of sacrifice, and Ekandem roughly plucked the five fowls and threw their feathers on to the mound. Tearing the bodies to pieces with his fingers, he distributed the flesh among the five head-chiefs and their principal attendants. He reserved a choice tit-bit for himself, and Akpan accepted my share. Finally, he arranged the heads of the five birds in a row on the top of the mound, and so left them.

Thus was Ederiobo re-opened without the shedding of human blood.

When we set out on our return journey to Ikot-Abassi, the five head-chiefs, hitherto at enmity with one another, were squatting around a little fire of sticks roasting their portions of fowl together in most amicable fashion.

CHAPTER XII.

A FUNERAL AND A FLIGHT.

During my stay in the Ikono country I saw so many curious sights that, if I were to tell you about even one half of them, I should never be able to finish this narrative of the quest of King Edward's Ring.

Much of my time was occupied in attending to my "patients." They came to me from all the neighbouring villages, and, remembering the advice given me by the chief of Itu, I never gave away my medicine, but insisted on the payment of fees. These were mostly paid in kind, in the form of live-stock, yams, and other vegetable products. Akpan looked after my little herd of goats and my poultry-run.

It was the dry season, and I visited a good many outlying villages of the Ikono sub-tribe, sometimes absenting myself two or three days from the Ikot-Abassi headquarters. Everybody knew that I was the King's guest, and everybody respected and feared me as the white medicine-man of great repute; so I went about quite unmolested. Of course I never interfered with the natives in any way whatsoever. I recognised that, their line of evolution having been for centuries entirely different from our own, the results must also be entirely different, and that it would be easier to divert the course of a mighty river in one day than to change their mode of thought and action in one generation.

The Ibibios are not a lazy people. Their wants are so few and so easily satisfied that to be "rushed" is quite an unknown experience to them; but they seem to be always occupied about something or other. What they do is done in a leisurely manner. Their work interests them, and, on the whole, they lead a happy life—far happier and healthier, and infinitely less monotonous, than that led by "the white slaves" of overcrowded European cities and of the fetid workshops of the sweating system. Their farms are, as I have already said, their chief care. The women attend a market nearly every day, keep their dwellings clean, and do the cooking. The men build huts and juju structures, hunt and fish, weave cloth, and make baskets. Some are carpenters and smiths. The children help their mothers, and do odd jobs, such as sweeping out the compound, and fetching water and wood.

Certain occupations are confined strictly to the different sexes. Thus cotton-spinning and cloth-weaving are done only by young men, while clay pottery is made only by the women. Their spindle greatly resembles that used by the ancient Egyptians, and they have two sizes of looms, the larger for weaving loin-coverings, bags, and satchels from the fibre of the wine-palm (*Raphia vinifera*), and the smaller for weaving cloth from locally-grown cotton. Their pottery is made without the help of wheel or of mould, the potter sitting on the ground and building the vessel up from its base by deft use of her fingers. They are ornamented with yellow bands of pigment obtained from the otun-shrub, and some are quite elegant in shape.

To catch leopards and smaller animals, traps of various sizes are built by the roadside and baited accordingly—a goat for the leopard, a few eben-dates for the little antelope, and so on. Birds are limed as follows: a stick is thrust upright in the ground, and on each side at acute angles from its base are set thin withes smeared with rubber-sap and palm-oil. Birds flying against them are captured, stuck thereto by their wings. Bats are snared in slip-knot nooses of fibre suspended from branches of trees, and from "bamboo" poles fixed horizontally across roads.

Fighting is almost a pastime with them, and is often conducted in quite "sporting" fashion. One day, while visiting a group of villages in the north-western part of the country, we came across the scene of one of their battles. Midway between two communities, which were at feud about some old dispute, a long narrow area had been cleared of the smaller kinds of undergrowth, but trees and bushes had been left standing. At both ends of this space trenches had been dug.

"What do these mean?" I asked my guide.

"This is where they fight," he replied. "They cannot decide their palaver by talking, so they have agreed to fight one another here on certain days. They helped one another to clear the bush."

"But," I said, "we have just passed through Itak [one of the two villages] and I saw nobody on guard, and the people were going to market just the same as usual. How is this?"

"Yes," he replied, "you are right; there is a truce to-day. When they are not fighting, they meet together, and drink palm-wine with one another, and talk over everything that happened during the previous day's fight."

"How many days does the fighting continue?" I inquired.

"It depends," he said, "on how many are killed. If one village kills plenty of men, and the other few, the fight ends; but, if nobody is shot, they may keep at it from time to time for several years."

Sometimes the boys of two hostile villages form themselves into companies and fight one another with bows and arrows. The latter are of split "bamboo" about a foot long, pointed at one end, and "feathered" with a leaf at the other. They are never poisoned, and do but little injury unless they enter the eye. They also throw at one another hard sticks pointed at both ends.

I used often to visit a grey-haired chief named Imuk, who lived on a hill two miles south of Ikot-Abassi. He was a juju-man, and dwelt in a hut in the middle of a small compound, which hut was full of all manner of venerated rubbish and dirt. He was emaciated and rather dirty, and wore nothing but an old loin-cloth, a bracelet on his left arm, and charms around his neck. He was blind.

"I have been blind five years," he told me. "A devil did it by poison. It came on quite suddenly. One day when I was returning from the yam-field to meet a guest who had come to see me, I had all at once to use my broom to feel the way."

The poor old fellow was always pleased to have me call on him, and it was from him that I heard the extraordinary conditions under which their King held his throne. Of this, however, hereafter.

Old Imuk was rather neglected, and left too often alone; but he seemed to accept his position as the usual fate of helpless old age, and he but seldom murmured against it.

"I don't go about much," he informed me, "for I never leave this compound except to attend meetings. When there are matters to be discussed, I tell my drummer to beat his drum, and then the people assemble."

One afternoon, on going to his place, I found that he had died a few hours previously, and that his people were already busying themselves about the funeral. His hut had been cleaned and put tidy. The body lay on its back on a mat on the floor, the head resting on a goatskin. Over it was spread a coverlet made of strips of native cloth sewn together, and on his breast lay a small fret-like frame used to hold fish. His bare right arm was kept up at right angles to the body by a cord suspended from one of the rafters. Tied to this cord was a European bell, and two manillas had been forced round the wrist.

I raised the cloth from his head. The eyes were closed, and a pigment resembling clay had been smeared over the face. Between his right side and the wall the embers of a fire were glowing.

"Why do you hang this bell here?" I asked.

"To be rung by those who wish to hold communion with his spirit," they explained.

Ringing the bell, I placed in the dead chief's hand my little silver match-box.

"Imuk," I called, "do you know me? I give you this snuff-box so that you may take its spirit with you into the spirit-world."

"You should break it, master," said Akpan, "for everything given to a spirit should be broken."

So, borrowing Amo's matchet, I bored a hole in the side of the box, and then replaced it in Imuk's hand.

His family were pleased with what I had done. The funeral was to take place the next day. I asked them to send a messenger to summon me when all should be ready.

About noon the following day the messenger arrived, and we set out in a broiling sun, Otu·leading one of my goats. In the roadway outside the deceased chief's compound men were running up and down, and others were beating drums. Inside the compound all the plantains had been cut down, and lay prostrate here and there. Straddlewise on the summit of the gable-roof of the hut in which the body was, sat a man on a goatskin holding a horn and an open umbrella; from his cloth a live white fowl was dangling by the legs.

Outside the entrance to the hut sat several children fanning with cloths a small wooden coffer, bespattered with pigments, and containing fufu, palm-wine, and other food for the spirit.

On entering the hut, I found the corpse lying as before, with the glowing embers of a fire between it and the wall. The right arm was in the same position, but had been put into a scarlet sleeve.

Then the body was placed on a bier, brought out on men's heads, carried nearly up to the exit from the compound, and there set down on the ground. The arm remained fixed in its upright position, with the bell attached to it, and, during the whole progress from hut to grave, a man kept alongside the corpse and never for one moment permitted the bell to cease jingling.

People of both sexes—some wearing idiong head-rings, and some smeared with yellow powder—thronged thick around

I

the bier. They led goats or carried fowls. A clay bowl was placed at the feet of the deceased, and, one by one, these victims were held over the feet while their throats were cut. The dripping bodies were thrown forward to fall in a heap against the exit from the compound, where the fowls fluttered about in most gruesome fashion. My goat was killed with the others—nine altogether. I did not count the fowls. Their blood ran over the feet and into the bowl. The bell was continuously jingling, and men beat drums and ran about striking iron gongs.

One of the most active of these runners was a young man wrapped in a scarlet cloth. When all the victims had been sacrificed, this cloth was taken from him and spread over the corpse. Imuk's principal widow took up the bowl into which some of the blood had dripped and placed it on her head, and another of his widows carried the box of food. Then the bier was lifted up and borne into the road. Meanwhile, the bodies of the goats and fowls had been removed.

The bearers ran backwards and forwards with their burden, the bell being made to jingle the whole time, while another man carried and flourished about a wooden shield and a short spear. Youths followed it, shouting and singing. First they took it down the road towards the town-place, and then, coming back to the spot from which they had started, they turned it round, and again went down the road. This was done several times. Then they went through the same action up the road. Next they went down the road again, and carried it by a back way into the compound, and so past the deceased's hut and out into the road again. (I think they were trying to deceive the spirit—trying to make the old chief believe that he was being borne to a feast and not to his grave.)

At last they all ran with the bier down the road, and through the town-place, to a neighbouring grove, where the grave had been dug. It was about five feet deep, and in one side at the bottom a long recess had been made. They lowered the bier with the strong rope-like coils of a creeping plant. Two men got into the grave, and, drawing the wooden bier from under the body, broke it up and handed the pieces to others standing up above. The corpse, wrapped in a new fibre mat, was put into the recess by the two men. Then the little coffer of food was passed down and placed in a smaller recess near the head, and a woman handed down an egg. The broken bier and its ropes were placed on top of the body; also a matchet, first broken in two by one of the men. Okono-branches were thrown in and arranged at the bottom of the grave. Then many people pressed forward and threw in, or handed to those nearest to throw in for them, small twigs broken from branches of neighbouring trees.

"Why do they do this?" I inquired.

"To salute the dead chief," Akpan explained.

Then earth was scooped in, and the two men stamped it down. When it was filled to within a foot of the top, the principal widow brought forward her bowl, and clay having been dipped into the blood, two round cakes were made. Then one of the men turned the bowl upside down at the head of the grave, and, a small stake having been cut and halved, one half was driven through the inverted bowl and the other into the earth at the foot. Imuk's widows wanted to retain the two cakes of clay and blood, but a man snatched them and threw them into the grave. Finally, it was filled up level with the ground.

Then all the people returned to the deceased's compound, and drank palm-wine, and received their portions of the sacrificial meat.

Thus did my old blind friend go to his long home.

As we walked back to Ikot-Abassi, I asked how it was that no human sacrifice had taken place on this occasion, and Amo, who generally managed to pick up all the news, explained it as follows.

"When dem old chief t'ink he go die, sar," he said, "he call plenty people for his house. He tell 'em white man—you, sar—be his friend, and come look him plenty times, and tell him plenty new t'ings. He say, 'Makara no 'gree for kill man, Makara t'ink dat be bad. What time I be young and lib for play, I kill plenty men, and t'ink dat be fine t'ing. Now I be old old man, Makara come tell me dat be bad t'ing. S'pose you kill man for me when I die, Makara no fit to be my friend no more. S'pose you kill man for me, my ekpo [ghost] go humbug you too much.' So," continued Amo, "dem people fear what dem old chief say, dey fear plenty. So dey no kill man for him. I t'ink, sar, dey be glad too much when you dash dem old chief dem small small silber box."

"Yes, by the way," I said, "what did they do with it? Did you see it in Imuk's hand at the funeral?"

"No, sar," Amo answered, "dem box no lib for his hand. I open dem long box, I look dem small silber box inside; plenty snuff lib dere."

Here Akpan broke in. "They have put so much snuff into the grave," he said, "and they think Chief Imuk's spirit will be so pleased with your gift, that he will spend all his time taking snuff,, and so will have no time to humbug his people."

Shortly after the funeral of Chief Imuk, we met with an adventure which nearly ended disastrously.

We had been visiting the country lying on the left bank of a little river called Onio. It was rather thinly populated, and most of the villagers were then at work all day in the fields. On every side they were cleaning the land, or planting yams where it had been cleaned. Women with toddling pot-bellied children, fat as little pigs, and mothers carrying infants astride on the left hip with their left arm passed round the child's body, were helping their husbands and brothers. Men were cutting down bush with their matchets, or working with their only other farming implement, the hoe. Here stood a man digging a hole with the long-handled hoe, and here was a skinny, ill-made boy, bending over the ground in back-aching attitude, using a very short-handled hoe to scoop a hillock of earth over a piece of yam dropped into the hole by woman or child. Others were cooking food on the edge of the clearing. They have no settled time for meals, but eat when most necessary or convenient.

About noon we entered the town-place of Ikot-Idem, and halted there for rest and food. It was badly kept. The ground was covered with dead leaves browned and curled by the heat, straggling weeds, and fallen branches. Little paths ran across it from side to side, and on it grew several large trees and an okono with tufts of sombre-green foliage. All around were the three palms—oil, cocoanut, and wine—clumps of plantain and a few low bushes. At the foot of the okono was a pile of juju objects—small blocks of stone, a broken glass demijohn in its wicker jacket, broken pottery, and broken gin-bottles.

The place was very still, and the village seemed to be quite deserted. My men wanted water, but could not find any.

At last Amo found a boy and brought him to me. "He say no water lib here, sar. Dem riber what dey call Onio be far. All people lib for farm. I t'ink we get cocoanuts, sar?"

Now the custom of the country is that, if a stranger lacks food or drink, he may help himself to cocoanuts without getting into trouble for trespass or theft.

So the boy fetched his climbing-rope with its two loops or stirrups, and, putting his left foot into one stirrup, and slipping the other above his right knee, climbed the rough trunk of a palm. In this fashion they ascend quickly and fearlessly, but on several occasions I saw boys swarm up a lofty palm using nothing but their arms and legs. On reaching the top, he threw down, first a number of dead brown branches, and then the nuts. He gathered them by twisting them round and round until the stalk broke, and they fell to the ground with a thunderous thud. Then my men hacked off the green outer shell with their matchets, and beheaded the hard brown inner shell, and drank the refreshing milk.

Wanting to see the head-chief, whom I was doctoring for a tumour on the arm similar to Okun Ibanga's, I sent Amo to the yam-fields to find him. Soon after he had left me, Otu, who had gone into the bush with Towzer to pluck the leaves of a certain plant to put into his soup, came running back calling in Ibibio, "Some man seize Towzer and take him away!"

We were in friendly country, and I was tired and sleepy I thought there must be some mistake, and was annoyed at being disturbed.

"Go, Akpan," I said; "take Otu and Isan with you, and bring the dog back. There must be some mistake about it."

So they went.

Nearly an hour later, Isan, who was headman of the carriers, returned running and out of breath.

"They are Anangs, master!" he gasped. "They have seized Akpan and Otu, and say they won't give them up unless we pay plenty of manillas."

"Did you tell them," I asked, "that you all belong to the white medicine-man?"

"No, master," he replied, "they know nothing of white men."

"Where are they?" I inquired.

"In a big compound not far from here," he said. "We are on the boundary of the Anang country."

I determined on the spur of the moment to attempt a rescue by "white man's bluff." Amo had been carrying my revolver for me, and had taken it with him to the yam-fields, and not one of my men was armed. I had a cane, and they had sticks.

Picking out two of the carriers to accompany me, and instructing the others to stay in the town-place with Akpan's boy Ima, I told Isan to lead on, and we set off at a good pace. It was a very winding path, running through plantations of wine-palms, and bordered here and there with eben-trees.

After going about a mile, Akpan stopped short and pointed to the gable-end of a hut visible through the ragged growth of a patch of cassava.

"See, master," he said, "that is the compound. It stands alone, I think; the village is further away."

"Have they guns with them?" I asked.

"No," he said, "only matchets. They are young men, about twenty of them."

I now took the lead, followed in single file by the three carriers. Making our way through the cassava, we reached the back of a large compound, inside which many voices were raised in dispute.

I had started in hasty irritation, we had walked quickly, and I arrived there by no means cooler in mind or body. The result was that I handled the affair with great lack of patience and tact.

Walking straight through a back entrance into the compound, I found myself face to face with about a score of excited youths. Akpan stood unbound in their midst, and they thronged around him wrangling and shouting. He was in vain trying to make himself heard. With his back to a wall under the eaves of a hut sat Otu, his hands bound behind him, but his feet unfettered. He was crying. On Otu's knees lay Towzer with blood trickling down from one of his hind-legs.

At my advent the noise ceased. They had never seen a white man before, and my sudden apparition was naturally rather a shock to them. I, however, must have looked anything but formidable. I was coatless, with shirt-sleeves turned up above the elbow, and my face and arms were dripping with perspiration.

"What does this mean?" I cried in their language. "First you seize my dog, and then two of my men. I am the great white doctor who lives with the King of the Ikonos. Aren't you afraid of my mbiam or magic?"

Now, although by this time, I could speak Ibibio fairly fluently I was by no means perfect in it, and, in the excitement and haste of the moment, I had made several blunders in what I had said. They understood my meaning, it is true; but it was expressed so queerly, and my "accent" was so foreign, that some of the boys laughed. This did not tend to lessen my anger.

"Release them at once," I shouted. "I am not a man to be played with!"

I looked round to see if the three carriers were with me, and the Anangs probably thought I had a body of men at my back outside the compound, for they retreated a step and stood as if ready to run.

Akpan saw his opportunity, and, leaving them, stepped up to my side.

"Some of them want to kill me, master," he said; "but some are afraid. They are going to sell Otu, and eat your dog."

Now the wisest thing to have done would have been to have sat down on entering the compound, and bluffed them by assuming an air of fearless composure. Also, if I had used Akpan as my spokesman, instead of making myself ridiculous, they would have listened, and all would probably have ended peaceably. The fact was—but this I did not learn till afterwards—that Towzer, seeing them cutting poles in the bush, had run up to them, and, not liking the look of them, had begun to bark. They were trespassing there, so, fearing that the dog would betray their presence, one of them threw his matchet at Towzer and hit him on the left hind-leg. Then, hearing Otu shout, they had seized the dog and run away.

If I had taken the matter calmly, and asked for an explanation, they would probably have been so astonished at my venturing almost alone into their midst, that they would have yielded through fear of some mysterious unknown power at the back of such fearlessness.

My blustering display of anger and blundering speech had brought me down to their own level, and consequently all they now feared was an attack from my rear.

As soon as Akpan said to me, "They are going to sell Otu, and eat your dog," I picked up a matchet from the ground, and, walking over to the boy, cut the cords that bound him. He lifted up Towzer and followed me to where Akpan and the three carriers stood.

"We will go," I said in a low voice. "Lead on, and be quick."

Otu was carrying the dog tail foremost over his shoulder, holding him by his hind-legs.

They filed out, and I brought up the rear.

The Anangs were so astounded at my action that they did nothing until we were half-way across the patch of cassava. Then they gave a yell, and swarmed out after us.

"Run!" I shouted. "Run! they are after us. Run for your lives!"

Then we ran. Good heavens, how we ran! Akpan led, then the two carriers, then Otu, Towzer, and headman Isan, and then I.

The twenty youths followed in hot pursuit, shouting to one another, and brandishing their matchets.

At first the cassava and the furrows of the cultivated land somewhat retarded progress, but we were soon on the "road," and then there was nothing to hinder us.

Akpan and the two carriers were well ahead, but Otu was

toiling with his load, and Isan, though he did not desert him, did not offer to relieve him of the dog. The brave little fellow began to lag.

"Get on! hurry up!" I shouted. "I will drive them back."

So, turning, I made at our pursuers—then about twenty yards behind—with my uplifted feruleless cane, yelling out epithets which I fear were not quite "parliamentary."

My absurd bluff was again successful. They must have taken me for a white "ekpo!" They turned and fled as fast as their legs could carry them.

Then I resumed my flight, but the Anangs, seeing my back, plucked up courage and renewed their pursuit.

I could see Otu and Isan a good way in front, but Otu was now quite staggering along.

"I must try the same trick again," I said to myself, so at the next corner, I turned round, and once more made for my pursuers.

This time only a few fled. The others came at me, yelling and flourishing their long knives.

Then I knew that I must bluff no longer, but take to my heels and run. So I turned and ran for dear life.

As soon as the Anangs saw my back just in front of them, they shouted something to one another, and began throwing their matchets and sticks at me. Several whizzed unpleasantly near my head, but fortunately—very fortunately!—the tree-bordered path wound in and out a good deal, and they therefore had to aim across corners and between trunks, and, moreover, the Ibibios are not "good shots!"

It *was* an exciting race—by far the most exciting that I had ever known—and, if I had not had my thoughts just then otherwise engaged, I might have remembered training for "the 100" at Cambridge, or thought on many a good run that I had had with the Epsom Harriers or the Needham Market Beagles.

The most exciting moment of the whole race was yet to come. Turning a sharp corner, I saw a few yards in front of me, on the left of the road, a large pit formed when building an adjoining hut, now ruinous. It so encroached on the road, that for a length of three or four feet, the path was only six inches broad. On the right there was a high bank.

Just as I reached the mouth of the cavity, a matchet, aimed more adroitly than the others, hit my left hand and fell into the pit. Had it come half-an-inch nearer me, or had I overbalanced myself in the slightest degree, I should have fallen in likewise, and then—well, I should not have been able to write this yarn.

However, I got safely over the perilous edge and continued

my headlong flight, and at last—when the pursuers' footsteps sounded very close behind—saw in front of me the end of the road and the open space of Ikot-Idem town-place, with a number of my men drawn up in line with matchets and sticks in their hands.

Putting on a final spurt, I outdistanced my pursuers, and ran almost into the arms of Amo. He carried my revolver. I was too breathless to say anything. I heard shouts behind me, then shots, and then I fell against a carrier, and we both rolled over.

It was Akpan who pulled me up. "The Anangs have all run back, master," he said, "and we have taken one prisoner."

On seeing my little force of carriers, to whom some of the Ikot-Idem people, arriving during my absence, had joined themselves, the enemy had beaten a hasty retreat. Amo had fired several shots at them, and had hit one in the foot, who had fallen and been captured.

None of us had sustained any injury. The flying matchet had merely grazed my hand. Little Otu was quite exhausted, but very delighted at having safely rescued his friend Towzer. I gave Isan a bit of my mind for not having helped the boy with his heavy load, but the headman said he didn't understand why he had been expected to risk his life for a dog.

We had had a really narrow escape. The chief of Ikot-Idem informed me that the Anangs of that neighbourhood were about to celebrate the anniversary of the death of an ancestral deity, a war chief of great renown. Human sacrifices were always made on this occasion, and, had we not escaped, they would probably have despatched our spirits to greet that of their ancestor in the other world.

I bandaged up our prisoner's foot, and, carrying him on a "bamboo" stretcher, we returned to Ikot-Abassi.

Otu now owed Towzer one life instead of two.

CHAPTER XIII.

IMPORTANT MYSTERIES ARE EXPLAINED.

The "sickness" with which Chief Esien was suffering was rheumatism in the left shoulder and knee. It was only a slight touch. Had it been severe, he could not have taken his daily exercise in wrestling. I painted the joints with tincture of iodine, and gave him a liniment, and he seemed quite satisfied with this treatment.

His attendant boys kept always so close to him that it was impossible for us to converse without their overhearing everything said. I often noticed a look in the chief's eyes which I interpreted into, "I have something I much desire to say to you, but I dare not for fear of these boys." They were always perfectly obedient and respectful to him, but there seemed to be some understanding between him and them which precluded their ever leaving him to himself. They were kept strictly to their duties—far more strictly than the majority of Ibibio boys—and any breach of conduct was punished by their instructors, and, if it occurred a second time, the offender was banished from the coveted post of "King's son."

It was not until I had been nearly two months at Ikot-Abassi, that I learnt the reasons for their constant attendance upon him. It was, as I mentioned in the last chapter, old chief Imuk who told me.

I went to visit him, accompanied only by Amo and Towzer, and we often found him quite alone. In return for my visits, and my little presents of snuff and tobacco, he would tell me what he knew of the history of the Ikono people. He was very aged, and often rambled on somewhat incoherently, but, little by little, by patient listening, and by putting questions to him and asking him to tell me the same thing over again, I learnt enough to explain the curious position of their "King."

I will tell the story as far as possible in Imuk's own words.

"Long, long ago," he said, "before the cloth and tobacco of the white man were first brought into our country, and when there were still a few elephants left where the forest had not yet been cut down, there was a great war in this land. In those days the Ikonos and the Anangs were one people, living together in the same villages and compounds, and obeying one king, who, with his chiefs, governed well and kept peace everywhere. When he died, he left two sons, full-grown men, the elder two yam-harvests older than the younger. Now the younger, Adong, was stronger and richer than his brother, and he wanted to succeed his father and to inherit a large share of his father's wives and cattle. In particular, he wanted a girl named Adiaha Abassi, who had been married to the old king only just before his death. But they both wanted her. So the brothers quarrelled."

"You have not told me the name of the elder brother," I said.

"His name was Ekpeng," he replied, and then continued, "This quarrel grew greater and greater, and some of the people agreed with one brother, and some with the other. At last the whole country was split up into two parties, and there was a great war. Ekpeng, though poorer than his younger brother, had the larger following, but Adong's wealth enabled him to hire men to fight for him, and these men were from Abam, big and strong, and great fighters.

"The war lasted four years. Many people on both sides were killed, and the country groaned under the cruelty and greed of the Abam soldiers, who burnt whole villages, seized women, and ate up all the land. The king of the Abams gave his daughter to be Adong's principal wife, and she bore him a woman-child, and, soon after her birth, Adong died. Some say he was poisoned.

"Then all the people cried out, 'Let us finish this war. We are tired of fighting. The Abams are become our masters, and our country is spoilt.' "

"So a truce was proclaimed, and a great meeting held, and the people clamoured for peace.

" 'Adong is dead,' they said, 'and leaves no son behind him. Let his brother Ekpeng, elder son of our late king, take his wives and goods and rule over us. Then we can send the Abams back to their own country.'

"But the son of the king of the Abams, whose sister had been married to Adong, rose up and said, 'My father, and we his soldiers who have had much hard fighting in your country, refuse to agree to this. Chief Adong's women and cattle and yam-fields now belong to us; we refuse to let Ekpeng have them. Moreover, my sister was Adong's principal wife, and has borne him a child. Would you have us hand them over to him?'

"Then the wise men who used to help the late king to rule consulted together, and answered, 'We do not want your sister and her child. Take them and leave us. We will give you many cows and goats, and will send you some every year, but we do not wish you to stay here. Go, we beg you, and leave us to settle the country ourselves.'

"But the Abams would not go. They threatened that, unless their terms were accepted, they would bring more soldiers and overrun the whole place, and burn, and kill, and seize everywhere.

"Our ancestors were not so strong as the Abams, and their best fighting-men were nearly all killed; so, to avoid a worse fate, they had at last to submit to the demands of these foreigners. It has always been said that the Abams themselves were also glad to avoid further warfare. They, too, had lost many men, so that in reality they could not have withstood the united forces of the two rival brothers; but

this our forefathers did not then understand. The Abams
deceived them by their big talk.

"When they at last agreed to these demands, a great meeting
was called to arrange evrrything, and to it came chiefs from
every village of what we now call the Ikono and Anang
countries, and also the king of the Abams himself."

"What was his name?" I inquired. "Do you not speak
it because you are forbidden to do so?"

"No," Imuk answered, "it is not forbidden, but my grandfather, who told me these things, had forgotten the king's
name. I think perhaps it was Abassi."

"Go on," I said, "tell me what they arranged at this great
meeting."

"Just before it took place," he continued, "Chief Ekpeng
also died, poisoned by the Abams—so some people said. Then
the chiefs of the country saw that if they disputed among
themselves as to his successor, there would be more fighting,
and the whole tribe would perish. So they consulted the king
of the Abams, and asked him to choose a new ruler from among
them.

"He consented to their request, and many of them secretly
gave him presents—slaves and cattle. He said he would
declare his choice at the great meeting.

"It was a very great meeting. Some say it was held in
Ikot-Abassi town-place, and some say at a village in the Anang
country called Ikot-Ekpene; but I do not know which
account is correct.

"Then the king of the Abams rose up and spoke in a
loud voice so that all the people heard him.

"'Chiefs and fighting-men,' he said, 'we are met here to
end this long war. Your rulers, Ekpeng and Adong, are
both dead. It was their disputes that began the war. We
must establish a new rule so strong that there will be no
more fighting. The chiefs of this country have asked me to
choose a new ruler from among them. If I do this, the
others will fight against him, and peace will never come to
you. To avoid this, I give you as king my own son. You
know him well; he has lived among you as leader of my
soldiers. Let him be your king, and let all your chiefs help
him to make good laws and rule the country of Chief Ekpeng.'

"Then the king's son—it was he, not his father, whose name
I think was Abassi—stood up, and all the Abam soldiers
shouted and waved their spears; but our forefathers did not
shout. He was a tall man, taller and stronger than all men
there except his father.

"But the king made him sit down again, for he had not
yet finished the whole matter.

" 'As for Chief Adong's country,' he said, "it has been held during the last four years by my soldiers. Your chief called us to help him, and we have done much hard fighting and lost many men. Adong married my daughter, and she has borne him a child. My will is that my daughter succeed her husband and become queen of his country, and that her daughter succeed her on the throne. I will appoint a company of my soldiers to live with her, to protect her from harm and to enforce obedience to her commands. Accept my scheme, and I will withdraw my men. Reject it, and we will wage war here until none of you is left alive. I have finished.'

"After spending two days in discussing this scheme, the Ikono and Anang chiefs, seeing no other course open to them, consented to adopt it.

"So it came about that the people of Chief Ekpeng were ruled by an Abam king, and those of Chief Adong by a woman who was also an Abam. The former were called Ikonos, and the latter Anangs.

"In consenting to adopt the scheme, the chiefs made certain conditions to which the king of the Abams agreed. Fearing that their new ruler might leave them and thus cause renewal of the war, they made a law that he should never go beyond the bounds of his principal town. Fearing that, as he grew old, the power would slip from his hands, and the people refuse to obey him, they made another law that, as soon as one hundred white hairs could be plucked from his head, he should cease to rule, and should be succeeded by a younger man.

"The Anangs likewise made conditions when they accepted a queen. At the bottom of their hearts they hated the Abams, and their consent had been obtained only because they looked forward to the day when Chief Adong's daughter, instead of her Abam mother, would be old enough to rule over them. Fearing lest Etuk Afia, the child's mother, should live to be an old woman and so be their queen for many years, they made a law that, when the queen lost her fatness, and became so thin that she could no longer outweigh a certain number of manillas, she should resign and be succeeded by her daughter."

"Have these laws remained in force up to this day?" I asked. "Do your King and the Queen of the Anangs still hold their thrones under these conditions?"

" "Yes," answered Imuk, "they have remained unaltered through many generations, for the country cannot prosper except we do as our forefathers did."

I recollected the date on Arthur Riversley's strip of cloth

—1677. When he "printed" that message with his dying fingers, there was a "Quene" in the Ibibio country. The laws made after the great meeting were therefore at least two hundred years old.

"Tell me," I said, "tell me who determines the time when the king must vacate his throne, and the queen resign hers."

"I must tell you the whole story," he answered. "Another condition made by our forefathers was that their Abam king should come to them alone. Each of the thirty-five villages of the Ikono people agreed to give him one girl, also cattle and goats, and also to send a certain number of men to work at certain times on his farm. They did so, and King Abassi lived with his thirty-five wives at Ikot-Abassi, and peace was restored throughout the land. He was a strong man, feared and respected by all.

"His sister, Etuk Afia, queen of the Anangs, was also a strong woman, and she ruled her people just as if she had been a man. She refused to take another husband, probably fearing that, if she did, he would usurp her power. The village where she lived was called Ikot-Afia-Ete. Her house was different from all other houses in this country, for it was round like the moon, and had a very high roof tapering up to a point. With her and her little daughter lived three aged Anang women, chosen by the queen because they were witches and knew all the secrets of the country.

"The circular house stood in the middle of a large compound, around which were the huts, built square as we build them, of her bodyguard of Abam soldiers—young fighting-men, picked out by the king of the Abams, the queen's father, because of their strength and valour. They were relieved every three years. During this period, they devoted all their time to protecting the queen, enforcing her commands, and practising feats of strength and endurance, such as wrestling, jumping, and running. They were not allowed to have wives, and had to keep their huts clean and do their own cooking. At the end of the three years, they returned to their own country with cattle and goats given them by the queen, and bought themselves wives and settled down there. Other young men took their place. Thus, every three years, was much wealth taken from the Anang to the Abam country. This custom still continues."

"And who," I inquired, "determines when the queen's reign must end?"

"Every year," replied old Imuk, "the Anang chiefs hold a great meeting, and the queen is weighed in the presence of them all. This meeting takes place at the feast of new yams.

"Once a-year in this the Ikono country, all we chiefs also

hold a great meeting, and the king's cap is removed, and his white hairs are plucked out and counted. Our meeting takes place at the end of the dry season, on the day after the first fall of rain."

"And, when the test goes against him," I asked, "who succeeds him? Is it always his eldest son?"

"No," replied the chief, "his son never succeeds, partly because the son would be the child of an Ikono mother, and so breed up strife in the land, and partly because our first king—Abassi, as some call him—had no sons. It was thus. He had thirty-five wives, and some of them bore him sons, and some daughters, but no man-child of his ever lived. It is said that the medicine-men always killed them.

"Then at last, when the first grey hairs appeared on Abassi's head, they began to talk of the succession, and the king of the Abams—one of Abassi's brothers, who had succeeded the old king—heard of it, and visited Ikot-Abassi with a great following, for he saw that the Ikonos were planning to cast off the Abam yoke. Then it was agreed that when Abassi became too old to reign, he should be succeeded by another Abam, a young man chosen from the bodyguard of the queen of the Anangs.

"So it has come to pass that every year at the time of our meeting a truce is proclaimed between us and the Anangs, and the Abam soldiers of their queen are present when our king's cap is removed, and, if the test goes against him, a great wrestling takes place, and the winner succeeds as our new king."

"And what becomes of the king whom he supplants?" I inquired.

"He has to wrestle with his successor," said Imuk. "If he, in spite of his grey hairs, can overcome his young opponent, he is allowed to retire to the Abam country, and to take with him all his wives, and children, and cattle, and goods. If, however, he be vanquished, he is sacrificed to our big town-drum."

"And his wives and children?" I asked.

"They are divided among the queen's bodyguard, who, though their period may not be ended, are allowed to return to their country with their booty. Thus have we done for many generations. Never, since the days of our first Abam king, have the grey hairs proved stronger than youthful vigour; all our kings have been sacrificed to the big drum."

"What becomes of the Anang queens when they lose their weight and have to resign?" I inquired.

"They are allowed to retire to their father's village," he replied, "for so did their first queen, Etuk Afia."

"And who succeeds?" I continued.

"Queen Etuk Afia," he answered, "was succeeded by her daughter, who was also Adong's child; but she refused to marry for fear of soon growing thin and so losing her power. So they had to make a new law, that, when their queen could no longer outweigh the manillas, all the unmarried girls of the country should be called together and weighed, and the heaviest of them all should be chosen as queen."

"How many manillas," I asked, "are they required to outweigh?"

"It all depends," he said. "The throne is given to the heaviest girl. During the first few years of her reign she grows fatter and fatter, but, after a time, the cares of her kingdom, and the jealousies and bickerings of her bodyguard, tell upon her, and her weight begins to go down; but as long as she is able to outweigh her original weight, less one hundred manillas, she retains her position. Since the days of Queen Etuk Afia, every queen has had three of the oldest men in the land to live with her, and it is said that they have sometimes put that into the queen's food which has tended to make her thin."

"One thing you have not explained," I said. "Tell me why is your king never left alone? Why are there always two Ikono boys in attendance on him?"

"The reason is," he said, "that one of our kings, the fourth after Abassi, obtained from a foreign medicine-man who visited him a medicine which, when rubbed on his head, removed all the hair. It could not grow again, so the test could not be applied. Therefore he was killed, and the succession continued in the usual way.

"After that, our forefathers agreed that the king must never be left alone, and so the company called 'the King's sons' was formed. Also, it was decreed that the king should always, day and night, wear a cap of leopard's skin, and that it should never be removed except on the first night of every new moon when his head is washed by a blind man in the presence of his twenty-four boys. They stand around him in a circle, but at such a distance that, when the cap is removed by the blind man, they cannot see the condition of his hair. Since I became blind, I have performed this duty. King Esien has plenty of hair, but of course I do not know if it is much greyer."

"Much greyer!" I exclaimed. "Do you mean that it is already losing its colour?"

"Yes, he replied, "last year, on the day after the first rain, when the annual testing took place, ten white hairs were plucked from his head. Probably there are now many more. His reign is drawing to a close."

"And will he be sacrificed?" I asked in horror. "Surely he is too popular a king for that. He is kind to everybody, and all men seem to like him. Can nothing save him?"

"Nothing," answered Imuk; "as our forefathers did, so must we do. His only way of escape is to overcome his successor when they wrestle together. That is why he wrestles every day. He is an expert wrestler and very strong, but the queen of Anang has many strong men with her, and all of them are younger than Esien. Never since the days of our first Abam king has the outgoing man escaped death. If fate has ordained that he should be overcome, he must die as all our former kings have died. Otherwise, the whole country will be spoilt."

The day after the old blind chief had told me the last details of this history, he died, and with him died my means of obtaining further information, for I had already discovered that the other Ikono chiefs, and many of the people, regarded me with considerable suspicion. I noticed the "King's sons" took special care to overhear every word that passed between Esien and me, and that there were sometimes spies placed upon my movements.

Amo had always accompanied me to Imuk's house, and so had heard the whole history, and he and I used to talk it over when we were alone; but we were cautious, and generally conversed in English.

It was now near the end of the month of February. The first rain falls usually about the middle of March.

Chief Esien's face sometimes wore a worried look, and more than ever did his eyes express that he longed to confide in me.

About this time Akpan informed me of the arrival of a "brother" of his at Use, and recommended that I should send my cattle and goats there, so that his brother could take them down the Enyong to Itu, and keep them there for me until my return, when I could send them to Calabar and realise a good price for them. He was careful to point out that, if I should proceed into the Anang country, it would be unwise to leave my property with the Ikonos.

So, thinking the suggestion good, I acted upon it, and sent my cattle and goats to the market, where Akpan's brother met and took charge of them. I little realised that the crafty Akpan was acting under the instruction of my wily host, Chief Udaw Idiong of Itu!

One day, when overhauling my stores, I opened a small case of toilet requisites—soap, tooth-powder, brilliantine, etc.

K

—which Pleasance had had packed for me by our local chemist. She had insisted on superintending certain parts of my kit, and had put in many things which were really unnecessary luxuries.

In this particular case, I found a bottle of colourless liquid labelled: "Hardy's Hair-Dye. Unequalled for strength, purity, and permanency. Of such matchless virtue that its merits are known all over the world without the proprietor having spent one shilling on advertisement. . . . Used by the Dowager-Empress of China, Mr. Rider Haggard's 'She,' and the King of the Kukubukuluku Islands, all of whom have signed testimonials in its favour," etc., etc. The directions for use were: "To turn white or grey hair brown, put one tea-spoonful of the dye into one pint of water, and rub this mixture all over the hair. To turn white or grey hair black, use two teaspoonfuls. In both cases, one application will produce a permanent effect. The dye will not injure or stain the skin in any degree whatsoever, and it has no smell."

"Here is the very stuff for my purpose!" I exclaimed to myself. "The difficulty is how to apply it."

To test its virtue, Amo and I experimented upon a piece of white goatskin. Amo rubbed it with the stronger dose of the dye, and the next morning it was perfectly black.

He and I discussed many plans for saving our good friend Esien from his probable fate, and at last we hit upon a scheme which seemed feasible.

The first difficulty was to communicate our discovery and scheme to the chief. We overcame it as follows. Twice every day the vigilant watch of "the King's sons" was somewhat relaxed, and this was when he was wrestling. The wrestling-ground was, as I have said, an oblong stretch of greensward. It was carefully measured out and surrounded by an edging of empty cocoanut shells, which, during a match, nobody was permitted to cross. If any spectator put even one foot over it, he had to give the wrestlers a fowl apiece. All around, banks of earth had been raised on which the umpires and spectators sat.

When the chief was wrestling, his two boys took charge of his leopard's skin and cowrie ornaments, for not even they were permitted "within the ropes."

During our stay at Ikot-Abassi, Amo had wrestled nearly every day, frequently with Esien himself. He had never succeeded in overcoming the chief, but the chief had now great difficulty in overcoming him, and, more often than otherwise, their matches were "drawn." Sometimes they struggled for nearly half-an-hour upon the ground.

Esien was teaching Amo many of the tricks and turns which he had picked up from a variety of opponents, and, during their struggles, he often gave him verbal directions, some of which were of course inaudible to the spectators.

Here was a means of communicating with the chief. It was Amo who thought of it, and it was Amo who carried it out, for, although I sometimes had a bout in the ring with Esien, my linguistic attainments were too imperfect to be relied upon in this serious crisis, and, besides, I was more suspiciously watched than Amo.

So day after day, when they were struggling together on the greensward, Amo told Esien, in a few words at a time, of our scheme for saving him, and he of course agreed to play his part therein.

CHAPTER XIV.

"THE TESTING OF THE KING'S YOUTH."

The "town-drum" of Ikot-Abassi stood in a little clearing at one side of the town-place where the Ekpo dance had been held. This drum was greatly venerated by all the Ikono people. It had been carved out of a section of the trunk of an enormous tree, and was said to be the largest drum among all the tribes thereabouts. I did not measure it, but, as far as I can recollect, it was about twelve feet long, and between six and seven feet high. It was carved into the form of a man's figure—a man with a tub encircling his body, his head and neck projecting at one end, and his legs at the other. His body (the "tub") had been hollowed out through two long holes at the top, and on it were carved: his arms and hands holding an "ngkene" gong, two coiled snakes, the head of each half-mooned with a manilla, two lizards, a small bird, the "ngkong-ngkong" or double gong, a tortoise, etc.

It was beaten only in time of war, to call the people together, and at the annual "testing." It was very ancient, older than the civil war between the rival brothers Ekpeng and Adong, for during that war it had been partly burnt by the Abam mercenaries, and was much blackened and charred on one side. They had tried to drag it away on rollers to the Anang country, but it had proved too heavy for them. Had they succeeded, it would have been a great trophy of victory.

For many generations every outgoing king, after suffering defeat on the wrestling-ground, had had his throat cut over this drum. The royal blood was collected in a clay vessel and poured through the holes at the top, and in time of war the spirits of all their kings were believed to assemble inside the drum, which, when beaten, gave forth their united voices calling upon the people to conquer their enemies.

Over this drum, to protect it from the elements, was erected the usual gable-shaped roof of the country, which it was the duty of a certain family to keep in constant repair.

The head of this family was called Akama-Mbuut-Mbong, meaning the keeper of the kings' skulls. He was so named because in a hut in his compound, which adjoined the town-place, were kept the skulls of all their kings. After the sacrificial ceremony over the drum, the head was handed to its hereditary keeper, and the body was carried with much pomp to its grave in Akai-Mbong, the king's grove.

This then was the fate which in all probability awaited Chief Esien.

The Akama who was then in charge of the royal skulls was a noted abia-idiong (medicine-man). His knowledge of the medical virtues of herbs and barks was unequalled in the whole country, and many resorted to him. I often visited him, and we used to exchange information. I taught him rudimentary surgery, and he told me the properties of local plants. His possible jealousy of me as a rival practitioner was thus avoided.

His compound was superior to all others except Esien's. On one side, surrounded by awbawti-trees, stood his idiong-house, a small hut consisting of two rooms one behind the other, and in front a porch with painted walls, furnished with clay benches for the use of patients awaiting admittance to the temple of mysteries. A very small wooden door opened from the porch into this temple, a room about eight feet square, containing a remarkable collection of juju objects.

Imbedded up to their eye-sockets in the clay floor were the white skulls of the Ikono kings, arranged so regularly that the general effect was almost that of a tessellated pavement. The Akama's clients had to squat on top of them, and were threatened that, if they told lies, the royal ghosts would visit and torment them.

The back wall of the temple was hung with fibre mats, and in the middle thereof was a circular aperture communicating with a still smaller chamber behind. In front of these mats was a "bamboo" frame supporting the idiong-master's stock-in-trade, a motley collection comprising small wooden images of women, of a dog, a snake, and a bird, large iron manillas, a bunch of goats' skulls, clay pots full of stinking rubbish, eggs of all ages, etc., etc. On the ground in front was a flat block of stone, on which lay a much-venerated aerolite or thunderbolt, and beside it were tortoise-shells, feathers, broken iron spuds, ekput-rattles, clay cakes, and various other odds and ends. Hanging from the roof was a dirty bunch of fibre to which were attached feathers, fish-frames, and dried herbs.

At one side of this back wall was a still smaller doorway giving admittance to the inner room, which contained a basket of "mbiam," several old rusty guns, and an assortment of Ekpo masks. At the back of it was a little door opening from the grove of awbawti-trees.

The Akama was a young man, a plump, jovial fellow who grew fat on his fees and worried about nothing at all. People who dreamed dreams told them to him, and he interpreted them according to the amount of the fee; women about to give birth to children brought him fowls and eggs, and he instructed them what sacrifices to make for safe delivery; girls wanting love-potions,' and hunters wanting luck— all resorted to his idiong-house, and he answered them through the hole in an oracular voice. He knew all the secrets of the country, and was as great a man as the king himself.

He lived uncommonly well—ate flesh every day, and drank gin whenever he felt inclined, which was far oftener than was good for him.

On the seventh of March there was a new moon, and on the next morning Chief Esien's head was solemnly washed by a blind man, while all "the King's sons" stood around him in a circle. I was not present, for I had feigned illness, and remained in my hut, to which Amo denied everybody admittance—even Otu and Towzer.

Chief Esien, in anticipation of the approach of the annual testing, had lately been very busy with juju matters, visiting shrines in different parts of the village, making sacrifices, and imploring the deities to give him another year's reign.

After having his head washed, he complained of renewed pain in the knee, and informed his boys that, having lost faith in the white doctor's medicine, he should that night visit the Akama to consult him as to a remedy. In this, he was acting on my instructions.

Late in the afternoon I was carried in my hammock to the Akama's idiong-house, taking with me six bottles of my own gin. I went in alone, as I had often done before, and asked him to cure me of a bad headache. He seemed rather flattered by my going to him as a patient, and rubbed a white earth on my forehead. I then called for the gin and presented it to him. He was delighted with this large fee, and asked me to drink with him in his inner chamber. He usually drank trade-gin. My gift was an almost unknown luxury to him.

So I told Amo and my bearers to sit down until I should be ready to go, and the Akama informed his people that he should remain there all the evening, and was not to be disturbed.

Then we retired to the room of oracles, and the Akama spread skins on the clay seats, and on the floor. On his left wrist he wore a heavy brass bracelet engraved with curious devices.

"This is good drink," I said, "so good that I give it to only my best friends. It is comfortable here. Let us drink a bottle each. Do you agree?"

My convivially-minded host readily agreed, so we each opened a bottle and prepared to spend a sociable half-hour.

Now two of the bottles, specially marked by me, contained nothing but water. I easily arranged that, while he drank the fiery gin—it was a good strong brand—I drank the water.

The Akama greatly relished it. His broad face beamed all over, and he insisted on repeatedly shaking hands with me. "It tickles the inside of my stomach," he said. "I will give you a cow for a case of gin like this."

We soon finished one bottle apiece.

"Let us each drink another," I said. "If we die to-night, we cannot drink them to-morrow."

He required no pressing; so we began on our second bottle, I drinking water as before.

I then asked the Akama various questions about his professional procedure, and he proved as communicative as I had hoped to make him. Towards the middle of the second bottle, his replies became quite incoherent, and his head began to nod. Then he slipped on to the floor, but still grasped the bottle, nor did he relinquish his hold until he had emptied it to the very dregs. Then it fell out of his hand, and he entirely collapsed—dead-drunk.

I am well aware, good Reader, that I was taking a somewhat immoral means to attain my end. You, sitting in your comfortable armchair at home, of course consider my conduct on this occasion to have been quite shocking, and feel that *you* would never have "lowered" yourself as I did! My reply is, "All's fair in love and war." If you wish to judge me with absolute fairness, leave your armchair, go among genuine savages, and then, having seen what they are really like, abuse me to your heart's content. I used my wits, and succeeded. You with your scruples might have failed."

I shook my prostrate host, I kicked him, I shouted in his

ears, I pulled his arms and legs. Nothing, however, had any effect upon him. He was as insensible to it all as an overfed pig at a cattle-show is to the proddings of the admiring dealer. He was, in short, quite *hors-de-combat*, and would remain so for many hours to come.

So, leaving him there, I passed into the temple, and out through the porch, and, getting into the hammock, was carried back to my compound. Amo told Akpan and Otu, and they spread it abroad, that the idiong-master had given me medicine, and had advised me to remain quietly in my house for a day or two.

Then I dressed up as an "idem," or superhuman being. I wore my suit of black tights, a girdle of fibre fringes, and a mask and huge shaggy wig. My face, hands, and neck were blackened with wood-ash applied on the top of vaseline. Tied to my girdle was the bottle of diluted hair-dye.

As soon as darkness set in—about 7 o'clock—Amo let me out at the back of my house, and I crept away through the bush and trees that separated us from the Akama's compound. I had nearly a quarter of a mile to go, but the night was dark, and, had anybody seen me, they would have taken me for an "idem," and run away. Nobody, however, saw me. I reached the awbawti-trees safely, and quietly entered the idiong-house at the back.

I lit the Akama's little lamp. He was lying exactly as I had left him. Again I shook and punched him, but he was wrapped in too deep a sleep to awake. Pulling off his curiously-engraved bracelet, I slipped my own left hand through it. The bottle of mixture I deposited in one corner.

Soon after my arrival, Chief Esien and his boys arrived. He was escorted by twelve of "the King's sons" bearing lighted taper-sticks. They all sat down outside, except the two who were taking their usual turn of attendance. The chief and these two entered the porch and knocked.

I was in the small inner chamber, seated behind the circular aperture, through which I could see into the temple.

"Come in," I called in a deep oracular voice, "come in, and close the door."

They entered. One of the boys carried Esien's lamp, lighted. It was a feeble flickering light, but it illumined the little temple just sufficiently to make the skulls and other paraphernalia look most grimly weird. The boys gazed around with awe and terror in their faces, and kept very close to their master.

"What is your business?" I inquired.

"I am Esien, king of the Ikonos," he replied. "I have long been sick in my knee. The white doctor's medicine does me no good, so I come here, and crave your forgiveness for going to him, and beg you to give me good medicine."

"What reward do you offer if I cure you?" I asked.

"I will give you to wife my daughter Nwa. You have often asked for her, but hitherto I have withheld my consent. Take away this pain" (he groaned) "and she shall be yours."

"Kneel down," I said, "and swear on the heads of your predecessors that you will indeed do as you say if I effect this cure."

"I kneel and swear," he replied.

"Put out your light," I cried, "and let all three of you kneel and remain in that position."

They obeyed my directions.

Then, disguised as I have already described, I entered the temple, and set fire to a little heap of powder previously placed there in a clay bowl. It burned with a ghastly green light and filled the place with suffocating smoke and smell.

"Ekpenyong Ibriitam [the great Ibo juju] is here to-night," I said. "He is jealous lest his mysteries be disclosed. Bend down all of you, put your lips to the heads of the kings, and swear never to reveal what you see and hear in this temple."

They obeyed.

"Behold this bracelet," I continued. "You have often seen it on my arm, but little did you think that the strange figures hereon were the work of Ekpenyong himself. If you value your lives, tell this secret to no man."

Then I made the two boys put on Ekpo masks with wigs so enormous that their bodies were almost concealed in them.

Returning to the inner shrine, I spoke through the aperture.

"In which knee is the pain?" I asked.

"In the left knee," Esien replied.

"In front of you," I said, "you will find a flat block of stone, and lying thereon a thunderbolt sent straight to earth by Abassi. Place your left knee on this stone, and rub the suffering part very softly with the thunderbolt."

Esien did as I told him, but, directly he applied it to his knee he yelled out, "It burns me, it eats into my skin, the pain is more than I can bear!"

"If you want to be cured," I said, "you must endure pain for a few minutes. Keep still while one of the boys rubs your knee with it."

As soon, however, as the boy touched his knee, he threw his limbs about, pretended to be almost frantic with pain, and pushed the boy away from him.

"This will never do so," I said. "I must give you medicine to quiet you. Put your mouth to the hole."

He did so, and I poured water down his throat.

"I feel better," he said, "I will be quiet now."

"Kneel as before," I said. "Place both your hands on the wall that separates you from me. I will hold your head, while one boy holds your knee down, and the other rubs it with the thunderbolt. Put your head through this hole."

The chief and his boys implicitly carried out my commands. Esien thrust his head through the aperture into the little room where I was.

While the boys occupied themselves with his knee, I quickly removed the chief's cap, and rubbed the hair-dye all over his hair, except just above both ears, where I left two little patches untouched. His hair was unusually thick and long. Then I replaced the cap, and whispered to him that I had finished. All this time he continued his groans and cries.

When I replaced his cap, he withdrew his head and stood up.

"I can endure no more," he said. "Let me go."

"The cure is complete," I replied. "The pain will be quite gone by to-morrow. You may go. Tell your two boys to leave their masks on the floor. Remember, all of you, the solemn oath that you have sworn. Before you go, drink this," and, so saying, I thrust a bottle of gin through the hole.

Esien made his boys drink enough to considerably increase their muddled condition—the smoke and their heavy headgear had combined to nearly smother them—and took a long pull at it himself.

Just as they were going, I called out, "Remember your promise to give me your daughter Nwa. I shall get her, for your knee is already cured."

Then they opened the door and departed.

After re-arranging the temple and inner room as I had found them, and restoring the bracelet to the Akama's wrist, I also went, leaving him still sound asleep on the floor. I regained my house in safety, and only Amo knew of my absence.

The next morning the chief sent his daughter Nwa to the Akama. She was escorted by the twelve boys who had accompanied Esien the previous night. Amo happened (!) to visit the idiong-master's compound at the same time, and this is what he reported to me.

"Dem Akama sleep all night for dem idiong-house. Dis mornin' he came out. He laugh plenty. He say he t'ink Abassi dash him gin, gin what be good too much. He say he drink, he sleep, he dream plenty fine t'ings, but he no fit for tell nobody what dem t'ings be.

"Den," he continued, "all dem small boys come. Dey bring dem woman Nwa. Dey say, 'Esien go dash you dis girl 'cause you make good medicine for him last night.' Dem Akama, he no sabby, he open his eyes like so" (Amo made a circle with his hands). "Den he rub his head. Den he look dem girl. Den he cry, 'Fool palaver lib for my head dis mornin'. First me no sabby, but now me sabby. Dem chief Esien come for me last night. I gib him medicine, he no be sick no more, he dash me dis woman.'

"He be glad too much, sar," said Amo in conclusion. "He play, he beat drum, he dash dem boys plenty palm-wine."

Thus ended my share in the preparations for the annual ceremony of testing the king's youth.

Rain being now probably not far off, the whole tribe busied themselves preparing for the reception of the bodyguard of the Anang queen. The compound annually occupied by them was repaired and cleaned, and furnished with "bamboo" beds, sleeping-mats, and skins, and cooking-pots and fuel were got ready for them. Attention was also given to the wrestling-ground, and to the banks or seats which surrounded it. Messengers were sent to all parts of the Ikono country, and also to Ikot-Afia-Elte, the queen's headquarters, warning everybody to prepare for a summons to assemble at Ikot-Abassi.

The first rain fell at daybreak on the morning of the 18th of March. Immediately the runners who for days had been held in readiness started out in every direction to call in the people.

Some of them arrived that evening. Some, travelling all night, arrived early the next morning. The Abam soldiers, who had furthest to travel, did not reach Ikot-Abassi until noon.

This being a sacred period of truce between the Ikonos and Anangs, they came unarmed, that is to say, without their guns, for, even where all is peace, the native but seldom lays aside his matchet. They carried long walking-staves, similar to that brought to Riversley by Daniel Wood.

They were a fine body of men, thirty or forty of them, so fine that nobody seeing them could be surprised that their tribe had so long held the Ibibios in subjection. None of them was so tall as Amo, but there were several quite six feet in height. Several were as short as five foot eight, but the average height was about five foot ten. Those lacking inches made them up in depth of chest and strength of limb. They were all in splendid form and training, and seemed quite unfatigued after their thirty miles' walk. Compared to the puny, thin, ill-made Ikonos, they were giants.

All were dressed alike in the time-honoured uniform of the Queen's bodyguard, consisting of an ikiko or civet-cat's skin round the loins, a narrow strip of blue-and-white cloth tied just above with matchet attached thereto on the left hip, and a scarlet feather stuck into their wool over the right ear. None of them wore any jewelry, nor did they shave their hair into patterns. They wore it rather longer than was customary among the Ibibios, and it was "parted" down the middle—*i.e.*, a narrow furrow of hair was shaved off, a fashion prevailing to-day among paddlers on the Gold Coast.

They came in in single file, and were received by the Akama and conducted by him to their compound. After bathing in the stream which runs at the foot of the Ikot-Abassi ridge, they were served with food cooked by the king's wives, and about three o'clock they repaired to the town-place and sat down on the left of the king's chair.

The Reader is already familiar with Ikot-Abassi town-place, for it was there that the dance of the ghosts was held. On the present occasion, the crowd was very much larger, for, not only had men and boys come in from all villages of the Ikono sub-tribe, but the women and children of the immediate neighbourhood were permitted to attend. They had put on their best frocks, that is to say, a few additional beads, shells, and metal ornaments, and they herded together behind their menfolk.

Except for a central space kept clear by "the king's sons," the whole arena was packed with thousands of squatting Ikonos. Late comers had to stand in the bush on the outskirts of the clearing, and the branches of the trees were black with adventurous boys who preferred to look down on the ceremony.

I and my little following, including Towzer under Otu's control, were on the right of the King's chair. (If, after seeing it at Riversley, you think it should be called "throne," I will submit to your better judgment.)

All were now assembled except King Esien and the senior chiefs of the Ikonos. Suddenly a great booming noise was heard. The big drum was being beaten by its four hereditary drummers, and the voices of their departed kings were speaking to the Ikono people. It hushed the great multitude into absolute silence, and the effect was really so wonderful that it sent a sort of thrill down my backbone.

Then down the avenue came the procession, a long procession in single file. It was headed by a boy beating a wooden hand-drum. Then followed about a score of Ekpo monsters intended to represent the spirits of all the dead kings.

Their limbs were blackened, and they wore masks and wigs, and round their loins the identical leopards' skins worn by the deceased monarchs.   One of them had no mask, but his head from the eyes downwards was concealed by a long fibre fringe.   He was quite bald; all his hair had been shaved off, and white earth rubbed over the crown.   He represented the king who had disgraced himself by using the foreigner's hair-medicine.

Next came three aged chiefs, the second of whom being quite blind, grasped the end of a pole held by the man in front of him.   Behind them were three men walking abreast, or, rather, a central figure flanked by two walking sideways.   He in the middle carried with evident trepidation and trembling a large china plate, while the others held under it a cloth which would break its fall if its bearer should have the misfortune to let it drop.

Then came King Esien, holding himself right royally, attired as when I had first seen him, and attended of course by two of his boys.

Six more chiefs followed him, and in the rear came his thirty-five wives in gala costume, tripping along, waving their fans, and singing.

As the head of this procession entered the town-place, the booming of the big war-drum ceased, and an orchestra hidden behind a clump of trees broke into a volume of noise which even the famous tribal drum had barely equalled.   Drums, horns, and rattles of every description belched forth a royal welcome, and the vast assembly rose and shouted with one accord.   Towzer's barks swelled the din, and the vultures sitting up aloft, forgetting for once their usual dignified indifference, flapped their wings and soared away to less noisy perches.

Esien walked straight to his chair, the chiefs and royal ghosts grouped themselves at his back, and the people resumed their seats on the ground.   He raised his long staff, and the music ceased.

"Chiefs and people of the Ikono tribe," he said, standing up, and speaking in a clear voice audible to the attentive throng, "we are once again met here to carry out our forefathers' yearly custom of testing the king's youth.   I give you all welcome.   Let us first, however," turning to the Abam soldiers on his left, "give welcome to our guests who come from afar, even from the country of my sister the Queen of the Anangs."

The people rose, and shouted, and sat down again.

Then one of the Abams led forward a pure-white sheep, and presented it to the king.   This was the annual gift sent him by the queen. Its left ear had been cut off, the ownership mark of the royal lady. Esien laid his hand on it, and one of his men led it away.

"I have but little to say to you," he continued. "I have ruled over you for ten years, and the country has prospered. I have besought Abassi and the spirits of our forefathers to grant me farther extension of my youth. At last year's meeting, ten white hairs were found on my head. If this year there be found ten for every one of those ten, I must hand over my kingdom to a younger man, to one of these our guests, and, if I be overcome on the wrestling-ground by my successor, I must suffer the fate which all my predecessors have suffered. I have finished. The day grows late. Let the ceremony take place."

Then, without further ado, the procession—with the exception of the monsters and of the king's wives, who remained in their places—re-formed and proceeded to the central space kept clear by the circle of "King's sons." Within this enclosure were also admitted I and Amo, Esien's principal wife, the Akama (who was master of the ceremonies), and six of the Abam bodyguard.

I had a good look at the precious plate. It was a specimen of old English delft ware, and an antiquarian friend tells me, that, if my description to him is correct, it was probably one of those made by Dutch potters who settled at Lambeth in the middle of the eighteenth century.

The royal chair was brought. Esien sat down on it. Breathless silence reigned, but everybody craned forward their necks as the old blind chief, guided by his friend, removed the cap from the king's head. Esien sat perfectly still with his hands resting on his thighs, but I could detect a slight tremor in his limbs.

Then the sacred plate was brought near by its three caretakers, and two of the other chiefs began a close examination of the royal head. Running their fingers through his wool, they peered here and there with the utmost anxiety, but could find no white hairs. They expressed their amazement. Then one of them made a little exclamation; he had found what he sought just above the right ear. Carefully he plucked out hair after hair, until twelve lay on the plate.

"I can find no more," he said.

Then the other chief examined the other side of the head, and he too was successful, and added nine more white hairs to the collection. Then, one after another, the remaining Ikono chiefs made individual examinations, but not one of them could anywhere find another incriminating hair. Then the six Abams had their turns, but they were equally unsuccessful.

"Are you all satisfied?" Esien asked.

"Yes, we are satisfied," they replied.

So the procession returned to the clump of okonos under which he usually sat.

Then the king's drummer beat his drum to command silence, and announced in a loud voice, "The testing is finished. Only one-and-twenty white hairs have been found in King Esien's head. Abassi has ordained that he reign over us another year."

Then the people rose and shouted.

The chiefs crowded round Esien to congratulate him on the result, and one of them, a queer-looking old fellow with a pipe in his mouth, an iron gong in one hand, and three little brass ornaments attached to his necklace, asked if the king could account for the white hairs appearing only just above the ears.

"Yes," replied Esien, "I will tell you. One moon ago, after I had sacrificed at the shrine called 'itie-ubong [seat of royalty]' I dreamed that same night a dream. I dreamed that two spirits came to me, and, removing my cap, and seizing me one on each side of the head, took me swiftly through the air till they brought me to a great king who had more cattle than there are people here to-day. They made me kneel down before him, and he laid his hands on my head and said, 'Return to rule over the Ikono people.' Then the two men brought me back to my compound here."

"But the white hairs," persisted the inquiring chief, "how did they escape the touch of the great king's hand?"

Esien smiled. "It was where the two messengers held me," he said. "They held me so the whole time, they did not for one moment let go of me; therefore the great king could not touch me where their fingers were gripping."

"Was he black or white?" asked the old chief.

"Black," said Esien.

Then the assembly broke up, for the sun was setting. They were all to sleep at Ikot-Abassi, ready for the great display of wrestling which would be held on the following morning.

CHAPTER XV.

SURROUNDED BY HOSTILE SAVAGES.

Rain fell again during the night, but the morning dawned with sunshine. The whole day was devoted to wrestling. Chief Esien seemed to have taken out a new lease of strength as well as of life, for he overcame every opponent, including the champions of the Abam bodyguard. Amo also distinguished himself, but was eventually defeated by one of the smallest but strongest of them named E'tuk Umaw. None of the Ikonos won prizes except a young man from Ndiya, whose physique was above the low Ibibio average.

That night a great "offiong" dance was held in the townplace. It began about 9 o'clock, and was attended by persons of both sexes, and of all ages, from the grey-haired elder who, leaning on his staff, talked of old times with old cronies under the trees, to the small naked youngster who with a band of playfellows tried his best to copy the antics of the young men.

There was no moon, but a pile of branches and dried grass was lit in the middle of the clearing, and replenished from time to time, and the people danced round it. The flames, now lighting up the circle of dancers and the varied foliage of the trees, and now expiring, produced a very picturesque effect. This dancing was a slow movement in a sort of cakewalk fashion, and they chanted rather than sang. Every now and then, one, who considered himself an expert, left his fellows and executed a pas-de-seul inside the circle. When one chant was ended, a voice from the throng would "set" another, and the others pick it up, and then the drums join in. The band was inside the circle, and consisted of four "obodum" and two "ibit" drums.

I had my chair placed on a little knoll from which I could see over the dancers' heads. Towzer lay beside me. Amo, Akpan, and our boys joined in the revels. Also the Abams, who could be easily picked out from the circling crowd by their superior height and size.

After watching them for an hour or so, I left the revellers and retired to bed, and was soon lulled to sleep by their monotonous drumming and chanting. When I awoke just before dawn the singing had ceased, but the drummers were still at it. They were finishing up with an orchestral performance, including some quite intricate measures.

The day following these orgies was devoted to much-needed rest. Otu and Towzer had had the good sense to retire early, so the former was in a fit state to attend to my wants. The less said about my other servants the better. Akpan did not show himself the whole day, and I found that Amo was better left alone. He had made friends at the dance with one of the Abams, and when I got up I found them both asleep on the verandah of my compound.

Later on, the Abam awoke and I entered into conversation with him, both of us speaking somewhat "broken" Ibibio.

"I should like," I said, "to visit the Anang country, and pay my compliments to your queen. Her fame has reached to my own land far away across the big sea."

"How is that?" he asked with surprise. "No white man has ever entered the Anang country, and we are far from the countries through which white men's trade comes to us."

"Long, long ago," I replied, "many generations ago, a white man visited the queen who was then ruling over the Anangs. He died at Iboku [Old Calabar], but he sent to his people a message telling them of the queen. He also sent home a staff like yours," pointing to that in his hand, "and he said that the queen's people used a certain mark. I will show it to you."

Then I produced a sketch of the "marke" on Arthur Riversley's strip of cloth.

"It is our nsibidi [private mark]!" he exclaimed. "See I have it here," and, pulling aside his ikiko-skin, he showed me a cicatrice or scar of like pattern on his right hip. "Only we of the queen's bodyguard may have it," he added.

"Have you never," I asked, "heard of this white man's visit to the Anang country?"

"It was not a white man," he replied. "It was Abassi Himself. All the Anangs know of it. He had a white skin like yours, but his hair curled and was long like an ekpo's. He came down from heaven, and visited the queen, and then suddenly disappeared. It was He who taught us to do this," pointing to the "parting" down the middle of his hair. "After His departure, the name of the queen's village was changed from Abak to Ikot-Afia-Ete [the people of the white father]."

"Is your queen ever called Adiaha Makara [the eldest daughter of the white man]?" I inquired.

"No," he answered; "but she is sometimes called Adiaha Abassi [the eldest daughter of God]."

Now Amo's mother had told me that Adiaha Makara was an occasional title of the Anang queen. Probably the old lady's memory had played her false. She had never really recovered from the loss of that favourite parrot at Lagos!

"You may be right," I said diplomatically, "but I heard it was a white man from my own country. It happened, however, very long ago."

"Did Abassi," I continued, "leave anything with the queen as a proof of his visit?"

"Yes," replied the Abam, "when He went away He gave her a ring, and said, 'Wear this till I return. It is a proof of my love for you and your people.' But, alas! He never returned."

I was becoming excited, but managed to maintain outward composure.

"And is this ring still worn by the queen of Anang?" I asked.

"Yes," he answered, "it is the most valued jewel of all. The queen has many fine cloths, and great wealth in beads, but this ring surpasses them all. It is green in colour like the grass."

"What!" I cried. "Green, did you say? Are you sure it is green? Isn't it blue like the sky or this cloth?" touching the strip of cloth to which his matchet was attached.

"No," he replied, "no, it is green, green as the grass and the leaves. Of that I am quite sure."

The careful Reader may perhaps remember that the ring given by King Edward to Walter de Riversley was a "Turquoise-Stone of a rich blue Colour set in Gold and having the royal Badge or Device of a Griffin."

Here was a shock for me! "Am I really on a mere wild-goose chase?" I asked myself. "Perhaps—nay, probably—Arthur Riversley was wearing several rings, and gave the queen one in which I have no interest. I can hardly believe that he would give her the famous heirloom of his family. Yet his written message calls it 'ye ringe.' Now, however, that I have got as far as this, I will not turn back. Quite possibly the old chronicler may be wrong, and quite possibly my informant here may be wrong."

"I should like to visit your queen," I repeated. "I have lived in this country for several moons. I can understand and speak the language, and I have learnt the customs of the people. I am a medicine-man; these Ikonos will tell you that I have cured many people by my skill. Would not your queen be pleased that I should visit her? Have you no sick people?"

"Many of the Anangs are sick," he replied, "but I do not know if the queen would like to see you. I will ask her. She follows in all things the advice of her three wise women."

On the following day the great meeting broke up, the Ikonos returned to their respective villages, and the Abams also de-

L

parted. Amo's friend promised to send me a message in a few days' time.

The Anang prisoner whom we had captured at Ikot-Idem town-place had expected to be eaten by us! The treatment he received was therefore a pleasant surprise to him. I had had him carried to my compound, and every day I dressed his wound, and doctored him for the fever which accompanied it. Okudi was his name, and he had a rather intelligent face. On becoming convalescent, he followed me about like a dog, and said he wanted to join my service. For some reason or other he took a dislike to Amo, and then the latter reciprocated it. Amo, being a Yoruba and a Mohammedan, looked down upon these pagan "bushmen," and was much too apt to show his scorn.

Averse from bickerings in my own little household, I got rid of the boy as soon as he was recovered of his wound. He did not want to go, and attributed it to Amo's influence. However, I sent him back to his own village, and told him to warn his people not to meddle again with me or my men.

Three days after the departure of the Abams, the promised message arrived from Ikot-Afia-Ete. It was to the effect that the queen would be graciously pleased to welcome me at her capital, and would send her bodyguard to meet me at the Kwa Ibo river at a place called Ikot-Osúrua. The two messengers would guide me there. The queen had sent forth runners to every Anang village through which we should pass, warning them that I was her guest, and that the roads were to be cleaned ready for me.

When Akpan heard that I was really about to go into the notorious Anang country, he expressed so many misgivings, and seemed so full of fear, that I decided not to take him with me. With Amo's help, I could now get on quite well without an interpreter. I therefore paid off Akpan and his boy Ima, and sent them back to Use with the remainder of my livestock, enjoining them to take charge of all my cattle and goats until my return to Itu.

Of my original following, there now remained only Amo, Otu, and Towzer.

Chief Esien was genuinely sorry to part with me. He had been a thoroughly good friend, always straightforward and sincere, and I—or, rather "Hardy's Hair-Dye"—had saved his life, for at any rate another year. We exchanged parting gifts, he giving me a fine leopard's skin, and a number of metal bracelets of native manufacture, and I giving him a meerschaum-pipe and a hundred heads of tobacco. He and all "the King's sons" accompanied me to the very edge of the Ikot-Abassi boundary. I shook hands with him in English fashion, and also with the plump Akama, now the happy husband of Nwa.

"Come back to us," they cried, and, climbing the hill on the other side of their stream, I shouted to them, "I will soon return."

On the previous afternoon about 3 o'clock there had been a small tornado followed by a heavy fall of rain. On the morning of my departure, the sun was shining joyously, a gentle breeze blowing, and all Nature looked greatly refreshed after the welcome rain.

The winding path took us through fields of yams trained to climb along cords of fibre, attached to trunks of palms, or to branches of the "ukang-ukot" shrub, just like ropes to a may-pole. In among the yams grew strong clumps of maize, the gourd, pumpkin, koko-yam, etc. Where it led us through villages, it was shaded by wine-palms and eben-trees, the latter a beautiful sight with its white bark and clusters of pink dates in striking contrast to the dark-green foliage. Then the water-tree with umbrella-shaped leaves, tapped for its sap when the season is unusually dry.

The flora of the Ibibio country is inferior to that of rural England, and the luxuriant greenery of the bush almost smothers the few blossoms that do venture to flourish. The vivid-blue pea which had bloomed freely during my stay at Use was no longer to be seen, but I noted the yellow marigold (in blossom all the year round), the magenta rock-rose, the yellow flower of the cotton-plant, a bush with bunches of bright scarlet blossoms, and quite a galaxy of mauve flowers, including a lovely vetch, the convolvulus, and the leafless crocus.

A tree, blown down by the wind, lay across the path, and, as we climbed over it one of my guides said to the other, "A man's soul lived in it; and, now that it has fallen, he is dead."

Every village contained several "ngkweme" or spirit-houses, erected by the roadside for the temporary abode of the spirits of departed friends. They are of two kinds—lofty with a gable-shaped roof for men, and low and long with an almost flat roof for women. They are never built over the grave, but are quite independent of the corpse, which lies elsewhere in some neighbouring grove.

The men's structures vary in height from fifteen to even forty feet; at the back is hung a curtain made of pieces of cloth sewn together in patchwork fashion; and in front, attached to a frame of poles and "bamboos," or placed on the ground, are all the utensils most valued by them while alive. Here also are deposited the skulls of animals sacrificed, the gin-bottles emptied, and the sticks of fish consumed, at the funeral. They represent the funeral-bill displayed for the spirit's inspection—"Behold how much we have spent for the good of your soul, and, beholding, leave us in peace."

A woman's spirit-house is far more elaborate. Sometimes it is divided with strips of painted matting into many small pigeon-hole compartments, and therein are placed her market-baskets, and cooking and other household utensils. Sometimes a long hut-like structure is built, and its walls white-washed inside and out, and thereon are painted, in black, yellow, and red, either intricate geometrical patterns, or representations of men, animals, and inanimate objects.

The back of a man's "ngkweme" is usually concave, so that between it and the cloth curtain there is a small apsidal or simicircular space. The back consists of a framework of poles and "bamboos," covered with palm-leaf mats.

It had been arranged that we should spend the night at a place called Mbiasu, an Anang village about twelve miles south-south-west of Ikot-Abassi. Something, however, happened to upset this arrangement. Our guides were by no means certain of the route, and, soon after we had passed from the Ikono into the Anang country, it became pretty evident that the queen's orders for cleaning the roads had not been carried out. They were mere tracks, in many places only eighteen inches wide, fringed with grasses and weeds, and every now and then obstructed by a fallen tree. They all looked alike, and, about 3 o'clock in the afternoon, when we had marched ten or eleven miles, the guides admitted that they had lost the way. The Ikot-Abassi carriers, who had agreed to take my loads as far as Mbiasu, were equally ignorant of the road.

"Push on," I cried, "when we come to the next village, we will get another guide."

After pushing our way for an hour or so along a bad over-grown path through low bush, but not so low that we could see over it, we caught sight of some huts half-hidden in trees on a hill, and decided to make for them. We crossed two small streams, and then ascended the rather steep hill. We passed an open juju-house by the roadside. An old man sat therein, but, on seeing us, he walked away and paid no attention to our questions.

The two guides were at the head of our line, then I, and then Amo. It was beginning to grow dusk under the trees, and I am rather short-sighted. As we neared the top of the hill, the path improved, and I saw before us a small circular town-place. Just as we entered it, the guides seemed to disappear, and I found myself at the head.

At that moment Amo called out, "Look, sar, dem man go shoot you! Look dem gun lib for his hand!"

I looked, and there under the trees on the opposite side thirty yards away stood several men, one of whom held a gun pointed straight in our direction. Had I been less short-sighted, I might have seen him earlier, and I *might* then have turned or moved to one side. Had I done so, he would undoubtedly have fired at me. Seeing me, however, immovable—for I had stopped short on hearing Amo's exclamations—he was so astounded that he lowered his gun.

Then, taking off my white helmet, I waved it in the air, and, walking into the town-place, sat down on the bank, and instructed my men to do the same.

Several other men joined the group under the trees, and stood looking at us. Our guides were nowhere to be seen. I tied my white handkerchief to my walking-stick, and planted it in the middle of the clearing.

Then I said, "I am the white doctor who has been living at Ikot-Abassi with Chief Esien. I am on my way to visit your queen. Her Abam soldiers are to meet me to-morrow at Ikot-Osúrua, and she has sent messengers to tell all her people of my visit. We have lost our road. We want to sleep to-night at Mbiasu. Please give us a guide to that place."

They came forward and stared at me, but said nothing.

"You seem afraid of me," I continued. "I am a peaceful man, and mean you no harm. Call your head-chief to come here, and I will explain further."

Then one of the men answered, "Our head-chief will not come here to see you. You must go to him. He lives in another part of our community."

"Very well," I said, "lead on, and we will follow."

So my carriers replaced the loads on their heads, and we followed three of the men. We were all unarmed. There was not a gun of any kind among us, and the two revolvers were locked up in one of my boxes. We had become so long used to living unmolested among the Ibibios, and we had believed ourselves to be going on such a safe journey, that we had actually forgotten the existence of the revolvers.

I walked behind the three men, and Amo just behind me. I could not catch what they were saying, for there is a slight difference between the Anang and Ikono dialects. Amo, however, understood them.

"Sar!" he cried in a tone which somewhat astonished me, "we all go finish now, they go kill we!"

"Nonsense, Amo!" I said. "Why do you think so? I see

nothing dreadful. We have got on all right so far. Surely you are wrong."

"*No*, sar," he said with emphasis. "I no be wrong. We all go finish dis time. I sabby what t'ing dey say."

"We shall get through all right," I said. "Tell the carriers to close up, and to walk quickly."

Our leaders were going along at a good rate. We came in sight of a market-place where stood about half-a-dozen men with guns.

"I t'ink dey go kill we here," said Amo.

Keeping as close as possible to the man immediately in front of me—a small active middle-aged fellow whom I took to be a minor chief—I shouted out to these men, "We are going to see your head-chief. Come with us."

They laughed by no means pleasantly, and fell in at the rear of our line.

The road we were following was fairly broad and well-kept, and gradually ascended a hill. Nearly half-a-mile after passing through the market-place, we saw before us a village and another town-place over which an enormous cotton-tree predominated. Just before we reached it, there was a commotion among the carriers behind me. Apparently, their loads were being taken from them.

"Let us hurry up and see the head-chief," I cried to Amo.

We entered the little town-place in safety, and I made straight for a small shed which stood at one side. It was similar to "the shed of the shades of ancient fathers" at Use, but contained no prostrate clay figure. Inside, there were several boys making baskets. On my approach, they rushed out at the other end, leaving their work scattered about on the floor.

I stood outside with my back against the gable-end of the shed. Amo was on my right, almost behind me, then Otu holding Towzer, and then the score or so of carriers, all of them mere boys. Their loads had been taken from them, and were now being piled up in a heap at the foot of the cotton-tree.

Thirty or forty men and boys had followed us from the hamlet where the adventure had begun. Many of them carried guns or brandished matchets, and they were all greatly excited. Others were running in from the road along which we had come, and others were joining them from the village to which the three men had led us. The basket-makers returned with other boys, and took up a position at my back inside the shed.

Then they crowded round us in a semicircle three or four deep, pressing so close that the nearest almost touched me. Behind them, in the open space around the big tree, some of the most excited did a sort of war-dance, presenting their guns as if to fire, or waving their matchets wildly in the air. They were of a very low type—skinny, ill-made, all but naked savages, their faces as inferior as their bodily physique. Some had daubed white and yellow pigments on their foreheads and chests with a particularly diabolical effect; some had bones and teeth hanging from their dirty necklaces; one man, whose face, if I had been born with "nerves," might still sometimes haunt me, had a bulging eye, only one ear, and a long-fanged yellow tooth bound to his right temple by a cord so tight that it was eating into the flesh.

This evil-looking crew gazed at me as if their salvation depended upon it, all the time jabbering, and disputing, and pushing one another.

"And you sometimes wake up in the dead of the night and see again their fiendish faces and hear again their discordant yells?" inquires the sympathetic Reader.

"Thanks very much," I reply, "I am sorry to disappoint you; but no, indeed I don't. I sleep always uncommonly well, and do not indulge in dreams."

I stood perfectly still with an expressionless face, returning their gaze with compound interest, but wondering all the while whether they would despatch me with gun, matchet, or in some lingering fashion peculiar to themselves. No, I didn't see all the events of my life pass before me in a flash as orthodox people should always do on such occasions; but, somehow or other, though with due appreciation of the humorous absurdity of the difference between stately Whitehall and my squalid surroundings, I thought of King Charles the First, who "nothing common did, nor mean, upon that memorable scene," and it certainly bucked me up. (Please pardon the slang.)

It is far better, I thought to myself, to die thus, than to rust out, and eventually die in my bed like a cow in the straw. I have had a very full life, there is nothing I regret, and, after all, what is death but a passing from one phase of life to another. If it were not for those two or three people at home whose life my death will darken, there would be nothing in it at all.

Then there floated across my memory the verse of a song which Pleasance used to sing:

"La vie est brève,
  Un peu d'espoir,
 Un peu de rêve
  Et puis—bon soir."

I could hear the tones of her voice, and see her face

illumined by soft candlelight in one corner of the Riversley drawing-room.

Then in a flash—all these thoughts had occupied my brain only a few seconds—life became very dear, and I strained my wits to their utmost tension. Were not Amo, and little Otu, and faithful Towzer, and all these carrier-boys dependent upon me? They were in my service, I was the cause of bringing them into danger, and I was therefore responsible for their lives. They, too, had homes and friends who would grieve for them.

Amo was trembling in every limb. As the basket-making youths behind us were unarmed, and seemed peaceably inclined and mere spectators, he had ceased to protect me in the rear, and had advanced to stand at my right side. He was a head taller than all the crowd, and most of them were too excited to look up to his face. I was glad of this, for his inability to restrain showing his fear was doing our cause no good. An expression of abject terror was on his face, and his very lips were trembling with it.

He began to speak to them very volubly, so volubly that I had difficulty in following him, especially as he used the Anang dialect; but, from a word understood here and there, and from the movements of his hands, I saw that he was imploring them to have mercy upon us.

"This will never do! I must give the situation a different turn," I said to myself.

So, laying my hand on Amo's shoulder, I said with a smile, "Come, old fellow, you must not talk like this. You and I have got safely through all sorts of troubles, and shall get safely through this. Don't show fear. Be a brave man, and buck up!"

He turned his face to mine with a pitiful attempt at a smile, and said, "O sar, dey go kill we! We all finish dis time!"

Then, holding up my hand to command attention, and using the Ikono dialect, which they understood, I addressed them as follows:

"I don't know why you are making all this noise. We are not come to fight with you. I am the white medicine-man who has been living at Ikot-Abassi. I am on my way to visit your queen at Ikot-Afia-Ete. She is expecting me, and has sent her messengers all over your country to tell you to receive me well. If you do us any harm, she will send her Abam soldiers to punish you. They are waiting for me not far from here. I fear nothing, and, if you kill me, my ghost will give you no end of trouble. Where is your head-chief? Call him, that I may speak to him."

My speech had, I could see, a favourable effect upon them.

Taking advantage of it, I spread out my arms, saying, "come, clear off, you are smothering me and my men."

My tone, that of one who quite expected to be obeyed, produced the desired result, for they moved somewhat further back.

Just then I saw looking round one of the huts a face which seemed strangely familiar, though it was disguised with dabs of clay and pigments. It was Okudi, the Anang boy whom we had captured at Ikot-Idem, and whom, after his cure, I had sent back to his own village.

I called to him, but he at once disappeared.

CHAPTER XVI.

ON THE PILLAR OF TORTURE.

Just as Okudi disappeared, the head-chief himself arrived upon the scene. He was a determined-looking old man with a satchel slung over his back, a matchet at his left hip, and in his right hand a curiously-barbed spear with a carved handle.

The crowd made way for him, and I held out my hand and smiled. He grasped it, and had a good look at me.

"I visit your town in peace," I said, "but your people treat me like an enemy. What does it mean? I am the white doctor whom your queen is expecting at Ikot-Afia-Ete."

The chief planted his spear in the ground at my feet, and, pushing his way through the crowd, went up to the big tree, and broke off a branch. Then he returned, and, shouting out words which I could not understand, began to hit out right and left with the branch. The crowd fled before him, laughing and shouting, but undoubtedly in flight. He ran all over the town-place driving them before him, and in a very few minutes had dispersed all the armed men who had come from the hamlet, leaving only those who belonged to his own village.

It was now nearly six o'clock. Darkness would soon be upon us, and we did not know how far from Mbiasu we were. It would be best to spend the night with the apparently friendly chief who had driven off our assailants.

"Thank you," I said, again shaking him by the hand. "You have done well. Night is coming on. We cannot continue our journey. Will you show us where we may sleep here?"

"Come," he said.

He took us to his own compound, just at the back of the shed against which I had been standing. A high fence separated it from the town-place, and I rather suspect that through it the old man had watched the whole proceedings. The carriers' loads had been left untouched. The only thing missing was one of two live fowls which a boy had been carrying; and, during the scrimmage, the other fowl had been killed.

We all climbed over a stile into Chief Okut Akan's compound, and he directed his people to prepare a certain hut for me. Meanwhile he conducted me into his own hut and gave me a goatskin to sit on. Several elders of the village were there, and other men and boys crowded in until there was no room for anybody else. The head-chief then brought me a white fowl, and asked me to accept it, and to drink palm-wine with them.

"Some of my people have behaved ill towards you," he said. "They belong to my community, but are a different family. Their late chief was younger brother to my father. Their present chief is a young man, and they are all wild and troublesome, but they fear me because I am a great juju-man."

"I will forget their bad conduct," I said. "Perhaps they were only playing with me, but such play is not good, and I am sure that your queen will be angry when she hears of it."

My host looked troubled. "I beg you," he said, "not to report it to her. I drove them away from you, and had no share in it. If the queen hear, she may send her Abam soldiers to trouble us."

"Very well," I replied; "you helped me, so I promise not to tell her of it. I accept your gift, and I will drink palm-wine to show I bear your people no ill-will."

So we went through the usual procedure, and it seemed to give them satisfaction.

Then, surrounded by an interested group of the chief's nearest relatives, I had a refreshing wash and changed my clothes in the yard.

Later on, the hut was declared ready, and I went inside to see about the arrangement of the bed. Amo was there, and he and I had a few minutes' private conversation together.

"Well, Amo," I said, "we're safe, you see. I told you we should get through all right. Do you feel happier now?"

"Me no sabby, sar," he replied, unable to shake off his late terror. "Dese be bad bad people. Me no sabby what t'ing dey t'ink for do."

"But surely," I said, "you don't think they will trouble

us any more. This old chief drove them away, and he seems quite friendly. What is it you fear?"

"Me no sabby, sar," he answered, and I could get nothing else out of him.

I went round to see the carriers. They had behaved extremely well in keeping so quiet, and showing no panic whatever. They were lodged in a hut somewhere behind mine. They seemed to have quite forgotten the unpleasant half-hour we had gone through, and were cooking food with their usual cheerfulness.

Then I had a warm "tub" inside my hut, and then dinner, and then went to bed, feeling too tired to bother about anything more. For security's sake, Amo, Otu, and Towzer were sleeping on the floor of my hut. My loaded revolver was under my pillow, and I had given Amo his.

I slept soundly, but awoke at dawn with a hazy impression that I had dreamed of hearing a cry and a shot. Peering out through the mesh of my mosquito-net, I could see Oto curled up on his mat, and Towzer sleeping at his head; but where was Amo? He had placed his mat near the door, but, though it was shut, there was no dark form on the yellow mat.

"He is gone out to look round, or to see to the carriers," I said to myself, and, turning over, I had another little nap.

Otu waked me up with a cup of cocoa in his hand.

"Good morning, Otu," I said. "Where is Amo? Call him, please."

"Me no sabby, sar," he answered; "me no look Amo dis mornin'."

Slipping on a coat, I went out. It was a fine fresh morning. Outside stood a little knot of the chief's family, looking curiously at me and my belongings.

"Good-morning," I said. "Where is my tall servant? I want him."

They shook their heads.

Just then Chief Okut Akan came up, and we exchanged greetings. I repeated my question to him.

"I don't know," he said, "but perhaps he is gone with my messengers to tell the Abam soldiers that you will reach Ikot-Osúrua to-night. I told them to go at daybreak."

"No," I said, "I don't think so, for he would not have gone without first telling me. He must be somewhere about the compound."

I went to the carriers' quarters. They were all astir, cooking more food. None of them had seen anything of Amo. I was beginning to feel alarmed.

On returning to my hut, I carefully looked around. His mat and pillow still lay on the ground, but the revolver was gone. I had seen him put it under his pillow before he went to sleep. In a corner stood his walking-stick; and the breeches, singlet (vest), and leathern belt that formed his usual attire were on the top of one of the boxes. At night he wore only a strip of cloth round his loins, but enveloped himself from head to foot, according to the fashion of his country, in a voluminous wrapper of some dark-blue material. This wrapper was missing. I concluded, therefore, that he had left the hut during the night, taking his revolver with him. But why? This I could not answer.

An hour passed away. It was now 7 o'clock. Amo, however, had not returned.

At 8 o'clock the chief came to me and said that, in order to reach Ikot-Osúrua before nightfall, it was necessary that I should start at once. He would give me carriers from his village, and would send the Ikono boys safely back to Ikot-Abassi.

"I cannot leave this place," I said, "until I find for certain where my servant is gone. I feel sure he did not accompany your messengers. If evil has befallen him, I will bring the Abam soldiers to punish those who have harmed him. I refuse to go from here until I see him."

Their faces were vacant of expression, but I thought I detected a boy smiling behind his hand.

The village was very quiet. Women and children went about their usual daily routine, and a few old men sat in the compound talking among themselves, but there were remarkably few young men and boys. Chief Okut Akan said they were all at work on the yam-farm.

I grew very restless, and kept wandering out into the town-place and a little way up and down the roads, but took care not to go far from our night's quarters. At first they watched my movements rather carefully, but, after a while, they grew tired of it, and left me to myself. I had my field-glasses with me, and swept the whole neighbourhood with them, for Okut Akan's village was on a hill.

It was a very hot day, one of those sultry days that betoken the near approach of a thunderstorm.

In the middle of the afternoon, my attention was attracted by seeing vultures from different part of the country all flying towards a grove of trees which stood on a hill in the direction of the hamlet where the man had pointed his gun at me. I wondered why they were all going in the same direction. There must, I thought, be something special to attract them. Then, all of a sudden, something seemed to tell me that their movements were connected with Amo. At first it came as a shadowy presentiment, but this grew gradually stronger and stronger, until at last I had a horrible mental vision of Amo hanging head downwards in that grove of trees suspended by a brass rod passed through his heels, with a flock of vultures pecking at him.

I was alone, and apparently unobserved. I thought of returning to the compound for my revolver, but, fearing to attract attention, did not do so.

Instinct showed me the road. I followed the previous day's path as far as the market-place where Amo had thought they were going to kill us, and then, leaving on the right the hamlet whence we had come, proceeded along a path to the left, and, crossing a little stream, saw the grove of trees on a hill in front of me only a quarter of a mile away.

I had walked very fast, and had seen nobody at all. After crossing the stream, I went cautiously, avoiding the road, and creeping from bush to bush. The hillside was clothed with clumps of bush interspersed with tall dry grass. As I drew near the top, I heard occasional shrieks of laughter I proceeded more and more cautiously, and crept away from the road towards the back of the hill. On getting to the summit, I found myself in a thick grove of palms and other trees. In front of me was the back of an "ngkweme," a man's spirit-house. It was about thirty feet high and ten broad. The thatched back was ruinous. I entered where the leaf-mats had fallen away, and then there was only a cloth curtain between me and the open town-place. The cloth was rotten from long exposure, and I had no difficulty in making a small opening where two squares were sewn together. Through this peep-hole I looked, and this is what I saw.

On a clay pillar in the middle of the clearing stood Amo, and around him in a circle squatting on the ground were two or three hundred youths and boys with bows and arrows in their hands. The sun breaking through a rift in the trees was shining full upon Amo.

The pillar was of red clay, unpainted, about five and a half feet in height, and having at its thickest part a circumference of about ten feet. This became gradually smaller near the top. which was quite flat. At one side were two square mounting-holes, one above the other.

Amo wore nothing but his scanty loin-cloth, which was so arranged that he was quite naked behind, except for the narrow connecting band passing between the legs. His ankles were fettered together, but the chain permitted him to have his feet as much as a foot apart. His whole body from the neck downwards had been smeared with some oily substance, which made his skin shine like highly-polished metal, and brought into prominence the great muscular development of his arms and back.

The young devils sitting on the ground were baiting him, and greatly enjoying their sport. His body was the target for their arrows. These, as the Reader may remember, were not of the long iron-tipped variety used by some tribes in war, but slender sharp-pointed canes about a foot long, feathered with leaves. They make little round holes in the skin, and of course draw blood, but, unless they enter the eye, or are shot with great force and at near quarters, do not cause serious injury.

These youths were shooting their arrows at Amo, but taking care not to hit his head. Half-a-dozen of them were sticking in different parts of his body, which must have been punctured all over, for blood was dripping and trickling off him. To add to their sport, they had provided him with a little wickerwork shield, eighteen inches long by twelve broad, and had left his hands free.

They did not all shoot at the same time, but took turns in leisurely fashion, three or four shooting together from different points of their circle. Amo afterwads told me that they had been at it for many hours, having begun a long time before noon; that when one set of boys had wearied of it, another had relieved them; and that the points of the arrows were smeared with honey so as to attract flies to the wounds made by them!

Flies of all kinds were buzzing around him, and his weary attempts to keep them off were causing his tormentors much amusement. His chief endeavours were to protect the front of his body. His back and lower parts behind had suffered most, and he was therefore most pestered by insects where he could least get at them. Several arrows stuck in his shoulders where he could not pull them out. Whenever he used his hands at the back of his body, they shot at the front part of his thighs and at his breast. Several arrows had grazed his cheeks and drawn blood.

He moved round on his pedestal, and thus from time to time faced all parts of the circle. His eyes, poor fellow, were full of an expression of agonised fear and pain, but I could see that he was still sane.

"Water!" he cried. "Give me water. I am dying of thirst."

His cry startled the vultures perched up aloft in the branches of the trees, waiting for their turn to come. Several of them, fearless because never harmed by the natives, were prowling about on the ground outside the circle of boys.

Then one of the tormentors, who had been sitting with his

back to me, rose up and walked round the pillar, and stood where I could see his face. It was Okudi.

"Ungrateful little devil!" I said to myself. "So he is at the bottom of all this!"

"Ha! ha! my friend," he cried, "your long body makes a grand target for us; you have given us plenty of sport. You're the fine fellow who scorned us 'bushmen,' and thought yourself as good as a white man. We have taught you to look down upon us—from this pillar! Do you still refuse to speak?"

"Water! Give me water," cried Amo, "and I will answer you."

Then another boy brought a calabash, and Okudi, fixing it at the end of a long pole, thrust it into Amo's hands. He eagerly snatched it, and gulped some of it down his throat, but quickly gave a cry.

"It is full of salt!" he exclaimed. "I will not speak unless you give me water."

They all shrieked with laughter. My blood boiled. I longed to have them all by the throat and strangle them.

"No, no, my friend," said Okudi in a mocking voice. "All day long you have refused to give us the information we require, so we are not going to give you anything, not even water. Unless you answer our question before the sun go down, we shall finish you off, and get what we want in some other way. Your master, 'the great white doctor,' as he calls himself, cannot escape us. Will you answer us?"

Amo folded his arms, but made no reply.

A young fiend, who looked about ten years old, stood up, naked as he was born, and, shooting his arrow, hit Amo full on the right knee.

He stumbled, and almost fell off the pillar.

"Take care," called out Okudi, "it's not a soft bed to fall upon!"

I looked, and saw that all around the pillar, to a radius of ten feet, they had covered the ground with the glass of broken gin-bottles. The lower parts were buried in the earth, with their jagged edges sticking out. Had Amo with his fettered feet attempted to jump from the pillar, he must have cut himself fearfully on this "bed."

There he had stood in the broiling sun, hour after hour, thirsty and exposed, tormented with arrows and stinging insects, and fearing lest at any moment he should overbalance himself and fall headlong on to the broken glass. It is a wonder to me how he had managed to keep himself from going mad.

Then there came a rumble of thunder from far away in the north-eastern distance.

"We must finish our job quickly," said Okudi, turning round on his companions. "I think a great rain is coming."

Then looking at Amo again, he continued, "We give you one more chance, but it is your last. Tell us by what magic your master, the white doctor, protects himself from us, and tell us how we can kill him so as to prevent his ghost from troubling us, and we will let you go. We will take an oath with 'mbiam,' so strong that he who breaks it shall not live to bury his mother. Will you answer?"

The sun, a glowing ball of fire, was sinking lower and lower in the heavens.

Amo had thrown away his shield, and stood as still as a statue with his arms folded across his chest.

"Will you tell us?" Okudi reiterated.

Amo shook his head.

Their arrows were nearly all expended, but twenty or thirty boys had at least one left, and, at a given signal, they shot together from around the circle. Amo, hit unexpectedly in different parts of his body, and almost dead with pain, fear, and exhaustion, lost his balance and fell.

The boys shouted, and I, in my momentary anxiety, cried out, but fortunately was not overheard.

He tottered and fell, and apparently they all thought he must fall on the bed of broken glass, for they scrambled up and rushed forward to it. Just in time, however, he recovered himself, and so swayed his body that he fell across the top of the pillar on his back with head and shoulders hanging over. The pillar was at least five and a half feet high.

Again there came a rumble of thunder, and this time considerably nearer.

"Let us finish," they all cried. "The hole is ready. Perhaps he will tell us when he sees what we have prepared for him."

Then they removed enough glass to clear a little pathway between them and the pillar, and six of them took Amo from his perilous position, and, carrying him along, laid him on the ground. He seemed unconscious, so they flung water over him. At last he groaned and sat up. Fortunately, no arrow had been sticking in that part of his back on which he had fallen. If there had been one there, it might have been forced into him and injured him internally.

They hurried through the next act of their programme Carrying him, two at his shoulders and two at his feet, they brought him towards the spirit-house where I was hid. Some twenty feet in front of it was the mouth of a small hole with the earth out of it lying heaped up all around.

They brought Amo to it, took off his fetters, tied his arms behind him, plucked out an arrow from his left thigh, and, taking him under the armpits, dropped him into the hole, and held him in a standing posture, so that just his neck and head appeared above ground. At first he stood with his back to me, but, one of the youths crying, "Let us make him look at old Chief Akarafo's 'ngkweme,' " they turned him round to face me.

His eyes were open, but whether he was still sane or not I could not determine. His face was smeared with blood, and his tongue protruded.

Then they shoved in the earth, but did not stamp it down very tight. They had, as will be afterwards seen, a reason for this. It covered his shoulders and came almost up to his chin. Then these devils—the word is most appropriate, so I must use it—smeared his face with something which I afterwards found to be honey, and placed a bowl of water just in front of him.

"Drink," said Okudi, pulling his victim's tongue, "we give you plenty of water now." They all laughed.

"Let us cover his head with a pot," said one of the boys. "There are several big ones in the old chief's spirit-house," and, so saying, he began to advance to the place where I lay hid.

"Stop!" shouted another. "If we cover up his head, he won't be able to see them coming."

So the first boy turned his back on me. I had had a narrow escape from being discovered, for these pots, three or four of them, were all *behind* the curtain!

Then they smeared a number of long "bamboo" poles with honey and palm-oil, and laid them on the ground from each side of Amo's head to the edge of the town-place.

Some of the crowd, weary of their "sport," were already gone, but the majority had remained to see the whole programme duly carried out. They now, however, took their departure, shouting, and laughing, and saying how hungry they were.

At last only Okudi and another young man remained.

Okudi said, "I shall stay here till the little people come. I want to see how he'll like them."

His companion muttered something which I did not understand.

"You can go if you like," said Okudi. "I am not afraid of ghosts, and can stay here alone. But here comes food. Cook and eat it here with me before you go."

A small boy brought them plantains and a calabash of water, and then went away again.

M

They made a fire at a distance from Amo, and sat there roasting their food, and laughing over the day's events.

Amo moaned, but so faintly that they could not hear him.

A number of vultures swooped down on to the ground, but the two youths drove them away.

"Their turn isn't come yet," said Okudi with a laugh.

Then his companion left him.

The moon appeared through a break in the trees, and flooded the scene with her silver light.

Okudi lit his pipe, and, strolling up, squatted down opposite his victim.

"Ha! my friend," he said, "if it hadn't been for you, I should have stayed with the white man, and got out of him what I wanted. Do you hear me?"

Amo moaned again.

"I can't see you well," continued Okudi. "We must have more light here. If I set fire to your hair, I shall see better."

He got up, and went over to the fire to fetch a light.

"Now is my time," I said to myself, and picked up the rusty barrel of an old gun which with other rubbish lay on the ground at my feet.

As I bent down, I detected that peculiar ammonia-like smell which denotes the nearness of "driver" ants, the black variety that march across the country in columns millions strong, biting to death every living thing that cannot escape from them. At once I understood the meaning of the honey on Amo's face, and of the trails of honey-smeared poles laid between him and the bush—it was done to attract these ants —they meant that he should be slowly bitten to death by them. It also explained why they had filled in the earth so loosely, for, had they beaten it down hard, it would have been impossible for the insects to reach his body below the head.

Okudi returned with a light, and he too at once detected the smell, for he threw down his burning stick, and, stamping it out, exclaimed, "The little people are coming. They don't like fire. I mustn't drive them away. It will be fun to see how my tall friend will welcome them. Do you hear?" he cried, pulling one of Amo's ears, and peering down into his face. "Don't you smell them? The ants are coming to finish you up!"

At that moment I knocked him down from behind with a blow of the iron gun-barrel, and he fell prostrate without a word.

On the other side of Amo's head, and within two yards of it, the whole ground was alive with myriads of moving black forms. The ants had, according to their frequent procedure, broken up their various columns, and were marching *en masse* upon the human banquet to which they had been invited. They move very quickly, and are almost irresistible. If I wanted to save Amo from their clutches, there was not a moment to be lost. The little warriors were already at my own feet.

Snatching up handfuls of sand, I flung it along the ground against them, and kept at it until my arms ached. Then, having created a temporary diversion, I picked up the sticky poles, and flung them to the ants. Then, rushing up to the smouldering embers of the fire, I seized the glowing wood, and, rushing back, made a barrier of it between Amo and his would-be assailants. Ants will never cross fire.

Then I knelt down, and, putting my mouth to Amo's ear, called him by his name. A faint moan came in reply. He was still alive. Picking up the bowl of water, I held it to his lips, and poured a few drops down his parched throat. He opened his eyes, but did not recognise me.

One of the diggers had left his hoe on the ground. Taking it, I began with feverish haste to scoop away the earth from Amo's shoulders.

When I had got down to his breasts, I felt a sharp bite and turned. The ants had executed a flanking movement, and were attacking me in the rear. So, leaving Amo, I fought them again, pelting them with sand, and at last drove them back. They had almost reached the senseless Okudi. Though he richly deserved to be tortured by them, I had mercy upon him, and dragged his body out of their way.

At that moment large drops of rain began to fall, and a heavy shower followed close upon them. This was entirely in our favour: it would drive the ants to seek cover, and would soften the ground for my digging, besides proving very refreshing to the wretched victim.

Then I put all my energy into the digging, and little by little got the earth away from Amo's body.

Meanwhile, clouds swept across the sky and darkened the moon, and thunder pealed in clap after clap, accompanied by flashes of vivid lightning. The refreshing rain was swept across the clearing, and ran in streams into the hole where I was working.

When I had scooped out the earth as far as his loins, he reeled to one side, and his head fell on to his shoulder. I feared for a moment that he was dead. He moaned, however. The rain was bringing him back to consciousness.

Having scooped out a little more earth—I was now lying on my stomach while I worked—I decided to try pulling him out. I had not yet loosened his hands.

Pushing him so that his back rested against the edge of the

hole, I put my hands under his armpits, and tried to pull him out. He was very heavy at any time, heavier now because of his inertness, and his legs were still buried in the soil.

The rain was falling in torrents, and I was already wet to the skin.

I pulled and pulled, but could not succeed in moving him; so had to dig out more earth. I went down into the hole, and worked till I had freed him as far as his knees. Then, getting out again, I pulled once more, almost straining myself to pieces, and at last managed to drag him out of his earthy prison.

He lay on his back without any movement of life. I cut the cords that bound his wrists. They were cutting into the flesh. I poured more water down his throat, and wished fervently for my brandy-flask. I put my hand to my pocket, and there it was—I had had it there the day before, and had fortunately forgotten to remove it at night.

I poured the brandy drop by drop down Amo's throat, and soon he stirred, moaned, and opened his eyes.

"It's I, Amo," I said. "You are all right now. Try to sit up."

He, however, was not yet conscious. He continued to moan, and to move his head from side to side.

His limbs and body were cold. I took to rubbing them, and the pain I thus caused his wounds did more than anything else to rouse him. I gave him more brandy, shook him, and eventually, slipping my arm round his shoulders, half dragged him up into a sitting posture. He opened his eyes again, seemed to recognise me, and said, "Dey go kill me, sar, but me no fit for tell dem nothin'."

"All right, Amo," I said. "It's all finished now. You are quite safe. I am here with you alone."

Little by little, for he was very dazed, he at length regained consciousness, and seemed to understand when I told him we were still in danger, and that he must exert himself to escape before daylight.

Then, leaving him for a few minutes, I returned to where Okudi lay. His heart was beating, but he was still quite stunned from my blow. Tearing his cloth into strips, I bound his feet and his hands, and, dragging him along, pushed him into the hole, and left him there. I replaced the old gun-barrel in the spirit-house, and threw into the bush the cords that had fettered Amo's wrists. There was nothing to show who had struck Okudi, or how Amo had managed to get out of the hole.

I had noticed on the other side of the clearing a half-ruinous woman's spirit-house, large enough to shelter us from the rain, now beginning to abate. I managed to drag Amo on to his feet, and, he leaning on me, we crossed the town-place very slowly, and I helped him inside, and made him lie down in the only dry part of the little building.

CHAPTER XVII.

"OUT OF THE FRYING-PAN INTO THE FIRE."

I consulted my watch. It was 8 o'clock. Night in the tropics is always long—there were nine hours before daybreak. It was quite unlikely that anybody would visit the town-place during the night, for, besides their fear of meeting ghosts and "idems," the weather would keep them indoors. The storm had passed over, but rain was falling very persistently.

Thinking that Okudi might perhaps regain consciousness, and call for help, I returned to the hole, and tied a cloth gag over his mouth. He was safe from ants, for they would not venture out of cover until the day broke, when in all probability some of his companions would arrive to see what fate had befallen their victim.

Then I bestowed all my attention upon poor Amo. He was terribly weak and exhausted. I gave him more brandy, but he was more in need of food, for he had eaten nothing since the previous evening. Meat was out of the question. Even if I had had a gun, and dared risk rousing the neighbourhood by using it, it would have been 999 to 1 against my bagging anything, for game does not grow on the bushes like blackberries, even in West Africa. Comfortable stay-at-home people, who rave about the "luxuriant productiveness" of tropical vegetation, imagine that vegetables and fruit are everywhere so abundant that all the traveller has to do is just to put out his hand and take them. Well, to put it shortly, they are quite wrong.

What was I to get for Amo? The yams in the fields would not be ready for several months, and I dared not run the risk of visiting a village to steal from a stack of the last year's crop. I walked round the clearing looking in the dim light for a clump of plantains, but was unsuccessful. At last, however, my foot kicked against something round, which, picking up and smelling, I found to be an orange. There were two trees, growing side by side. Pulling down a branch, I gathered and bit into one of the fruit, but found it to be of the bitter variety. The other tree, however, yielded sweet oranges; so, gathering some, I took them to Amo. He ate half-a-dozen, and they helped to revive him.

Then, using one of the spirit's clay bowls for a bucket, and also one of the deceased woman's old cloths, I washed the honey and blood off his face, and then proceeded, very gently and carefully, to wash the wounds which covered his whole body. Though it must have pained him a good deal, he made no sound, but bit his lips once or twice. In one corner I had made a small fire of some of the dry rubbish lying about. Then I induced him to stand outside propped up against a tree-stump, so that the rain might cleanse and refresh him. His arms gave him considerable pain, for they had been tied tightly behind his back and kept in that position by the earth pressed down upon and around them.

Crossing over to the ngkweme from which I had watched him being tortured, I tore down a large section of the cloth curtain, and carried it over to Amo, who, after drying himself at the fire, wrapped himself in it, and lay down to get a little sheep. I, meanwhile, took off my wet clothes, and tried to dry them at the fire, but without much success.

Just before midnight the rain ceased, and the moon and stars reappeared. It was important that we should get far away from this place before the return of day.

I waked Amo. He seemed very dazed, and groaned with stiffness and pain, but I at last made him understand the situation. We then discussed it in all its bearings. We were entirely ignorant of our whereabouts, not knowing even the name of Chief Okut Akan's village. All we knew was that Ikot-Afia-Ete, the Anang queen's headquarters, lay about a day's journey to the south-west. Had we been certain of the road, we would have returned to Chief Esien's country.

There were Otu, Towzer, and the Ikono carrier-boys to be considered, but it would have been most fool-hardy madness to return to the compound for them. Even if Amo had been in a fit state to fight, we were unarmed and therefore powerless. The best thing to be done for their safety was for us to reach a friendly village, or join the Abam soldiers, and bring force into operation for their recovery.

Chief Okut Akan had been a friend to us in need, and he evidently stood in fear of the queen's wrath. We might trust to him to take care of the boys. It was, however, very unpleasant to feel that our plucky little Otu and faithful Towzer were in the midst of enemies.

We decided to push on.

"Come, Amo," I said, "you are better now, and can walk with my help. I will give you an arm, and you can have a long stick in your other hand. Come, we must stay here no longer, but take to the road and try to reach a place of safety before dawn."

So we set out.

I had got into my clothes again, but they were very wet and uncomfortable. I should have done better to have carried them, and made a temporary covering of more of the curtain from the old chief's spirit-house.

We were a ghostly-looking pair—Amo's tall figure, enveloped from head to foot in the patchwork wrapper of cloth, chiefly light in colour, and I in breeches, grey shirt, and white pith helmet. I felt quite prepared to make unholy noises if any night-prowler should meet us.

We went slowly at first, but the cool air—much cooler after the storm—and the delightful feeling that he was actually free again, and had escaped the horrible fate from which escape had seemed impossible, gradually put more vigour into Amo, so that, after the first mile or two, we accelerated our pace, and proceeded at the rate of three miles an hour.

Avoiding villages as much as possible, and thereby of course making our journey more circuitous than it need have been, we kept to the least narrow roads, and at length arrived at one lately cleaned.

"This must be the road we should have followed the other day," I said. "These people have cleaned it according to the queen's order."

"Me no sabby, sar," said Amo. "Me no t'ink dese people fit for obey dem queen. Dey all be bad too much. S'pose we go back for Ikot-Abassi, dat be good, sar."

"I agree with you," I replied; "but we don't know the road. Let us follow this, and see what it leads to."

A mile further on we began to descend, and then came to a river crossed by a rickety bridge.

"This must be the Kwa Ibo," I said. "If so, the queen's village lies somewhere on the other side. It is deep and rapid, but not so broad as I expected to find it." (I afterwards learnt that this was the Onio just above its junction with the far larger Kwa Ibo.)

We managed to cross safely, and then took half-an-hour's rest on the right bank, I sitting, and Amo lying down, in a little shed built there for the convenience of fishermen. We had, up to that point, happened on no human being whatever, but, passing through one village, we had seen torches moving about among the trees, carried by people searching for snails—the large edible snail called "ekwong." During the day they cut a rough track through the bush and strew it with certain leaves which attract the snails at night.

On resuming our journey, we soon became involved in a network of paths, and, eventually, went—as I afterwards discovered—north-west instead of south-west.

After having covered altogether about twelve miles, Amo declared that he could go no further. He would have fallen several times if I had not supported him. Want of nourishing food, and the terrible experiences of the preceding day, had combined to make him as weak as an invalid.

"Lef [leave] me, sar," he exclaimed. "Me no fit for walker no more. Me tink me lib for die. Lef me, sar, and go away plenty quick from dis bad bad country, I beg you, sar!"

"Nonsense, Amo!" I replied. "I am certainly not going to leave you. You and I must stick together, and come out of it all right as we have always done. Take another little rest here, and then we'll go on to the next village, and try our luck with the people."

"You be all same bruder for me, sar," said Amo. "S'pose dey go kill we, me t'ink my ukpong [spirit] go for same place what your ukpong go for, sar. Den one dey we come back for here, and we fit for humbug dese people *plenty!*"

"All right," I answered, "we'll die together if die we must, but, first of all, we'll do our utmost to live together. You must buck up and help me."

We had left behind us the hilly country which prevails in the eastern and north-eastern parts of the Ibibio district, and were on the table-land which extends over all the remaining parts.

After my companion had had another short rest by the roadside, I made him get up again, and we went onward at a very slow pace.

Just as the darkness was fading before the approaching dawn, we entered a village and halted in a little clearing under the trees. In the middle of it lay the various drums of an "offiong" orchestra, indicating that probably the villagers had been dancing there during the early hours of the night. On one side, against the trunk of an "otinsak" —a tree with reddish bark and green orange-like fruit, growing in clusters on its trunk, and containing a substance used for bird-lime—stood on end the "bamboo"-and-mat roof of a hut with its inner side turned to us. We sank down on the grass beside it, both of us thoroughly worn out.

Amo lay at full length wrapped up in his patchwork garment, and at once fell asleep, but as quickly awoke, moaning, and calling for water. I found some in a clay saucer at the foot of an awbawti-tree, and we both drank. I sat up, my back leaning against the framework of the roof, and Amo lay with his head on my knees. For a few moments I drowsily

watched the first shafts of light stealing into the little clearing, and then my head drooped, and I knew no more.

I was aroused by a sharp exclamation, and, opening my
eyes, saw a figure kneeling on the ground poring over Amo.
It was an old man with a patch of white painted round his
left eye. He had pulled aside Amo's wrapper, and seemed
to be fingering and examining his loin-cloth. Then he crept
on his knees up to me and peered anxiously into Amo's face.

"No," he said to himself, "it cannot be. This man is not
of our race. He has none of our marks upon him, and yet he
wears the sacred symbol of my deceased mother. How can
this be? They are both strangers, and one has a skin like an
Abiriba. Perhaps they are messengers from the spirit-world,
sent to me by my sister Adiaha." (The Abiribas are a family
or sub-tribe of Ibos whose skins are sometimes very light-
coloured.)

"Greeting, friend," I said. "Was the mother of whom you
speak called Adiaha Ediaw Ituen, and did she live at Ikot-Afia-
Ete?"

The old man jumped up and stood before me, trembling all
over.

"Fear not," I said, "we are men like yourself. We have
come from a far country to visit you. We come from your
sister Adiaha, who is still alive. This man," touching Amo,
"is her own son, and I am his friend."

Then the old man dropped on to his knees, and touched the
ground several times with his forehead.

"It is Abassi returned to us!" he exclaimed. "Who else
should know that my mother was Adiaha Ediaw Ituen, and
that she lived for a while at Ikot-Afia-Ete?"

"You are right," I said, "but tell it to no man. We are
both sick, and very tired after our long journey. Take us
secretly to your own compound, and let us rest there until
we feel able to deliver our message."

The old man stood up on his feet again.

"It lies over there," he said, pointing through the trees. "It
is not far distant, and it stands alone. Only my wife and
our two sons are there. Come quickly before the village is
astir."

So I laid Amo's head on the grass and got up. I felt very
ill and tired, and had difficulty in standing upright. I, however, pulled myself together, for our lives were probably
dependent upon my attitude.

"Adiaha's son is too sick to walk," I said. "We must carry
him. You take his feet, and I'll take his head."

He was very heavy, but somehow or other, we managed to
lift him, and, the old man leading the way, we stumbled along

with our burden. We had to lay him down several times before we reached the compound, but at last we did reach it —a small, compact square of huts standing alone on the edge of a great yam-field.

A woman and two young men were there, and stood transfixed with amazement on seeing us.

"Explain to them," I said to my guide. I was almost at the end of my tether, and could hardly get out the words.

Then the old man explained it all to his wife and sons.

"We are very sick and weary," I gasped out, "and my friend, Adiaha's son, has been badly used by an enemy. He wants medicine on his wounds. My clothes are wet. Please give me a dry cloth to wear. We can tell you nothing further till we are well again. Keep our arrival here secret from everybody. Otherwise, trouble will come upon you. We are. . . ."

Then I felt myself falling, and heard the crash of my fall, but was conscious of nothing else.

*　　　*　　　*　　　*　　　*

During the period indicated by the above five asterisks, I lay in that little compound in utter unconsciousness of all that went on around me, in the throes of a raging fever. Amo, who, as soon as he awoke from the long sleep into which he had fallen, nursed me through it with untiring devotion, said to me afterwards:

"Plenty days you lib for talk fool palaber, sar. Me no sabby what t'ing you say. One big word you say too much often. Dat be 'Ribersley.' Me t'ink dat be for juju, sar? Sometimes, me t'ink you die one time, sar. Den me say, 'S'pose my white bruder no lib, me no lib.' Big knife lib for my hand, sar, me fit for . . . " and he drew his hand across his throat.

"How do you manage to keep people away from the compound?" I asked.

"Dem old man," he replied, "dem man what say he be bruder for my muder, he tell ebery man dat his son be sick for 'mfatitu [¿he small-pox],' so nobody no come, sar."

Malarial fever, however, comes to an end like all other things. Those who have been blessed with a good constitution often recover from even the severest attacks, but—well, it is such a terrible enemy that, unless science can altogether expel it, West Africa will never become "a white man's country." Nature has made it a black man's country, and Nature probably knows what is best.

On regaining consciousness, I found Amo at my side. He gave me a drink of water—knowing what I had always done, he had insisted on having the water boiled before giving it to me—and helped me to sit up. I lay in a room about fifteen feet long by nine broad. It was clean and neat. The walls of light-brown mud were perfectly smooth, as was also the hard black floor. In one corner was a fireplace with "bamboo" fender, and above it a shelf for pots and calabashes. On a row of wooden pegs let into the wall hung various articles —a satchel, a string of cowries, a head of maize, a gourd-cup, an old cloth, a bow, and so on.

"Well, Amo," I said, "I think I've been very sick. How are you? How are your wounds?"

"O, sar," he cried, "me be plenty glad you lib for talk agen. Me be glad too much! Dem woman gib me good medicine, sar. Me no be sick no more."

His wounds were, indeed, all but healed. The negro recovers from wounds and cuts far more quickly than the European.

Amo gave me soup several times during the day, and on the following morning I had an interview with the old man who had befriended us.

Both parties entered into explanations. His name was Ekandem Ituen. He was son of Adiaha Ediaw Ituen, and therefore brother to Amo's mother. His mother had been for a few years queen of the Anangs, but had been deposed on losing her weight. Finding us sleeping on the grass in the early morning, he had carefully examined us, and had found, attached to the string of beads which Amo wore round his loins, the pendant given him on Calabar beach by his mother. It was this that had procured us such a friendly reception.

The old man made much of Amo, for Adiaha had been his favourite sister, and, during my illness, Amo had recounted to his uncle all the history of Adiaha's slavery and life in the Yoruba country.

I could see, however, that he regarded me with anything but favour. My illness and weakness had banished his pleasant theory as to the return of "Abassi," and I suspected he had by now heard from his neighbours of the white doctor who was travelling through the country.

It was about ten days since we had left Ikot-Abassi. Surely the Abams awaiting us at Ikot-Osúrua must have been making inquiries for us.

I asked our host.

"No," he replied, "we have heard nothing."

"Is the queen's place far from here?" I said.

"Yes," he answered, "far off, so far that I don't know where it is." He glanced at me suspiciously.

On the third day after my return to consciousness, he informed us that news of our presence had—he did not know how—got abroad, and that a "stranger" wanted to see us.

"He is living here with the Inokuns," said Ekandem. "My grandfather gave them land here, and they have a large compound."

"Do they come from Ibum [Aro Chuku]?" I asked.

"No," he replied, "they are from Obinkita, a village near Ibum. They trade with us and buy slaves."

"I did not like the way in which he looked at me.

"Who is this stranger?" I inquired.

"I don't know," the old man answered, "but he says he knows you, and has been looking for you. He does not belong to this country."

Probably, I thought, it is Akpan. Yet it was unlike him to venture into the dreaded Anang country.

"He will come here this afternoon," added Ekandem, turning round and walking away.

Late in the afternoon a crowd of people entered the compound, and stood staring at Amo and me—who were sitting in the shade of the eaves—and laughing and talking among themselves.

They were superior in all ways to the Ibibios—of better physique, of greater intelligence in the face, and infinitely better dressed. They were, in fact, very well dressed, quite as well as natives at Lagos and Old Calabar, and their attire was picturesque, and the colours blended well with one another and with the hue of the wearers' skins. There were as many women as men. One carried a sleeping baby in her arms, but the most conspicuous was a girl in a cloth frock with a pattern of great yellow butterflies all over it. Their coiffures were quite extraordinary, and two ladies who stood together had three rows of raised cicatrices beginning below the chin and running down the body between the breasts.

"Greeting," I said. "If you are come to visit me, you had better sit down over there out of the sun," and I pointed to the verandah at right angles to where we sat.

They laughed and said nothing, but looked back as if expecting somebody.

"Here he comes!" they cried.

Suddenly a man pushed himself through them, a man with only a stump where his right hand should have been—*Ikong!*

A feeling of great relief came over me. "He is come to our rescue," I said to myself. "He has heard of our predicament, and, remembering how I saved his life at Use, is come here to help us in our present need. I will quote this as a lesson to those who told me that the negro was never grateful!"

I looked up with a smile. "Well, Ikong," I said, "how did

you get here? I am pleased to see you. I suppose you heard we were in trouble, and came to help us out of it?"

For answer, he walked slowly up to me and spat in my face!

Amo sprang up in a moment, and, hitting him straight between the eyes, knocked him over sprawling on the ground.

The next instant, however, two stalwart Inokuns caught Amo's arms, forced them behind his back, and pinioned them there. He struggled and tried to free himself, but more men fell upon him, and quickly bound his feet also.

I rose, but two men pushed me down again, and sat on on each side of me grasping my arms.

"Put them together," said Ikong.

So they lifted Amo and sat him with his back against the wall next to me. Then they formed around us in a semi-circle, Ikong standing in the middle.

"Caught at last!" he exclaimed. "This man," pointing to me, "pretends he is come here to establish trade between you and the Efik traders, but his real object is to get to know all about your country so that he may return and bring soldiers to conquer it. It was he who cut off my hand," holding up the stump, "and it was his tall servant," pointing to Amo, "who ate it afterwards. They meant to kill me, but I escaped. I have followed them here, and now I will have my revenge."

So we were out of the frying-pan into the fire!

"This man lies," I began. "Listen to me, and I will ——"

But one of the men who held me, and who seemed to be under Ikong's commands, put his dirty hand over my mouth and silenced me.

"Do not listen to him," Ikong continued; "he is a great liar. I am come here to save your tribe from him, and you must help me. It is not often you get a white man to sacrifice. I want a good price for him. The tall man is very strong. He would make a good slave to work in the lead-mines you have told me of," and he turned to one of the Inokuns."

Here Ekandem Ituen interposed. "The tall man is my sister's son," he said, "and wears the sacred charm reverenced by all Anangs. I will not have him sold. He will stay here, and live with me. I care not what becomes of the white man; I am quite willing to sell him. I found him, so he belongs to me—not to you," speaking to Ikong.

Then a great hubbub arose, Ikong and old Ekandem disputing, and the latter's family and the Inokuns joining in. They chattered like a colony of nsiat-birds building their nests in a grove of palms, and once or twice they got almost as far as blows.

Eventually, however, they agreed among themselves that Amo should stay with his newly-found uncle, and that the Inokuns should buy me for ten thousand manillas (about thirty guineas in English money), payable in six months, and to be divided equally between Ikong and Ekandem Ituen. Some stinking "mbiam" was produced on which they swore in mutual agreement, and the Inokuns sent for, and paid on the spot as earnest-money, one thousand manillas to each of the vendors.

Then they drank gin together, Ikong sitting on a little stool opposite me, leering at me with his ugly goggle eyes, and every now and then spitting in my face.

"I give you compliments, *sir*," he said in English, with mocking emphasis on the last word. "I have at length eventually circumvented your peregrinations. You cannot escape the pleasant death these aborigines are preparing for you. 'Idem-Inyang' is enjoying his revenge, the savour of it is sweet unto my nostrils, sweeter also than honey and the honey-comb!"

"You d—— ungrateful hypocrite," I began, but the dirty hand stopped my words, and then they gagged me and carried me off. I heard Amo's voice shouting, and saw him struggle to get at me, but my captors hurried me quickly away.

CHAPTER XVIII.

I BECOME A SLAVE.

I was carried to the Inokuns' quarters, and there they ungagged me. It was a large, well-kept compound, with goats, pigs, and dogs running about in the central yard. I could not, however, see any indications of furniture or mode of living superior to what I had noticed among the Ibibios. The higher intelligence of these Inokuns had made them wealthier than the indigenous people in whose country they had settled, but they expended this wealth upon their persons. A few young mango-trees flourishing by the side of the road leading up to the compound were, however, a sign of "foreign" occupation.

They treated me well, permitting me to sit on the verandah so as to enjoy the cool breeze, and taking pains to give me good food. I was, nevertheless, carefully guarded. They all understood and could speak the Ibibio tongue, but among themselves they spoke Ibo, of which language I knew nothing. When I addressed my guards, they shook their heads and smiled.

I did not see Ikong there. That night I slept in a little inner chamber, confined with leg-irons, but in other respects fairly comfortable.

Early the next morning they waked me, and told me they were going to market, and that I was to go with them. At my request, they brought me water to wash with, and they gave me food before we started. Rain fell all the way to the market, and they lent me a European umbrella! In spite of the rain, the market-place was full of people, but they were sheltering under the trees and under the thatched roofs of two or three open-sided sheds.

A little crowd gathered round to stare at me, and, having nothing else to do, I counted the varieties of "umbrella" under which they took refuge. Those of the smart set, including of course my Inokun owners, were provided with cheap European articles; well-to-do men of conservative principles who disliked innovations carried, balanced on their heads, a large circular structure of plaited palm-leaflets; a few women-and youths of an adaptive turn of mind kept off the rain with a thatching-mat, taken from the reserve stock which all good householders should have; and, lastly, there were some of the poorer sort, and many little naked urchins, holding over themselves a koko-yam leaf, or a plantain leaf, or even a branch of foliage broken off some tree.

The Inokuns permitted no liberties to be taken with me, for I was their *rara avis*, for whom they had paid a great price, and on whom—as it soon transpired—they intended to make a big profit.

The rain having abated, business recommenced, and the place soon became a buzzing hive of trade. I was led round to a particular section of the market which, had they understood the alphabet and indulged in the fashionable vice of advertisement, would have been labelled "SLAVES." Seated on the ground in three rows were a score or so of persons of both sexes, but chiefly women and children, who were for sale just like any other commodity there.

A large proportion of them owed their captivity to a pernicious custom which prevails throughout the Ibibio country, namely, that of avenging an injury, not on the aggressor, but on a third person, who as often as not has neither participated in nor had knowledge of the evil deed for which he is made to suffer. He, in his turn, avenges himself on a fourth party, who perhaps retaliates on a fifth, and so it often happens that a very small crime—the trespass of a pig, or the theft of a few yams, for instance—may be the eventual means of stirring up strife between half-a-dozen villages. When you thus avenge yourself on an innocent third party, you are said to do it "against" the owner of the straying pig, or the man who stole your yams.

I recollect an example which was brought to my notice while at Ikot-Abassi. On 7 February a woman A of K was seized by B of L, because on 25 January a woman C of L had been seized by D of M, because five years previously D's pig had been killed "against" a brother of the husband of the said C of L, because he had committed adultery with E!!!

Another instance was as follows. The bush of the village of R adjoins that of the village of S. Some people of R were burning their bush prior to clearing an area for yam-planting, and the wind carried the flames on to the S bush, but no real damage was done, for the people of S intended to shortly burn that identical piece of bush themselves. It, however, was an excuse for a quarrel, so the S people went to R and killed "against" the burners of their bush a goat belonging to W of R, who had *not* been present at the burning. The S people took the goat home and ate it. W was naturally much upset at losing his goat merely because some of his fellow-villagers had accidentally been the cause of the burning of the S bush. Instead of avenging himself on these fellow-villagers, he gathered together X, Y, and Z, furnished them with loaded guns, and led them to the S yam-farm to seize two children in revenge for the goat. The S people were unarmed except for their matchets and farming implements. W and his gang seized two children. While getting them away, a fight ensued, and five of the S people were shot or otherwise wounded, two very badly, and a month later one of them died of his wounds. Then a state of war obtained between these two villages. The origin of it all was that blast of wind which had carried the fire from one bush to another!

This pernicious custom, which, however, is the law of the land handed down to the people by their much-revered forefathers, keeps the whole country in a constant state of petty warfare and reprisal. Women and children go to market in fear and trembling, and nobody ever feels safe.

Their seizer hurries them off to a place of concealment, which is generally not his own village, but another allied village some distance away. Usually a period elapses before they are sold, for their husbands or fathers may prove willing to redeem them, and the seizer is by no means averse from opening negociations.

The captives hardly ever attempt escape, for the simple reason that they do not know the road home. They have never ventured outside their own village boundaries, and so are absolutely ignorant of the surrounding country. If they should take to the bush, a worse fate might befall them.

Pray, gentle Reader, restrain your tears, and also your imagination. These captives are invariably well treated, and they are almost always indifferent to their "fate." It is, after all, only a change of ownership, and they lead just the same life as they were leading before. Women and their children are the husband's chattels. The children belong to him because their mother belongs to him, and not because he is their father. Often he isn't. The woman is frequently quite glad to get a change of husband, and the children quickly adapt themselves to a new home. Those who most deserve your pity are the hapless husbands who have, often for some misdeed of which they are entirely innocent, thus lost the most valuable part of their little property. Probably they had invested all the hard-earned savings of their youth in the purchase of the wife. In losing her and her children, they have lost both capital and interest.

The captives squatting on the ground in Edet market were by no means the miserable-looking creatures that you, kind Reader, may have imagined them to be. Three or four were tired after a long journey, but they had all been well fed, and the women were reclining in luxurious ease, instead of haggling over petty bargains like the "free" women all around them. Some of the most presentable of them, conscious of their charms, were ogling possible purchasers. The children were quiet and somewhat frightened, for they had not lived long enough to have learnt that change is not necessarily an evil.

The Inokuns gave me an empty gin-case to sit on, and there I sat wondering what was in store for me. The fever had made me weak and thin. For the first time since I had left Old Calabar, I was quite separated from my men, alone in the midst of savages with whom deeds of atrocity were of almost daily occurrence, being, in fact, an important part of their religious system. All things considered, they were not, after all, nearly so much to be condemned as those religionists of Christian Europe—the inquisitors of Spain, and both parties in sixteenth-century England, for example—who used to torture and burn men and women simply because of a difference in creed. These reflections, however, did not then comfort me much!

My greatest comfort was the knowledge that Amo was free

N

and in the near neighbourhood, for I felt quite certain that he would do his utmost to rescue me.

The Inokuns wanted to sell me at a profit, and also to get rid of the responsibility of having a white man on their hands. Many purchasers looked at me, but the price was high, and there might be trouble with my ghost, and—well, I was a new commodity, and they would rather that somebody else should take the risk.

The owner of about half my fellow-slaves—I was now a slave!—was a plump and jaunty idiong-master, who, judged by the respect and attention generally paid to him, was a man of wealth and importance. He wore a pink-and-white loin-cloth, an idiong-ring round his head, and a necklace of black and red beads, with a small pendant hanging down behind. On his left wrist was an ivory bracelet, and over his left shoulder a strip of native white cloth, to which was attached a matchet in a light skin sheath. His right arm was quite bare.

He exchanged greetings with the Inokuns, but took no special notice of me, though I could see that he frequently eyed me, and kept his ears open to all that was said concerning me.

When the market seemed to be breaking up, he strolled over to where I sat, and asked a few questions of the Inokuns. Then I had to stand up, and, to my disgust, he pulled me about and felt my limbs, just as if I had been a horse or a bullock.

"He's very thin," he remarked. "We want a fat man to sacrifice and eat at our feast of new yams. This man has no flesh on him."

"He has been sick," said Ezume, the head of the Inokuns, "but is nearly well again. If treated well and given plenty of food, he would be fat by the time you hold your feast."

Then the idiong-master, who had already made up his mind to buy me, began haggling with my owners, and eventually they agreed to take five girls in exchange for me. I saw the damsels picked out and given over to become concubines to the Inokun men and handmaids to their wives, and so had the rare privilege of knowing the actual value at which other people rated me!—

> O wad some power the giftie gie us
> To see oursels as ithers see us!

It would have been mere waste of breath for me to protest. I was quite helpless. The best thing to do was to take it calmly, and hope for escape or rescue.

They drank a bottle of gin over the bargain, and politely

asked me to take a sip, but I declined their courtesy with thanks. Then they nodded to one another and parted.

My new master, whose name was Udaw Afia Udaw, called his half-dozen boys together, and we set off. They left my legs and arms free, but tied a cord round my waist, and I walked in front of the man who held the end of it. They all had guns except the idiong-master, who carried over his left shoulder an umbrella with the handle behind.

About a mile after leaving the market, we crossed, by a fairly good bridge, a river which was broader and deeper than any that I had seen since leaving Enyong. It was, in fact, the Kwa Ibo. Then we proceeded south-west, and walked five or six miles through a perfectly level country, and at length, just as the sun was setting, reached our destination.

I was given a good meal, and, at my request, they brought me a cocoanut, the milk of which I preferred to the muddy water they had provided. I slept in an inner compartment of my owner's hut, with my feet passed through a log, and fettered, as had been done with Ikong at Use.

The next morning the whole village called to inspect me. They offered me no incivilities, but, on the contrary, treated me with a sort of respectful awe.

"Abassi has blessed us greatly," said one pleasant-faced old chief, "in sending us this white man for our yam-feast. The white men are far wiser in most things than we—so those who have met them in the countries bordering on the great sea have told me—and those of us who eat of this man's flesh and drink of his blood will take some of his wisdom into our own bodies, and hand it down to our descendants. Abassi be praised!" and the venerable gentleman raised his eyes to the heavens.

"We must take great care of him," said another villager. "He is so thin now that, unless we can manage to put more flesh on his bones, I fear there will not be enough meat for all of us. The best morsels must of course be offered at the principal shrines throughout the community."

"Yes," said a third, with a wink, "'offered' certainly, but not necessarily left there. Let the deities consume the ukpong [soul] of the meat while we eat the flesh itself."

A grey-haired hag, who was my master's mother, and, therefore, a matron of rank and importance, gently requested me to stick out my tongue.

I complied, at the same time thinking that the old dame must be learned in medical symptoms; but I was far from the mark!

"It's a small tongue," she said with a sigh. "I always

think the tongue is the tit-bit of all, and my good son has promised me this man's, but, alas! it will be but a morsel."

A disrespectful beauty giggled, and said to a companion round whose neck her arm was twined, "Old mother Ankama has enough tongue of her own already. If she eat this white man's, there'll be no more peace for any of us!"

A tall, thin, cadaverous-looking worthy, who had hitherto remained silent, remarked, "Give the tongue to the women. For my part—and I speak from experience, for this will be the tenth man I have helped to eat—I much prefer the fingers. There's a flavour about them which reminds me of that delicious delicacy, a rotten crocodile's egg. Thin fingers are nearer that flavour than fat, and the bones make a very nice soup," and he licked his lips at the very idea of it.

Their remarks were hardly the most cheerful that could have been made, but this point of view did not occur to them. The more educated and cultured one becomes, the more points of view does one see at the same time, and so life is made very difficult and complex. These simple folk had not reached such a high standard.

Meanwhile, Udaw Afia Udaw and the chiefs of the village had a private consultation in their juju-house. I could see them from where I sat. Their debate was evidently full of knotty points, for it lasted almost until noon.

Then at length they dispersed, and the idiong-master, coming up to me, spoke as follows: "We have bought you at a great price, and for a certain purpose, and we cannot afford to lose this chance of benefiting our country. I mean we must kill and sacrifice you. For three years the yam-crop has been unusually bad. Last year we sacrificed three girls, but the crop was no better. Then I went into inam [seclusion], and, on coming out, cast lots, and the spirits of our ancestors told me that a white man must be sacrificed. Then I went to Edet market, and saw you there, and knew at once that Abassi had sent you to us. Do you understand, Makara?"

"Perfectly," I answered. "How long shall I be permitted to live?"

"I will tell you all," he replied. "Three moons will come and go before our annual feast takes place. Until then you will live and grow fat, and we wish to make your life as pleasant as possible. We are anxious, Makara, that your ghost shall not trouble us after your death. We hope you will understand our difficult position, and try to make it easier for us, and that, if we treat you very well, you will rest quietly in the spirit-world.

"We do not intend to put you in fetters, or to tie you up like a goat, but we shall take you to our sacred island, from

which escape is impossible. You will be supplied with plenty
of good food, and as much gin and palm-wine, and as many
cocoanuts, as you require, and, moreover, we have, after much
debate, decided to allow you three wives. In our village
are three widows whom nobody has yet bargained for. They
will live with you on the island, and cook your food, and keep
your house clean, and amuse you. More than this we cannot
do. Do these arrangements please you, Makara?"

This simple ingenuousness, the appeal to my sympathy, the
fear of supernatural retaliation, the determination to avert
at all costs a fourth bad yam-harvest—what a medley of primitive ideas to lay before a nineteenth-century Englishman!

Much might happen in three months. I would lie low
and think out a plan of escape. Surely Amo would take
action, and probably the queen would send her Abam bodyguard to effect a rescue.

So I answered, "I am not prepared to say anything. I
fear nothing, and am quite indifferent whether you kill me
or not. I have no power over my ghost. However well you
treat me, it will undoubtedly humbug you considerably if
you kill me. I have no more to say, except that nothing
will induce me to take the three widows. I would much
rather be shut up with three baboons. Please thank the
chiefs for their thoughtful offer, but please ask them to keep
all widows away from your sacred island."

Udaw Afia Udaw looked rather discomfited.

This sacred island—I speak from after-experience of it—
is of very small extent, fifty yards long by twenty broad. It
lies in the middle of the larger of two lakes situated in the
bush which extends west of the village. They are entirely
overgrown with the yellow-green "water-cabbage" which I
had first seen on the Enyong. These little plants cover the
expanse of water so closely that the effect is that of a well-
kept lawn—the water is nowhere visible. These lakes are
deep in places, but elsewhere are so shallow that wine-palms
grow therein. Their shape is irregular, and they have no
defined banks, but are surrounded by swampy ground.

On the day after my little conversation with the idiong-
master, I was led out of the compound, and then along a
narrow winding path to the edge of the swamp. Several
boys accompanied us, carrying bundles of leaves of a cactus-
like plant whose juice has a most pungent smell.

Across the fifty yards of swamp which separated us from
the edge of the cabbage-covered lake was a sort of bridge
or jetty of "bamboos" resting on piles.

Udaw Afia Udaw smeared the boys' legs up to the knees
with a green paste, and they then went along the bridge

strewing the cactus-leaves before them, and returned empty-handed.

Then he smeared his own legs with it, and also those of a tall young fellow, whom I afterwards called the ferryman, and of an old deaf and dumb man who had joined our party. They hoisted me on to the ferryman's shoulders, and, following Udaw Afia Udaw, and followed by the old man, he carried me along the bridge and put me into a canoe moored to the further end of it. The idiong-master and the old man also got into the canoe, which was chained to a post and secured by two heavy padlocks. It was full of the same pungent leaves. The ferryman produced keys and freed it, and then he paddled and poled us across the lake to the island—a distance of about 150 yards.

On one end of this islet stood a hut, and at the other end were one of the enormous silk-cotton trees so often alluded to in this narrative, and a little clump of plantains and orange-trees. All around the shore grew a thick hedge of the cactus-like plant.

They put me on the ground on the further side of this hedge, and all three of them led me to the hut. It had evidently been prepared for me, the roof had been patched with new mats, and it was clean inside. It consisted of two rooms, and these rooms contained hundreds and thousands of skulls. The hut was, in fact, the charnel-house of the neighbourhood. The walls were lined with them, neatly arranged on "bamboo" trellis-work; great bunches of them, covered with cobwebs and dirt, hung from the rafters, and the inner chamber was packed with them almost up to the roof. Goats' skulls were most numerous; next in number were those of men and women, and then followed a variety which would have furnished a learned scientist with enough material for a year's study and a ponderous tome.

"This is your dwelling-house," said Udaw Afia Udaw, with a sweep of his hand. "We have had it repaired and cleaned for you, and have provided you with a sleeping-mat, a stool, cooking-pots, and all things needful. This old man will remain with you to wait upon you. His name is Mbokk. He is deaf and dumb, but will soon learn to understand your wants. A supply of food will be brought you every morning by this man," pointing to the ferryman. "You will be frequently visited by me and the other chiefs. We hope you will eat plenty, and soon become quite well and fat."

Then he took me round the island. The fringe of swamp encompassing the lake was so full of wine-palms that no view was anywhere obtainable through them. None of them, however, grew within fifty yards of the island.

My guide pointed to the encircling expanse of cabbages. "The water beneath them is in some places very deep," he said, "and the whole lake is full of a small green snake, whose bite is most deadly. We have no cure for it. Long ago one of our forefathers discovered that they abhor the smell of this plant," touching the hedge of cactus. "He killed all snakes on the island, and planted this bush all round to keep them off, and since then the island has been free of them. We also have a medicine which, smeared on our skin, keeps them away. If you attempt to escape, the snakes will bite you. Abassi has given you to us, Makara. We must carry out his desire, but we will make the end of your life as pleasant as possible. Sometimes the boys shall come here to play and dance."

I of course thanked him for all these well-meant courtesies. Had I been a god, they could not have treated me better. I afterwards learnt that there survive among them traces of an ancient belief that the human victims whom they sacrifice and eat are temporary personifications of their deities, and that therefore the feast is looked upon as a solemn sacrament —the eating of the flesh and blood of a god.

Then they left me with old Mbokk.

Since then, I have never anywhere complained of feeling lonely, for no isolation can bear comparison with mine on that island. Every morning the ferryman came with food and water. He was always accompanied by two youths, who, during the handing over of the supplies to my keeper, stood with guns ready pointed in case I should attempt to board the canoe.

Udaw Afia Udaw and other local magnates occasionally paid me a visit, but, somehow or other, we did not make much progress towards sociability. They were always full of tender inquiries concerning my health and condition, but, in spite of it all, I did not wax fat. I am not made that way, and the awful monotony of my life and horrible fate awaiting me were not conducive to that cheerfulness of mind which tends to create flesh.

I induced Mbokk to teach me how to make baskets, and in the cool of the morning and late afternoon I did a little gardening, and all the while I of course turned over in my mind every possible means of escape.

CHAPTER XIX.

ESCAPE.

To add to the dreariness of my life on that island, the weather during the first week of captivity was most depressing. It rained persistently every day, and the air was full of mist and vapour. No sunshine appeared. Every evening, as soon as darkness began to set in, myriads of croaking frogs tuned up one after another, and sang melancholy dirges the whole night through.

There are no monkeys in that part of the country, but I often heard the cries of other beasts. The ferryman told me that a small variety of crocodile lived in the lake, but I never saw it. In the hottest part of the day, hundreds of long, thin-bodied, green snakes used to bask on the top of the cabbages.

Old Mbokk spent a good deal of his time in sleep, leaving me to my own devices. One day I noticed some long ropes of creepers hanging down from a branch of the great cotton-tree. Its trunk was too big and smooth to scale, but here was a means of climbing. So I pulled myself up hand over hand, and, at a distance of sixty feet from the ground, reached the branch. Then I climbed along it, and gazed around.

The result was disappointing. Encircling the lake was a fringe of wine-palms, never exceeding about thirty feet in height, and beyond them there stretched in all directions a perfectly flat country, covered with palms and bush, the monotony of which was absolutely unbroken except where here and there a cotton-tree reared its majestic head above the common level. I could see neither road nor dwelling—every sign of human occupation was concealed within the overwhelming mass of greenery.

Nevertheless, I continued this exercise every day. It was something to do, and it kept the muscles of my arms in good training.

Ten days passed away. Every morning I drove a little stake into the ground, getting the idea from some tale read in my boyhood—*Robinson Crusoe* or *Swiss Family Robinson*.

Deliverance, however, was near at hand.

The nights were dark. On the tenth night, about an hour after the last glimmering of day had faded in the western sky, I was startled by hearing a shrill noise, half whistle and half hoot, which seemed to proceed from the southern side of the lake. My keeper was of course quite unconscious of all sounds.

I stood out in the open. After a minute's interval, a shout was borne to me across the water. It came again and again, and at last I distinguished the words "All right." Then, making a trumpet of my hands, I shouted back, "All right." Immediately afterwards the same shrill noise was repeated, and then all was quiet again.

You may be quite sure that I did not go to sleep that night. We had an ample supply of fuel, so I made up a blazing fire, opened the door of the hut, and stood in the doorway dressed in my breeches and shirt and wearing my helmet, so that any friend—it must be a friend, I concluded—on the edge of the lake could see that the figure was that of a European.

I kept the fire blazing until daybreak, but of course did not stand in the doorway the whole time. Nothing, however, happened.

"They will come again now that they know I am here and alive," I said to myself.

Mbokk kept no watch whatever over my movements. He had been stationed there to wait upon me, not to guard me.

I slept during the day, and the next night I made a bright fire when dusk was falling, and, too restless to remain still, walked up and down the little island, and in and out of the hut.

About the same time as on the preceding night, the same shrill whistle came from the southern side of the lake, and was followed by the shout.

I shouted back "All right."

Then all was still. I stood there listening intently. Presently I heard a sound above the croaking of the frogs, a little splashing sound which came gradually nearer and nearer. It was that made by a swimmer.

"Good heavens!" I exclaimed. "Surely Amo isn't swimming out to me! He will be bitten by the snakes, and reach this island only to die on the shore. Yet how should he know of their existence?"

I was in an agony of anxiety.

The splashing came nearer and nearer, and at last a dark figure jumped over the hedge and rushed up to where I stood in the light which came through the doorway of the hut. It was indeed Amo.

We did not shake hands in the "Dr. Livingstone, I presume," style. Amo, in fact, gave me no opportunity to do or say anything. He fell upon me like a madman, and began to tear off my clothes.

"The snakes have bitten him, and he is mad," I thought, as I struggled to release myself.

"No plenty time, sar!" he gasped. "Dem Anangs hear me.

Dey lib for canoe. Dey come quick. No fight me, sar. Me put good medicine for your skin."

"The snakes," I said, "the snakes in the water have bitten you."

"No, sar," he replied, "medicine lib for my skin what snakes no like. Me bring medicine for you," and, so saying, he pulled a bundle off his back, tore it open, and began rubbing some mess on me.

His meaning suddenly dawned on me. He had obtained Udaw Afia Udaw's green paste, and so been able to swim across the lake in safety, and I was to escape by swimming back with him.

Just then another sound came across the water, from the northern side of the lake. There were voices, and a clanking which was undoubtedly that of unmooring the canoe.

Amo was rubbing the stuff on my back. I tore off my breeches and boots, and began rubbing it all over my body. The smell of the paste was very strong; it made me feel sick and almost smothered.

"Quick, sar, quick!" Amo exclaimed. "No plenty time. Dey bring gun, me t'ink. Shut eyes, sar."

I obeyed, and he smeared the stuff all over my face and head.

The sound of the paddles was now very near. They could see our forms silhouetted against the light of the fire.

Suddenly a shot pinged over our heads.

"Dis way, sar. Run!" cried Amo.

I followed him round to the other side of the hut.

"Me carry you, sar. Me fit for swim so," and he made as if to take me on his back.

"No, no!" I exclaimed. "I can swim it quite well. We shall go more quickly if we keep apart. Lead, and I'll follow."

So he pushed himself through the hedge, and I followed. He plunged into the water, and I did likewise.

The canoe grated against the shore of the island. There were several voices shouting and calling to one another.

Amo struck out, and I kept close behind. The water was not cold, but the cabbages somewhat impeded progress. Amo, going first, had more trouble with them than I. The sense of danger just behind us quickened our speed, and we were soon twenty yards away from the island. Turning my head, I could see several forms running hither and thither. Another shot was fired, but not in our direction.

"All right, Amo," I cried. "They can't see us. They think we're still on the island. "What's that? Look ahead of you?"

A light gleamed among the trees, low down, and about a hundred yards in front of us.

"Dat be my friend, sar," he replied. "He lib for help we. He fit for show what place we swim for."

So we made straight for the light.

The water was warm, I hadn't a shred of clothing on to encumber me, and I was buoyed up with the excitement of the escape.

As we approached nearer and nearer to the fire—it was a fire of brushwood—I could see a man bending over it. He stood on a tiny islet formed of tussocks of grass and reeds strengthened by the roots of half-a-dozen palms. He pulled us up on to the bank, and then I saw that he was the young Abam with whom Amo had made friends on the night of the offiong-dance at Ikot-Abassi.

We were all three stark naked, and smeared all over with the green paste, and Amo and I had water-weeds and bits of cabbage clinging to our bodies.

"Quick!" exclaimed Amo. "No plenty time, sar. We fit for go long way dis night."

He and his companion lighted taper-sticks at the fire, and gave me a long stout walking-staff. The Abam led the way, I followed, and Amo brought up the rear.

Our leader plunged into the water on the other side of the islet, and we followed him. It came up only to my waist.

After wading slowly through some fifty yards of this swamp, the water seldom coming higher than our middles—once, however, I sunk over my head into a hole—and more often no higher than our knees, we at length reached dry land.

A little shed stood under the trees, built for the accommodation of those who came to tap the wine-palms. Here the Abam and Amo had left their clothing and matchets. The former resumed his ikiko-skin, and the latter, cutting his fibre loin-cloth into two, shared it with me.

Then Amo opened a gin-bottle which was half full of liquid, and offered it to me.

"What is it?" I asked.

"Gin, sar," said Amo; "no good for white man, but fit for make you hot inside."

So I swallowed some of it. It was very fiery, and exceedingly nasty, but it probably did something to keep the cold out of me and to invigorate me for the longish journey that lay before us. It was trade-gin. I had never "sampled" it before, and have never had occasion to do so since.

My two companions emptied the bottle between them, and then we set forth, but they first extinguished their torches.

We walked as quickly as the darkness permitted, I keeping

as near the Abam as possible. Whenever he came to a tree across the path, or to any irregularity in the ground, he politely stopped to indicate it to me.

It was one of those incongruously queer situations in which the educated, up-to-date Englishman of all periods of our history has always delighted to find himself. Here was I without the least outward mark of civilisation, my only article of clothing consisting of a scanty strip of "cloth" woven from palm-fibre, following through the mysterious depths of the West African bush a genuine savage, who would think as little of knocking me on the head as we at home think of killing a fox or an otter. True, I had my faithful Mohammedan servant with me, who had of course reached a far higher standard of culture and intelligence than the Abam, but, had *you* seen him on that particular night, I doubt if you would have called him anything but a "savage." He was as scantily clothed as myself, and the mixture of green paste and mud which covered him from head to foot made him look a real "wild man of the woods." Of all three, perhaps I looked the most "unpresentable," for here and there, where paste or mud had disappeared, there were patches of white skin visible, the general effect of which was to give me a leprous appearance. I am quite certain that any native meeting me unawares would have taken to his heels and fled.

Our guide seemed to have a thorough knowledge of the road, for without any hesitation he threaded his way through the network of narrow paths which covers all parts of that densely-populated country, avoiding villages, and also yam-farms, as often as possible.

After proceeding without a halt for what I judged to be nearly two hours, we took a short rest, and Amo briefly explained matters.

"Dem old man Ekandem Ituen like me too much," he said. "He no want me for foller you, sar. Dey keep me prisoner all dem night. Den me humbug 'em. I say, 'I no like dem white man. I glad you sell him. Now I lib for free, I sit down here, I work for you, you gib me wife, I no go away no more.' Den dem old man, he glad too much, he cut dem ropes what bind me. Den I sit down softly softly for three-four days. I 'tend I be sick, I sleep plenty, I listen for my ears. Den I hear man say what place dey take you for. Dey lib for talk about dem big water and dem bad bad snakes. I sabby dem snakes, I sabby medicine what dem snakes no like. I go for bush, I look plenty medicine lib dere."

"What is it?" I asked.

"Dem people call it otu," he replied.

"One day," he continued, "I lib for market. I meet my friend," pointing to the Abam. "He like me too much. We drink palm-wine. Den he say, 'What place dem white man lib for? Dem big woman what be chief for Anang, she send me eberywhere for look him.' Den I tell him ebery-t'ing. He say he sabby dem big water. So we 'gree for—for—"

"Rescue," I suggested.

"Yes, sar," he went on, "for rescue you. We walker softly softly, sar, we look dem canoe, but we no fit for take it. Dem locks be strong too much. Den I put plenty medicine for my skin, and I swim for you, sar. All finish."

These explanations ended, we continued our journey, and three miles further on entered a village, and soon came within sight of a little clearing wherein burned a fire, around which dusky forms were moving. They were chanting, but there was no music.

I expected the Abam to turn into a side path, but he kept straight on.

"Are they friends?" I asked, speaking over my shoulder to Amo.

"Yes, sar," he answered, "dey be dem Abam men."

Our guide shouted something to them, and they stopped their dancing and came to meet us. There were a dozen of them, and nobody else was there. The queen had sent them out on duty, and they were spending part of the night in the by no means unusual amusement of dancing by themselves.

They welcomed us in their own cheery fashion, and chaffed my two companions a good deal on their appearance. We were quite near the right bank of the Kwa Ibo, so they accompanied us down to the water and helped us to clean ourselves. In the excitement of the escape, I had given my bare feet hardly a thought, but on washing them I found they had sustained several cuts and scratches.

"Are we far from Ikot-Afia-Ete?" I asked.

"No, quite near," said Amo's friend, whose name was Chuku. "We will sleep here till the light begins to return, and then we will set out and reach the village long before the sun is at the top of the sky."

A sort of rest-house stood at one side of the clearing. They lignted a fire in the middle of it, gave me a mat in a corner, and, arranging their own mats on the floor all over the one room, lay there with their feet towards the blaze. They all had their guns beside them, but nobody in the Anang country would have dared to attack these Abams. After all we had gone through, I was very glad to get a few hours' rest and sleep.

Amo waked me just before daybreak, and, there being no toilet to make, we started at once, going, as far I could judge, in a south-westerly direction.

After walking about five miles, they pointed ahead to a grove of trees seen across a farm-clearing. It was Ikot-Afia-Ete.

"I can't go before the queen in this toggery," I said, touching my one and only garment. "You must please lend me some cloth."

"Chuku say," said Amo, "dat all your box lib for dem queen, sar. He say dey catch dem Chief Okut Akan, and ebery-t'ing. Me t'ink dey catch my two box, sar."

"Otu and Towzer also?" I inquired.

Receiving no reply, I looked round, and saw that Amo was holding an earnest conversation with Chuku.

"He go beg dem woman-chief for box, sar," he informed me, "but he no t'ink she 'gree."

"Tell him," I replied, "tell him to give my compliments to the queen, and to say that, according to the custom of my country, I cannot pay my respects to her in person unless I put on proper clothes. Tell him to say that the great White Queen who rules over all white men would be angry with me if I should fail to treat their own queen with all due respect."

Chuku departed with this message, and Amo went with him to point out what box it was that I wanted.

Meanwhile the other Abams conducted me to a compound at the entrance to the village, and there I sat awaiting the messengers' return. Women and children gathered around and gazed curiously at me. I felt something like what Captain John Good, R.N., of the eyeglass and dapper appearance, one of the heroes of *King Solomon's Mines*, must have felt when the ladies of Kukuanaland insisted on seeing his "beau-tiful white legs." But, alas! I had not even the "flannel shirt and a pair of boots" which the gallant naval officer was permitted to retain. The Abams, however, did not permit these people to approach me too close.

After waiting there until about noon, I was glad to see Amo returning, and, with him, carriers bringing the boxes on their heads.

"Dem queen no 'gree for long time, sar," he said, "she no like for gib we dem box. Den old woman, who be old too much, she talk plenty for dem queen. Den she 'gree, and Chuku show me what place dem box lib. Den I catch 'em and bring 'em, sar."

It was indeed pleasant to get into decent clothes again. I rigged myself up in a grey flannel suit, and had to wear a thick felt wideawake in place of the helmet left behind on the island.

Amo retired with Chuku and his precious boxes into one of the huts, and took a long time over his toilet. The result, however, was hardly a success. He had left Old Calabar looking like a magnificent brigand of romance, but he emerged from that hut in an attire which was "neither one thing nor the other." He himself, however, was evidently quite satisfied, and the Abams crowded round him with expressions of admiring envy; so of course I said nothing.

He had, with his friend Chuku's help, got himself into his exceedingly tight buckskin breeches, and as they would not now meet round the middle—for they had shrunk after his plunge into the Cross River to kill the crocodile—he wore a scarlet canvas belt. On his head was a long white "stocking" cap with a scarlet tuft at the end. He wore neither vest nor shirt, but had on a long-tailed dress-coat, which had of course been originally black, but was now shiny and green with age. With this costume, Amo assumed all those swaggering airs of a drum-major which had so delighted the fair ladies of Calabar.

We set out, Chuku leading, then I, then Amo, and then the Abams and those who carried the boxes.

I had quite expected to be taken straight to the royal compound, but, though we caught sight of it standing in a very large clearing, we were conducted to another compound quite half a mile to the left of it.

"Will not the queen see me to-day?" I inquired.

"Chuku no sabby, sar," replied Amo. "He say dere be sick old woman lib for dis compound what want medicine."

"Who is it?" I asked.

"She be old woman what lib always for dem woman-chief's house," he said.

We entered the compound, and I was at once led into a hut where an aged dame sat on a little stool crouching over a fire.

I greeted her with the respect due to old age, and asked her what ailed her.

She shook her head and moaned, but said nothing.

"It is dark in here," I said. "Will you come out on to the verandah, so that I may see you more clearly?"

She complied with my request, and I then had a good look at her.

She was clean, and wore a good deal of cloth superior to what most Anang women wore, and she was loaded with beads and trinkets. Her face was deeply lined, and there was a wicked look in her old eyes.

I felt her pulse, and at my request she stuck out her tongue, but she would not reply to my questions.

Turning to the Abams, I said, "Can any of you tell me what ails this lady?"

They all drew somewhat back.

Then the old woman, who had seemed afraid to speak to me, called out in a quavering voice, "Come hither, Chijoke, come hither, and speak for me."

A tall young Abam, looking anything but pleased, advanced, and falling on one knee in front of her, said, "O damsel, fair as the lily of the bush, what is it that you desire me to say?"

Placing her right hand softly on his head, and leering hideously, she replied, "Tell the great white medicine-man that the pain is here," and she spread her other hand over the region of the heart.

He repeated her words to me, and then continued, "Fairest lily, damsel of the long neck and burning eyes, what else shall I say?"

"There is nothing more to say," she answered, and sighed gently.

Then the kneeling Abam arose, and, retiring backwards, rejoined his fellows, who slyly chaffed him.

Suddenly the situation dawned upon me; the ancient dame was suffering with nothing more serious than old age, and was sad at heart that she could no longer enjoy the pleasures of her youth. Apparently, the three "witches" who lived with the queen, and through her ruled the country, made the soldiers of the Abam bodyguard treat them as if they were still young maidens.

"A drop of good gin and a little flattery," I said to myself, "will soon put her right again."

So, standing in front of her, and making obeisance, I said, "Fairest lily of the bush, may I hold your hand and look into it?"

She extended her hand with a sort of smile, and I made careful examination of the lines on the palm.

"Go, Amo," I said, "go and bring me a bottle of my best gin."

Meanwhile, I turned aside, and with my stick drew mystic figures in the sand.

Amo returned with the bottle, and I borrowed a gourd-cup.

Pouring out a liberal dose, I handed it to her, saying, "Drink, maiden of the long neck, damsel with a skin as black as the blackest night, drink this medicine, and let it flow into your heart."

She drank it, and asked for more!

'Not now," I said, "lest your beauty blossom forth too quickly, and all men kill one another because of it."

"Listen, fair one," I continued. "I have looked into your hand, and have there read what it is that troubles you. Far away in the bush in a compound surrounded with wine-palms, there sits a man, neither too young nor too old, who frets because of you. He has much cattle and many goats, but he loves his wives no more, for he has heard of you, 'the fairest lily of the bush,' and he can neither sleep nor eat for thinking of you. It is this grief of his which is making itself felt in you, and therefore you are sick."

As I neared the end of this speech, the old lady rose little by little from her stool, supporting herself on a stout carved stick, and, by the time I had concluded, she was standing upright.

"Bring drums," she shrieked, "and let us play. Hurry! hurry! Let there be no delaying. The medicine works quickly and well. I feel that I must dance."

Flinging away her stick, she executed a sort of pas-de-seul. The Abams made a circle round her, and clapped and shouted.

"Ha! ha!" she cried, "'tis fun to dance 'offiong' once again. See, I trip it like the youngest of them all," and she capered and pranced in really wonderful style.

When she grew tired of it, she made one of the Abams escort her back to her stool, but I met them halfway, and requested to have the honour, and so led her to it.

While the drummers drummed, and the youth of the compound "danced" around them, I carried on a mild flirtation with the ancient dame, and won great favour thereby.

"When am I to meet your queen?" I asked. "After seeing you, I no longer care to see her, but the great White Queen whom I serve will ask me concerning your queen, and therefore I must pay my respects to her. I hear it said on all sides that, when you are at court, no man has any eyes for the queen."

"It is so, you are right," she answered with a gratified leer. "But tell me, what is the name of the man who sighs for me, and what is the name of his village?"

"Those questions," I replied, "I may not answer until after I have been admitted to your queen's presence."

The old lady promised me an audience on the following morning.

The Abams afterwards told me that the queen was a mere tool in the hands of her three "witches," and that, if I had not found favour with Mother Umana (such was her name), admittance would have been altogether refused to me.

CHAPTER XX.

"THE TESTING OF THE QUEEN'S WEIGHT."

The wonderful recovery of Mother Umana was noised abroad all over Ikot-Afia-Ete, and every telling of the details sent my fame up higher and higher. Amo informed me that the queen and the two other old dames were now quite eager to see me.

It was about 8 o'clock in the morning when we were admitted to the royal compound. Since the days of Etuk Afia, first queen of the Anangs, the arrangement of the buildings had been somewhat changed, for the present queen's residence occupied one side of the compound instead of standing in the middle of it. I learnt on subsequent inquiry that the site of the circular house remained the same, but that the position of the Abams' huts had been altered.

The compound was about a hundred yards square. It was surrounded by a high fence of leaves of the oil-palm packed into a framework of poles, and the only entrance was exactly in the middle of one of the four sides and faced the queen's quarters on the opposite side of the square. Thus her majesty could see all who came in or went out. A long broad avenue bordered by trees of various kinds, among which the eben, wine-palm, and ukana were most frequent, led up to this entrance.

Chuku had been detailed to conduct me to the royal presence. Amo was the sole remaining member of my original suite, but he made up in size and deportment for a host of lesser satellites. He had again donned his get-up of the preceding day, and had added a pair of old scarlet and white epaulets, an accompaniment to a dress-coat never sanctioned by the great house of Poole. He also increased his swagger several degrees. Had he walked in front of instead of behind me, I should have been quite unable to maintain that dignity of mien which befitted the occasion.

Behind Amo followed a crowd of those of the Ikot-Afia-Ete people who had preferred accompanying us to squatting in the compound to await our arrival, as hundreds and thousands of their fellow-villagers were doing. Both sides of the avenue were lined with women and girls, for no member of their sex was allowed within the compound except to be tried in the queen's court or to give evidence in other cases.

The entrance was an ordinary doorway only three feet wide. Over it was a little roof put up to protect a bundle of "medicine," and on each side stood an Abam with a drawn matchet in his hand. At my approach, they lowered their weapons, and stood to attention.

We entered. The lower half of the great square was packed with squatting men and boys, and an orchestra of twenty drums was making a considerable din.

A straight passage across the middle of the compound had been kept clear for me, and up it we three walked, Chuku, I, and Amo, in the same order as, but in rather different attire from, that of my night-escape from the sacred island. In front of us was a little grove of trees, among which appeared the high conical roof of the queen's circular dwelling.

The royal party was grouped in a semicircle under a sheltering clump of okono-trees. In the middle on a stool sat Her Majesty Queen Inuberi, and on leopard-skins at her feet crouched the three old dames, for, after finishing her revels of the preceding night, Umana had resumed the usual routine of court. Drawn up in a semicircle behind these ladies was, Chuku and the two warders at the entrance excepted, the full complement of the Abam bodyguard, all dressed alike—ikiko-skin round loins, blue-and-white girdle just above, and scarlet feather over the right ear—and each man carrying a long carved walking-staff.

On the queen's right stood a little man, a crippled dwarf, and on her left was another figure, a boy clad in a blue-and-white loin-cloth and leathern belt, white vest, red fez, and scarlet brass-buttoned waistcoat. It was little Otu! He was grinning from ear to ear, but stood strictly at attention.

The queen held something white in her arms upon which she appeared to be bestowing caresses and a good deal of attention. I am, as I have said before, somewhat short-sighted.

Halting at a respectful distance, I removed my wideawake with a tremendous flourish, and called out in a loud voice, and in her own language, "Greeting, O Queen!"

The words were hardly out of my mouth before Her Majesty's white nursling struggled violently, tumbled off her lap, and, yapping in frantic joy, rushed wildly up to me. It was dog Towzer!

Forgetful of the royal presence, and of all etiquette and decorum, he jumped round me, barking, and wagging his stumpy tail, and would not be quieted until he had leaped high enough to lick me on the nose, and I had patted him and called him "good old dog."

The queen was expostulating, but all her court, including

the three old witches, laughed.   Towzer had "broken the ice" for us all.

I called Otu. He advanced, halted, gravely saluted, and said, "Gooder-mornin', sar.   Me lib."

"So I see," I replied, "and I'm very glad of it; but take charge of the dog and keep him quiet."

When Otu resumed his place at the queen's side with Towzer in his arms, the royal lady's brow cleared, and, smiling complacently, she extended a fat hand to be licked by the dog.

Queen Inuberi was decidedly plump, but not nearly so fat as the bride whom we had seen at Itu. Her arms and shoulders were bare.   She wore two wrappers, one tied round the waist and extending down to the feet, and the other tied round the body under the armpits, and extending down so as to overlap the first.   Both were of orange-coloured silk embroidered with little bunches of green leaves.   On her head was a nodding structure of pink ostrich feathers, and she wore a great deal of jewelry—many fine coral necklaces of different lengths, an extraordinary variety of bracelets on both arms from wrist to shoulder, and, on her fingers, a similar collection of rings.   I could not of course then see if King Edward's Ring was among them.

The three old dames were also much bejewelled, but their attire was less gorgeous than that of their royal mistress.

"Greeting, great queen," I said, standing near, and bowing low.   "Your fame has reached even to my own country far away over the big sea.   I have travelled many moons and been through many dangers to visit you, but the sight of the splendours of your person and your court is sufficient reward for all that I have gone through."

Her Majesty's fat face was particularly unintelligent, and I don't think she understood much of what I said.

"I take your dog," she said, patting Towzer, "and I take your boy," pointing to Otu.

"Take everything I possess, O queen," I answered.   "I am happy that you like them."

The queen looked relieved and smiled.

"I must tell you, however," I continued, "that my dog has a devil inside him, which sometimes gives trouble; but perhaps your majesty has no fear of devils."

The good lady looked troubled.   "I must ask my three maidens," she said.

Then she yawned—a very big yawn—and, fumbling among her silk garments, produced a piece of raw flesh, and held it out to Towzer, who greedily swallowed it. She thus enticed him back to her lap, and began fondling and patting him.

Towzer turned up the whites of his eyes, and politely pretended to like it.

The three old ladies winked at one another, and I stood there feeling the situation somewhat helpless and absurd.

Mother Umana rose up.

"Come, Inuberi," she said, "let us go to the council-chamber. Come, sisters, let us go."

The queen sighed, but obeyed. She gave Towzer back to Otu. Two of the Abams helped her to rise, and Umana's two "sisters" each gave her an arm, and, thus supported, the royal lady waddled away towards her circular house. Umana beckoned to me and Amo to follow, but, with a wave of her hand, indicated to the bodyguard and the dwarf that they were not to accompany us. Otu carrying Towzer had followed the queen.

The topmost point of the conical roof was about thirty feet from the ground. Just outside stood a tree with a string of jaw-bones encircling the trunk, and at its foot was an irregular pile of bottles and skulls. The circular wall on which the roof rested was five feet high, and was pierced by four little doorways. Inside, the diameter was about twenty feet. Smouldering logs and a few small drums lay about the floor. Attached vertically to the great central post, which reached up to the apex of the roof, were two ladders giving access to a sort of platform built high overhead.

The doorway facing the main entrance gave admittance to a series of little low rooms built on at the back.

I had followed Umana through the little opening, and Amo followed me. The queen and her two other "maidens" were already seated on one of the four clay couches which had been raised around the wall. Umana seated herself beside them, and pointed to where Amo and I were to sit.

"We have grave affairs of state to discuss," said Umana, who was evidently the chief of the three. "You, white man, are a great doctor, learned in the wisdom and medicine of your country over the big sea, and we hope you will be able to help us."

She paused, and I said, "You are right, fairest lily, I am indeed a great doctor, and I carry mighty secrets in my head, and powerful medicines in my boxes. If, however, we are going to discuss any matter which you do not desire should be noised abroad, it would be better to send my boy outside," and I pointed to Otu.

The queen put on a fretful expression, and seemed inclined to resist my suggestion, but the old ladies overruled her, and turned out Otu and dog Towzer.

"My man here," I said, glancing at Amo, "may hear everything. He is faithful, and will help you as much as I."

"We have an ancient custom in our country," began Umana, "which I must fully explain to you. It concerns the succession of our queens. Long ago——"

"I have already heard it all," I interrupted. "Your queen is weighed at her succession, and reigns as long as she do not fall below that weight less that of one hundred manillas. Is not this so?"

"Yes, you are right," she replied, looking, however, somewhat disappointed at being done out of the telling of a long story, "I see that you know it all."

"Well," I said, "what is your trouble?"

"Our present queen," she said, "the beautiful Inuberi whom all the Anangs fear and obey" (the old hag winked at her two "sisters"), "has reigned over us five years, and all the land has prospered and been at peace. It would be well if her reign might extend to another five years, but, alas! Abassi has decreed otherwise; she is far less fat than she used to be, and is quickly losing weight, so quickly that at our next yam-feast she will probably be found wanting and have to resign her power to another. In that case, I and my dear sisters will also have to retire, and give place to three other maidens," and, so saying, she sighed deeply.

"Ho! ho!" I said to myself, "so now the cat's out of the bag. These good dames feel their brief period of authority slipping from them, and are dreading to have to become mere nobodies again."

"I will give this matter due consideration," I replied.

Then, addressing the queen, I said, "Cheer up, your majesty, it is the thought of resigning your throne that is worrying you into thinness. You musn't lose hope. I will do my best for you, and I trust you may reign for many years to come."

The royal lady sighed and yawned.

"I don't worry about that," she said in a languid drawl. "I don't mind about losing my weight, and I don't care if I am not queen any longer. Life here is awfully dull" (she yawned again). "I would rather be an ordinary girl, and dance 'offiong,' and have a husband, and go to market. As queen, I am not allowed to do anything, and—O, life is most awfully dull!" and the poor thing gaped again and again.

"Hush, my dear Inuberi!" cried the three witches, "you are most ungrateful. We do all we can to amuse you, and you have more cloths and beads and jewels than all other women in the country. If you complain in this fashion, we shall not allow you to look on at the next offiong-dance."

They treated her like a naughty child. She was, indeed, nothing more than a child in their wily old clutches.

"She is tired," said one of the three. "Let us adjourn."

In taking my leave, I held the queen's right hand, and bowed over it long enough for me to see that the ring was *not* there.

That night I cogitated long and earnestly upon the problem before me. Here was I, actually in the village of Arthur Riversley's "Quene of Ibibio," and yet I could not see how to recover King Edward's Ring, of the very existence of which I was indeed in considerable doubt.

The next morning I devoted to getting my stores into order, for, thanks to Umana, all my property had been returned to me. Then there happened yet another of those extraordinarily fortunate incidents which belong rather to a tale of fiction than to a sober narration such as this. You will hardly believe me when I tell you that, on opening a case labelled "Ideal Milk," I found it to contain twelve dozen tins, not of the milk, but of that well-known food which, quoting from its label—said to be the composition of a certain great man of letters noted for the dignity of his style—"has converted the puny, sickly infant into the elephantine healthy man, the anæmic invalid into the lusty prize-fighter, the gaunt lamp-post-like spinster into the portly matron, the. . . . . ." but really this food is so well-known that I need not mention even its name.

"What a fortunate mistake those people at the Stores have made!" I exclaimed to myself. "Three months must elapse before the celebration of the feast of new-yams in the Anang country. Surely, if Queen Inuberi can be induced to take the food regularly during the intervening period, she ought to put on weight. At any rate, we will try it. 'Never say die.' There are, say, ninety days. I will allow her a tin and a half per diem, and, just at the end, two per diem. Surely this should produce the desired result."

The three witches thoroughly approved my plan, having first personally tasted the stuff and declared it to be uncommonly good. The queen was too languid and lazy to offer any objection. So we fed her on it at regular hours every day, and after ten days' treatment, the royal lady began to put on flesh, or, as Amo said, "dem woman-chief lib for grow fine too much, sar."

Meanwhile, what of Otu and Towzer? Well, not wishing to in any way give the queen cause to fret, I waived my claim to them, and permitted them to attend daily at the court. The consequence was that they both got to think "no small beer" of themselves, and that my active little terrier waxed almost as fat as his royal mistress.

As soon as I became settled in my own quarters, I made inquiries as to Otu's presence at Ikot-Afia-Ete, and then at last the whole matter was explained.

First of all, then, those two messengers who had arrived at Ikot-Abassi three days after the Abams' departure had been sent, not by the queen, but by that scoundrel Okudi, who thus had hoped to get, and had all but succeeded in getting, his revenge on Amo, and to carry out his schemes—whatever they were—against me. The messengers had of course purposely led us astray.

Chuku had delivered my message to the queen and her three old dames, but the latter had disagreed as to whether or not to receive me, and, while they were thus debating, we were undergoing the series of adventures which began in the hamlet near Chief Okut Akan's village and ended with my incarceration on the island in the middle of the snake-infested lake. Okut Akan's village lay in a remote corner of the Anang country, on the boundary which separates the Ibibios from the Ibos, and therefore its people were but little under the queen's control.

The day after our escape from the place of the pillar of torture, news of our plight had reached Ikot-Afia-Ete, and the queen, or, rather, her three *gouvernantes*, had despatched the Abam bodyguard in all directions with orders to rescue us and bring us to the court, and to arrest all the principal offenders.

Ten of these soldiers had visited Okut Akan's village, and had there found, safe but under detention, little Otu, dog Towzer, and the Ikono carrier-boys, together with all my baggage. They took the boy, dog, and baggage to Ikot-Afia-Ete, and sent the carriers back to Ikot-Abassi. They also arrested the old chief, though he pleaded not guilty. At his entreaty, they scoured the country for Okudi, and at length caught him and carried him along with them. He had, as I had foreseen, been pulled out of the hole and freed of his bonds by his fellow-accomplices who had visited the place of torture early the following morning.

The Abams, however, had quite failed to discover what had become of Amo and me. They could find no traces of our whereabouts, and had at length begun to conclude that we had made a supernatural departure. Then one day Chuku had met Amo at a market, and they had planned my escape as has been already told.

At the same time, the Inokuns, hearing that I had lived long an honoured guest at the court of the king of the Ikonos, and that the queen of the Anangs desired to entertain me in a similar capacity, became afraid of what they had done, and, to save themselves, accused and betrayed that arch-fiend Ikong into the Abams' hands, and he too had been carried a prisoner to Ikot-Afia-Ete.

Thus was explained to me all that concatenation—the mention of Ikong has brought this long word to the end of my pen—which enabled me to see clearly the course that our affairs had taken.

Amo supplied another link.

"You have never told me," I said to him one day, "why you left Okut Akan's compound in the middle of the night. I awoke in the morning thinking that I had heard a cry and a shot. What was it?"

"Me lib for sleep, sar," he replied. "Den somebody make softly tap-tap for door. Den me open and look Okudi. He say, 'Dem people go kill dem white man. S'pose you foller me softly for bush, I fit for tell you eberyt'ing.' I put small gun [revolver] for my cloth, I foller him. Dem when we catch [reach] dem road, plenty boys lib for bush. Dey run for me, I holler, I fire dem small gun. Hundred boys come, me no good for so plenty, dey catch me, dey carry me away quick."

Everything was now quite clear to me, and I hope I have made it equally clear to the Reader.

One of my first inquiries was for old chief Okut Akan, who had rescued me from the howling mob of savages by his prompt use of a branch of the big juju-tree. I found him living in the Abams' quarters, well-fed and comfortable, but a prisoner, and in great terror of his captors. The sight of me seemed to cause him more fear than pleasure. Probably he expected that I meant to take vengeance upon him for what had happened to me and my men at the hands of some of his people. I, however, assured the old man that I was his friend, and would try to procure his release.

So I laid the whole matter before the sisters three, and my influence was such that the old chief was permitted to return to his village. I gave him a liberal present of cloth and tobacco from my store, and, shaking him cordially by the hand, thanked him again for what he had done for us, and assured him that, if he treated all white men thus, he and they would always be excellent friends.

"Now for Ikong and Okudi," I said. "Where are they?"

"Come, sar," said Amo; "me fit for show you."

I followed him, and Chuku accompanied us.

He led me behind the queen's side of the compound, and along a winding path through the bush. After pursuing it for a quarter of a mile, we suddenly entered a clearing, and there facing us was a sight which filled me with horror and disgust.

Two lofty scaffoldings of poles and "bamboos" had been erected, and thereto were attached crucifixion-wise the bodies of two human beings. A strong cord passed round the waist bound the victim to the stout framework at his back, his arms were extended as far as they would stretch and then tied round the wrists, and his legs, stretched out in spread-eagle fashion, were tied at the ankles. In each case, the head had dropped down on to the breast.

The stench was very bad. Vultures sat there pecking at the bodies, and up and down one pole an army of driver-ants was ascending and descending.

"Well?" I inquired, holding my nose, and turning away from this horrible spectacle.

"Dey be Ikong and Okudi, sar," said Amo. "Dem woman-chief and dem old womans, dey hold court one time [at once], dey find dem two men guilty. Den Chuku's bruders, dey make dese trees," pointing to the scaffoldings, "and dey tie dem bad men, and so dey finish."

"Did they give them gin?" I asked.

"Yes," answered Chuku; "they each drank a bottle of gin."

"Were Umana and her 'sisters' present when these men were tied here?"

"O, yes," replied Amo, "dey lib, and plenty womans and pickins lib. Dem queen, dey no 'gree dat she come, but she cry plenty, she make big palaber. Den dey 'gree, and she sit here, and she glad too much."

Amo and Chuku laughed, but I turned away, and pleaded sickness as my excuse for not visiting the court that afternoon.

* * * * *

During those three months spent at Ikot-Afia-Ete, I saw many strange things which space forbids me to describe here. I visited some of the outlying Anang villages, but never without a strong Abam escort. The Anangs are quite as "savage" as the Ikonos, but, living nearer the Ibos and nearer the old trade-route to "the Coast," they are somewhat better acquainted with European prestige and commodities, and so will perhaps more readily submit to the sword of Civilisation which hangs over them.

I must, however, devote a few lines of description to something which, as far as I can ascertain, is peculiar to the Anangs and their immediate Ibo neighbours. I refer to the kind of pillar upon which Amo had to stand while they shot arrows at him. I saw specimens of it in nearly every village on the right bank of the Kwa Ibo. It stood usually in the middle of the town-place, and was called "mbut-mbopo." It was a solid mass of clay, and varied in height from 3¾ to 9 feet, but the average was about 5 feet 9 inches.

The finest of all was that at Ikot-Afia-Ete. It was 7 feet 6 inches high, with a circumference of 137 inches, and was coloured and painted with belts of symbols resembling the signs of the zodiac, the most frequent of which was the "marke" drawn on Arthur Riversley's strip of cloth and tattooed on the right hip of the Abam soldiers.

Most of these pillars were provided with a little mounting-block with foot-hole above. Some had a thatched roof erected over them, while others were protected from rain by just a few leaf-mats laid across the top. Some were unpainted and quite plain, but some, though unpainted, were carved with bold geometrical patterns. On the ground at the foot of many of them were buried, neck downwards, five or six gin-bottles.

I was informed that these pillars played an important part in the local ceremony of marriage: when the bride came out of the fattening-house, the bridegroom had to stand on the top of the "mbut-mpobo" and dance, and then jump to the ground without bending his knees. If he failed to perform this feat successfully, he had to give up his claim to the bride.

I did not see any specimen of these pillars in the whole of the Ikono country.

* * * * *

At last the great day when Queen Inuberi would be weighed drew near. The three witches and I had but little doubt that our treatment had been entirely successful, for our patient had waxed monstrously fat, and we had taken every means to keep her in a good humour.

Umana almost daily asked me the name of her love-sick swain, and of the village in which he lived, but, though I kept her excitement alive by glowing accounts of his increasing unhappiness on her behalf, I postponed giving her the desired information until after the great day.

At length the fourteenth of July arrived, and all the Anang villages poured out their men, women, and children to attend the great meeting at their capital. Although it was now about the middle of the rainy season, no rain fell on that auspicious day. It was, in fact, real "Queen's weather." The country was looking very different from what it had looked when I had left Ikot-Abassi. Then the maize had been green and strong, now its stalks were brown and broken; then the fruit of the eben-tree had been a beautiful pink, now it was purple-black; then the yams were covered with tender green leaves, now they were shrivelled and old, and were yielding up their tubers to the feast-making husbandman. Some villagers were celebrating the harvest by cleaning their "roads."

The ceremony of testing the queen's weight was held in a large square clearing lying just outside the village. The people began to arrive at dawn, and by nine o'clock there were tens of thousands of them patiently squatting on the ground. A large orchestra of drums discoursed sweet music in a corner. The space reserved for the queen and her court was surrounded by all the fattest damsels in the land. How some of them had managed to journey so far, I really do not know. Some of the men looked particularly tired and irritable, so perhaps they had had to carry these ladies. They had all just come out of their fattening seclusion, and were gathered together here in case the present queen should have to vacate her throne in favour of one of them.

I had lent Queen Inuberi my hammock for the occasion, and eight of the strongest of the Abams had been detailed to act as bearers, four relieving the other four. According to ancient custom, she had discarded all her gorgeous robes and jewelry, and wore nothing but a pure-white garment which I believe Shakespeare calls a smock.

A drummer led the royal procession. Then followed twenty Abams walking two and two—a survival of Arthur Riversley's training of the bodyguard—then Otu in all his finery, carrying fat Towzer, then the hammock with its white-clad occupant, and two of the relief-carriers walking on each side of it, then I, Richard Wood, trying to feel dignified, then the magnificent Amo, then the three weird sisters tottering along arm-in-arm, painted, bedizened, and bejewelled in wondrous wise, then the dwarf, and then another score or so of the Abam soldiers two and two.

As we entered the square, the drummers beat out their noisiest welcome, and all the people, rising simultaneously, shouted "Long may Inuberi reign."

In the middle of the clearing stood a tall erection resembling a gallows. A very strong rope ran in a groove cut in the cross-piece, and at each end of the rope hung a large wooden tray. On the ground lay many bags of manillas.

Mother Umana, ringleader of the three wise women, should rightly have made a speech, but the expectation of hearing the name of her lover, and the excitement of showing off her fine clothes before such a vast assembly, were so great that she had quite forgotten what were the right things to say, and for the first, and, I fear, only time in her life, was a really wise woman in that she said nothing. She whispered to me to speak, but I shook my head, so she cried, "Let the ceremony proceed."

Now, I have not the least intention of satisfying the curiosity of fair Readers by telling them the exact weight of Queen Inuberi, for a lady's weight should never be mentioned, not even in print. Bag after bag of manillas was placed in one of the wooden scales, and then at last the royal lady was assisted out of the hammock, and, with one of her maidens on each side to support her, she waddled to the other scale, and was carefully helped into it.

There she sat in rather an uncomfortable position, but with a smile of indifference upon her broad face.

The "clerk of the scales," a benevolent-looking chief wearing an idiong-ring and a shabby military tunic in addition to his loin-cloth, had carefully counted the manillas in each bag before the beginning of the ceremony.

Queen Inuberi's scale was a little higher in the air than that containing the manillas. The three old dames clung to one another trembling with excitement.

"The test goes against Her Majesty," said he of the idiong-ring. "Abassi has seen fit to decree that she be deposed."

"Wait!" I cried. "What about the hundred manillas that should be subtracted in her favour? Have you done so?"

"Great Scot!" exclaimed he, or words to that effect. "How stupid of me to forget!"

Then he opened one of the bags, and began to take out manillas five at a time, and laid them in fives on the ground. The scale gradually went up, until at last, when the hundredth manilla had been removed, there could be no possible doubt that the queen's weight had won the day.

Inuberi sighed, and begged to be carefully released from her crouching position, the three witches wept tears of joy, and all the people shouted "Long live our queen!"

Then the procession re-formed, and we returned to the village.

That same afternoon Umana and her sisters paid me a state call, and thanked me for having averted what would have meant social ruin to them. I entertained them, not with tea and buns, but with gin and biscuits, and the usual small-talk flowed freely on.

Then Umana drew me aside.

"Tell me," she said, "pray tell me the name of that dear man who frets so much because of me."

"His name, Madam," I answered, "is Akpan, and he lives at Ikot——Ikot——I really cannot recall the end of the name, but perhaps I may dream it one of these fine nights."

Now "Akpan" means eldest son, and is the commonest first-name in all the Ibibio country, and "ikot" means people, and is the most frequent prefix to place-names.

The old lady, however, was quite pleased, and danced up and down with joy. It was, indeed, all that I could do to prevent her from giving me an affectionate embrace.

"And now, ladies," I said, "I wish to speak with you upon a subject of the greatest moment. I have been instrumental in enabling you to keep the reins of government for yet another year, but the food is exhausted, and I fear that, without its nourishment, Queen Inuberi cannot maintain her present splendid condition. I have consulted the stars, and I find that something is working against her—a something which has shortened the reign of very many of your queens."

"What is it?" they all breathlessly asked.

"A ring," I replied, "a ring left here many many generations ago by a white-skinned man whom some of you call Abassi. Now, listen to me. That ring, when given to the queen with whom he stayed, was blue. It has since become green, and it is this fatal change in its colour that is working against queen after queen of your tribe. Unknown to the royal ladies though this fact be, it is nevertheless to this cause that they owe those worries of the mind which make them tire of their sovereignty and grow thinner and thinner. If the ring could be changed back again from green to blue, all would be well with them."

The three old dames gazed at me in amazement.

"The ring!" they cried, "how should you know this great secret? You are indeed a mighty magician," and they fell with their foreheads touching the ground.

"Can you change the colour for us?" eagerly inquired Umana. "Our forefathers used to say that it was blue at first."

"No," I replied. "I cannot change the colour, but I can give you another exactly like what it should be, on the condition, however, that you hand over to me the ring that has lost its virtue."

Putting my hand into my pocket, I drew forth a gold signet-ring containing a turquoise with a griffin engraved thereon. I had had it made for me in London by a skilled jeweller, who had copied the design from a collection of fourteenth-century rings preserved in the British Museum.

"Is this anything like your ancient ring?" I asked.

The old ladies took it eagerly, and examined it closely and carefully.

"It is exactly like it!" they exclaimed. "You are indeed a mighty magician. Give us this ring, and we will gladly hand you the other."

"Where is it kept?" I inquired.

"In the roof of the council-chamber," Umana replied. "Let us go at once."

So we went.

We found Queen Inuberi sitting there, fondling Towzer, while Otu and the dwarf were playing some boyish game close by.

"Climb, Etuk Owo," said Umana to the dwarf; "climb up to the treasure-chamber and bring me the calabash painted white and red."

The poor little fellow, crippled and dwarfed from birth, quickly did her bidding, for he had long been trained to this climbing, and descended with the calabash.

Opening it, Umana disclosed a medley of gewgaws and trinkets, and there in the middle lay King Edward's Ring, the ancient heirloom of the Riversleys of Riversley!

"Here you are," said she, handing it to me. "Now then give me the other one."

I took the long-lost ring. The stone was green, but a griffin was engraved thereon, and there could be no doubt of its ancient workmanship. I put the two rings side by side and compared them, and at once realised the difference between the work of a fourteenth and a nineteenth century artist.

Giving the old lady the modern article, I slipped the other on to my finger, and made a silent vow that I would not remove it therefrom until I should stand face to face with Pleasance to give an account of my quest.

CHAPTER XXI.

HOME.

Having at last, after all those months of wanderings, waitings, and adventures, recovered the Ring, the quest of which had taken me out to that land of savage cannibals, I turned all my thoughts towards home, and determined not to lose a day about setting out.

Umana and her "sisters" were really grateful for what I had done for them. I told them that I could not leave Otu and Towzer behind, however much Queen Inuberi might desire to keep them, so we arranged that my departure should not be revealed to her.

As far as I could judge from my own observation, and from what the natives told me, Ikot-Afia-Ete lay about two days' journey west of Itu, and my nearest way back would have been to go through the Ikono village of Ndiya, and thus approach Itu from behind. The attitude of the people east of Ndiya seemed, however, rather doubtful, so Amo and I decided to return through Ikot-Abassi, King Esien's capital.

On the second morning after the ceremony of testing the queen's weight, we set out with a strong escort of Abams to conduct us as far as the border of the Ikono country, where we expected to meet another escort sent out by Esien, for a runner had been despatched to inform him of our movements.

I took a tender farewell of the three dear old ladies, promised to send them several more cases of the wonderful food, and whispered into Umana's ear that I hoped on my next visit to find that she had made "Akpan" happy.

We crossed the Kwa Ibo, and about noon reached the first Ikono village, and there found many old acquaintances awaiting us. So we took leave of our Abam escort, Amo and Chuku embracing one another after the fashion of our good friends across the Channel.

That same evening we arrived at Ikot-Abassi, where Esien and the Akama welcomed us most heartily. With them, we spent the whole of the next day, recounting our adventures and hearing the Ikono news. I was glad to know that all the carrier-boys had returned safely from Okut Akan's village.

It was arranged that we should join the river Enyong, not at Use, of which place I did not hold pleasant recollections, but at Ikpe-Ikot-Nkun, a market-town much higher up the river. It had the advantage of being an Ikono community within King Esien's domain, and also it was frequented by traders from Old Calabar.

So we set out early on the following morning, Esien and the Akama accompanying us, as before, to the bank of the Ikot-Abassi stream.

I have told you that Esien's chair is now at Riversley. This is true, but it was on my *second* visit to the Ibibio country that I acquired possession of it. If this present narrative find favour in your eyes, I may venture to write another yarn about "King Esien's Chair."

We reached Ikpe-Ikot-Nkun safely, slept one night there, and left early the next morning in a large trade-canoe bound for Itu and Old Calabar. It had a score of lusty paddlers, so we reached Itu the same night.

It was delightful to be on the water again, and every ripple of the rapid current seemed to speak of going home. There is no space left to tell of all the interesting birds and flowers that I observed on the way down. We passed Use beach, and thought of little Otu's adventure in the "miry clay," and. in passing the mouth of the short Asang creek, we laughed over the midnight episode on the juju-island, and wondered if fate had in store for Chief Enia Eke any punishment as terrible as that which had befallen his accomplice Ikong.

It was dark when we reached Itu. On the following morning, we climbed the hill to Chief Udaw Idiong's place.

The old man overflowed with cordial expressions of welcome, but I had by now acquired considerable experience of native faces, and could detect that all this gush of good phrases was put on to conceal something from me.

"Where is Akpan?" I asked. "Hasn't he heard of our arrival?"

"He is away in the bush," replied the chief, "and I don't know when he will return. He will be sorry to have missed seeing you."

"I will spare him that sorrow," I said, "for I shall stay here until I see him and obtain from him an account of all my cattle and goats. Where are they kept?"

"In the bush far away at the back of Itu," he answered. "Akpan has taken much trouble with them; but, alas! many have died of disease, and several were drowned on their journey down the Enyong."

"I shall wait here till his arrival," I said. "Please send for him at once."

The chief demurred, but I established myself, with Amo, Otu, Towzer, and the scanty remains of my baggage, in an Efik trader's compound, and, when Umaw Idiong saw that I really meant what I had said, he at last sent for Akpan.

Two days later, that worthy arrived, with fear and crafty guile written all over his face.

After the usual interchange of greetings, I called for an account of my livestock, of which some had been committed to the charge of his "brother," and the remainder handed over to Akpan himself when he had left Ikot-Abassi.

Then followed a long tale of misfortune: drownings, disease, thefts, and so on.

"Now, look here, my good friend," I said. "I know you pretty well, and I regret to have to say that I don't believe you. I am quite willing to pay you for your trouble, but I am equally unwilling to have the greater part of my property stolen by you and your excellent family. You will remain here with me, and, if my cattle and goats are not forthcoming within three days, you will accompany me to Old Calabar,

P

and the whole case will be submitted to the British Consul there. Do you understand?"

"Yes, master," he replied, "I understand, but indeed you do me wrong."

To help his understanding, I borrowed from my landlord a pair of handcuffs, and had him carefully guarded.

Well, to cut a long story short, on the third day after my little conversation with Akpan, all my cattle and goats were handed over to me—not one of them was missing! Then, releasing Akpan, I paid him for the trouble that he had had in looking after them, and hired several large canoes, which, loaded with these animals—my medical fees!—went with me down the Cross River.

We reached Old Calabar on the last day of July, just over a year since I had disembarked there from the "Africana," and to my great joy I found that a homeward-bound ship was due to sail a week later.

Mr. Johnston welcomed me back with amazement. They had all long ago given me up as lost in the Ibibio bush, for many melancholy stories of my fate had found their way down river and been more or less believed. I stayed with him till my departure, and gave him a full account of all our adventures.

And what of Adiaha? Was she still alive and fretting because she had not been allowed to accompany us to the land of her birth? Not a bit of it. The old lady had made the most of her little property—goats, cat and kittens, fowls, ducks, and parrot—and had traded with such skill that she had attracted unto herself another husband, a middle-aged Efik trader who owned the compound of which I had taken out a year's lease. We found this pair living very happily together. Adiaha was plump and gorgeously gowned, and no longer hankered after that burial-grove in the Anang country of which we had at first heard so much.

And Madame Amo? This lady had, during our absence, presented her husband with a fine boy. On our return, a sort of christening ceremony was held, to which all the *élite* of Calabar society were invited. The infant's parents, grandmother, and step-grandfather were splendidly arrayed, and I had the honour of paying the expenses and of bestowing my name, Richard, on the son and heir.

Long and earnestly did Amo and I discuss the future. He wanted to accompany me back to England, but, though for many reasons I should have liked to retain his services, I saw there was much to be said against it; so eventually he made up his mind to live at Old Calabar and trade between that port and Lagos.

I of course endowed him with all the cattle and goats, and gave him a sum of money upon which to start trading. I also promised to write to him from time to time through one of the missionaries, who also kindly undertook to write Amo's replies to me. Moreover, I promised that I would pay him a visit during the next few years.

Otu made his home with his sister, Madame Amo.

There is really but little more to tell. My wife, indeed, who has had the patience to read to this point, says, "Pray finish now, and leave Readers to imagine the rest for themselves"—excellent advice, doubtless, but my natural obstinacy prompts me to finish otherwise.

I do not intend to dilate upon my parting with Amo or Otu's with Towzer. Partings are exceedingly unpleasant things, and should be slurred over and cut superlatively short.

My former cook, Tom Peter, and his little "brother" Jim George, had worked for a year at "Priscilla" Factory, and were now hoping to return to "we country." I therefore engaged their services for the voyage, more on Towzer's account than on my own, and they furnished me with daily amusement until I parted with them at Monrovia.

One strange detail remains to be recorded. When I had placed King Edward's Ring on my finger in the circular council-chamber of Queen Inuberi, the stone had been of an emerald hue, and it so continued until about half-way through the voyage. I often looked at it—it meant so much to me—and one day I thought I detected a slight change in it—the green seemed to be yielding here and there to a bluish tinge.

One of the passengers on board had been in Persia, and had visited the celebrated turquoise-mines near Nishapur. I showed him the ring, and asked if he could explain what was to me quite a phenomenon.

"O, yes, easily," he replied. "The colour of the turquoise is much affected by the atmosphere. Yours has suffered through being subjected to the great heat of the tropics, and is now regaining its natural colour because we are getting into the temperate zone. It is possible that by the time we reach England, it may be quite blue again."

And so it actually happened, for, when I set foot on English soil, the stone was in colour a true cerulean blue.

*   *   *   *   *

Riversley Park, the old oaks and bracken flooded with the glorious light of the setting sun. Under Queen Elizabeth's oak, the oak with the rustic seat lettered "SEMPER EADEM," stand the same two figures that filled the foreground of a former picture. The girl is slipping on to her finger a ring which the man has just removed from his.

* * * * *

Extracts from the *East Anglian Daily Times* of 19th April, 188—:

No. I.

"Her Majesty the Queen has been graciously pleased to "grant that, on the death of Mr. Riversley of Riversley, the "estate of that ancient family shall descend to his only child, "Miss Riversley, on condition that, immediately after her "marriage to Mr. Richard Wood, he shall lay aside his own "name and arms, and adopt those of Riversley only."

No. II.

"WOOD—RIVERSLEY.—On April 18th, at St. Mary's "Church, Riversley, by the Rev. D. Wood, rector, father "of the bridegroom, Richard Wood, to Pleasance, only child "of Mr. Riversley of Riversley."

THE END.

www.ingramcontent.com/pod-product-compliance
Lightning Source LLC
Chambersburg PA
CBHW020654030726
47498CB00002B/502

* 9 7 8 1 9 0 5 2 1 7 2 2 9 *